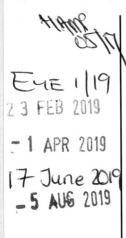

BY MARY WOOD

The Breckton series

To Catch a Dream
An Unbreakable Bond
Tomorrow Brings Sorrow
Time Passes Time

Proud of You

All I Have to Give
In Their Mother's Footsteps

The Cotton Mill saga

Judge Me Not

Tomorrow Brings Sorrow

Mary Wood

PAN BOOKS

First published 2012 by Books by Mary Wood

This edition published 2017 by Pan Books
an imprint of Pan Macmillan
20 New Wharf Road, London N1 9RR
Associated companies throughout the world
www.panmacmillan.com

ISBN 978-1-4472-6746-1

1 3 5 7 9 8 6 4 2

A CIP catalogue record for this book is available from the British Library.

Typeset by Palimpsest Book Production Limited, Falkirk, Stirlingshire
Printed and bound by CPI Group (UK) Ltd, Croydon, CR0 4YY

For my mum and dad,
Dora and Edward Olley. You gave me love,
you cared for me and taught me how to live
and how to seek out my dreams.

And for my mum- and dad-in-law,
Edith and Jim Wood. You gave me your son,
Roy, and a wonderful second family.

I love and miss you. It is in knowing
I would have made you proud that I find strength.
Thank you.

1

Sarah & Billy

The Visit

Loose pebbles crunched under the wheels of Sarah's car. The sound warned her how close she was to her ordeal. Applying pressure on the brake, she slowed the car, not wanting to come to the end of the long driveway.

Menston Mental Hospital – 'the madhouse', as the folk of Leeds called it – loomed ahead. She could see its landmark Gothic clock tower and could almost feel the chill of its endless corridors, peopled by the shuffling insane: a stark contrast to the autumn sun outside.

Guilt had long since left her and resentment had replaced it, as the shackles of fear bound her to promises that she'd made in another lifetime.

Billy's ways had eroded the forgiveness she'd found, and her love for him had eroded along with it. She'd tried to accept that his mental illness had caused him to commit such vile acts, but over the years of visiting him here she'd seen the truth – Billy nurtured a destructive hate. He didn't try to control himself, but instead used bullying tactics to get his own way.

Stepping out of her car, Sarah walked towards the building. Once inside, she glanced at the clock: five past twelve – she

1

was already late, and no one was at reception to enable her to sign in. Ringing the bell, she willed the clerk to come quickly, for Billy would be getting agitated and that wouldn't bode well.

At last she made her way towards the visiting room, and as she did so, a shadow danced across the corridor ahead of her. Billy must have seen her coming. Had he been hiding behind the curtain, watching her? Her gut clenched in the same way it had three days before, on 3rd September at eleven fifteen in the morning, as she'd listened to Neville Chamberlain announcing, 'Britain is now at war with Germany' – a sentence that seemed to shroud them all in a fear of their own and their loved ones' imminent death, although for her it had held added dread. Thinking of this now, Sarah slowed her step as she neared the large doors.

Billy stood in the doorway, with a menacing stance in his strong, but not tall, frame. His dark hair shone with the Brylcreem he'd used to plaster it back. His half-closed, coal-black eyes had an unfathomable, dull depth to them. When he spoke, his voice mocked. 'So, you came then?'

'Aye, I came. Not that you deserved me to, after what happened last time.'

'Eeh, don't go over that – we've not got long. I take it they've told you as we could have some time alone?'

'I'm not in agreement with that, Billy. I should've reported you.'

'Just try, and you know what'll happen, don't yer? Now, let's get inside, eh?'

The room's dingy appearance did nothing to ease Sarah's fear. Sage-coloured paint peeled off the walls, dirt from a thousand pairs of hands marked the doors, and the oilcloth on the floor had the appearance of a broken jigsaw puzzle in the way its pattern had peeled off in places. A small, high window, mottled with mildew, refused the sun entry.

The 'interview rooms' – as the powers-that-be called this room, and the one like it along the corridor – sometimes accommodated private visits with trusted patients. Trusted! How Billy had convinced them of his worthiness to use the room, she'd never know.

'Come here, me lass.'

'No, Billy. Not unless you promise not to—'

'Sarah, can't you leave it? I said I were sorry. Anyroad, you're me fiancée – I'm entitled. And you didn't help things by wearing that dress as Mam had made for you. It showed most of your tits, so what did yer expect?'

'Don't talk like that, Billy. And it didn't; its square neckline just showed a bit of cleavage. All the girls wear that fashion now.'

'You're not wearing it today, I see. You couldn't get a cardigan to fasten higher than that one does. Undo a few of the buttons, lass. Give me a treat, eh?'

'Oh, Billy, when did you change so much? You used to love and respect me. Everything was going to be right between us. We discussed that we'd wait until we were wed.'

'Aye, but when will that be? How can I wed you, when I'm stuck in here?'

Inside, she hoped that would always be so, but she knew it wouldn't be. 'Look, let's change the subject. I've brought you some stuff. Your mam sent you a hamper and a letter, and Granna—'

'I don't want stuff!' The chair in front of him clattered to the floor, echoing off the walls and striking a terror through her. Billy stood close, his angry eyes boring into hers. 'I want you, and I want me freedom. Can't you understand that,

3

Sarah? I want out of here. I want us to be together, like we were meant to be. I'm not for taking much more of it.'

His anguish didn't arouse her pity, but added to the dread that had settled in her. The news she had for Billy signified the changes that the future held. 'Well, there is some hope it could end soon. Your mam has a lawyer working on your case. He sounds promising. He'll come and see you, when he has things in order. You're to act right with him, Billy. Keep your temper and be polite.'

Billy sat down, his face hungry for more of the same news. 'Go on – what's he said? Has he said owt as can give me hope?'

'There might be a way. He's looked at your reports, and there's nothing there to say you're not fit. The fact that the psychiatrist no longer works with you, that you're not on medication and that there haven't been any outbursts for a few years all look favourable. But you'll have to play along with the lawyer's suggestions.'

'I'll do owt he says, I promise. What he's come up with, then?'

'He reckons that, with us declaring war on Germany, if you apply for the army—'

'Christ, give up one institution for another!'

'Well, he thinks it might be the only way. If he could go to a judge with your record, a good reference from here, and wanting to fight for your country, then he's sure it will be a foregone conclusion that they will let you free.'

The ensuing silence gave her time to think. Billy free! Free to do what? Only she knew that he hadn't really changed. Only she knew that the years of incarceration – having been sectioned to an institute at the age of eleven – hadn't made any difference to him. His jealous rage had led to the vile killing of her beautiful Mongol sister Bella, and to the more excusable killing of Billy's brutal dad. She'd seen the evil core of him, but she also knew he could hide and control the depths of it at will, so long as nothing marred his good record. Despair overcame her. *Oh God! The price of that will once more fall on my shoulders, for with Billy's freedom there will be no avoiding marrying him.*

Maybe the war would change things – a terrible thought, but if the war went on long enough, it would keep them apart, maybe even forever . . . No! She'd not think of the possibility of Billy being killed as being a way of freeing herself of him, because that would be the death of her Aunt Megan, Billy's mam. Her own liberation wasn't worth the hurt it would cause Aunt Megan.

Sarah sighed; she'd just have to take whatever life with Billy threw at her. Doing anything else would cause so much pain.

Billy's eager voice cut into her thoughts. 'I'll do it, lass. Aye, thinking on it, it's sommat as would appeal to me, anyroad. I'd enjoy getting stuck into them Germans. Eeh, lass, no more talking now – I've got to hold you. I've got to feel your body near mine. They'll be along in a minute to shift us into the communal area.'

Every sinew in her stiffened as Billy took her into his arms. Memories of fighting off his wandering hands on her last visit sickened her: his brutal handling of her, like an animal playing with its prey; and then, when he didn't get his way, his flaunting of Dilly, the poor, sick young woman who followed him about like a lapdog. '*Dilly'll give me what you won't, won't you, Dilly? Come on, Dilly, lass, come with me into the bushes and I'll show you a good time.*' His laughter had vibrated through Sarah. Dilly's slack grin and obvious happiness at his suggestion had made her pity the situation the woman found herself in. As Billy had walked away with Dilly, who shuffled behind him as fast as she could, she'd wanted to shout, 'She's welcome to you!', but she'd kept quiet and accepted her humiliation.

The grip of his arms tightened around her now. 'Oh, Sarah, lass . . . Christ, I've got to have you, Sarah – I've got to!' His mouth covered hers. The force of the contact pushed her backwards. The wall stopped her from falling as his body crushed against hers. 'Sarah, Sarah.' The moist feel of his lips on her neck shuddered through her.

'No, Billy. Not here. Not like this. Soon.'

'I'm not waiting any longer. I can't, Sarah. What's the odds, anyroad, as we'll be married when I get out?' His fingers kneaded her breasts, his thumbs rubbed her nipples. She tried to stay his hands, but couldn't. Pinned by his body against the rough plaster, she could do nothing as he leaned to one side, reaching for the hem of her skirt. Her skin crawled as his fingers traced a path up her thigh.

The leg of her knickers tightened with the intrusion. She could feel him probing her and knew now that it wasn't just his hand. Panic gripped her. 'No, Billy.' But he took no heed, and her resistance proved futile.

It hadn't lasted long. Sweat from Billy's forehead dripped onto her as he pulled himself from her. Wiping it from her face and neck with the back of her hand, Sarah remained slumped against the wall, bending her legs a little to try to ease the soreness and bruising that the stretching sensation had caused her. The bruising extended to her heart, and she felt her pride, her self-worth and all that she had been up to this moment desert her.

Billy didn't look at her or speak to her as he concentrated

on putting himself away and buckling his belt. When he did look up, his flushed face bore the expression of someone who didn't care for her feelings. 'There, lass. You're mine now, without doubt. And it were good an' all. Eeh, lass, I'll not be having that Dilly any more, I promise. Come and give me a cuddle.'

Hating him, but hating herself more and with no fight left in her, Sarah allowed him to hold her. In the warmth and strength of his embrace, she found some recompense for the tears she couldn't give release to. Ignoring the smell of his unwashed clothes and body, she let her mind wander.

How different things had been when they were children: she and Billy, the best of friends, giggling about being boyfriend and girlfriend, playing together in a carefree world. And then the day came when her world had spun – like the spinning top she'd received for the last Christmas she remembered before the nightmare had begun – and everything had changed.

As the recollection gathered pace, it made her want to pummel Billy to death with her fists. But instead she'd take all he put her through, for the sake of so many people, especially her Aunt Megan.

It was funny, but though more of a mam to her than anyone could be, she'd never called Aunt Megan 'Mam'. She still remembered her own mam. She'd had a lovely name: *Cecelia*. 'I gave her a right posh name,' her Granna Issy had said, and then had made Sarah laugh by adding, 'Aw, but though it were posh, we always used the short form – Cissy – so no one'd think as she were one of them with their knickers trapped in the crease of their bum.' She had some sayings, did her granna; but then Aunt Megan had said her mam had been the same and could floor you with the shock of what came out of her mouth at times.

Cissy. Just thinking the name conjured up the sound of tinkling laughter and happiness from a distant time that Sarah couldn't touch – a time that lived on inside her, where her mam took on the form of an angel, all fluffy and pretty and with mounds of curls, and was safely locked in a corner of her mind where nothing bad lurked.

Listening to Aunt Megan, and sometimes to her dad and granna, telling stories about her mam helped to keep Cissy alive for Sarah. She loved to hear how her mam and Aunt Megan had been close from the age of thirteen, when they'd both become seamstresses, and how they'd looked out for each other. Strange that they should both be in her thoughts at this moment. She supposed it was because right now she most needed a mam by her side, to hold her and soothe away her shame and hurt. Aunt Megan had done that for Sarah all her life, even before her mam had died.

A longing came into her. If only she could share with someone what was happening, and could ask someone to help her. But who? She couldn't tell Aunt Megan, and telling her granna or her dad would result in Aunt Megan finding out.

Maybe Aunt Hattie? Another of her surrogate aunts, who'd been in her life for as long as she could remember. But then what could Aunt Hattie do? Whatever anyone did would result in Billy's anger being so great that she couldn't imagine what the consequences might be.

The situation was hopeless. The more she pondered on it, the more a deep loneliness lay within her – even though she was surrounded by the love of strong women, who'd all been to hell and back and would give their lives for her. Everything in her world hung as if from a fragile spider's web. Any action she took to break away from Billy would be like taking a broom to her life and sweeping that web away. Billy would see to that. Billy would take his revenge, and he'd take it on everyone she loved – especially Aunt Megan, because he still felt a loathing in him for her: his own mam, the woman who least deserved his hate and who loved him beyond anything. The blame he'd unjustly placed on Aunt Megan's shoulders, for him killing his dad, hadn't diminished over the years and would mean that she would suffer the most. No, Sarah couldn't be responsible for that happening.

This knowledge tightened the chains that bound her to Billy and filled her with a horror of her own future. But although her heart bade her to end this sham, she knew there was no escape.

Billy's smile held satisfaction as he watched his beautiful Sarah cross to her car. He admired her slim body, her rounded little bottom and her fair hair, styled in the latest fashion and swept back into two rolled waves that extended around to the back of her head. And her eyes – her lovely blue eyes. She was his, all his. *God, I hope with everything in me that what I just done to her means she'll have me babby in her – that will seal things good and proper. She'll have to marry me then.*

Seeing her walk like an injured animal cut him to his heart, but she'd brought it all on herself. Sarah hadn't been the same of late. There wasn't the love in her – it was all forced. He'd make that right, if only he could get out of here. How could it not come right? He loved her. Always had done. Nothing, and no one, could separate them. At least they'd to think on before they tried, as he'd not stand anyone getting in his way where Sarah was concerned.

The fury of this possibility trembled through Billy and lit

the demon rage that lived within him, burning a painful fire through his veins. *Take deep breaths. Control it. The time will come to unleash it, but not now. Now I need to concentrate on pleasing everybody – it's the only way. If I don't, I'll not have a hope of getting out of here.*

2

Megan

The Past Lingers

Megan hung the receiver back on the wall, her smile – the last remnant of the belly laugh she'd shared with Hattie – lingering on her lips.

'What's Hattie been on about this time? I thought as you'd wet your knickers, with how you were laughing.'

'Oh, Phyllis, it were one of her customers. Hattie said this woman came into the emporium, looking like she'd not eaten for days, then by the time she'd gone around all the counters her belly had grown like she were ready to drop twins!'

'What? How come?'

'The crafty mare had sewn a pouch into the front of her coat. Hattie said she had the woman hopping like a kangaroo before she was done with her. Then loads of Hattie's stock kept dropping out – jelly moulds, scrubbing brushes, peg bags. The woman denied all knowledge of them, but to top it all, Hattie ended up giving the poor soul a job! Turns out she's five kids to feed and no man. So she's to get to the store at closing time and work along with the other cleaners. It just tickled me. Anyone else would have sent for the police, but not Hattie. She sorts the woman's life out for her.'

'Aye, that's typical of Hattie. Look how she sorted me and Daisy out.'

'And me, and she did her best for me mam,' Sally chipped in.

'Well, I could say that an' all,' Megan told them. 'It was Hattie as first started me on the road to having a business. So I reckon young Freda should make a pot of tea and we'll have a toast to our Hattie, eh?'

Freda, the latest apprentice and, to Megan's mind, a good girl, jumped up without protest, though she did have a cheeky quip as she went towards the kitchen. 'Glad to. It'll take me away from you lot, as you sound like you're going down memory lane again.' Megan saw Freda just manage to dodge the pincushion that Sally threw at her. They all laughed at this.

The banter didn't continue. Instead, the hum of the sewing machines resumed, leaving Megan looking at six bent heads, three of which belonged to women who were very dear to her.

How different their lives were now, she thought, as she carried on sorting through swatches of material samples. And yes, a lot of it was down to Hattie. Hattie had helped her through the worst of times, had given Megan her first chance to set up on her own and, after she'd lost it all, had encouraged her to start over again, once she had the means to do so. Now look at where she was; she had all of this: a dress shop and design studio, as well as this making-up room where all her drawings became a reality. It was just like Madame Marie's place had been – the studio of the woman who'd taken her on as an apprentice from the age of thirteen until her marriage.

Part of Megan's mind closed at the thought of her first marriage. She couldn't dwell on any of that. It was all too painful, and a long time ago now. And as the world goes, some good had come out of it: her son Billy, for instance. Yes, there were bad times with the lad, but no matter what, she loved him. And then there was her being with Jack – not that she'd ever have been with him if Cissy had lived. Cissy had been Jack's first wife and a very special person. The bond she and Cissy had shared had been strong. Megan had loved Jack all the time he was married to Cissy, but had never shown her feelings then. To have done so would have hurt Cissy badly. *Oh, Ciss, lass, I still miss you. But thou knows, you live on in your Sarah. She don't look like you – she looks like Jack – but she has your kind ways and bubbly nature.*

The bustle of activity in the room around her reminded Megan of Madame Marie's, as did the smell of the fabrics and cottons, though a new odour mingled with these familiar ones: that of warmed oil, as the electric machines whirred away and heated up. During the Madame Marie years there had been few machines, and those that there were had a treadle to work them. *Eeh, if I spent a day on one of them, the backs of me calves knew it.*

Those years had shaped Megan's dream to own her own place, but what she had now wasn't what she once wished for. She'd gone from wanting to design exclusives for the rich, as Madame Marie had done, to wanting to have as little as she could to do with any top-drawer folk. So now she designed everyday wear and Sunday best for the middle classes, and she was working on a new line for Hattie's emporium – off-the-peg, affordable clothes for the working class. However, she still did exclusive designs for Lady Crompton and her daughter over at Hensal Grange, and their friend Lady Gladwyn. She owed that much to Lord and Lady Crompton, because indirectly it was their money that had given her this second chance to set up.

But then, they owed her, an' all – owed her for all she went through at the hands of Laura Harvey, Lady Crompton's sister. But no, she'd not think about all of that. She'd forgiven the woman as she'd lain on her deathbed, and that was how it would stay. She'd had to, or she and her Jack could never have moved forward.

Sally's laugh echoed across the room, cutting into Megan's thoughts and bringing her back to the present. Sally had stood up to help Freda, who teetered across from the kitchen bearing an overladen tray and looking as though she would drop it at any moment. The smile she'd lost came back to Megan's face at the antics of the girls teasing and having fun at Freda's expense, though she checked on her apprentice to make sure she was taking it all in her stride.

With the tray safely on the table, Sally turned and indicated that she would pour Megan's tea for her. Megan felt sadness enter her as she looked at Sally – beautiful Sally, fragile, not in stature, but inside where it mattered, damaged by the horror she'd endured as a child when she'd been raped by a sex fiend. If only the tendrils of pain that clung to her would heal and allow Sally to seek real happiness. But she wouldn't hear of looking for a husband, or even think of loving any man in that way. At twenty-one, she had carved out a place for herself *on the shelf*, as they described unmarried girls of her age, and that's where she wanted to stay.

As she made her way across to Sally and Freda, Megan saw Phyllis and Daisy rise from their benches to join them. Their appearance demonstrated the changes that Hattie had helped bring about in their lives. Their hair – once permanent-waved into the latest fashion to increase their chances of attracting 'customers' – was now worn in a natural bob and tied up in a headscarf while they worked. As they no longer had to prostitute themselves, the make-up they had once used to plaster their faces was gone, as were their flamboyant clothes.

They lived a happy life together as a couple, though of course few knew their real status. Most thought they were just spinster-friends, no different from many others who hadn't been lucky in finding a man, out of the few who came home from the last war. *God! It's hard to believe we are now at war again.* Megan's mind went to Billy. Somehow it felt like she was trading his freedom from that awful place for his life in trying to get him released to the army. This thought set a tremble running through her. *Please, God, keep him safe if it works out that he does have to go to war.*

Daisy lifted her cup. 'To Hattie, for all she's done for us all, and to the continued success of her and Harry's emporium.'

Megan raised her mug and clinked it against the rest. Freda giggled. The girl didn't really know what all the fuss was about, but Megan and the others did. They knew they were all the stronger for having Hattie in their lives. Suddenly Megan couldn't wait for the evening to come. Hattie and Harry were coming over for their tea – a distraction she needed at the moment. Because although she'd let her mind wander around all sorts of events in the past, there were things in the present that were niggling at her – not that she could share them, but it was enough just being with Hattie, her friend from the moment they were old enough to make friends thirty-eight years ago. And even before that according to what they had been told.

Within weeks of their birth they'd been taken from St Michaels, a home for unmarried mothers, to a convent orphanage, and had often been told by Sister Bernadette, the nun who'd devoted herself to them, that they were much happier when together as little babbies than they would have been if she separated them. *By, it beggars belief that me and Hattie are going on forty now. Where have all the years gone? And how did we weather it all? I don't know.*

Megan shrugged. One thing she did know: having a hug from Hattie would, and always did, make her feel better about everything.

3

Terence & Theresa

The Seeds of Revenge

Terence Crompton paced up and down the lawn, as boredom – his constant companion – made him restless.

The late-September sun warmed his back and bathed the stunning Hensal Grange in a soft light. He loved this place and always had done since, as a child, he'd visited his poor Aunt Laura, whose home this used to be.

Everyone always referred to Aunt Laura – the late Laura Harvey – as *poor Laura*. Dogged as she'd been by unhappiness, the description suited her memory, what with Laura losing her only child at birth and then losing her husband in the so-called 'Great War', before dying from TB at a very young age. Although, before doing so, Laura had rather blotted her copy book by committing the ultimate faux pas of falling in love with her stable groom!

That very groom was now the cause of most of Terence's discontent, owning as he did the best stud farm in the county. And all courtesy of a very big slice of what should have been part of *his* inheritance from Aunt Laura.

'That was a big sigh, Terence. You will become the master of sighs at this rate. For goodness' sake, why don't you do something with your life? Join the army, or something?'

'Ha! You're one to talk – lazing around, sunning yourself. I don't see you, dear sister, engaging in useful employment.'

'A privilege given to the fairer sex, dear.'

'Oh, go away, Theresa. I can't be doing with you at the moment. And your privileges should not be at the expense of Pater.'

'And yours should, I take it? Anyway, that was not a kind remark. You know I can't do anything other than rely on Pater, until my divorce from Raymond sorts itself out – at which time, half of what is owned by that wretched pansy I married will become mine.'

'Have you heard any more on that front?'

'Yes, his lawyers are trying for an annulment, as they are saying the marriage wasn't consummated! And if they get it, that will be the end of that. So, would you have me out on a limb?'

'You could live on your inheritance from Grandfather and Aunt Laura. You haven't touched it yet.'

'No. Unlike you, I let Pater invest it for the long term – which I am very happy about, because, with the money tied up, I can't show that I have adequate means to support myself. If I could, I would lose most of what I stand to gain. Look, you know all of this, so why bring it up now? Mater and Pater are happy to have me home, so why can't you be? You're my . . . my soulmate – my twin, for heaven's sake!'

'Oh, sorry, old thing. Here, shift up and make room for me. We'll snuggle up, like we always used to, and stop this fighting. We need each other, right now more than ever. Look, surely you could play the "Give me what I want, or I tell all" card?'

'Yes, that is the next step – a quiet settlement and divorce, citing his adultery with a maid or something, within days of our marriage. Such a story will leave me embarrassed, but with my reputation intact.'

'Your reputation! My dear, you haven't had one of those since you were a youngster.'

'Terence, don't. I'm not in the mood.'

'You never are, these days.'

'Oh, shut up and get in!'

Theresa's warm, delicious body welcomed him next to her in the ample-sized hammock. Slim and very pretty – in fact beautiful; the most beautiful woman he knew, and the female *him*, really – his twin had attributes that mirrored his own: he was tall and elegant, with dark hair and large brown eyes flecked with hazel and framed by sweeping eyelashes. They were both always at the centre of northern and London society, but they were lost, too.

At twenty-eight years old, they lived aimlessly from day to day and held a secret that burned into them both; but more so for Theresa, since her failed marriage. *Thinking of which, fancy old Hawthorn – the school bully – turning out to be a faggot! Who'd have thought it?*

Terence himself had suffered under the gang that the Honourable Raymond Hawthorn had accumulated around him. He'd taken him to task over it, too, when Hawthorn had stepped up as a beau to his sister. But then, as Theresa told it, Hawthorn had cried like a baby on the first night of their marriage, begging her to live a sham life with as many lovers as she wanted as long as she turned a blind eye to him having as many male partners as he wanted. It all beggared belief, as they said around here. *But it pleases me, all the same.*

As for himself, Terence had failed in his education and hadn't taken up a position in the family bank – not that he couldn't, as Pater would make a place for him, but he simply couldn't face the humiliation of being unable to grasp the business. All those figures scared the hell out of him.

His only interest was racing horses. Riding them, breeding them and owning a top earner occupied all of his dreams. And that's where that blighter Jack Fellam put an obstacle in his way. Pater wouldn't hear of Terence starting a rival stud farm to Jack's, even though Aunt Laura had run one from this estate that was in direct competition with Smythe's Stud Farm, which Jack now owned.

All the stables Aunt Laura had built were still in good condition, but with Pater overseeing the business side of Fellam's stud, he saw it as a betrayal of Jack Fellam's trust if he funded Terence to run a similar business. His father's objection was impenetrable. But, that aside, what stuck most in his craw was that Fellam had used the legacy Aunt Laura had left him to buy bloody Smythe's Stud Farm in the first place. *A legacy that should have come to me.*

Aunt Laura's affair with Jack Fellam had brought her nothing but pain, but she'd become riddled with guilt after she'd tried to stop Jack from marrying Megan, the woman he'd fallen in love with. And from what Terence had heard of the consequences of Aunt Laura's actions, Megan Fellam had nearly been killed by the vicious man she was then married to, but had tried to escape from. All the same, Aunt Laura shouldn't have tried to make amends by leaving Jack a huge slice of her wealth!

'What are your plans, my little brother?' Theresa often addressed him this way. She'd been born a full half-hour before him and thought it funny to emphasize the fact. He didn't mind, as he adored her – when he wasn't irritated with life, that is.

He pulled her closer to him. She didn't scold him, but

snuggled into him, as she knew he liked her to. 'God knows. I know one day I will inherit all of this, but what is it, other than a beautiful country pile? I've no interest in administrating the estate side of things or running the farm, so I would employ a manager for that, as Pater does. And though I rue the proceeds going to Fellam, I'm jolly glad Pater sold the mine and that it took care of Fellam's share of Aunt Laura's legacy. Ugh! The very thought of being involved in mining repulses me.'

'Yes, it was fortunate it fetched such a good price, otherwise we wouldn't be living here, as there was very little money left once Aunt Laura's estate was settled. At least the stinking mine did that for us. But, you know, sometimes I miss living in our own home in York. I wish the parents hadn't sold our pile there. It would be lovely to go back in the winter for the party season.'

'Oh, that doesn't bother me. I prefer to go to London, and Christmas here is right up my street, with the house full of guests and the shooting parties and . . . Anyway, we digress. I am the topic of the conversation, and this isn't helping me.'

'Really, Terence, you can be so boring sometimes. Surely you can find something to do?'

'Thank you for that. But no, finding a position in life is easier said than done. I have few options, sister dear. I can't take up politics. Pater's title – being an honorary one – doesn't pass to me, so I don't qualify for the House of Lords. And so I am stuck. That is, until I can do with my inheritance as I wish: a state of affairs that I am not looking forward to, as I don't wish Pater's demise, lovely old thing that he is. I am very fond of him, as you know, but it is Pater and his stubbornness that are stopping me doing what I want to do.'

'Darling, there is a war on. Oh, I know – at only a few weeks old, nothing is happening yet, but it will. I have listened to conversations, and everyone believes it will be a long haul. Many lives will be lost, and much property destroyed. The economy will be a mess. There's even talk that they will conscript all the young men. Racing and gambling will be the last thing on people's minds. Shouldn't you think about becoming an officer or a pilot, or something? Before all the best positions go, I mean. After all, if you don't, you could find yourself having to take orders from the gardener's lad.'

'Heaven forbid! Besides, as you say, it's early days yet, and I can't see anything coming of it. It's ridiculous: some screaming German chap bombing us! It *ain't* going to happen, dear. Anyway, I fancy a smoke. Have you got yours on you?'

'No, but I brought my bell out with me. I'll ring for Frobisher. I think the old thing could make it out here. He can organize us some tea and bring some cigarettes out for us.'

'It's time he was put out to grass, poor thing. He must be a hundred.'

Theresa laughed at this. Her brother loved to make her laugh. Although Terence had said she shouldn't be here, he hadn't meant it. He was jolly glad she was. In fact, he didn't know what he'd do without her.

Terence climbed out of the hammock and helped Theresa out. She linked his arm in hers as they walked over to the summerhouse, where they ordered their tea to be set. She looked lovely in her calf-length white linen dress, with its flowing skirt. She had picked up her straw sunhat, trimmed with a yellow bow, and placed it on her immaculately cut, shining hair. The picture of innocence that she portrayed suited her. They matched rather well, he thought – he in his white slacks and shirt, and sporting a yellow cravat.

They didn't speak, and he found that his mind wouldn't let

go of the Fellam question. He needed to do something. The conversation he'd had with his friends, Godfrey and Cecil, came to mind. During the shoot in August, he'd told them of his feelings and ambitions and Cecil had said, 'Well, why don't we fix it? We could make it look like an accident. What about a fire?'

The notion had shocked Terence – even more so when he realized that not only was Cecil being serious, but that Godfrey agreed! Oh, he knew they were a couple of wild things. Rich beyond imagination, they looked for any prank to amuse them, safe in the knowledge that their money and position would bail them out, but he hadn't thought they would go that far.

Why he was even mulling over the stupid idea was beyond him, but it did have some merit. It would finish Jack Fellam. Pater had said that the stables, buying the land and house and setting up his wife, Megan, in that dress-making business she ran, had taken all of Fellam's inheritance. Yes, they were all making a good living – they weren't wanting, and he supposed they were comfortably off – but not so as Fellam could start again. That would take an immense amount of money – money that, surely, his father would rather invest in his son than in some groom who had brought scandal to Mater's family?

Convinced of this, the idea began to appeal to Terence. He would have to plan it well. No suspicion could fall his way, and no one must get hurt – not human beings anyway, although he supposed he'd have to destroy a few horses. That would be difficult, but then: needs must. As for Fellam, he owned acres of land that he used for no more than training and grazing the horses, so he could turn that into an arable farm. The country would need home-grown supplies. The government had already started to encourage people to grow their own vegetables during the last few months, when war had seemed imminent. Fellam would have to take up the challenge, as they all would. He'd make a good living from that. Nothing to worry about there.

Perhaps he should befriend Fellam: take an interest in his stables, maybe even offer to help out, on the pretext of wishing to acquire knowledge. *Yes, that would be the thing. No one would think I'd have anything to do with destroying something that I took an interest in. I could offer to ride the horses – I'd love that.*

Yes, suddenly the whole plan seemed a real solution: a fire would wipe out Fellam's business in such a way that he couldn't start again; and until the right opportunity presented itself to put that into operation, Terence thought, he himself could spend his time around those magnificent racehorses and studs.

Happy with his plans, he decided to talk to Theresa about getting involved with the stable. See how she reacted. If she didn't suspect there was any more to it then he'd know it wasn't a foolhardy plan. Anyway, whether it worked or not, just thinking about it had made him feel better. He started to run. 'Come on, sis. Race you.'

4

Jack

A Father's Concern

Jack Fellam closed the last of the stable doors just as Sarah's car pulled in through the gates. There was no sign of Megan following behind; it was just wishful thinking that he'd expected her to, when she'd warned she could be late home.

Sarah didn't alight from the car immediately, but hung her head over the wheel. Jack looked away; he'd not intrude, even though when Sarah – his only living child – hurt, he hurt. Poor lass, it couldn't be easy for her, having the man she loved locked away, as Billy was. Her pain was natural, and it was bound to visit her more when she'd had to part from Billy after visiting him. There was nothing he could do to lift that pain from her, or to make things better for her. Not that he wanted to make everything better for her, because although he let Sarah think he was happy with the situation, deep down he wasn't, and he wished she wasn't in love with Billy.

He had to console himself with the fact that there no longer seemed to be any harm in the lad now, though Billy's actions in the past still visited Jack in the wakeful hours of the early morning and filled him with dread.

Pulling himself up, Jack told himself that he had to move on; after all, Billy had only been ten when he'd committed the first heinous crime that had changed their lives, and he'd suffered terribly at his father's hand. Had seen things, too, that no lad should see – things that had turned his mind and made him think it was right to deal with anything you didn't like by using violence. Then there was Megan, his own lovely Megan, who had been part of the violent past Billy had witnessed, as she'd been beaten near to death and raped by her then-husband, Billy's father. The memory of this clutched painfully at him.

Sarah lifted her head and looked over towards him. She didn't return his wave but got out of the car, turned from him and hurried towards the house. Jack's heart lurched. He couldn't bear anything to trouble his lovely Sarah. He hesitated, wondering if he should go after her, but thought better of it and busied himself picking up the horses' feeding buckets.

'I'll see to them, Jack. I've another half-hour to kill before I knock off.'

Glad of the distraction, Jack glanced over at Gary, his head trainer. 'I'll take you up on your offer, Gary, lad. I'm supposed to check on my ma-in-law to make sure she's coping when it comes to cooking the meal for us all. She's not getting any younger.'

'Eeh, you're under the thumb good and proper, Jack. Go on with yer. By, I'm glad my Jenny don't work like your lassies do! At least I don't have to get stuck into women's work when I get home.'

Jack laughed at this. He didn't mind the banter. He and Gary had known each other for years, having worked together for Laura Harvey. Gary often ragged him about having a working wife, but he'd have it no different. It wasn't the done thing, but it made Megan happy, and that was his main reason for living: seeing her and his ma-in-law and Sarah happy. His worries about Sarah revisited him. She'd acted strangely; it wasn't like her not to greet him when she returned home, and she'd always have a word with Gary or any of the lads around the stables whenever she came into the yard. The niggling within him turned to deep concern.

As he went through the gate leading to the path that would take him through the beautiful gardens at the back of his house, Jack felt the usual disbelief. This grand house, with its six bedrooms and two parlours – or 'withdrawing rooms', as top-drawer folk called them – was far beyond his own and Megan's beginnings. He looked up at the building. The sun, now low in the sky, reflected back a golden light from the many windows. His heart jolted with pride. To think that he and Megan owned and lived in such a place!

In the end, they had a lot to thank Laura Harvey for. He could think of her now without guilt. He and Laura had been two lonely young folk drawn to each other. Their affair had taken place two years after Cissy died, and before he'd woken up to realize that the feelings he had for Megan were more than those of just good friends. What Laura's jealousy had caused, once she knew he'd fallen for Megan, wasn't easy to come to terms with. Nor what it led Billy to do. But Megan had forgiven him, and had forgiven Laura in the end, so that helped.

'Take them boots off, Jack Fellam!'

'Eeh, Ma, let me in the door afore you start. By, woman, a man ain't a man in his own house these days.' He crossed the kitchen and tugged at the bow tying Issy's apron. Once loosened, the pinafore hung from her neck and drooped around the front of her. Her reaction wasn't as quick as it would have been in years gone by – he'd have been in for a clout then –

but still he dodged out of her way as, wielding a floury rolling pin, she turned towards him.

'Jack Fellam, you're worse than having a babby around. Give over, or you'll find your lugs reddened with this.'

'Ha, you'd never catch me! With you waddling like a duck, I'd be long gone. Here, give us a kiss and greet me as you should greet the head of the house.'

'You may be head of the house, lad, but that don't include me kitchen, so in here you'll do as I say or you'll find yourself as a filling for one of me pies. Now come here and stop taking me on.'

All his worries left his shoulders as she encased him in her warm embrace and planted a kiss on his cheek – his ma-in-law, Isabel Grantham, always known as Issy, had stood by him, no matter what. She'd taken him in as a lad just home from the last war. His brother and da had been killed in the trenches, and his ma had died with the shock of the news. He'd been a lost soul seeking a new beginning, and he'd found it in her home.

There he'd first met Issy's daughter, Cissy, and her friend Megan. He'd fallen deeply in love with Cissy. They'd had a blissful marriage, marred only by the miscarriages poor Cissy suffered after having Sarah; but then along came Bella. Cissy had died giving birth to Bella, making Jack feel as if his heart had been ripped out of him.

He shook his head as he remembered the awful events of the following years. It all seemed like a lifetime ago. Bella – *me little defenceless Bella*. Hatred, never far from his bones, trembled through his body, and he knew that if Billy, his little girl's killer, stood before him now, he'd strangle the life from him.

'Eeh, lad, it'll never leave you.'

He hadn't spoken of it, but she'd known. It was like that, with Issy. She knew when you were troubled. He came out of her arms. 'No, Ma, I don't suppose it will, but like you've said many a time afore, we've to find a way to live with it.'

Brushing the flour from where it had rubbed onto his shirt, Issy retied her apron, then surprised him by echoing his own worries. 'Aye, and to deal with it an' all. It ain't over, Jack, not whilst Billy's still alive, it ain't. Oh, I know I shouldn't think like that, as the lad's doing his time and has had help for his unstable condition, but the fear of him doesn't leave me, and I worry for our Sarah.'

'I know, but don't say owt to Megan; she's enough on her plate, with how Billy is. He's started being a bit cutting with her of late, and Megan thinking as he didn't blame her any more. By, it beggars belief how he could even think her responsible for everything in the first place.'

'Well, his dad was responsible for him thinking that way. Bert Armitage was more than evil – he even had Megan thinking she was the cause of his violent ways towards her; so it's not surprising a young 'un would take it as a truth. But what are we to do about Sarah?'

'There's nowt can be done. She loves Billy – always has done – so we're to leave well alone. Where is she, by the way? Poor lass seemed very upset when she arrived back. Didn't greet none of us, which ain't usual.'

'She didn't come in this way. I heard the front door go, and then she called out that she'd see me in a bit, as she wanted to get a bath. By the time I'd gone through, she'd disappeared up the stairs. Oh, Jack—'

'I know, Ma. I fear for her an' all, but like I say, there's nowt can be done. We just have to be here if she ever needs us.'

'If only Sarah could return the love Richard has for her.

29

How much better our lass's prospects would be then. Eeh, that'd be the best thing as could happen, in my books.'

'You're an old romantic, Ma. Those feelings you think Richard has for Sarah are all wishful thinking.'

'No, lad. They're true all right.' Issy touched her nose. 'I know.'

Jack smiled to himself. Young Richard would be the perfect husband for Sarah. A long-lost brother of Megan, Richard was a handsome, well-set-up lad. He took after his father in wanting to become a doctor and was just beginning his training.

Bridget, Richard's ma, had given birth to Megan when she'd been a lass of just sixteen. Her circumstances had been such that she'd had to give up her babby. When, by an amazing coincidence, mother and daughter were reunited, Megan found she had two half-brothers, Richard and Mark. And lovely lads they were, too. By, he'd love Richard and his Sarah to get together. But there was no use speculating about it. Sarah loved Billy and always had done, since they were young 'uns together. He couldn't see that changing.

Jack shuddered as he thought this and, though he was not given much to praying, he directed a plea at the God that he'd often felt had let him down. *Please look after me little Sarah. Let there be no more – please don't send us any more to bear . . . But if you have to, then let it be on my shoulders, not Sarah's, and not Megan's or Issy's.*

5

Richard

Life's Tangles

'Bridget, darling, what is it?'

'I don't know, to tell the truth, Edward. It is nothing Megan has *said* in her letter, more what she *hasn't* said. I've just got this feeling . . .'

'That's your imagination, dear. Your motherly instinct is always in top gear, making you think something is wrong with Megan. It's always the same, and then you find you had nothing to worry about.'

'No, not always. The whole time we were trying to find her, I used to say I felt things weren't right for her – and I was right then.'

'Let's start with what the letter *does* say, shall we?'

'Megan says she's trying to get Billy released. She feels he may do something really bad if he is cooped up in that secure mental hospital much longer. But she doesn't sound happy about it.'

Richard had let his parents' conversation go over his head. He'd been engrossed in what the post had brought for him, but now unease entered him on hearing his mother's words.

Billy, free. But that would mean Sarah and he ... Oh God!
'Is it likely they will set him free, Father?'

'It's possible. It has been nine years since his incarceration. I haven't kept up with his medical condition lately, but I'll see what I can find out. I'm due at a meeting of the Trust this afternoon, so I'll look up Dr Hutting's number in the directory of psychiatrists that's kept at the hospital. Last I heard, he was in charge of Billy's case.'

Richard nodded. He knew the *finding out* wouldn't be a chore. A vibrant personality at seventy years old, his father would still be going strong in his career as a surgeon to this day, had it not been for the slight tremor that now afflicted him. As it was, he remained active as a member of the Leicestershire Hospital Trust and enjoyed getting involved.

As a lad, Billy had been in a secure mental institution in the area, but had moved up to Leeds at the age of sixteen. Since then Richard hadn't seen anything of him, and didn't wish to, either. He voiced that now. 'Well, I – for one – hope he doesn't come out. Oh, I know I haven't met him many times, but when I did, I didn't like him. Sorry, Mother, I know he is your grandson and my half-nephew, but, well . . .'

'I know, dear. We can't choose our relatives. I'm always wishing things were different – not about finding Megan, of course. The years after she was taken from me, at her birth, were hell for me. Finding her was a completion of who I am. Her circumstances, when we did find her, were appalling enough for us all to come to terms with. But to have the problem of her son, my grandson Billy, on top of that, and all he was capable of and carried out – well, that marred the reunion of Megan and me.'

'Look, old girl, I've told you before that you cannot change things; and Megan is happy with Jack now. All the violence she suffered is behind her, so you have to stop worrying about it all.'

'I don't think it is behind us, I—'

Richard rose and left the room. His mother looked close to tears, and he knew it was best to leave his father to comfort her.

They made a striking couple, he thought as he reached the door and looked back. They were holding each other: Father, tall, slender and with white-grey hair, and Mother, younger than his father by about twelve years, and still retaining her graceful beauty. A rush of love for them both assaulted him.

Although he had inherited his father's love of medicine, Richard took after his mother in looks, having the same very dark hair and oval eyes. Many times she'd told him he was a mirror image of her own father. 'Every time I catch sight of you when I'm not expecting to, my heart stops, as it seems that my dad has come back to me. You look exactly like him – the same deep-blue, smiley eyes and your tall, strong build, though my father got his physique from working down the pit from the age of six or seven.' She'd go on to say that sometimes her dad's image was like a haze in her memory, and at other times was crystal-clear. 'I was only little when he died, but the locket my mam gave me, which had a picture of them both, kept him alive for me.'

Going off at a tangent, she'd tell him how she'd left the locket with her baby, and how it had been the cause of her and Megan finding each other all those years later. Then she would resume talking about Richard's resemblance to his grandfather. 'You know, my mam once told me that my dad had an Italian in his ancestry, but that nothing was known of him.'

Richard smiled at this romantic notion as he walked

through the hall. Catching a glimpse of himself in the mirror as he passed by, he thought there might be some truth in the Italian heritage and vowed to get his mother to tell him more about her family. There seemed such a mystery surrounding his maternal grandparents, and nothing about their names gave a clue to anything out of the ordinary: Will and Bridie Hadler. *Definitely not Italian-sounding!*

Wanting some air and some time to consider his own thoughts, he took his jacket off the coat stand and went outside. The chill in the air surprised him. The last few days had been warm and sunny, making all the speculation about war seem as though it belonged somewhere else. The buff envelope with its War Office stamp that had arrived for him this morning had reminded him that it didn't.

Crossing the cobbled yard, he reached the gate. Beyond lay acres of softly rolling landscape. Their house, on the outskirts of Market Harborough, stood on an incline, affording them views far and wide of this part of Leicestershire, on the border of Northamptonshire.

To his left he could see the many church towers and spires of the villages, dotted here and there amidst the farmland. Some of the fields had been harvested and ploughed, whilst others were pastures with herds of cows idly chewing away on the grass; and some still boasted their crops of wheat swaying in the breeze, making the scene look like a patchwork quilt of browns, greens and yellows. To his right lay the more densely built-up area of the town itself, a place with much history to it. In particular, he loved the seventeenth-century grammar school building at its centre; criss-crossed with old beams and looking as though it was supported by stilts, it told of a bygone age.

As Richard leaned on the gate, the only sounds to disturb

his thoughts were those of the wildlife variety: birds twittering, and the occasional sheep or cow telling the world whatever. He looked back at the rear of their home, a large detached house – rural, peaceful; a happy place – the front of which looked out over the Welland Valley, with its ever-changing kaleidoscope of colour reflecting the seasons. A lovely place, but one that belied the trauma that the two loving people who lived there had experienced, before marrying and giving life to him and his younger brother Mark. Their heroic actions in the Great War were enough for anyone to endure in a lifetime, working as they had done in sparse tents behind the front lines. His father being a surgeon and his mother a nurse, they had battled to save lives, with minimal equipment and in horrendous conditions. But even worse than that was what his mother had suffered as a young girl.

It had been a shock when they had decided to tell Richard the truth about how he came to have a much older half-sister. The story angered every bone of his body. To hear of the rape of his mother, when just a young girl, and having her child taken from her – only to find her years later, and to have to face the shocking truth that her long-lost half-brother, Bert Armitage, and her daughter Megan had met and married, in ignorance of their relationship to each other – had been devastating to him. Added to that, the product of that marriage, Billy, born unwittingly of incest, had been inflicted with mental-health disturbances, resulting in him committing vile acts that had blighted all of their lives.

The tremble shaking his body and stippling his arms with goosebumps unsteadied Richard now. He thought he'd come to terms with it all. He was in his last year at university and was hoping to go to medical school, to become a surgeon one day; at the age of twenty-two, he should have been able to deal with it, but he couldn't, not really. And now there was the possibility of that monster Billy gaining his freedom!

Sarah came into his mind: his fear for her and – yes, he had to admit – his longing for her. Despite the horror of the revelations concerning Megan's birth, he'd been quite proud to find out, at the age of twelve and a half, that though he and Sarah weren't blood relatives he was a step-uncle by marriage to her, and half-uncle to Billy, without being much older than them. But now those relationships meant very different things to him: he hated his nephew and was in love . . . *No!* He must stop thinking like this! Sarah belonged to Billy. Always had done and always would.

The sound of horses' hooves from the direction of the lane that ran by their house caught his attention. Its rider – beautiful, raven-haired and elegantly side-saddled – called out to him. 'Hey, Richard, are you all right?'

'Yes, I'm fine. I'm just pondering things.'

'Nothing too serious, I hope. You looked very downcast.'

'I've had one of *those* envelopes! Have to report for a medical next week. Not looking forward to it, or to the interruption of my studies.'

'Oh no! So soon? God – that nasty, moustached little . . . Oh, I don't know, there doesn't seem a name that would fit Hitler, or describe what I think of him. He's going to spoil all of this. Us, and what we have.'

She dismounted and walked towards him. Her horse, held by the reins, pulled against her, poked its head over the gate and nudged Richard, knocking him backwards. The action made him laugh and gave him an excuse to try and get away. 'He's not happy at having his ride interrupted. I won't keep you, Lucinda. I have to go in and break the news of my call-up to the parents. I've been avoiding doing so.'

'Oh, don't mind him. And you're not stopping his exercise – he had that earlier. I rode over specifically to see if I could catch you. We have something to talk about, remember?'

Richard's heart sank. Damn his stupidity for kissing Lucinda at the autumn ball! She'd been trying to snare him for ages, and would now read more into the kiss than there was. How was he going to get out of this?

Everyone seemed to assume they would marry one day. His mother had hinted at it, and his father had said he couldn't do any better for himself. His parents and Lucinda's, who were wealthy farmers, had been friends for as long as he could remember. He and Lucinda had grown up together. He'd never had feelings other than friendship for her, but even their own circle of friends seemed to take it for granted that one day he would formally court her. God, what a mess!

'Well? Have you a moment to talk? I mean, Richard, we should sort things out. Even more so, with the possibility of you having to go to war.'

'I – I know. Sorry, look, I – I acted very foolishly the other night. I didn't mean to compromise our situation. But—'

'But you do love me, don't you? So why don't you take it further?'

'I can't, and I don't know. I mean, now isn't the time. Our lives are going to change. Besides, I'm not of independent means.'

'Which way around did you mean all of that, Richard? I hope you haven't misled me? You must realize I can't hang around much longer. This is very unfair on me. Surely we can make it official for now? Once you are my fiancé, well . . . well, we wouldn't have to stand on ceremony. We could get a lot closer.'

The insinuation she put into this took him aback. 'I can't

promise myself to anyone, Lucinda. I . . . Look, you're right, we do need to talk. Are you free this evening? Perhaps we could drive out and find somewhere to have dinner where no one knows us, so we won't be interrupted. A hotel in Northampton maybe?'

'Yes, I would love that.'

'I'll arrange everything and pick you up at seven.'

Her body swayed towards him, her face upturned. There was nothing he could do, without embarrassing her, other than kiss her. He managed, though, to avoid her lips and peck her cheek instead.

As she rode away, Richard felt despair at the situation he'd created. Somehow, tonight, he had to find a way of letting Lucinda down gently. *But how? Whatever I say, I'll look like a cad. Maybe I am one. What kind of man falls in love with someone who's practically a relative?*

The shudder that went through him was a throwback to the horror of what had happened to his half-sister, Megan. But Sarah herself wasn't related to him. He must remember that. She was the daughter of his half-sister's husband. There would be nothing at all wrong with a union between them. *If only it would happen . . . If only.*

6

Hattie & Harry

The Past Rises to Taunt

Hattie stared at the newspaper. Shock dried her mouth and shook her body. Arthur's wife dead! The paper became scrunched in her grip, before she dropped it to the ground. *Why? Why does that news drum up old feelings?* Feelings she'd thought long dead. Feelings that had belonged to a different person – the person she had been in those days.

The sound of the paper being gathered up caused her to turn round. Harry stood looking at her; she hadn't heard him come into her office. His face held concern. 'Is there something wrong, Hattie?'

Trying to keep her voice from shaking, she said, 'No, nothing. I lost me thoughts for a mo. I were looking for that advert you mentioned. Someone selling a van? I think you're right: we need to cover all angles, with this war. It could work – if we can't get deliveries to the shop, we'd have to fetch our own stock. Then there's that delivery service you were on about . . .' She stopped, realizing she was rambling.

'The advert wasn't in *The Times*, love. Why you have that paper, even occasionally, is beyond me.'

'I – I like to keep up. Get to know how the top-drawer lot

are thinking. We have a few accounts with them lot, so it pays to know what they're about.'

Harry didn't say anything. As she took the paper from him, he left without even telling her why he'd come into her office. Without giving a thought to this, Hattie spread the newspaper out on her desk and found the obituary page once more:

The death of Lady Greystone, which took place in Kenya two months ago on 2nd September 1939, has shocked society. Lord and Lady Greystone had been on holiday in Kenya when Lady Greystone suffered a bite from an unknown insect. Within hours she was in hospital fighting for her life – a fight she lost at 10 p.m. that night. The body was interred in Kenya. Lord Greystone sailed into Southampton a week ago. He has announced that a memorial service will be held in three weeks' time.

The article went on to give more information about Arthur: his First World War heroics, his injuries, and the mystery concerning where he'd disappeared to for all those years afterwards. *It were no mystery to me*, Hattie thought. The happiness of those years with Arthur was etched into her, and always would be, as was the pain of his leaving her.

A tap on her door and the sight of Megan entering made the pain resurface and clutch at her heart. Her eyes filled with tears.

'Hattie, love?'

'Oh, Meg, we went through sommat, didn't we? And, when we least think of it, it pops up to sting us again.'

'Eeh, lass, what's brought this on?'

Hattie pointed to the article.

'It still hurts, after all this time then, Hattie, love? By, we thought Arthur different, didn't we? Come on. It does no good thinking on it all now.'

'I know, but I still love him.'

Neither of them saw Harry move back from the door.

'I can understand that. It ain't easy to fall out of love. Look at me: I loved Jack from the moment I saw him and it never went away, no matter that he chose Cissy. But it turned out right for me. And I thought it had done for you, love?'

'It has. I'm being silly. It were seeing that article. It brings it all back. Anyroad, what brought you here in the middle of the day? Oh God, we had a meeting, didn't we? Where's Harry? He should be here.'

Something didn't sit easily with Hattie. Harry had come because of the meeting and she hadn't even acknowledged him.

The door opened. 'Did someone mention my name, and in a tone that suggests I might have to take me slippers else-where tonight?'

'Eeh, you daft ha'p'orth, Harry. You should have reminded me.' Hattie couldn't look at him. Panic rose within her. How long had he been outside?

Harry's taking charge of the situation eased the atmos-phere. Greeting Megan with a kiss, he quickly turned towards Hattie and took her arm. The squeeze he gave her was com-forting, but at the same time compounded her worry that he had heard what she'd said. But he gave her no time to dwell on this. 'Right, we best get on. Megan hasn't got all day. I've organized some tea and cakes for us. I don't know about you pair, but it seems a long time since breakfast.'

The air hung heavily between Hattie and Harry as they dis-cussed the new line, looked at samples that Megan had brought with her and haggled over the price.

Concluding business, Harry stood up. Hattie felt his eyes bore deeply into hers. 'Well, we've done well. It's only just on three. Did you say you haven't to go back to lock up your place, Megan?'

'Aye, that's right. Sally will see to things.'

'Well then, if I see to things here, I don't see why you two can't take yourselves off for an hour. Have a bit of time together – go shopping or sommat.'

'Shopping! Are you as daft as you look, Harry? We sell everything I'd want to buy!'

'Go to that tea room down the road, then. That one as puts an extra "p" and "e" on the end of "shop". It looks right posh. Or anywhere you fancy really, but have some time away from here and with Megan. It'll do you both good. You're never on your own together these days.'

The tea room lived up to being called 'posh', with its tables dressed in white lace cloths, adorned with little silver vases holding freshly cut flowers. The high-backed chairs were carved in a deep mahogany. The red carpet gave a soft tread, and the waitresses in their long grey skirts, white mob caps and white aprons reminded Hattie of her days in service, but added a touch of something special to the atmosphere.

After ordering, Hattie came straight to the point. 'Harry knows. He heard us. Oh, Megan, whatever possessed me? It ain't even how I feel. Not really. It just felt like it, when I saw Arthur's name.'

'Don't worry about Harry, love. He's always known your feelings. Happen he'd hoped he weren't second best, but he ain't as daft as you paint him.'

'But it's not true. It's not . . . Anyroad, you look like you've sommat to share. Let's forget my silly trip into the past. I'll pour. Eeh, look at these silver teapots. Their spouts are that snooty-looking, it's like they don't want us to handle them.'

Giggling at this, and with the tea poured and them both tucking into cucumber sandwiches as if they hadn't just had cake, or anything to eat for hours, Hattie felt better, though there was still the question of what was on Megan's mind – as if she couldn't guess.

'Come on, then, out with it.'

'It – it's Sarah. And Billy. And, oh, I don't know – the war . . . the possibilities of—'

'Eeh, one thing at a time, love, eh? I know as sommat's up with Sarah, as Sally told me. She's reet worried for her. But, thou knows, it's more than likely nerves over Billy coming out, and how it will be for them both. It can't have been easy for the lass.'

'Did Sally say as Sarah were sick at work?'

'Aye, but don't worry. No, you're not on with thinking – she can't be, Megan. How? When? No, she wouldn't. She has some morals, has Sarah. She . . . no. Billy hasn't—'

'Aye, that thought had occurred to me, so don't worry about saying it. He could, and he would. I have to face it.'

'Oh no, it ain't all starting again? You can't let it, Meg, love. You can't let Sarah go through what you did with Bert. Look, I know Billy's your son and all, but no.'

'I don't know what to do. I don't even know if I'm right. Oh, it's a mess!'

'Well, you have to find out. And if he . . . I'm sorry, Meg, I know you love Billy, and I know how it feels to do so, cos if it's anything like what I feel for Sally – and her not even me own – then it's painful. But if Billy's done owt to Sarah, then you have to rise above that, for Sarah's sake.'

'I know, and I will. But first we have to be sure. D'yer think you could talk to her? I've tried, but she brushes me off or makes some excuse to take her leave of me. I thought maybe you could get Sally to invite Sarah over. Pretend she wants to talk about girls' stuff.'

'Aye, I will. I'll find out for you, love. But if it's right, what we're thinking, promise me that'll be an end to it.'

'It will.'

'Reet, what's the other lot you lumped with this worry? It can't be any worse, so we may as well clear it all.'

Megan echoed all the concerns Hattie herself had over what might happen in the coming months. But Hattie knew they were tripled for Megan, because she feared for the lives of Billy and of her half-brothers, Richard and Mark, and even for Jack. He'd been a soldier in the last war, and it wasn't impossible they could call him up again.

'I thought Jack had started to plough up most of his fields by the back end of October, in line with the government ordering that all spare land must be turned over to producing food for the nation?'

'He has.'

'Well then, putting himself down as a farmer will keep him out of the army. All farmers are exempt, as Britain needs food. There'll be none getting in from abroad.'

'Do you really think that will keep him out? I mean, Gary has had his papers; Jenny's fraught with worry over it. As have all the other young lads who work in the stables. Jack's saying he'll have to close down the stables and get some Land Girls in to help him with the farming side. He needs to get a bit of money for the horses, though, as up to now he's borrowed equipment from neighbouring farms, but he'll need his own to hand.'

'I don't think you'll have too many worries on that score. It'll be survival of the fittest, and Jack were saying as he's only a small cog in the racing world. There's plenty as will keep their stables going and will take the stock Jack has. Now Billy, Richard and Mark – they're a different story. It ain't going to be easy for you, once they all get involved. But I'm here for you, love; we'll get through it all somehow. It'll take more than an upstart like that Hitler to beat us, Meg.'

Although Hattie made herself sound cheerful and managed to bring a smile to Megan's face, she didn't feel it. Her own insides were being churned up, and not just with what they might all have to face – or with the unthinkable having happened to Sarah. No, she'd felt demons rise up inside her, and she had to fight them. And no one could help her, not even Megan.

7

Terence

A Plan Thwarted

By the time Terence entered the dining room, his mother, father and sister were already seated. 'Sorry, I was delayed at the stables.'

'Oh, that's all right, my boy. Glad to see you doing something and enjoying it. Frobisher, will you serve now, please?'

'Yes, m'Lord.'

Amidst the gentle clatter of cloches being removed from serving dishes, his mother asked, 'So, what are you doing exactly, dear?'

'A variety of jobs and, I must say, now I'm getting to know Jack Fellam, I'm finding him to be a jolly good sort. Never had time for the fellow before . . . Well, not that I knew him, but I felt a bit on the jealous side, what with his history, and how well he came out of it all. It—'

'Terence, we won't talk about that in front of the servants, if you don't mind.'

'Sorry, Pater. Just saying: he's a decent chap, and very knowledgeable about the horses and the farming game. I've been helping out there, too. Learning a lot. Which brings me to something I want to discuss – maybe over brandy after dinner, Pater?'

'Of course. Now, Daphne, my dear, what is it that you are worrying yourself about? Is it something you want to talk over with us all, while we dine?'

'Not in terms of finding a solution, Charles. Well, not at this moment, but I am increasingly concerned about the number of staff receiving notice of their imminent call-up.'

'Yes, I know. It's the same with the farm manager and labourers. They are exempt, of course, but one by one they are saying they want to go anyway. Admirable, but it does pose problems that we need to address.'

'I'm surprised *you* haven't been called up, Terence. It would bloody well do you good.'

'Oh, shut up, Theresa. If you haven't anything useful to say, just keep out of it. Anyway, I have—'

'No! You can't! I mean—'

'It's all right, Mater, old thing. I doubt it will come to anything. I still don't believe any of it. It is as everyone is saying: a phoney war. Obviously we have to prepare, and that is all that is happening. The government has set the ball rolling in getting those of fighting age medically tested and trained. It will all be over soon, you'll see.'

'Exactly.' The look his father gave Terence as he said this told him this wasn't his real feeling, as indeed it wasn't Terence's own, but it was better to perpetuate the pretence for a while to allay his mother's fears. She had never really got over her sister's death and remained vulnerable to breakdowns. For a long time after Aunt Laura's demise Mater's mental health had given them all extreme concern, and she had seemed very frail since the first mention of war.

As Terence entered the drawing room to await the chat with his father, he saw that a fire roared up the chimney, warming every corner of this elegant room. He remembered this being his favourite room as a child. He'd loved the pale greens and silvers, and still did. The soft blend of colours lent a calm and beauty that were complemented by the highly polished oak of the occasional tables and display cabinets.

His Aunt Laura had once told him that her mother-in-law had chosen the room's colours; although Laura had never met her, the tales she'd heard of her being a frumpy misfit of a wife for her father-in-law, but a wonderful person and adoring mother, had made her keep the room as it was.

Mater had never wanted to change it, either. In fact, if it was left to her, everything about the house would have remained the same as the day they'd taken it over, and they'd be living in shabby surroundings as the house deteriorated around them. But Father had prevailed, and most of the place had been refurbished. Terence was glad that it hadn't included this room. At least not in changing it; it had simply been given a good freshen-up.

He swirled the brandy in his glass, then a satisfying and smooth yet sharp tang tinged his throat at his first sip. He relaxed in the high-backed wing chair, took a ready-cut cigar and accepted the light that the butler offered. 'Thank you, Frobisher. Pater will be in in a few moments, if you would wait for him.'

'Of course, Master Terence.'

This form of address would have annoyed him if it had come from any of the other servants, but Frobisher had known him since infancy, and although he and Theresa often had a joke about him, they held him in high regard.

'How are you, Frobisher? Are you still coping? We don't put too much on your shoulders, do we?'

'I'm very well, thank you, Master Terence, though I do

share your mother's concerns. Life downstairs is getting harder by the day. Two of the footmen have gone already, and the groom and chauffeur have both had medical call-ups.' Frobisher's shaky old voice held a hint of fear.

'I'll speak to Pater about it. He does take it all very seriously, you know. But poor Mater . . . well, it is a lot for her to cope with.'

'I understand. And I would be grateful if you could discuss the situation, thank you, Master Terence.'

'We'll sort it. I'm sure there are a lot of women in the town who would love to take up the positions the men are vacating.'

The look of utter disgust on Frobisher's face was a picture! The thought of a woman doing a footman's job seemed abhorrent to him. The opening of the door and Lord Crompton's arrival couldn't have happened at a more opportune moment. It stopped the laugh that was bubbling up in Terence, which he knew would have seriously offended Frobisher, and he'd never willingly do that. It would, however, be a source of entertainment when he spoke to Theresa later . . .

'Now, Terence.' His father paused while Frobisher finished ministering to him. At one time the butler had caused no disturbance, as he gracefully glided around them, carrying out his duties. Now he shuffled. The glasses that he had once filled with just the satisfying tinkle of syrupy liquid now clinked alarmingly, and his once indiscernible closing of the door had become a noisy operation as he let it bang behind him, no longer able to hold his tray in one hand while he closed the door with the other.

Terence waited, watching his father and allowing him to

gather his thoughts in his own time and open the conversation again.

Looking every inch the lord, his father held the title well. Of average height, and trim of figure, Charles Crompton had a quiet elegance about him, and a dignity in everything he did and in all his dealings with people. Taking a sip of his brandy and following that with a deep inhaling of his cigar, he sounded troubled as he exhaled, and weary. 'There is a lot to talk over, Terence. Not least you having had word from the War Office and, on top of that, the expectation that our whole way of life will be disrupted.'

Thick smoke curled in the air between them, filling the room with the distinct aroma of good Havana tobacco. Nerves fluttered in Terence's stomach. He couldn't tell if his father would be averse to him thinking of getting out of going to war or not. He decided to remain silent and listen.

A moment went by before Lord Crompton spoke again. 'Well, we'd better start with your position. I am concerned for your mother, if it should happen that you go to war.'

'I must say, I'm not without my own worries on that score, and it is what I wanted to speak to you—'

'Let me finish.' The stern tone surprised Terence. His father seemed almost angry or . . . Did he discern a note of . . . well, slight disgust?

'I'm not going to dress this up, Terence, but you are not exactly officer material.'

Despite feeling piqued at this, Terence was aware of another emotion overcoming him: that of shame. He hadn't made a success of anything, or even tried to prove his worth, so he shouldn't be surprised at his father's disdain, but it still felt uncomfortable to have this man he loved and admired spelling it out.

'Therefore,' his father continued, 'you can only look towards having to fight amongst the ranks, even taking orders from the working class! Your mother is very worried. To the extent that she could have a relapse, and I can't let that happen.'

'Not to mention the possibility of your son being killed!'

'Sorry, no – of course I didn't mean it to come across like that. It isn't easy . . . I mean, I am sure you want to go to war, and if it was possible I would buy you a commission, but I suspect, as things are in today's world, money isn't enough to secure your safety.'

Although he was uncertain whether his father was simply paying lip service to these sentiments, Terence didn't really care. The fact was that he had no intention of fighting for King and country, and it looked like Pater was of the same persuasion.

Picking up on this, Terence jumped in. 'Naturally I want to do what I can, Pater, but I don't think the country – or anyone else – is best served by me making a hash of things and getting in everyone's way, so I was wondering about you appointing me manager of our farming estate? That would exempt me and, I can assure you, I would take that exemption, if only for Mother's sake.'

This last he added to give weight to his suggestion, but to give it further credence he added, 'You need someone, Pater. I spoke to Earnshaw earlier, when I came back from Fellam's, and he is adamant that he and all of the younger ones are going to war. Hensal Grange Army, he called them. It appears that he sees himself as the sergeant and the farm hands as his troops, and he has already been drilling them as they carry out their work.'

'Yes, I know. Admirable. I'm very proud of them, though sorry at the same time. They have become like a sort of lower family, and it is distressing to think of them going. Anyway, I had thought of asking Fellam to oversee things, but it will be too much, now that he has to farm his own land, and with the horses as well.'

'Not that I am saying you should ask him, but hasn't he told you he has to give up the stables? There is already a rumbling that leisure pursuits will be the first thing to be curtailed – can't have the privileged enjoying themselves, what!'

'Don't be flippant, Terence. What exactly did Jack say?'

'That he would have to sell. Demand is already waning for his stud horses, and besides, he needs machinery to farm the land, and seeds and labour, though he accepts – like me – that we will probably have to rely on Land Girls. Makes sense, I think, him concentrating all his efforts on arable and dairy farming, with all that fertile land he has, and it being the flattest around here. It's—'

'But I haven't heard anything of this. It's ridiculous. I must speak with him. Yes, he will have to take things to a lower level, but he should keep his breeding programme. He has some of the best stock going, and when the war is over . . . well, it could make him a lot of money. I can't believe he hasn't talked this over with me first.'

'You mean you'd be willing to fund him to keep going?' The trickle of apprehension that Terence had experienced earlier revisited him. He'd thought it was over, this rivalry. He'd thought he had only to get to the end of the war and he'd be able to achieve his dream, and then there would be no objection from his father, with Fellam already out of business. After all, Fellam would be fine: he'd have his farm established by then, and his wife would be well set up.

'Of course. The future prospects are tremendous. Think of it: at the end of all this, racing will resume and all the main players will want good stock. If Jack has that, well . . .'

'But what about me? You know my ambitions. This could have been my chance.'

'Your chance? Oh, for heaven's sake, Terence—'

'No, Pater.' He could no longer sit; frustration was agitating his entire body. Pacing the room, he felt very angry. 'This is so unfair.'

'Just stop there a moment, Terence. Am I to believe that you hoped you could step into the breach and take over what the war might take away from Jack? That's preposterous.'

'Why is it? I didn't start the bloody war. There are always winners and losers. And besides, Fellam will have his farm well established by then. The stable *should* be mine. Aunt Laura always wanted it to be here. She even started up once, and everything is in place. All I need is the funds.'

'And the downfall of the man who least deserves it.'

'Least deserves it! God, have you forgotten what he did, in having an affair with Aunt Laura and then thwarting her? The shame he brought down on this family, and what it all did to Mater?'

'You know nothing, Terence. And I didn't plan on having an argument with you. Let's just deal with what we are facing, shall we? And for goodness' sake, drop this notion that you might even be capable of running a stud farm, let alone owning one!'

With his father in this mood, Terence supposed he had no option, but it did feel as if all his hopes had been dashed. Granted, he'd probably been saved from the rotten job of going to war, but . . . No, he'd not give up. There was always his other plan. It wasn't one he wanted to put into action, particularly now that he knew Fellam better, but what other choice had his father left him?

8

Sarah

Unwanted Preparations

'Sarah? Is that you, love?'

'Aye, sorry, did I wake you?'

'No, love, I was just resting me eyes. Come here and sit with me. I don't get much chance to talk to you these days.'

Sarah put another log on the already blazing fire and sat herself down on the couch next to Granna Issy. She sank into the feather cushions. She, like her granna, loved the late-autumn evenings.

The light had faded, banishing the shadows that the disappearing sun had thrown up. Only the flicker of the flames lit the room, but she didn't turn the lamp on. That would spoil the cosiness.

'Everyone's busy these days. Jack's allus on with his work in the stables and getting the land ready; Megan's life is lived in a whirl; and you, Sarah . . . by, you're a clever lass. Megan tells me as you're brilliant at taking care of all her dealings, where money's concerned. I'm reet proud of you, thou knows. Eeh, I reckon as you have a lot of your Granddad Tom in you. He was clever with numbers.'

'Well, I have the hard work of Aunt Megan and Dad to thank for that an' all. It was them as saw to it that I had a chance to go to the grammar school. Not that I were happy there, as they all thought themselves better than me. That was until they needed help with their homework.'

'Aye, I know. Still, you got through it, and with all your school certificates. Who would've thought it, eh? Your mam would've loved how you've turned out. And as for us living like we do, she'd have had something to say about that an' all. By, we'll be taking over Hensal Grange yet.'

'Oh, I don't think so. They must be millionaires.'

'Aye, got rich by making good marriages in the first place, they did. Eeh, I could tell you stuff about them. Not this lot that have it now. That Lord Crompton seems a decent bloke, and Lady Crompton ain't a bit like her late sister, Laura Harvey. But them as went before, and the old Mr Harvey – Laura Harvey's father-in-law, as passed on before the last war – there were some goings-on with him, I tell yer.'

Sarah remembered that Issy had told her this many times over, but she didn't say so. Instead she sought a distraction. 'Shall I get Fanny to make us a pot of tea, Granna? I'm reet parched. I've had a long day.'

'Aye, lass, that'd be nice. And see if she's got some of them scones made. I'd like to see if she's learned yet how to make them proper, like I showed her.'

Sarah laughed as she went in search of Fanny. Her granna was a one. She'd not wanted any hired help; the kitchen was her domain and had remained so until recently, when it had all become too much. For her body, that is, not for her spirit. Not that they could stop her altogether – she still oversaw all the meals.

Tiredness ached in Sarah's bones as she headed towards the kitchen. Tomorrow was decision day. The medical team had already sat and pronounced Billy suitable for release, and

Grandpa Edward had assured them that he'd looked into Billy's case and everything pointed to him being mentally fit. The final decision would be down to the court. The lawyer was sure it would all go well, but the outcome that he thought good was far from being so to her. The only good thing would be the end to her visits, but she'd rather endure them than have Billy free. Not that there had been another visit since . . . No, she'd not think on that. There'd been letters, though – letters written as if from a perfect lover. It all sickened her.

This thought had hardly settled in her when the walls of the hall closed in on her. Unable to see, and with her ears zinging, she groped for the hall stand. Clutching it, she steadied herself. Sweat beaded on her forehead. Her mind wouldn't tell her what was happening. She thought her body would sink to the floor without her being able to stop it. After a moment, the feeling calmed and everything took on its normal state. She gave herself time, telling herself it must be the stress coupled with, perhaps, the onset of her monthly, which – by her reckoning – was well overdue. She'd already missed one and was due again, but then, with her not eating well and fretting, it wasn't surprising. *Maybe tonight. Yes, all the signs are there. I'm sure to start me monthly tonight.*

Feeling better now she was back in the sitting room, Sarah felt glad that no sign of the incident had shown itself to her granna. Forgetting about it, she threw herself into the situation that she could see brewing, as Fanny put a tea plate of perfect-looking scones in front of them.

Issy took one, but made no comment. As she bit into it and

caught the crumbs from falling into her lap, she grunted. The look of surprise accompanying the grunt spoke volumes.

Sarah winked at Fanny, telling her, 'They're delicious. The best I've ever tasted.'

This set Fanny scurrying out of the room, and Issy choking as she said, 'By, lass, I'll say one thing for you. You not only look like your dad; you've got his cheek, all right.'

'Well, Granna, you are naughty. You put the fear of death into poor Fanny. She tries her best.'

'Aye, I knows, lass. I just can't get used to someone else in me kitchen. But you're reet about these scones, and though I'll bide me time, I'll tell her so one of these days. Anyroad, it's not scones as I want to talk to you about. Tell me what you've been buying.'

Trying to drum up some excitement for something she'd found a chore, Sarah giggled. 'Oh, I had a good day. I found just the headdress I was looking for.' She took the white skull-cap from the box she'd discarded by her feet when she sat down. 'Look, it's perfect! Aunt Megan's going to make some lilies out of the silk she is using to make me frock, and she'll attach them here at the back. And not only that, but I've found the perfect thing for Sally's hair, too. Look at this. It's the exact match for her dress material.' She displayed the small swatch of Sally's bridesmaid dress that she'd taken with her, and the two tiny roses on a silver clip that were an identical shade of rose-pink.

'By, lass, it's going to be a beautiful wedding. You're going to look lovely. Like I said, you're a picture of our Cissy. Eeh, she'd have been reet proud of you.'

'I still remember her, Granna. And Bella. I'll never forget them.'

'I knows that, me love. And all as she'd want is for you to

58

be happy. Are you happy, lass? Really happy, I mean? You're not drifting into marrying Billy, are you?'

'No! Of course not. I – I love him. It may be that our wedding is sooner than I thought, but then it's like that for a lot of young couples, with this war and talk of all the men going away.' Wanting to change the subject, Sarah asked her granna's opinion of the war. 'What do you think about it all, Granna? Will it be as bad as everyone says?'

'Aye, I think so, lass. If it's owt like the last lot, it won't be very nice. But then it's right as this one could be worse, cos it's likely it'll be fought at home as well as abroad. So God above knows what we're in for. Anyroad, sit down a minute, lass, and tell me. Are you sure you are doing the right thing? Is it just talk of war that's spurring you on, and the fact that you've been Billy's girl, so to speak, since you were little? What I mean is: don't you think as what you feel for him might just be a feeling as you'd have for a brother?'

'No. No, of course not. I – I love him. I – I don't know when it happened that our childhood love turned to a true, deep love, but one day it did.' Averting her gaze from her granna's knowing look, Sarah tried to cover the lies she felt forced to tell. Yes, she had some feelings for Billy. How could she not? They'd grown up together, had been inseparable as children and, even after what he'd done, there was no chance of him not being in her life. His mam, Aunt Megan, had become her stepmother. It was expected of her that she would visit him, but if Billy and his mam, and Sarah and her dad, had gone their separate ways then maybe . . .

As it was, whenever she'd visited Billy with Aunt Megan and her dad, they had always allowed her and Billy to go off together around the grounds. In her innocence, she'd continued in the same easy way they were used to with each other,

her own temper often keeping his in check and making him laugh. But then, as they got older, Billy had become serious about their relationship, obsessive, even. And she had become more and more afraid of him. The threats he aimed towards his mam were the main reason why she'd allowed things to drift and herself to become looked on as Billy's girl. Now, she was trapped by fear.

'That were a big sigh, lass. You knaw as you can tell your granna owt, don't you?'

'Aye, I do, granna. Eeh, I'm being silly. The war has speeded things on a bit for us, and I – I didn't expect to be preparing for me wedding so soon, but, well, it – it's given Billy a chance at freedom, and we said we'd marry when that happened, so I'm glad. Happy . . . well, just a bit nervous, that's all.'

'Eeh, lass, lass. I just don't want you making a mistake. You're only nineteen. It's very young to be wed. You don't seem to have had much chance to meet other young men, to even compare them with Billy.'

'I've met a few, Granna. There were a lot of young men on the accountants' course, and then I've known Richard and Mark.'

'Aye, Bridget's lads. By, I reckon as Richard's allus been sweet on you.'

'Granna, I have to go. I've to unpack this lot and get sorted for Aunt Megan coming home. And you shouldn't be on with talking like that – Richard's my step-uncle, and he'd be mortified if you thought him taking an interest in me were anything other than caring about me in the same way he cares about us all.' Trying to hide the blush that had overcome her, Sarah busied herself repacking the headdress. 'Granna, please don't talk of such notions in Billy's hearing. You know how jealous he can get.'

Her heart thudded at the thought, because an occasion came back to her when she'd mentioned Richard and Mark visiting for a weekend. Billy had thrown a fit at the thought of Sarah in their company, making threats that had some danger in them, as did all of his ranting. Nothing he said in anger could be taken lightly, and she couldn't bear Richard or Mark to suffer at his hands.

Because of this, she'd never allowed herself even to think of either of them in any other way than as friends. Easy to do with Mark, but when it came to Richard, she had to admit she'd had longings. She'd never tell her granna, though, and she'd hide them forever in a secret part of her heart. But then again, she supposed every girl would have such thoughts about Richard. He was so handsome, and so different in his looks. He took after his grandfather – what was his name . . . ? Will – Will Hadler. Yes, that's what her granna had told her, on one of the many occasions Issy had discussed that side of her younger days. Funny how it all turned out, with her granna knowing Richard's grandparents and mam. Anyway, what she felt for Richard was only a fancy. A silly thing, really. She was Billy's girl and always had been.

'You've gone quiet, lass. What's troubling you, cos I know as sommat is on your mind, and now's the time to speak up, afore it's too late.'

Granna was getting too close to subjects that Sarah didn't want to tackle. 'I'm fine, really, Granna. And I'm very happy to be marrying Billy. Now, you finish your rest and I'll take me parcels up to my room. I'll see you at dinner.' Giving her granna a quick kiss, she avoided the hug Issy tried to give her. It would have been her undoing.

Once in the hall, Sarah breathed a sigh of relief. The prying love of her granna had made the feelings she'd managed to suppress rise up and threaten her peace of mind. Closing the door on her granna didn't put an end to those emotions.

When she reached her bedroom, the bed accepted her into its soft embrace as she sank down into the feather eiderdown and lay back on the pillow. Stinging tears hovered below the lids of her closed eyes.

Three weeks – the time it took to post the banns – and, no matter what, she would be Billy's wife. That's what they had arranged; or rather, it was what she'd gone along with. With Billy's imminent release, and his enlistment, that had seemed the sensible thing to agree to. But how was she going to face it? *How?*

9

Megan, Sarah & Billy

Family Tensions

With her family all around her and Billy home, Megan should have felt at peace, but tension sizzled in the drawing room, where they all milled around trying to enjoy a pre-dinner drink.

Jack hovered close to her, seeking answers to questions that he asked only with his eyes, where his concern for her showed. But she couldn't give him any answers. Who knew how this welcome-home party that she'd arranged for Billy would go; and no, she was not *all right*! And neither was anyone else, by the way they all tried to make it look and sound as though they were.

Issy didn't help the situation, trying to cover her discomfort by fussing over everything and in the process driving Fanny – and the help Fanny had brought with her – to distraction. 'Eeh, Megan, lass,' she'd said a million times, 'what possessed you to have this do so soon?'

Looking over at Sarah increased the worry that was niggling at Megan. The poor lass looked as wound up as a coil of wire – held together, but ready to unravel and fall into an untidy mess at any moment. *And then there's me mam, acting*

*as though she's on hand to save me from hurt, no matter what;
and with Edward in tow, as if to do the same for mam.*

In another corner of the room, Megan's two half-brothers
Richard and Mark stood trying to make conversation with
Billy, but although he was jubilant at being free, he was surly
with them. For what reason, she didn't know. They'd never
done him any harm. Billy's attitude to her, she could understand. He'd never really forgiven her, and had let her know
in no uncertain terms that she'd done the wrong thing in
arranging this coming-home celebration. 'Christ, Mam,' he'd
said, 'what were you thinking? I don't want to be with all the
so-called long-lost relations, when I'm just out of that bloody
institution. I wanted a quiet weekend to get used to this new
place, and to being with Sarah and all of you. You've bloody
got no idea. You always did mess things up, and you haven't
changed, have you?'

His scowl bored into her, and she sensed that something
awful was about to happen. Looking at the clock offered her
some relief. The time was approaching when the rest of their
guests would arrive.

Sarah caught Megan's eye and responded with a smile, but it
did nothing to settle Megan. She so wished Hattie would come
soon. Hattie would sort everything out. She always did. She had
a knack for making things right when they weren't.

And there would be the distraction of Hattie's husband,
Harry, too. Good, dependable Harry. He always brought a
calming influence, which hopefully Billy would respond to.

Hattie was bringing young Sally, and Phyllis and Daisy, with
her, so the atmosphere should improve as the room filled with
everyone's chatter. These thoughts eased Megan's fears a little,
but she still harboured some doubts. She knew Billy would be
okay with Sally, as he'd known her from childhood and, like

them all, felt deeply for all that Sally had been through. But she did wonder if he would be respectful with Phyllis and Daisy, or even with Hattie for that matter, despite knowing that he'd get short shrift from her if he tried anything.

Phyllis and Daisy's past, working as prostitutes – and now being a couple – would give Billy plenty to deride. Megan couldn't see him looking beyond their situation and seeing the lovely women they were. *Oh dear, what have I done? Billy was right – I should never have thought this welcome-home party a good idea.*

When the doorbell rang, Megan jumped, and she flew towards it as if propelled by wings. Hattie instantly made her laugh. 'Eeh, it's that cold out here, your breath catches in your lungs. Hey, Megan. By, that's a warm welcome – you at the door before I let go of the knocker. Makes me feel like I'm Queen Victoria or sommat.'

Issy, ready as usual with a quip, came up behind Megan. 'Well, that ain't a good way to feel, Hattie, seeing as she's been dead this thirty-odd year and more. By, it's good to see you. Come on in, lass. Thank goodness you're here. This one's like a cinder girl on hot coals.'

Megan didn't ask what a cinder girl was, but was glad Issy was being Issy at this moment. It took everyone's attention, and stopped her from grabbing Hattie like the lifesaver she thought she was.

'Reet, I gather it's not going as well as you'd hoped, Megan, love? Never mind, reinforcements have arrived. It were bound to be strained, but the more people you have to break things up a bit, the better. Is Billy playing up?'

'Well, he's not reet pleased with me for arranging this, and at the moment he's taking it out on Richard and Mark. Oh, Hattie. What have I done?'

'Never mind that – it's done now, so let's get on with it, love. Take our coats and let's get in.'

As they entered the room, Hattie said to Sally, 'Right, lass, go and greet Billy like a long-lost friend. I know you only met him a couple of times, but after you've said hello and how nice it is to see him, get the lads talking and I'll take over with Billy. Go on, lass. He won't bite.'

As if she hadn't orchestrated it, Hattie went to Bridget and Edward first, hugging them before saying, 'Well, I have to greet the lad whose honour we are all here for, so I'll be back with you in a mo. Billy! Come here, lad. Eeh, it's good to have you back with us. Look at you – you remind me of that picture of your great-grandma, Bridie. I was only looking at it the other day in your locket, wasn't I, Megan? It's your eyes. They're Irish eyes. By, you've made a handsome young man! Now, how are you?'

Like magic, the atmosphere eased as Sarah joined Hattie and Billy. Megan was puzzled as to why Sarah hadn't stood with Billy when he was talking to Richard and Mark, instead of letting the situation get as it had; but knowing Sarah, she'd have her reasons. No matter, everyone seemed happier now.

'Are you all right, Megan, dear?'

'Yes, Mam, I am now. Sorry, love. Things were a bit—'

'There, that's better. Now, I think I deserve a drink.' Hattie had come up to them and didn't give them a chance to continue.

'You do, Hattie, love. Ta for that. Reet, let's start to enjoy ourselves. Jack, see to the drinks whilst I go and see what Issy and the others are up to with the food. Be back with you in a mo, Mam. Don't worry, everything is all right now.'

When Megan showed them all into the dining room a few moments later, it was with pride. She'd picked the longest of the downstairs rooms to convert for this purpose the moment they had settled into this grand house. She'd found it to be the only room in which she could fit a table long enough to seat all of her family and friends. At the far end of the room, glass doors opened onto the garden, creating lots of light, which reflected off the summer blue in which she'd had the walls painted. The curtains were white with dark-blue cornflowers adorning them, and the carpet matched the colour of the flowers.

The table looked grand, set with her best china. That, too, had a cornflower pattern on it. The overall picture was one of calm and elegance. A fire, huge and spitting resin from the burning logs, gave warmth to the scene. As she sat down, with everyone in the place allocated to them, her nerves eased. *By, it's sommat an' all, me entertaining like this.*

Though she'd done it many times over the years since their good fortune, she never got used to it, and each time it gave her a special feeling. Looking at her family, now chatting easily, she thought everything was going to go well, and she'd been silly to think otherwise.

Billy ate his hot soup. He looked around as he did so. What a load of codswallop. His mam was the worst, acting like she was a lady or sommat. Christ, if his dad were here, he'd put her in her place. All this fancy stuff – and at the cost of his dad's life. And his own, for that matter, as they'd both suffered because of his mam's actions. Carrying on as she did, building a nest-egg behind his dad's back, and all with the intention of leaving him. Once she'd achieved that, all hell had been let loose when his dad found them.

The memory shuddered through Billy as he looked at his Uncle Jack. He'd always loved Jack, and it had been trying to save his life that had led to all that happened. *Aye, and it were all me mam's fault that I killed me dad. Oh God!*

'So, Billy, I know you've only been home a few days, but how are you finding it?'

Edward was supposedly his step-granddad, but he wasn't anything like a real grandpa, though Billy could say as the 'grand' bit was spot-on – too grand for the likes of them. Still, Edward wasn't a bad bloke.

He'd not let any of them off the hook, though. He'd tell it as it was. 'It's strange, to tell the truth. It don't seem like I belong here at the moment. When I left, we lived in a flat above a shop, having just left me dad in our miner's cottage, and now I've come back to this! Takes a bit of getting used to.'

His step-granddad nodded and smiled, but Issy butted in. 'Eeh, you soon will, lad. I feel as though I were born to it. By, I can be reet posh if I want to be.'

It sickened him how they all laughed as Issy, the old bag, lifted her little finger off her spoon and held it in the air, like she thought it gave her airs and graces or something. She always did think she could solve everything by making a crack.

Billy didn't join in with the laughter as it all looked false from where he sat. His anger unleashed some of the bitterness he felt at the way they all acted. 'Aye, but there is a saying as you can't make a silk purse out of a sow's ear, and there's a few of them here today, I reckon.' He enjoyed the silence that fell. Sarah tapped his leg with her foot, but then she had a side to her as well, like she'd forgotten how it all used to be. Well, he was of a mind to remind them, and he'd start with them as were no better than the scum on the street. 'So, it ain't as if you've forgotten the *selling yourself* days, then?' He looked at Hattie, then Phyllis and lastly at Daisy, before turning to his mam. 'And you, Mam. You must remember how it was, when you were deceiving me da—'

'Billy! None of this is called for, lad. It's reet as things have changed since you went away, but everyone here deserves what they now have and how their lives are better than they were, so however bitter you feel about things, they can't be undone. We all did the best we could.'

'You did, Uncle Jack, and perhaps you, Granddad Edward – you tried, though you forgot about me in the last few years. But the rest of you, especially—'

'Don't even say it, Billy. You've nowt to pull any of us up for. *Nowt*. And I'll not have you trying.'

Billy had had enough. His chair clattered to the floor as he rose. The sound cut off the sound of his Aunt Hattie's ranting. She had a lot to talk about. She was nothing but a prostitute in her past, and you couldn't wipe that from your slate.

As he walked out, slamming the door behind him, he felt something eating him up inside. They all acted as if he'd been the only bad 'un, when in fact he were the only one as had paid for what he'd done. All the others had been rewarded.

Breaking into a run thwarted the cold that chilled his shirt-sleeved torso. The late-November air held a damp mist. Turning towards Breckton, Billy planned to run the four miles to the town and go into the pub for a few beers. He checked his back pocket. Aye, his wallet was there, and he had a pound note tucked in it – Sarah had given it to him for his journey home, but he'd not needed it. After he'd visited the recruiting office with that lawyer bloke – a condition of his release – the man had given him a lift home. That had turned out to be an experience in itself, as the man's motor car had been a revelation to him. Thinking of it made Billy regret his outburst. Hadn't he meant to be on his best behaviour so as to please Jack and his mam in the hope that, when he asked, they would agree to let him have a motor of his own? Well, he'd blown that. And Sarah wouldn't be pleased with him, either. Oh, bugger the lot of them. He'd drown them out in a few pints.

'Sarah, don't worry. He'll just have gone off to the pub or something. He'll find it difficult to settle for a while. It's to be expected.'

Richard's voice, coming from behind her, had Sarah wiping her tears, embarrassed that he might see her cry. She'd grabbed her coat and run outside after Billy, but hadn't been able to stop him. She turned from the gate to face Richard. Her heart leapt at the sight of him standing on the path, framed by the fading light of the late-evening sun. Tendrils of his hair fell forward onto his forehead. His beautiful liquid-blue eyes held hers. Her mouth dried. She had no conscious awareness of either of them moving, and yet his body came so close to hers that she could smell the freshness of his crisp white shirt and feel his warm breath brushing her face as he spoke her name. 'Sarah . . . I – I have to tell you: I have feelings for you. I—'

There was no need for him to finish. And Richard turning away from her did nothing to prevent his message from reaching her. But then, had she imagined it? Confusion reddened her cheeks, because when he turned back to face her, his voice lightened. 'Well, let's hope Billy's back in time for the wedding, eh? Can't have the blushing bride left at the altar, can we? Besides, I'm looking forward to the day. It has been ages since I went to a wedding, though there's a few arranged now,

with the fear of everyone leaving their girlfriends behind. I'm
even thinking of it myself.'

This shocked her. 'You have someone in mind then?'

'Yes. Lucinda. You met her last time you came down. The
raven-haired girl at the summer fete that Mother held on the
lawn. We . . . we have a sort of understanding.'

Understanding! If she lived to be a hundred, she'd never
take in how the classes above her own went about things. But
then wasn't that what she had with Billy – an understanding
of sorts?

'I'm happy for you. I found her to be a nice lass.' Her
words belied the way she felt. Inside she wanted to scream
out: *You can't! You can't marry her.* But what was the use?

'Yes, I've known her all my life, and our families get on well.
She knows me, almost better than I do myself, and – well . . .
it'll be nice to know she is waiting for me when I return—'

'Return? You're going off to war? I thought, as a trainee
doctor, you'd not have to go. I mean, the likes of you will be
needed here.'

'That's just it. *Trainee*, not qualified. No, I have to put all
that on hold and do my bit. I'm going into the RAF. I go to
Uxbridge in a couple of weeks to start my pilot's training.'

'Oh, Richard, I can't bear it.'

'Sarah, I – I must say it. I must speak. I love—'

'I've brought your coat, Richard.'

'Father! I didn't hear you coming. Thanks, yes, it is nippy.'

'Here you are. At least Sarah had the sense to grab hers
before she came out. Anyway, Richard, I think you should go
in. Your mother is upset, as is everyone. I'll stay with Sarah, if
she cannot face it all yet.'

'Thank you, Edward, but I'll go in an' all. I'm sorry about
the upset. It ain't Billy's fault. It were too much for him. Aunt

Megan should have given him longer to get used to being out, and with the family again, before—'

'Yes. Perhaps that is so. I'm sure she meant well, but I agree. Billy isn't ready to take it all in yet. Can't blame the lad. Everything has changed since he was sectioned. Well, dear, take my arm and we'll follow Richard back into the warmth, eh?'

Holding his arm, Sarah wondered how much Edward had heard, and even if his coming out to them had been because he suspected something might happen. As they walked up the path, she allowed her mind to wander. *Was Richard really about to declare his love for me?* Oh God! But no, she couldn't even think it, or create any room in her heart for Richard. Her destiny was mapped out for her, and she had to stick to it – for everyone's sake.

10

Billy

A Seductive Encounter

Panting from his run, Billy felt better for having left the whole lot of them behind. He'd needed to escape the confines of what his family had become. Let them all stew – he didn't care. His mam should have given him more time.

As he reached Breckton, everything that was once familiar now seemed alien to him. He just couldn't put his finger on why.

Walking along the Miners' Row, where he had lived until that day his ma left his dad and took him away with her to Leeds, he met no one he recognized. Crossing the road, he decided he'd walk down the lane before going into the pub, even though he had a strong urge to down several pints.

The trees still hung over the road and the cottages remained as they were all those years ago, though the folk living in them weren't all the same ones as had lived in them when he were a lad. Issy's old cottage, where he'd played with Sarah for hours and hours, looked different too, and he wondered who lived there now – whoever it was hadn't kept the old place looking as nice as it used to. The roses hanging over the doorway had turned to brambles through the lack of care shown to them. And there was a new lot in old Henry

Fairweather's place. The old git had chased Billy many a time from places he shouldn't have been. He remembered that Sarah had come in with the news of his death on one of her visits, her eyes full of tears, but he'd felt nothing. There were no place for old 'uns. They'd outgrown their usefulness and were a burden to everyone. Sarah was even worse when old Gertie died – breaking her heart, she were.

As he passed by the cottage where Gertie had lived, and where her son Gary still lived, he thought about the day he'd had some fun at Gary's expense. Feeling bored, and with Sarah tied up keeping Bella, her halfwit sister, amused, Billy had gone off to find his Uncle Jack. He'd come down this lane – in fact, this was where it had happened! Aye, the very spot. By, it'd been a bit of sport, making the horse rear and throw Gary. Gary could've won the Olympic Games with the way he flew through the air.

Laughter at the memory bubbled up in Billy. As he released it, the laughter echoed, bouncing back off the silence and splitting the air. A shudder trembled through him at the sound, sending him back to those years as if it were now. And the thought came to him that nothing had ever been right for him. He'd been happy when it was just him and Sarah, but then her mam had died having Bella, and things had changed. Rage boiled his blood, just thinking of Bella!

At the end of the lane he could see the gates leading to Hensal Grange. Turning to his left, he saw that the stile was still there. He had a fancy to climb it and head for the beck, but memories of the last time he was up there stopped him. He wouldn't put it past that ugly, stinking halfwit to haunt the area. This thought stippled his arms with goose-bumps and raised the hair on his neck. A voice in his head told him not to be so daft. To prove he didn't care, he climbed over the stile and ran towards the thicket. He slowed his pace when he reached the tree that he'd stood behind on that day, long ago. He looked in the direction he remembered Bella coming from. He could hear her calling, 'Biwwy, Biwwy . . .', and remembered the fear turning him to a statue, just before he'd beaten her to death and thrown her stinking body down the mineshaft. The same feeling seized him now and the atmosphere clawed at him.

A twig snapped. He stood still. A female voice came to him. A posh, top-drawer voice.

'Bother! Well, I'll just have to walk. Come along, Lady, we can't stay here . . . Oh, you startled me. I didn't know you were there—'

'Sorry, Ma'am. I hope as I'm not on with trespassing. I were just out for a walk.'

'I haven't seen you around here before. Are you from the town?'

'No, Ma'am, I live over on Fellam's Stud Farm.'

'In that case, as a stable-hand, you may be able to help. Lady – my horse – stumbled and now she's lame.'

'I'm no stable-hand. I'm stepson of owner. Me name's Billy Armitage.'

Her hazel eyes changed as he spoke, as did her beautiful face. It had been poker-like in its cold expression and her eyes had held disdain, but now they showed fear and her cheeks flushed. This shocked him.

'There's no need to be scared of me. I'll not bite.'

'No, of course. I – I . . . Look, can you help or not?'

'If you tell me who you are, and if you stop looking at me like I were scum, I might consider it.'

'Really! You are very rude!'

This came with the hint of a smile. He decided to seize the

advantage he'd gained. 'Eeh, how can you say that? I'm just a bloke out for a walk. It were you as were rude in your manner towards me, but I'm not one to fall out with a pretty girl. I'll take a look at your horse for yer.'

Something about the way she looked at him tickled a muscle deep in his groin, as she spoke in a much softer tone, and one that put him on an equal footing with her. 'I'm Theresa Hawthorn. Hawthorn is my married name. I'm the daughter of Lord and Lady Crompton, and we live at Hensal Grange.'

'Pleased to meet you, Ma'am. I've not long come home. I—'

'Yes, I know all about you. But you don't look like someone who would kill anyone.'

This came with a naughty aspect to it, like she was taking him on. It further aroused him. She stood by her horse, inviting him with her eyes. But then you couldn't trust her lot. If he took her up on what he read in her manner, she'd more than likely have him hanged. 'Well, you're right with your thinking, cos I didn't kill anyone. Not intentionally, anyroad.'

'Tell me about it.'

'I'm not in the mood to rake over it. I've had it up to here, and I ain't been home five minutes. So I reckon as now we know one another, it'd be best for me to take a look at your horse, then get on me way.'

Unsure what he was looking for, he lifted the lame leg. A piece of twig, about two inches long, stuck out from under the horse's shoe. After telling her what it was, Billy asked, 'Have you owt on you as I could use to prise it out? It must be giving her some pain.' Without saying anything, she took a pin out from her hair, allowing her locks to cascade around her shoulders. His throat instantly dried. She let her fingers brush his as she handed him the pin. Holding her gaze, he said nothing. Didn't trust himself to. She leaned towards him. Her face was near his, and he could smell the perfume on her and read the need in her eyes. But once again he cautioned himself. Women like her could be dangerous – not that he'd had any experience of them, but he had a sixth sense about it. He turned to get on with relieving the horse of the twig, asking as he did so, 'Your husband staying at the Grange with you, then?'

'No. We're getting divorced, as it happens.'

That explained a lot. He was right about her having a need, and he had a mind that she liked the thought of him seeing to it. The muscle in his groin tightened even more. He held himself in check – after everything that had happened, he couldn't risk anything going wrong now. He'd concentrate on the job that he had to do.

'It's lovely out here, don't you think, Billy? So quiet and . . . well, secluded. You could be out here and not come across another soul, except that I did today, of course. What brings you this way? And with no coat on. You must be frozen!'

'If you must know, it were me anger. Me mam thought it right to have a family do, to welcome me, and it went wrong. I didn't have a mind to act like everything is as it should be when it ain't.'

'You sound very bitter. I don't know everything that happened, but I know you've been away a long time. It can't be easy to come home and have to try and fit in again, especially as everything has changed. I mean, I understand your family didn't have money when you went away, and now they do; and on top of that, they are business people living in a big house. Quite a difference from a miners' cottage.'

'Aye, well, that were down to your lot. A cover-up, it were, but then you seem to know all about everything, so there's nowt as I can add to it.'

'Oh, I should think you could. I know my aunt had something to do with it all. An affair she got herself embroiled in, I believe. My twin brother, Terence, and I have never known the full facts, though.'

She'd moved close to him once more. Her perfume did things to him. He had to fight the urge to take hold of her and have some of what his Uncle Jack had had with her aunt, but he checked himself.

'Here, it's done. Your horse'll be reet now. I've to get on me way.' His hand went to rise to his forelock, but he stopped it. Instead he nodded his head towards her.

'So soon? You haven't told me about what went on. Are you going to be coming to Breckton again? Perhaps I'll see you. I ride out every afternoon at about this time.'

'Aye, I might, though it shouldn't be long afore I get me call-up. I've been in to sign up. They said they'd send for me to have a medical, then if that were reet, I'd go off for six weeks' training.'

'We'd better make it soon then.' She'd swung into the saddle, and as she looked down at him, she teased him once again. 'I'll look forward to it. You fascinate me, Mr Armitage. I like bad boys.'

Her laughter lingered in the air as she rode off. *By, I need that pint more than owt now.*

Although the family had continued with dinner, the atmosphere had been tense. Sarah couldn't engage in any of the conversations; her mind was in turmoil and her stomach churned. She feared for Billy's return: how would he behave when he came home? But then a sense of wonderment and confusion filled her as she remembered what had happened with Richard in the garden; what he'd said had lifted her, and yet increased her despair and compounded her sense of feeling trapped.

Besides feeling shackled to Billy because of her dread of what he might do, she now had another fear and, if it turned out to be true, she'd not have any choice other than to go through with their marriage.

The sickness and dizzy bouts she'd experienced hadn't resulted in her having her period, and that meant only one thing. She swallowed hard. *I have to stay strong. Whatever happens, the family can't know of this until after the wedding. I can't bring the shame of being pregnant out of wedlock down on them. I can't . . .*

Something Grandma Bridget said suddenly brought Sarah out of her thoughts. She and Granna Issy were doing their best to lift her spirits as they stood together in the drawing room. 'Just act as if nothing has happened, when Billy returns, darling – it's the best way with men.' Nodding her agreement, Sarah looked for a distraction. She'd listened to their advice for a good ten minutes now and was on the point of not knowing what to say next. Laughter coming from across the room drew her attention. Mark and Sally stood in a corner, enjoying a joke.

Sarah smiled at her grandparents. 'Ta, I will. I'll do all you say, I promise. I'll come and talk to you again later, but I think now, if it's all right with you two, I'll go and see what's causing the merriment over there. I could do with a laugh.'

Neither of them stopped her. As she headed towards Sally, she saw Richard out of the corner of her eye, heading in the same direction. When he spoke to her, his voice sounded as if nothing had happened earlier. 'I see you have the same idea –

gatecrashing the only people in the room who seem to be having any fun . . . Now then, you two, what are you up to? Share the joke.' But then what he said didn't match the way he looked at her. There was so much in his eyes. How was it she was so tuned into Richard that she could almost read what was in his mind?

'We're actually talking about the war, believe it or not. I know – not an amusing subject, but Sally tells me she is thinking of joining up, and we had this picture of all these women in high heels, brandishing handbags and brollies and terrifying the German army as they charged towards them! No need for you and me, big brother. The ladies will sort Hitler out for us.'

The idea tickled Sarah so much she laughed as she hadn't done in ages, and it felt good. It released a lot of the tension she'd held inside her. Richard joined her, touching her arm as he leaned forward, dabbing his eyes and adding to the picture: 'The Petticoat Army – ha, the very thing. Some of them can carry custard pies to throw. That should do the trick.'

This doubled Sarah over even more and weakened her knees so much that she clung onto Richard to steady herself. But then, without warning, a pain ground into her, as if someone had dug a knife into her back. She stumbled, and Richard grabbed her. 'What is it – oh God, darling, what is it?'

'Let go of her, you bastard!'

Richard took the full force of Billy's fist and his body shot towards the door, blood trickling from his nose.

Sarah could do nothing, let alone sort out in her head where Billy had come from. Pain gripped her in a spasm that took everything from her. She wanted to cry out for Billy to stop. She wanted to go to Richard, to hold him, comfort him, but all of those wishes went into a black hole as she sank to the floor.

The scene held all of Megan's nightmares. It seemed that her world would end; she'd no one to call out to. All were involved in one way or another: Hattie and Sally tending to Sarah while Jack, Mark and Edward were trying to get Billy off Richard; and her mam held Issy, stopping her from ploughing in, although physically restraining her didn't stop the tirade of abuse coming from Issy as she screamed, 'Stop it, you scum, you murdering scum! You're not fit to be in the same house as that lad—'

Oh God, for the first time in her life she wanted to claw at Issy, stop her, clog her mouth, as her heart screamed, *That's my son, my son . . .*

11

Theresa & Rita

An Unnatural Feeling

Riding into the stable yard, Theresa tried to calm herself. The encounter had affected her and had aroused feelings she found difficult to suppress. *God, I'm not cut out to live the life of a spinster!* True as it might be that her marriage hadn't been consummated, she'd had experiences. Some she should never have had at such a young age, nor with the person with whom she'd had them – it had been an illicit awakening of each other, fun at the time, but haunting now.

Besides that, there had been parties where she'd allowed more than she should, in some secret corner or other, giving in to the aching need that had lain within her since her first awareness. Not that any of the fumbling, or even the only time she'd been penetrated, had really given her the satisfaction she knew was possible – that was a discovery she'd made by herself in the safe haven of the night hours, and now an activity that she indulged in often. The shame of this tinged her cheeks, increasing her sense of discomfort.

As she reined the horse to a standstill, the last person she wanted to see right now came round the corner. *Oh, botheration!*

'Well, well, my dear older sister returns. How good life is

for some, while others toil. That must have been some ride, by the look of you, but Lady isn't sweating? Come on, out with it, what have you been up to? You have the same air about you as you did that day I found you kissing the footman at Lord Plaitman's daughter's coming-out do. What was her name? Silly thing. You remember, she had a wet mouth all the time – ugh! Anyway, out with it.'

'I haven't been up to anything, more's the pity. You'll never guess who I met up in the woods, though.'

'Who?'

'Only the notorious murderer! Handsome beggar. He helped me with Lady. She went lame on me, got something stuck in her shoe. Anyway—'

'You didn't—'

'No, but I wanted to. He has a magnetism about him. He's surly, very rude, but fascinating. I just hope I get another chance.'

'You're disgusting. You're supposed to be a lady – or had you forgotten?'

'Oh, come off it, Terence. I've seen you lusting after that Rita, or whatever her name is.'

'Yes, sorry, old girl, but she has some of the qualities you say your murderer has. Gets me where it's difficult to deny.'

'And that's not disgusting? She's nothing more than a Land Girl and a common slut from London's East End!'

'If you weren't my sister, I'd say you were jealous.'

'Don't start that again. Help me down, little brother. Or should I say "farmer boy"?'

'That's below the belt.'

On second thoughts, she would dismount by herself. She didn't want Terence pawing at her, as was his wont at times. She'd already been visited by the guilt and shame of yesteryear, although rejecting Terence wouldn't make things any better. To her shame, she still carried within her a deep love and attraction to her brother, of the type that she shouldn't; and she knew he did for her, too. As she touched the ground with one foot, he reached out for her.

'Big sister isn't cwoss with little bwover, is she?'

She couldn't resist him. Besides, she needed to be held and to savour the manly smell of him. His kiss lingered on her lips, adding fuel to the fire smouldering inside her. She pulled away. 'No, Terence, you know it's wrong—'

'It may be, but we both want it.'

'We can't. We must never let it go further, you know that. Now, let go of me. Go and fuck that big-breasted Rita, and the other one, if you must. What's her name?'

'Penny. Ha, I wouldn't touch *her*! Have you seen the colour of her teeth? And her eyes and mouth, covered in sores? Revolting, darling. Even the servants have complained to Mater and Pater about her. They don't like her having her meals with them. Bloody jumped-up lot. Still, I don't blame them. I wouldn't go near her either, let alone shag her. Ugh!'

She laughed at him. The unnatural feelings they had for each other were something they fought off on a daily basis. As children they'd often petted each other, touched private parts, and had long kissing and fumbling sessions. It had been their secret, and something they had both enjoyed. And even when, at times, they'd fallen asleep and Terence hadn't tip-toed back to his own bed, no one had suspected. The parents had simply put it down to them being twins and needing each other, but it had been more than that. Much more.

They had grown out of it for a while. School years had meant long separations, but their feelings had simmered under the surface. The only time she hadn't dwelt too much on them was when she had been on an extended holiday in Paris, living with her very best friend, Monique. What a wonderful two months that had been. Theresa had loved everything about France and its vibrant capital. And as a fore-runner to her 'finishing' year in Belgium, it had served as an excellent opportunity to brush up her French, in which she remained fluent to this day. Terence wasn't fluent, but he got by, and they often conversed in what she thought of as a beautiful language.

Her marriage had brought her relationship with her brother to the fore again. Terence had broken his heart the night be-fore it, and they had clung to one another, seeking pleasure in a lustful way that left only the final act of coupling undone.

Taking the reins from her now, he tilted his head. 'Anyway, I'll have to do something. Perhaps I will go and try my luck. See you later, old thing.' His smile nearly undid her. It tore at her emotions as she watched him walk in the direction of the barn.

The word she'd used to describe Billy Armitage came to her mind as she thought of Rita. Magnetism – animal mag-netism, in fact. They both had that quality: a dangerous element that drew you towards their sexuality. Rita wasn't beautiful, or even pretty. Her hair, shoulder-length and with the front rolled back, was a mousy colour, and her features, though not plain, were ordinary. It was what she did with her-self, and what she exuded, that set her apart. Not to mention her hourglass figure, large in all the right areas. It was the way she wore her clothes – even the overall they'd supplied her with, or the bib and brace, as it was known. The bib perched on the tip of her breasts, with the blouse she wore under it open to a plunge-line showing a mound of cleavage. The trousers she tucked into her wellingtons, emphasizing her rounded bottom and slim hips. Her face was never without make-up, and it was skilfully applied, making her eyes bigger than they were; and her lips . . . well, red, juicy and full. Kissable. *Good God! I've taken in a lot about the girl.*

Once more Theresa blushed as the reason suddenly hit her. She bloody fancied the girl! A groan bordering on a moan tightened her throat as she realized the depths of her being. Her sexuality was capable of anything. Anything!

Maybe she'd done the wrong thing. Perhaps if she'd stayed in her marriage, the freedom it would have given her, under the facade of propriety, would have allowed her to explore all avenues. But then she would have missed Terence so much . . .

Rita saw His High-and-Mightiness, Terence Crompton, coming across the yard. There were several places where the barn needed repair, making good peepholes through which to keep watch and look busy when she needed to. Trouble was, it made it bleedin' cold up in the loft where she and Penny slept, though on the plus side, it did provide her with fresh air to breathe and diluted the smell of Penny's body odour.

The holes had given her a view of something that had surprised her: the toff's little tryst with his sister. A bit queer, that. It made her feel sick, but still, it could have got him ready. If she knew anything, he'd be fish for her bait. She had to get rid of Penny first, though. ''Ere, Penny, leave us alone for a while, sweetheart.'

Penny stood up. Neither of them had been doing what they were supposed to be doing: swilling out the cowshed behind the barn, laying fresh straw on the floor and filling the feeding troughs for when the herdsman brought in the cattle at night. Made you bleedin' sick, the stench of piss and cowpats, so they put it off for as long as they could. Besides, they were both feeling disgruntled.

Standing up, Rita stubbed out her fag and then straightened her clothes, widening the gap in her blouse neckline and plumping up her hair a bit, before finding a lipstick in her pocket and refreshing her lips. Anticipation cheered her.

Being a Land Girl wasn't the cushy number they had thought it was going to be. It was dirty, stinking work, miles from anywhere, with just one pub for entertainment. Well, there was the miners' social, but that was a washout. They said they used to have dances there on a Saturday night, but she hadn't heard of any. It was a men-only domain most of the time, and when the women did go, there were limitations. No going in the men's bar and no buying drinks – only the men could be served. Bloody Northerners, they had no fun in them – though she'd met a couple of hot-blooded ones. *Nah, I'm not for this lark. I wish I'd gone into the munitions. At least they were in bigger towns and cities, giving you a chance of having some fun.*

His lust was obvious in the toff's eyes. It seemed she was to get what she'd been after. She'd be set for life, if she could hook him. Not bleedin' marry him, though! She wasn't that daft as to think he'd have her. But she could get a few things on him and screw him for some lolly – have his baby, even. That'd see her right for life.

'Hello, Rita, how is it all going? Are you and Penny settling in?'

Bleeding toff. As if he cares. 'We are, sir. Me and Penny are all right. The quarters you've given us ain't up to much, though; we feel like rabbits in a hutch, and it's getting bleedin' cold at night.'

'Oh? I'll have to look into that. I think there will be a room vacant in the servants' quarters. Will that suit you better?'

'Yes, ta very much. At least we'll be warm.'

'I'll arrange it. Rabbits, hey? Ha, somewhat strange metaphor. You're not partaking in their favourite occupation up there, are you?'

His guffaw sounded silly, childish. The joke wasn't that bleedin' funny. 'Chance'd be a fine thing, sir, but nah, we're more like bleedin' virgins.' She let her laughter tinkle and looked up at him from under her eyelashes.

'Hmm, shame. Should do something about that. Yes, can't have that. It's a sorry state of affairs for anyone.'

She moved closer to him. 'What do you propose then, kind sir? I hope you ain't got ideas?'

He blushed at this and flustered. 'No, of course not. Um . . . er, no, I was thinking we should make some entertainment for you.'

'Ha, I'm only having you on. But too right, I think you could provide me with entertainment, mate.' She indicated with her eyes where she thought he could entertain her, by looking up towards her own and Penny's bedroom above the barn. 'Though it might make a chap like you tired, climbing that ladder.'

Beads of sweat stood out on the toff's forehead. His lids half closed and his tongue slid over his lips. *Time to make a move and make something happen.* Turning from him, Rita swung her hips as she glided over to the ladder. At the bottom, she looked back at him and raised her eyebrows. He followed her like a horse after a lump of sugar.

Fired up for it now, she wouldn't have bothered with the kissing and groping, but she were bleedin' glad she let that part of it happen. His skill heightened every sensitive part of her. His kisses, deep and sweet-tasting, had her emotions swimming. His hands caressed her like she was something special, finding places she didn't know she had. *Oh God*. Her whole being released itself onto him. Wave after wave of pleasure consumed her. His flesh yielded to her grip on his back as the spasm taking her turned her into an animal and she clawed at him, her throat painful from the moans rasping from her. Her head stung as he grasped handfuls of her hair and forced her head backwards, stopping her from resisting his violent thrusts, when all she needed was to clench onto him.

Shattered by the intensity of it, her reward was to be taken where she'd never been before. She'd had plenty of blokes, but none came near this toff, this giant of a man. He splintered her very being.

Disappointment came at the end. Despite his coarse hollering of swear words – the like of which she was more likely to hear down the Old Pig and Whistle – showing her the depth of his feeling, he pulled out of her at the last second. It didn't make no odds to her enjoyment, but she were hoping he'd let go into her, giving her the possibility of sealing a hold on him. Still, there'd be another time. There were no doubt of that. And now she knew of his fancy for his twin sister, he wouldn't stand a chance. Besides, she'd be ready next time. He'd not escape her legs. She'd wrap them around him like a vice. She were a bleedin' match for any man.

As he tidied himself, he looked up, his eyebrows raised. The little smile on his lips begged for praise. *What the hell – he had some coming to him, didn't he?*

'Bleedin' hell, guvnor. You're a bleedin' tiger.'

The laugh he let out rebounded off the rafters, then he shocked Rita by taking hold of her and kissing her again. No bloke had ever done that before. Not after they'd had their way. Bleedin' hell, there were no accounting for bleedin' toffs.

'He did it then?'

'Of course. Couldn't resist, could he?'

'I – I ain't never had it. What's it like?'

'Bloody lovely, Penny. Well, it is with a bloke as knows what he's doing, and that toff knew what he were doing all right. He were the best I've had. So you're a virgin then, mate?'

Penny's face flushed and Rita instantly felt sorry. She hadn't meant to embarrass her. She'd thought, from how Penny spoke, as she were beyond that. 'Look, it ain't no bloody big deal. We were all virgins once. But if you want to change it, you need to do something with yourself. You ain't unattractive, but . . . well, a good bath wouldn't go amiss. And that hair of yers is like bleedin' straw. Didn't your mam introduce you to a toothbrush? I mean, I know times have been hard, but us lot shared one and used the soot from the back of the fire to clean our teeth. Bloody good stuff. Gets them white as anything.'

Seeing the distressed look cross Penny's face, Rita felt a rare moment of compassion for another. She wished she hadn't spoken so harshly.

'Look, mate, I can sense as there's sommat making you deeply unhappy, and it ain't bleedin' right that anyone should feel as though they have such little self-worth as to let themselves go like you have. Is there anything I can help you with, love?' Her feeling of being a bitch increased as she saw tears trickle from Penny's eyes. 'You can tell me, mate, and if I can make it better for you, I will.'

Penny took a moment to answer, but when she did, her

words compounded Rita's feelings of guilt over how she'd treated her.

'I ain't got a mam. And I didn't want to be attractive to me dad. Me sister were, and I seen what he done to her. He bleedin' killed her. He wanted her and she resisted. He slapped her about. He's in jail now, and he'll bleedin' rot there. After Ruby died, I just didn't care anymore.'

'Blimey! I'm sorry, mate, that's a lot for anyone to contend with, and I can understand your thinking. But look, love, we can't change the past; we can only make our future better. If you want me to, I'll help yer get yourself sorted. You're a lovely girl, and I want folk to know that. Let's start by getting you cleaned up, eh? If you get clean, you'll find that your eyes won't be all sore and matted, and those sores on your mouth will go. That'd be sommat, wouldn't it? I tell you what: you get on with shifting some hay and I'll go over to the house and have a word with the housekeeper. I'll see if she'll let us have a bath tonight. She's a bit of a cow, but we've been here a while now and ain't bothered her much.'

More tears dropped from the corner of Penny's eyes. *Poor cow.* But though Rita's heart felt heavy for Penny, she had no inclination to comfort her with a hug, not like she'd do naturally. No, she couldn't bear the thought, but she'd help Penny. It'd be a good job to get done too, for the smell and sight of her had been a bit much to live with.

When Rita got to the house, the housekeeper shocked her as she told Rita to follow her up the stairs. 'Blimey, I only asked for a bath, not a tour of the place. Where you taking me?'

'Master Terence said you're to come into the house for the winter, but I ain't happy about it. These bedrooms are for household staff and we're short of them, so if we take on more, you'll be back in that barn. And while I'm on, I want you to do something about that other lass. She's a disgrace!'

'Keep your bleedin' hair on. I told yer: that's what I came to ask for. Besides, you don't know the circumstances of her. Now, show me the room and how we go on for a bath. We've managed with a bowl and jug since we got here, and it ain't good enough.'

The housekeeper huffed, but didn't say anything. She simply shoved open the door of the room they were to occupy and then pointed down the landing. 'The bathroom is down there. You two can occupy it after dinner. No, make that before, because I can't face another meal with that girl stinking the kitchen out. I take it she will be bathing as well?'

Rita chose not to answer. She knew it would rankle with all the staff, having her and Penny here. *Toffee-nosed bleeders.* But she couldn't argue with what they said about Penny.

Once the stiff-backed spinster had turned the corner and was out of sight, Rita took a proper look around, clenching her hands with the excitement that seized her. She'd never seen the like of a room like this. Her home in London was squashed with bodies – there were ten of them altogether, all occupying two rooms above a shop. You could fit both of their rooms into this one. And the smell of wax polish everywhere made you feel you were one of them posh lot.

It was hard to take it all in. Two beds with a chest of drawers next to each and a big wardrobe took up most of the space, and a marble-topped washstand with a china jug and bowl perched on it stood under the window. It had a towel rail on one side with, she noted, one towel. Well, she'd ask for another, as she wasn't about to share. The walls were covered with a pink paper with daisies all over it. Though faded, it gave a light feel to the room. Bouncing on the bed, Rita giggled. *Blimey, Ma O'Reilly! I've come up in the world!*

Showing the place the reverence it demanded, she almost tiptoed along towards the bathroom, scared to make a sound, although what she saw when she opened the door changed that. 'Bleedin' hell! Call that a bleedin' bath? It's more like a swimming pool.' Clasping her hand over her mouth, she looked back along the landing, but there was no one around.

The water gushed out of the taps as she turned them on, and steam rose to the ceiling. Turning them off, Rita hugged herself before running back the way the housekeeper had brought her. She had to find Penny. They had to move in this minute. And she'd get that Penny scrubbed clean quicker than the bat of an eyelid.

Penny took the first bath; Rita left her to her own devices, afraid she'd be sick if she had to take in the smell of Penny when she was wet. But after that she made sure she supervised her, and worked on her matted hair. It had been a challenge, but now, as she looked at Penny a week later, it was a challenge that she was glad she'd taken on.

'It don't seem a week since we took this room, does it, Penny? Though looking at you, and the difference in you, you'd think it was more like a month. That frock suits you – you can keep it if you want. 'Ere, sit still, will you? How's a girl meant to put make-up on you, when you keep moving?'

'Sorry, Rita. I'm just excited, and it keeps making me want to pee. I ain't never been to no wedding before.'

'Well, you ain't going to this one, either. Not to the church do and breakfast – not official, anyway. But I've a plan. We're meeting up with them four girls from over at that stud farm. They're coming over to Breckton to see the service, but they're free after that until the party later. So we're all going to have a cup of Rosie Lee and a chinwag in that tea room.'

'But we're invited to the party later, ain't we? A lot of the servants are going.'

'Well, that's because they know the family, you daft cow. Anyway, it ain't official, but we might get in. Come on, let's have a look at you.'

The transformation in Penny was hard to believe. Her dark hair now shone. It fell into natural curls, and looked lovely with a side parting and clipped back. Her spots had all cleared up, and her eyes . . . well, that's where the biggest change had taken place. No longer crusted, they had widened out and were a lovely velvety blue. She had a pretty face and a good figure.

'You could catch any bloke's eye now, Pen, but keep your maulers off his Lordship. He's mine. He's been sniffing around again. Came into the barn earlier, but that sister of his called him out. Queer, the relationship between them – have you noticed?'

'No, can't say I have. Anyway, can we go now? I can't wait any longer. We ain't hardly moved from here for weeks. Though how you arranged where to meet them girls beats me.'

'I sent word. The minute I heard of the wedding in the family they work for, and that it were going to be over in this town, I took care of things, so me and you could get a look-in. Like I said, I'm reckoning on them helping us. We all got on well on our journey up here.'

''Cept that posh one. She were quiet. I think she realized what she'd let herself in for when she met us. I reckon as she should have done some other kind of war work.'

'Well, we'll see. P'raps she's found her feet now. Give her a chance. At least she's giving something a go. Not many toffs are. Come on, we're going to be late.'

Rita couldn't contain herself as they left the room, and she did a little hop, skip and jump at the pleasure of finally having the prospect of some light relief. *It's all going to be bleedin' lovely and, with a bit of luck, His High-and-Mightiness will be there. I could do with a repeat performance.*

12

Megan

Doubts Creep In

'Are you ready, Megan, love?'

'Yes, Jack. I'm as ready as I can be.'

'You look reet bonny, lass. By, that navy costume were best you could pick, and putting it with that green blouse . . . well, you look a reet picture.'

The making up of the outfit she'd designed for herself she'd left to Phyllis. Whenever she did this, Phyllis would choose something to contrast with green. 'It goes with your hair, lass,' she'd say. 'Eeh, I love the colour of your hair. I had mine dyed red just like it once, remember?' Megan had, and she'd hoped it hadn't been *just like hers*, as the resulting orangey colour that Phyllis had ended up with had attracted many a smirk when she wasn't looking.

Checking back in the mirror, Megan had to admit the suit was beautiful: a calf-length, pencil-slim skirt, fitted jacket with a wide collar and padded shoulders and flaring out from the waist. And with the soft-green silk blouse under it, it looked very chic. Just right for a wedding – any wedding, but something in her wished with all her heart it wasn't Sarah and Billy's wedding that she was wearing it for.

'Hey, what's that look all about? It's meant to be a happy day. Come on, me little lass.'

She went willingly into Jack's open arms. The warmth there encased her in his love for her. The way he snuggled her to him stirred the memory of their love-making the night before.

Fraught with worry over all that had happened, and what her mind suggested might happen, she hadn't been able to relax at first. But, as always, Jack had helped her, and she'd found herself feeling more passionate than she'd been for a long time. Together they had ridden the heights they were used to reaching, and the experience had left her fragmented.

'Eeh, I love you, Megan, thou knows. I love you with all that I am. Nothing will hurt you again, love. It's all behind us.'

'Is it, though, Jack? Will everything be reet?'

His answer told her that he'd misread her concern for Sarah's future, and thought she was referring to the awful night of the welcome-home dinner for Billy. 'It will, lass. Billy apologized to Richard, and to us all. Richard understood and accepted the apology, you know that. He could see that it must have looked bad to Billy, him holding Sarah and calling her "darling". And, like we said, Billy ain't used to these posh sorts. He don't realize as they use words like that to each other all the time. He understands now, so that's that.'

'But Sarah still looks so fragile.' Megan didn't tell him it was the result of a miscarriage. Only she, Hattie and Issy knew that. Everyone else thought Sarah had succumbed to a sickness bug. Megan had to explain the blood; it had started leaking from the poor lass as they'd carried her out of the room, so she'd told her mam and Jack it were just a very heavy monthly bleed. She'd have said more, if Sarah had allowed her to, but the lass hadn't wanted anyone to know that she'd allowed Billy to have her before they were wed. You couldn't blame her. Folk looked down on anyone as didn't wait.

Jack's reply told her that he didn't suspect any different from what he'd been told. 'She's bound to, love. She were reet poorly, and it's only been four weeks since.'

'I know. It seems so soon for her to go through with the wedding, but what choice is there? If they wait until Billy has his next leave, which Billy is adamant he won't do, they wouldn't have any time together. At least, by marrying now, they know they have two weeks before he has to report.'

'Well then, you have all the reasons why it's going ahead. Everybody and everything is ready for it, so come on, let's make it the best day we can for them, eh? I've a big job to do today. I've to give away me little lass in marriage, and that ain't easy for me, so I could do with you cheering up. And if you don't put a smile on your face, I might just have to take your knic—'

'Eeh, Jack, lad, you'll do no such thing! By, there were no carrying on like that when I were a lass. Now get out, while Megan helps me into me frock, or I'll have to go to the wedding in me housecoat!'

They both laughed at this intrusion from Issy. It sometimes annoyed Megan how Issy went around the house with no thought for what folk might be doing, but mostly she didn't mind. Issy were like a mam to her, and had been since she were a lass of thirteen. Even though she'd since found her own mam, the feeling she had for this wonderful stalwart of a woman hadn't diminished. Having no time to scold her for the umpteenth time for barging into their bedroom, Megan just took the gown, shooed Jack out and got on with sliding the dress over Issy's head. With this achieved, she stood back. 'By, you look grand, Issy, love.'

'Not me usual fat lump, then?'

'Don't be daft. That's not how you feel, is it, love?'

'Naw, not in this frock anyroad. By, it's lovely. Ta, lass. You did me proud.'

Issy held her arms aloft and twirled around. The skirt of the royal-blue and white frock flared out at the hem. The style of the fitted top and mermaid-shaped skirt really did slim her, and she looked younger. Beautiful. An overwhelming love for her seized Megan. She opened her arms. Issy came to her with a look that held relief. 'Megan, love, I – I haven't said owt about what happened and about me ranting on.'

'Don't mention it, Issy. It were the heat of the moment.'

'I have to. I have to say as I'm sorry. Thou's reet in saying it were the heat of the moment, but I said some terrible things. It were like all me pent-up feelings were released, and I have to say I feel better for it. Maybe I should have done it when it happened, but it's out now. I've said sorry to the lad and explained, and he seemed to understand. He were very good, and now I want to say sorry to you. No mam should hear someone going on like that about her son.'

Megan hugged her close, releasing her before her emotions got the better of her. 'Right, let's get you into your jacket and sit your hat on your head.'

The flared royal-blue jacket completed the picture. Issy looked lovely, with her grey curls forming a halo around the brim of her hat. 'Eeh, love, I can see Cissy in you. She'll be there with us, Issy, thou knows that, but you have to be as if you are her, for Sarah's sake. Take the lead in everything, just like you were the bride's mam, eh? It's your rightful place, love.'

Issy wiped her eye once more. 'Ta, lass. It's good of you to give me this honour, which by rights should be yours, you being her stepmam. Seeing to Sarah, as Cissy would have, will help me – help us both, as it happens. Especially as she's going to be wed in the same church as Cissy were to Jack, and me to my Tom. And you – well, there'll be memories for you there an' all, and not all of them good. Not to mention that we pass by the graves of my Tom, Cissy and little Bella.'

'I know, love – it's a big day for you. Put them shoulders of yours back and get that lovely smile on your face, eh?'

'I will, lass, I will.'

'And that other . . . Well, you're to think no more of it. I know how it's been for you. Now, off you go. Check as Sarah and Sally are all ready, and have their bouquets and gloves and everything. Oh, just a minute. Here, I haven't heard mention of the "something borrowed, something blue", so give Sarah this hanky to tuck into the ribbon holding her flowers. I made it for her. Look, I've embroidered a blue daisy in the corner, and feather-stitched the edge near the lace in the same silk an' all. I used the remains of the silk thread I had left over from a skein that I once prettied up a plain blouse for Cissy with.'

'Eeh, it's grand, and I remember that blouse.' Another tear had to be wiped away, but it was done in one quick action and the smile was back as Issy's old shoulders straightened. 'Anyroad, the "borrowed" is them pearls from Hattie – them as that Arthur bought for her. By, lass, everything brings back sommat to think on, don't it? Right, let's not start. Keep it all on a happy note, eh? See you at the church, love.'

As she walked outside to get into the car, Megan shivered. Even though the sun was high in the sky, it held no warmth, and remnants of the winter frost still glistened here and there.

She was glad she'd made a shawl for Sarah; it would give her some protection from the cold.

Her heart ached every time she looked at her beloved, frail stepdaughter. It seemed to her that history was repeating itself. She hadn't been fooled by the explanation given for Richard's term of endearment. The tone of it, as it had echoed around the room, had held a deep love. It was a love of the kind she wanted for Sarah – not the possessive love Billy had for her, as if he owned her. His actions were so like his dad's at times. *Oh God*. But then Sarah insisted that this was what she wanted. Even so, that didn't stop Megan feeling as if they were leading the poor mite to the slaughterhouse.

As the car swept down the drive past the stables, she saw Dorothy and Iris, two of their Land Girls. Four had arrived last week and were settling in well. Jack had converted the top half of the barn into a flat for them. It looked grand, and was something he'd talked of doing for Sarah and Billy, but in the end they'd decided to take the only cottage on the estate. It hadn't been lived in for a while, but was in good condition, and it hadn't taken much to get it right for them. It nestled in the only part of their land that wasn't flat: a small valley on the east side, about a mile from the main house. Sarah had fallen in love with it as soon as she'd seen it and had spent many hours playing there when she was younger.

Dorothy looked up and waved. She and Iris loved to work with the horses. The gesture compounded the good news that Jack would be able to keep the horses. It'd been grand to hear Lord Crompton confirm this in the meeting they'd had with him, and to know that his bank would also back her in her new project.

Iris also looked up and gave a more frantic wave. The lass were only eighteen, love her heart. It were young to leave home, but Dorothy had taken Iris under her wing. She were a lovely lass, Dorothy. Though she looked nothing like Cissy – who were what you'd term pretty as a picture, and dainty with it – Dorothy's ways brought her to mind. She had an easy nature, laughing a lot and always having something to say at the right moment. She and Iris were learning all about the stables and looking after the horses. 'It's like they were born to it,' Gary had said. *Oh God, it's hard to believe as Gary has to report for training on the same day as Billy.* But she wouldn't think of that. He and Jenny had been looking forward to today. They were treating it as a last good day together before he left.

Passing the bottom fields, Megan saw Mildred and Louise, the other two Land Girls, hard at work. One drove the tractor and the other had a pitchfork in her hand. It seemed strange to see young women doing such work, especially that Louise – a lass who spoke like she had a plum in her mouth, well educated and from an upper-class family. You'd think she would turn her nose up at it all, but no, she was as willing as the rest of them. She loved to train the horses and was a good rider, but she was happy to let the others do the stable work. As it happened, all four girls were turning out to be a real help, and easy lassies to get on with, even though they came from down south. Funny, that: northern folk never had a good word for southerners, and she'd not looked forward to these London girls coming to the farm.

Ranging in age from the youngster, Iris, to Mildred and Louise in their early to mid-twenties, and Dorothy, a widow of thirty-five-ish, they were a mixed bunch. It were good to think they were all coming to the party after the wedding breakfast.

Oh God, the wedding breakfast. How would they all get through it?

Shaking this thought away, Megan called out to the girls. 'Leave what you're doing now. Jack gave you the afternoon off. If you hurry, you'll have time to get to the church to see Sarah.'

'Thank you, Mrs Fellam. I'll tell the others. We're all so excited and have our clothes out all ready.'

Megan smiled as the girls dropped their tools and ran back to the barn. They'd have plenty of time, as Jack and Sarah hadn't left yet.

This distraction cheered her. Everything would be all right, she told herself. She was just being silly. Sarah wanted to marry Billy. Billy wanted to marry Sarah. The picture of Cissy – invoked by Dorothy reminding Megan of her – conjured up Cissy again. How lovely if she could have been here for her daughter's wedding. *Eeh, Cissy, lass, help Sarah. Look after her. Me heart won't lighten about her marriage to me son. I pray she's doing the right thing. I pray she's not walking into what I went through with Billy's dad*. A desperate tear plopped onto Megan's cheek. She wiped it away. There was nothing she could do and, as always, she just had to get on with things as they were.

13

Richard & Hattie

Avoiding Heartache

Richard paced up and down the corridor, his body at odds with his mind. He had to find a way of living with what was happening today. Thank God he had got out of attending the wedding. Sarah wouldn't know he wasn't there until she reached the church. He'd left it until the last moment to ring his mother and tell her the lie he'd conjured up: 'Stuck in Glasgow, sorry. Training schedules altered. Nothing I can do about it. Have to go. Give Sarah and Billy my best wishes, and my apologies to Megan and Jack. Hope I don't upset the seating plan or anything. I'll ring Lucinda. She may go with you anyway. I'll see what she says.'

Lucinda had chosen not to go, thank God. Somehow he hadn't wanted her there, with or without him. *Oh, Sarah, why? Why?* He was certain he'd read reciprocation for his feelings in her eyes.

'Lieutenant Chesterton, are you not meant to be in a lecture? Don't think for a minute ye know it all, lad. Clever or not, ye've a lot to learn, I'm telling ye. So look smart, or ye could find yourself cleaning the car park with a toothbrush.'

Richard jumped to attention, faced the huge Glaswegian professor who was now an officer involved in their training, and saluted. 'Good morning, sir. No, I'm on a twenty-four-hour pass. Supposed to be at a family wedding, but . . . well, things are complicated.'

'In that case, you'd do well to use the time productively. Join my lecture. I can promise you it won't send you to sleep, nor will you forget the fascinating facts I will tell you. Och, twenty-four-hour pass – they're making babies of ye! This is war, man. All that stuff has to go out of the window.'

'Sir!' Clipping his feet together as he once again executed a smart salute, Richard marvelled at how quickly he'd got used to deferring to another. Not that it came as any difficulty with this man. He greatly admired the professor in aeronautics, who'd been heavily decorated for his contribution in the Great War and had come out of retirement to train recruits in aircraft dynamics. Far from nodding off in his lectures, Richard had found them fascinating and could see the value of them. Knowing how your aircraft works and what it would stand up to was, in his opinion, going to be invaluable. Besides, it would take his mind off everything. Once again he found himself asking: *Why?* Why did Sarah have to carry out a promise that she'd made as a girl? She was about to tie herself to that bloody bully, and there was nothing he could do about it. How he was going to live without her, he didn't know.

'I see the medal that you arrived with has now cleared up.' The general indicated Richard's eye. 'Good, it bodes well that you are a fighting man, Lieutenant. The country needs such men. Come along.'

Following the professor to the lecture room, Richard knew his face was colouring. Arriving with a black eye hadn't been the easiest of things. Nor had reporting to Biggin Hill with the visible aftermath of Billy's attack on him – at that ill-fated party Megan had thrown for Billy's homecoming – helped him get off to a good start. Though all of that had paled beside the awful worry of trying to get news about Sarah. His father, as indeed he did, thought there was more to the bleeding that occurred on that night and to Sarah fainting. Megan hadn't let them near Sarah, saying she'd call their own doctor. It had all been a bit crazy really, and it had been a relief to hear from his mother that, although she had been laid low for a few days, Sarah had recovered and was busy getting ready for her wedding. His heart ached at the thought.

They'd reached the lecture hall, where the buzz of student noise from his fellow trainees hushed. How he was to get through the next few hours, Richard had no idea. As he slipped into a bench next to Victor Hughes, a man he'd really connected with from day one, Victor leaned towards him. 'There you are. I heard you hadn't left. Well, there was a call for you, from a Miss Lucinda Palmer. She said to tell you she is getting the overnight train, so don't let go of your leave pass.'

The groan came from deep within him, but Richard suppressed its exit and coughed to cover it up. 'Thanks. Well, I'm sitting in on this as something to do, beside the fact that I enjoy Professor McCleod's lectures, but I haven't made any formal arrangements to relinquish the time granted to me, so nothing lost.'

Nothing lost! The last thing he wanted was to entertain Lucinda.

Richard's taxi pulled up at the station. His heart drummed with the decision he'd taken. He couldn't marry Lucinda – it wouldn't be fair to her or himself.

Her wave held eager anticipation. Her fresh-faced beauty

and the shining excitement that she exuded compounded his feeling of being a cad of the first order.

'Darling, why so worried? Aren't you pleased to see me? A whole weekend together, and no parents around. Take me to the nearest hotel . . .'

'Lucinda . . . I – I need to talk to you. I – I—'

'Cold feet, eh? That'll soon pass. Come on.'

'No! I – I mean. It won't pass. Look. I have a taxi waiting. We need to go somewhere quiet. The driver knows of a restaurant where they have booths. We'll go there, you must be starving.'

Lucinda didn't answer this. Richard hoped she'd taken in the message that he was trying to convey.

The Charles Brae restaurant was typically Scottish, with a fair smattering of tartan and sprigs of heather in small vases. As the taxi driver had said, there were booths dotted around, which afforded a lot of privacy.

Once seated, Richard took a deep breath, but before he could speak, Lucinda said, 'Let me do this. We're not right for each other, are we?'

Richard could only stare.

'I have to be honest with you, Richard. I've fancied the pants off you for ages. I thought I'd come up here and let you bed me, and then make my mind up as to whether I could convert that feeling into something that would last us both a lifetime. I suppose a girl like me becomes desperate, in the normal run of things. There are so few "suitable men" to choose from. But I'm not on the shelf yet.'

'No, of course not. You're a very beautiful and desirable woman, Lucinda. I'm so sorry we cannot make a go of it, but please remain my friend.'

'I will. You won't be too broken-hearted, will you?'

This surprised him. He decided to leave her thinking that he still wanted her; it was the least he could do. 'Disappointed, of course, but I believe we both need our freedom right now. Who knows, in the future . . . ?'

'That's how I feel. If we survive this bloody war and neither of us has hooked up with someone, then we could give it another go.'

'Yes. I agree.' How cold such an arrangement was, but then it was wise to leave open the way forward. Both of them wanted marriage and children, and they got on very well together, when the question of a long-term relationship wasn't marring things. It was ideal for both of them really. Have a look around, but if no one else came up, there was always each other.

A smile curled across his lips.

'What's so amusing? We should be crying. We've just split up, haven't we?'

'Oh, I do feel pain, of course, dear Lucinda. I was just amused at us making an arrangement to be the last choice for each other. Ha – I find it rather funny.'

Lucinda giggled with him. 'You're my insurance, darling, and a very nice one too, so look after yourself and don't go getting killed, or anything like that.'

'I will. Now, let's order breakfast. I didn't have any before I went in for a lecture this morning, and I'm starving. Then we'll enjoy a lovely fun weekend together, with no strings attached.'

'Does "no strings" include sleeping together, purely for enjoyment? If so, I'm up for that.'

A flush reached Richard's cheeks, but he wasn't averse to the idea. Lucinda had always been very forward. He doubted she was a virgin, and yes, the idea of sleeping with her appealed. 'Hmm, maybe – just maybe.'

Lucinda laughed out loud. He joined her, but felt deep inside him a stirring of anticipation. Everything had turned out well, and he had a treat in store later, by the sound of things. One that would serve to keep his mind off the bed that he yearned to be climbing into tonight, with Sarah.

Shaking these thoughts from him, Richard concentrated on Lucinda and what she was telling him about her horses, while entwining her stockinged feet around his and running them gently up and down his leg. The feelings he was experiencing told him that he could get through today. He had to.

Hattie pulled on her gloves. 'Eeh, Harry, it's a cold one. I hope Sarah and Sally aren't going to freeze.'

'They'll be fine. They'll have the excitement of it all to keep them warm. At least it's a dry, sunny day. "Happy the bride the sun shines on", eh?'

'I don't know about that. I have a foreboding about it all. I just can't get my thoughts around Sarah wanting to marry Billy. She looks poorly, thou knows, love. I'm reet worried for her.'

'I know, but then nerves can't help. Stop being like a mother hen and come here. I could do with a cuddle before we go. You've not been generous of late with your cuddles.'

A slither of guilt assaulted Hattie. Why couldn't she stop thinking about Arthur? Harry was a good man; he'd rescued her when she most needed it, and been there for her ever since. But it didn't matter how she wrapped it up: he wasn't Arthur, and that was that. 'Hey, pack that in. You'll ruffle me dress. What a time to start your games! We're leaving in fifteen minutes.' She slapped Harry's hand away from her breast. He'd taken her in his arms from behind, kissing her neck and caressing her stomach before moving up higher. She could feel his need as he pressed against her. 'Harry, love, we've no time.'

'Well, it'll give you something to think of during the day. Every time you catch me eye, you'll know I'm lusting after you. Then when we get home you'll not be able to resist me. Don't forget: Sally's staying at Megan's tonight, so we'll have the house to ourselves.'

Again he kissed her ears, nipping the lobes and snuggling into her neck. Nothing in her responded – and hadn't done since she'd seen that newspaper article. A deep regret entered her. Harry didn't deserve this.

Turning in his arms, she made a big effort and kissed him deeply. 'Are you trying to drive me crazy, or what?' Telling Harry she loved him gave her the reward of his lovely smile. Her eyes filled with tears, which she tried to blink away. One escaped and ran down her cheek.

'Don't cry, love. It's all right, I understand.'

And she knew he did. This compounded her guilt, but she had no time to deal with it. 'Eeh, there's nowt to understand. It's natural to have a little cry on a wedding day, especially when your man shows you how much he loves you. Now, we must go.'

'Hattie, I do love you. And what I said about catching your eye during the day – I will, you know, just to reassure you and keep me promise.'

'I know, Harry. I'll be reet. Now stop worrying and hurry up!'

Still flushed from the feelings that were assailing her, Hattie shivered as they walked towards their car. Waiting for Harry to unlock the doors and crank the engine into life, she looked around. Another car parked a little way down the road caught her eye. Her mouth dried. *Oh, stop being silly. It's just another posh car, that's all . . .*

Once they were in their car, the one that she'd spotted drove past at walking pace. A face – still so scarred, so dear, so loved – looked out at her. Her heart stopped. *Oh God, Arthur . . . Arthur . . .*

14
Sarah & Billy

The Wedding

'Well, we're here, lass. Eeh, you look lovely, Sarah. Come on now, I know as you're nervous, but a nice smile for all them as are waiting to greet you will make you feel steadier.'

Sarah obliged, for she didn't want to upset her granna, who sounded nervous herself as she took charge.

'Sally, love, you get out of the car first and help Sarah out. Then you'd better come around this side and give me a pull. I've right stiffened up.'

'I'll help you, Ma. Leave Sally to take care of Sarah.'

'Aye, well, ta, Jack, but don't be making a big thing of it. Thou knows what yer like.'

Sarah held her breath. Although it was normal banter between her granna and her dad, she didn't want any of it today, and prayed that her dad wouldn't take the bait. Sally stopped any further goings-on by saying, 'Oh, look, there's the Land Girls from yours. It's nice of them to have come. Who're the other two with them?'

'Happen that's them from Hensal Grange. Come on, lass – get yourself out. We haven't got all day.'

'Sorry, Aunt Issy, I'm getting out now. Ooh, it's all so exciting!'

Sarah knew some of Sally's excitement was forced, and for her benefit. But though it was a nice try, it didn't lift her spirits.

The sensation of going to her own funeral lay heavily within her: how was she going to face seeing Richard with his girlfriend, and how was she going to get through all of this without upsetting everyone; and, most of all, how was she going to face up to tonight, when she had to get into the same bed as Billy?

Waving to old neighbours who stood in groups oohing and aahing over her gave Sarah a brief respite from her fears. As she passed the Land Girls, Dorothy said, 'You look lovely, Sarah, love. Good luck. Enjoy every moment of today. Lock it into your memory.'

She nodded. She found it difficult to think of a reply, knowing that Dorothy had lost her husband in an accident and must be thinking that Sarah herself had more than a little chance of losing Billy to the war. The brash-looking girl standing next to Dorothy saved her any embarrassment as she piped up, 'You won't mind if we join the party, will you, Miss? Only me and Penny here, we're Land Girls working for the Cromptons, and we ain't had no fun since we got here.'

'Rita!'

'Oh, shut up, Penny. You don't get nothin' if you don't ask. It stands to bleedin' reason. How're we going to get an invite, if Sarah don't know we want one?'

'Aye, we'd be glad to have yer. Just come along with our girls. Eeh, you've made me laugh, and I didn't think to do that with how nervous I feel. What's your names?'

'I'm Rita, and this is Penny. Pleased to meet you. And I have to say you are looking lovely – and you are lovely for let-ting us come to your do. We're ever so grateful. See you later, then. Now you'd better get on in there and get wed, so we have something to celebrate.'

Her granna had joined them and laughed at this, but in her role of taking care of everything today she replied, 'Eeh, you're a one, I must say. Well, ta for making me Sarah laugh, but I'm to hurry her along now.'

'Right you are, Grandma. See you later.'

Sarah had to hold her sides at this comment from Rita, as her granna gave a look of astonishment, then indignation. 'Come on, Granna, don't take heed. These lassies are from London. They're a different breed to us.' But as she took her dad's arm she said, 'I like them, though. They have you smiling when you least think you will.'

'And it's good to see, lass. Eeh, you've had us reet worried this last couple of weeks.'

'I know, Dad, I'm sorry. None of it's been easy for me. First, Billy home after all this time, then the wedding to sort out. But we're here now, so let's get on with it, eh?' Clinging onto her dad's arm helped to steady her.

Without turning her head in a way that could be construed that she was seeking someone out, Sarah let her eyes glance around the church, covering this by smiling at everyone as she recognized them. *He's not here!* Disappointment mingled with relief. But, no, Richard wasn't present. Surely if he were, he'd be sitting with Granddad Edward and Gran Bridget, but only Mark sat there, his eager eyes passing her by and settling on Sally. Poor Mark. Little did he know that Sally had sworn off men for life.

Billy turned around from where he stood at the altar, and for a moment Sarah's heart skipped a beat. She'd never seen him looking so handsome. Dressed in a dark suit and a dazzling white shirt, with a tiny collar framing a black bow tie and his tall frame upright, he was a real sight. She smiled at him and found it easy to do so. He smiled back and winked. The action caused his head to bob to one side, releasing a curl from his sleeked-down hair. It flopped onto his forehead, giving him a rakish appearance. As she came up to him, his lovely eyes sparkled as if filled with water. Irish eyes, folk said. Billy's grandmother had come from Ireland and he'd inherited many features from his Irish ancestors. The effect of his look was to give Sarah a sense of relief. Suddenly everything seemed all right. A huge sigh expelled itself from her as she passed her bouquet to Sally.

Releasing her arm from her dad's wasn't easy. His hand tightened, his fingers dug into her. Looking up into his eyes, she saw his pain. Her confidence wavered. What was she doing to this man, who loved her beyond anything? The shock of not having realized this before shuddered through her. Always she'd thought of the consequences that might befall Megan if the marriage didn't go ahead. But now she saw that she was putting her dad through just as much, as he was being forced to give his one remaining daughter to the man who'd deprived him of his youngest. Was he going to refuse to do so at this eleventh hour? Touching his hand, she gave him a smile that she hoped would give him some reassurance. But, inside, she wanted to plead with him to take her away from all of this.

The sound of sobs came to her as she turned back to Billy. She knew they would be from her Aunt Megan and her Granna Issy, but that was natural, wasn't it? Tears always flowed at a wedding. She wished she could turn around and reassure them, too, but she had to concentrate – she had to get through the next half-hour.

Looking once more into Billy's eyes, she returned his smile. As he slipped the ring onto her finger a few minutes later, she thought for a moment of Richard, but banished the thought. She was marrying Billy, and that was that.

His look of triumph, and not of love, gave Sarah the feeling that she was a prize won – but by the wrong man. *Oh, Richard!*

However, with the sound of the bells pealing joyfully as they came out of the church, and with rice raining down on them – something she hadn't expected, with all the talk of food shortages, and which caused a sharp tingle as its grains caught her face – the rejoicing took over the space around her and Sarah found herself joining in the laughter with everyone.

Billy latched onto this. 'We're going to be happy, aren't we, lass? Me and you were allus meant to be together, weren't we?'

There was a plea in his tone. 'Aye, we'll go on fine together, Billy. We'll need to work at making things alreet, but we will. I'm certain of that.'

'What d'yer mean: work at it? It's what we both want. Why shouldn't we just be happy? You're not . . . ?'

'I didn't mean owt, Billy. Calm down. Every couple has to make an effort to adjust to being married and to make sure they make their husband or wife happy. That's what I'm going to be doing. Now, stop scowling – folk are looking at us. Look, Dad's got his old camera out.'

Sarah felt Billy relax. His smile came back and he squeezed her to him. 'I'll definitely be making you happy tonight. Eeh, I can't wait, Sarah, you're me lass now. Me own lass.'

Once again a shudder shook Sarah's body and she wished Billy hadn't mentioned what was to come, because she didn't know if she could face it.

The wedding breakfast had passed without incident, and Sarah felt her mood lifting and a kind of happiness settle in her. Her worries had been unfounded, and she was glad now that Richard hadn't been able to make it. She'd never have relaxed with him here.

Other guests had now joined the party and a band had struck up. Everyone looked happy. The cider and sherry flowed, and the dancing had been under way for some time.

'Will you look at him, Penny? He ain't looked over at me all bleedin' night. He's only got eyes for her. Rotten bleeder.'

'Who're yer talking about, Rita?'

'Mr Bleedin' Terence Crompton, who do yer think?'

'I know you mean him, but who has he only got eyes for?'

'That posh cow, Louise.'

'Someone mention my name?'

'No – well, not in a way as there's anything to say to you. I were just having a bit of fun with Penny. Have you noticed our boss? He's got a fancy for you.'

Rita saw Louise blush. She'd noticed all right.

'Don't be silly, he's just looking around the room. Anyway, it seems to me he is taken – or, as you put it, "he's got a fancy for" – the dark-haired girl he is with. Can't say I blame him. She's very beautiful.'

'Nah, that's his sister. They're twins,' Penny said.

'Makes no odds, Penny, and I'll tell you both something. It ain't natural how they carry on.'

'Oh? In what way?' Louise asked.

Much to her annoyance, Rita didn't have time to answer this. She wished to put Louise off the toff, but before she could, Terence Crompton stood in front of them and bowed to Louise. 'May I have the pleasure of this dance, Miss . . . ?'

'Rothergill – Louise Rothergill.'

'Not a member of *the* Rothergills from Surrey?'

'No, well, not exactly. They are my uncle and aunt, and my

cousins. My branch of the family live in Kent, and we are not titled. Daddy is the younger brother.'

'How fascinating. What on earth possessed you to take up the work of a Land Girl?'

Rita felt like punching him in the face. *He's got a bleedin' cheek, ignoring me as if nothing has happened between us, and saying 'Land Girl' in that manner, making us out as if we are muck under his boots.* She watched as he swept Louise onto the dance floor and started a waltz with her. Grabbing Penny, she said, "Ere, come on. Let's dance, eh?'

As they passed by Theresa, Rita was shocked to notice a weird expression on the girl's face. Surely she wasn't going to show her feelings for her brother in public, was she? But no, the look wasn't one of jealousy. It was more like sexual hunger. She knew that feeling and had conveyed it across many a room. Following the direction in which Theresa was looking gave Rita a further shock. She was only giving the bridegroom the eye! *And now it looks like she's going to take her chances* . . . Rita watched as Billy moved away from his wife and Theresa walked over to him. *Bleedin' hell, it all goes on, up here in the country!*

'So, you are a married man now? That will clip your wings a bit, won't it?'

Billy laughed. The looks Theresa had been giving him since she'd arrived at his wedding party had excited him and prompted him to position himself well away from Sarah. 'I doubt it. I have what I want now, but a man can still have some fun, can't he?'

'Oh? Your bride is what you want? Forgive me for thinking you are disillusioned, sir.'

Her laugh after saying this quietened the anger inside him,

which pleased Billy. He hated it when anger overtook him; it closed him down, covering his mind in a red mist that he had to fight his way out of. His voice held steady as he replied, 'Aye, she's all I've ever wanted, but there's room for me to indulge meself. As long as it don't interfere with what me and Sarah have.'

'I wouldn't think that privilege of having *other indulgences* extends to her – am I right?'

'It seems to me you think you can poke your nose into business as ain't nothing to do with you. You posh lot are all the bloody same. Well—'

'Sorry, didn't mean to touch a raw nerve. Thought you were above that. Didn't have you down as being like the rest of them.'

'What d'yer mean by that?' The girl was beginning to rile him. He'd best move away.

'Don't go. It was a compliment. I meant that I thought I could exchange intelligent banter with you. Have some fun. Use innuendos – that's all.'

'Well, whatever they are, they ain't for me. I like straight talk.'

'Right, in that case, I'll be out riding in the woods tomorrow afternoon at two. I'll head for this side, so you haven't far to walk from your cottage.' Before he could say anything more, she turned. 'Pater, there you are! You promised me a dance, to keep me from getting bored.'

'Theresa!'

The look of embarrassment on Lord Crompton's face was a sight that Billy would not have missed. That daughter of his was a bitch. Her invitation – because that's what it was – had left him feeling his need. He'd have to get Sarah away soon. It wasn't done for the bride and groom to stay long at the wedding party, anyway.

Sarah's laugh met Billy as he went back to her. She was standing with the Land Girls. There was a couple of them he fancied an' all. He'd give that Rita a go, and her mate. Rita'd be good – experienced, he'd imagine – but the other one looked like no one had been there. Might be a challenge. Trouble was, he'd so little time left: two weeks . . . Part of him was excited about that. He relished the thought of war, battle, guns and explosions. He couldn't wait.

When Sarah spotted him, she didn't look pleased to see him. *And this being our bloody wedding day, an all!* She was different of late. Though, if he was honest, she'd been that way a while now. Well, she'd have to change her attitude, because he wasn't for having a surly wife. He wanted her how she used to be: feisty at times, and taking him to task, but all done with love. That's what was missing – love. It confused him as to why. *Richard!* Anger surged through him as this thought hit him like a bullet. There was something between her and that bastard, Richard fucking Chesterton!

The sudden and painful grasp of her arm startled Sarah. She'd seen Billy coming towards her and was making her excuses to the girls when it happened.

'Billy, what's wrong?'

The Land Girls moved away, their faces averted in embarrassment.

Billy snarled through his teeth, 'You – you're what's wrong. This is our wedding day and you spend it with everyone except me.'

'But you left me. You went and talked to Miss Crompton. I couldn't do owt about it, seeing as my new husband didn't choose to take me with him to talk to her. Now, let go of me arm or I'll scream the place down.'

'Ha! That's more like what you used to be like. Only with one difference.'

'Billy, I ain't going to talk over whatever you imagine is in me head, not in front of guests. You're making them feel uncomfortable. Now don't be daft. Look, your mam's looking over.'

'Aye, well, she's the same an' all. But I'll sort the pair of yer out, you—'

'Sarah, I believe this is my dance?'

'Oh, I – I . . . Aye, it is, Granddad Edward, ta. Let me put me drink down.' Grateful for the interruption, Sarah could have jumped for joy, but then she saw Aunt Megan just behind Edward and her heart sank. *Not now, please not now . . .* As Edward swept her into a quickstep, she could only pray as she watched over his shoulder and saw Aunt Megan approaching Billy. *Please God, let Billy be kind to his mam.* But deep inside her she knew there was no chance he would be.

Not wanting to ask him, and knowing what the answer would be, Megan summoned all she had in her. 'Billy, shall we dance, love? I'd like it if we did.'

'I don't want to dance. Anyroad, while we're on, what game are you playing at, eh, Mam? Feathering your own nest and acting like gentry do. Well, you just remember where you came from and how you got your money. And who died because of it all.'

'I'm not playing any game, Billy, and now isn't the right moment to talk of what's worrying you.'

'No, it never is. I'm telling you, Mam, sommat's changed around here. Sarah ain't the same. And I can't forget how you were with me dad – not just like that, I can't. I tried to while I were in that place, but it lay in me no matter what; and now it's harder out here, with seeing you with everything you've got. Me dad never had nowt, and you hurt him bad. I'm telling you: you do the same again and I'll kill you. Even if I have to swing for it.'

'I never had any intention of hurting your dad, Billy. I had no choice but to leave him. I couldn't take any more, and neither could I see you brutalized like you were, for nowt. I didn't take up with Jack afore I left your dad, if that's what you think. I'd planned on leaving long before I knew Jack loved me. And yes, while we're on, I ain't going to stand for you threatening me. In fact I have a warning for you: don't you ever do to Sarah what your dad did to me, or it won't be you doing the killing.'

She didn't wait for a reply; Billy's shocked expression was enough. She turned and walked away. Her eyes found Jack and she made her way towards him.

'By, me little lass. I keep saying it, but you looks grand today. And what does you think to it all, eh? Our young 'uns wed to each other . . . it puts a seal on everything, doesn't it?'

She managed a smile for him, and as she did so she looked back to where Billy was still standing, watching her. The look of hate that crossed his face sent fear trembling through her.

'Don't worry, lass. He'll change. They all do, when they have some young 'uns of their own and realize what it's all about.' Issy was standing at Megan's other side and had whispered this into her ear.

Megan touched Issy's shoulder and whispered back, 'Ta, Issy. I hope so. I really do.'

'What's worrying you, Megan? Is everything alreet?'

'Aye it is, Jack. Me and Issy were just musing on how

things change when the young 'uns have nippers of their own.'

'Aye, there's that to come an' all. Eeh, I'm looking forward to some little ones about the house. Our own grandchildren, Megan. It makes you think, doesn't it?' He pulled her to him and she snuggled into him, although it didn't help. The feelings inside her had taken root. What had they done? Why hadn't they stopped this wedding? *Dear God, let Sarah be all right.* She shook herself mentally. Of course Sarah would be fine. Billy loved her, didn't he?

The dance came to an end and Edward glided Sarah back to Billy. Megan held her breath as she heard Edward say, 'Your turn, Billy. I've brought your lovely wife back to you. Time for the bride and groom to have their last waltz, I think.' Turning to where she stood with Jack, Edward called over, 'What do you say, Megan?'

She didn't have time to say anything, as Hattie had come over to them and took charge. 'You're reet there, Edward, and none of us can let our hair down till the happy couple leave. Ha, funny that, but that's the way it is. Everyone has a good time at a wedding except the bride and groom!'

'I agree: our last waltz, Billy. Come on, down on your knee and ask me to dance. Eeh, I'm that excited for us to get off together and start our married life.'

Grateful to her Aunt Hattie, Sarah had taken her lead. She knew how to manage Billy. She just didn't feel inclined to do so that often, but now was the time to pull out all the stops. Leaning forward, she put her arms around him and kissed his cheek and, with every effort she could muster, said, 'I love you, my husband.'

The change was instant. Billy smiled down at her as he replied, 'Eeh, me little lass!' And, as tradition dictated, he knelt before her. But then he surprised her: his mood lifted and he made a bit of fun out of it, asking in a posh voice, 'Will you do me the honour?'

For just a moment, something of what she'd felt for him in the past came back to Sarah. She could make this work. She had to.

15

Sarah & Billy

A Path Chosen

Despite Sarah's bravado, once they had got into the car and everyone had waved them off, she'd begun to dread the moment that was now upon her: coming together with Billy as his wife. No more resisting; she had to forget that last time, and its consequences.

But though she tried, it was going badly. Her body felt cold and closed.

'I never thought as you'd be like this, Sarah. Come on now, you has to let me. It's our wedding night. Or is it cos I'm the wrong bloke, eh? That's it, ain't it? You're thinking of Richard, ain't yer?'

'No, Billy. It's you I love. You know that.' *I have to pretend.* 'I just need you to take your time a bit. You're hurting me, with how rough you're being. I thought we'd kiss and cuddle first. Love each other into it.'

'Look, Sarah, you're me wife now – and it ain't as if we ain't done it afore. We're supposed to come together tonight, thou knows that.'

'I just didn't think it would be like this. You're—'

'So it's me to blame, is it? I don't know you any more, Sarah. You've allus been me lass. I'm reet, aren't I? You're thinking of that Richard. The bastard! He got at you while I were away . . . Where're you going?'

'I'm not staying in bed with you, Billy Armitage. It's our wedding night and you're treating me like an animal, and saying things to me that aren't true and never have been. I'd rather sleep on the floor.'

'Oh no, you doesn't. You're going to be me wife proper. And while we're on, you can stop being Miss High-and-Mighty. You're Sarah Fellam as was, from Breckton, a groomsman-cum-chauffeur's daughter, not Lady Duck Muck.' He caught hold of her. She tried to pull away.

'You're hurting me. Billy, no! Billy!'

The blow caught her arm and sent her reeling back onto the bed. His weight crushed her. With his knee, he prised open her legs. The force with which he penetrated her seared Sarah with pain, as the tension in her tightened her muscles. She cried out, begging him to stop, but the more she begged, the harder he thrust himself into her. At last, his face contorted, his throat released a deep-seated groan and he pushed hard into her.

She hadn't wanted it to be like this . . . Not forced on her. Oh God, she'd wanted to be loved and cherished; taken to a place where she'd want to have Billy make love to her.

'Oh, Sarah. Sarah, me little love. Me lass, I'm sorry, Sarah. I'm sorry.'

With one hand on either side of her head, he lifted his body and looked down on her. He didn't remove himself from her, but her insides relaxed. His sorrow, and now his gentle wiping away of her tears, made it easier, but then his words made her tense once more.

'I didn't want to do you like that, Sarah. You made me.

Why – why are you like you are with me? Say sommat, Sarah, say sommat.'

'I – I don't know what to say. I . . .' Suddenly she knew that if she really was going to salvage something from this, she had to swallow her pride. 'I'm sorry. I shouldn't have been so silly. You were bound to be eager. I should have realized. But promise me, Billy: promise me you won't ever hit me again. That has hurt me more than the hurry you were in, and the rough way you were with me. It has hurt me inside.'

Shame etched his face, allowing her to give in to her anger.

'And I'm not for standing for it, so don't even think of doing it again, otherwise I'll tell me dad and he'll have sommat to say about it.'

'You do that and you'll—'

Rage reddened his face and made the veins in his neck bulge. Fear sat heavily in every nerve of Sarah, but courage came and blocked it from making her cower to him. 'Don't even think about threatening me, Billy. This has to end – and end now. If it doesn't, I'll walk out, and whatever that makes you do, you can take the consequences of, as I will an' all.'

Shock registered in his expression. His eyes stared down at her, their glare kindling a dread in her that belied the brave stance she'd taken. Still lying underneath him, she realized her vulnerability and the thought bathed her in sweat.

After a moment Billy's muscles relaxed. His body seemed to fold as he laid his full weight on her, his arm lifting her head and finding a way under her shoulders, his grip like a vice and yet expressing whatever love he was capable of giving. 'I'm sorry, Sarah, love. Don't ever be for saying as you'll leave me.'

Hearing what sounded like a sob, she put her arms around him. 'It doesn't have to come to that, Billy. Just take care in your treatment of me, and I will love and respect you. We can find happiness, despite everything we've had to face. It ain't going to be easy, but we're in this together, thou knows.'

'Eeh, Sarah, I want to make you happy. I want to conquer what I have in me. I love you and always have done, but you must take some of the blame. You didn't act as you should tonight, and haven't done for a while.'

'I know. It's all been a lot to take on. Let's start again, eh? Begin as if nothing has happened. It's our only chance.'

'Aye, you're reet.'

His kiss surprised her. The gentleness of it – the giving, not taking. It was something she'd not experienced with him before. It lit a flame inside her, and her body arched. Billy responded, his movements gentle inside her. The flame intensified, becoming an ache that throbbed a need into her.

Billy's moans joined hers. His thrusting heightened her feelings. Something was going to happen – something she wanted, needed . . . Oh no! No, not yet! Billy slumped onto her, and his guttural groan in her ear brought her the disappointment of an ending before she reached that elusive feeling, which she couldn't name, but needed so badly. It wasn't going to happen.

Billy's words of love helped, as did his kisses and thanks as he released himself from her; and, though she felt deflated, it set up hope in Sarah for their future. Now she knew that she could want him, want to make love with him and, with experience, would maybe find the completion of all her needs with him . . . *Or is it only Richard, my one true love, who can do that for me?* This thought shattered the peace she sought, for instead of her newfound hope for the future, before her lay a void that would live inside her till the day she died. But she had to accept that, and bear it. She was Billy's wife now. She'd chosen her path.

There was a happy, relaxed atmosphere when they woke and the morning went well. They breakfasted late, sitting in the warmth that the winter sun managed to project through the windowpane of their cottage. No one visited, as they'd all promised they wouldn't, but knowing the worries Aunt Megan and her dad had for her, Sarah decided that she'd like to contact them.

Dipping the half-peeled potato in the muddied water that was holding the other two unwashed ones, she felt Billy's eyes on her. She turned to see him sat with the paper on his knee, which the delivery lad had left in the letter box yesterday. His gaze was soft and kind. Smiling at him, she said, 'I hope I don't poison you. I'm not much of a cook. I've only had a few tips from me granna to help me.'

His laugh was relaxed. 'Well, we'll get by. I have a bit of knowledge, as we had to do kitchen duties in the institution, but I'd probably make enough for four hundred instead of two!'

Their giggling settled a homely feeling in her, as did all that surrounded her. The deep-pot sink at which she stood over-looked the garden at the back of the cottage, from where, if she looked up the small hill behind them, she could see the much larger hills, standing tall and majestic – as if they would call themselves mountains – towering in the distance. Behind her and opposite the sink, a table and chairs stood under the far window. In between these, in this living-kitchen with its shiny stone floor covered in a huge rug, stood two high-backed wooden chairs, one on either side of the fireplace, a large, black ornate range with side ovens, and a hob-plate and kettle stand that swivelled over the flames to become a hot-plate. A dresser, made of oak and lovingly polished, adorned the back wall. It held all the china she'd collected as she'd prepared her bottom drawer. Pretty lace curtains draped the tiny windows with their leaded lights, though a stark reminder of what might happen in the near future assaulted her as she looked at the regulation blackout curtains tied back on each side.

Music filled the room as Billy switched on the wireless – a big brown box with a golden latticework speaker at the front. It stood on the edge of a shelf holding dainty knick-knacks. And it looked like an intrusion from outer space. The screech-ing and whining it emitted made it sound as though it objected to Billy turning its dials. 'I were hoping to tune into the news, but we don't seem to have much of a signal. I were wondering how the war is progressing, as I need to keep up with it all.'

'Oh, I'd forget it for a couple of days, love. There's time enough. Look, I know we said we'd have no contact, but how about I give your mam and me dad a ring – let them know we're all right and happy, like?'

'Aye, I was thinking the same. A good idea. In fact I might walk over there while you finish getting dinner. Get out from under your feet, eh?'

'Ha, you're not under me feet. But, yes, if you like. And call in at the pub and bring a couple of bottles of brown ale. It'll be nice to have them with our meal. Like a celebration.'

His kiss as he went to leave wasn't what Sarah expected. 'Hey, you'd think we were an old married couple, instead of newly-weds. Give me a proper kiss.' It was good to feel this relaxed – like everything was going to be right between them. And good, too, to be in Billy's strong arms and to feel his lips on hers, and to experience the tickle of quieted muscles jumping to attention, in anticipation of what might happen later. 'Eeh, Billy, I do love you.'

And she did. A good love – one that she could live with – would help her to cope with the other, more vibrant emotions that she held for Richard. *Oh God, will I ever have an intimate moment with Billy without thinking of Richard?*

16

Billy & Theresa

A Fateful Tryst

'I thought you would come. And you haven't kept me waiting long. So, what was it that brought you to me? Little wifey not satisfying enough? Or you are sorely tempted by what I might have to offer? Which one is it, Armitage?'

'Keep me wife out of this. And who's to say I'm here to see you, anyroad?'

Theresa fascinated Billy, but also irritated him; what with her being who she was, he had to watch what he said to her. Though, inside, he felt he could smack her smug mouth.

Standing under a tree, with her horse tethered nearby, Theresa snapped her riding crop against the bark. 'So, am I to take it you are going to remain faithful and are here because you wanted to stretch your legs? Funny you should need to, just at the time I am out riding . . . Oh!'

Striding towards Theresa and grabbing her in his arms seemed the only way to shut up Her Hoity-Toity High-and-Mightiness. Once he was there, she looked him in the eyes. Billy realized she was taller than him, but luckily she'd placed herself where the uneven ground dipped a little. He stared back at her, registering her breath coming in small gasps. It had a sweet scent to it. A heady feeling seized him and

132

connected with the muscles clenching his groin, as the musky perfume she wore assaulted his senses. The shadow of fear left her face, but before she could start talking again, he covered her mouth with his.

Her response shocked him: a hunger and frantic need that he could almost taste turned the kiss into a frenzy of touching, grabbing and thrusting of her body towards his. Taking his lips from hers, breathless and out of his depth, Billy saw a raw passion that he'd never experienced. 'Eeh, lass, what am I to do about you? You're a lot for a man to handle.'

Caressing him through his trousers, she whispered, 'I think you are more than up to the challenge.'

Lost in the pleasure she gave, he could only croak, 'Where?'

Taking his hand, she turned and ran. His mind registered the old mineshaft as they passed it, but he didn't give a thought to the memory it should have evoked, as the thicket became denser. Branches pulled at his shirt as if they'd not have him go any further or complete his mission, but he ignored the scratching and tearing at his clothes as the demands of his body freed him of all sense of guilt or the need for caution.

They came into a clearing. A large sign declared 'Private, Keep Out'. Though he'd played around these parts as a young 'un, he'd never been in this neck of the woods, as far as he could remember. And he'd definitely never seen this field. He'd heard tell of a place as the Harveys used for picnics a few years back, and assumed this must be it. The field stretched long and narrow, and in one corner stood a shed-like building. At the far side he could see a gate – the normal entrance, he assumed. Did he imagine it, or had he seen a figure disappearing through it? He could have sworn he'd seen that tasty bitch who had been at his wedding. One of them Land Girls. Well, if she was a Peeping Tom she'd see a good show and would likely be after some of it herself in the near future. The thought excited him.

'I have a key.' Theresa pointed to the shed as she said this.

The interior further surprised him. It was equipped with a stove, ready-laid with kindling, and there was a pile of logs in one corner, one of those sofas with only half a back along the rear wall, and a thick rug on the floor. It looked cosy, though crowded with stuff in the near corner: cricket bats, balls and a stack of deckchairs and folded rugs, creating little room to move around.

'Well, will this do? Do you think you can handle me here?'

Watching her sitting on the sofa, patting the seat next to her with one hand and undoing the front buttons of her blouse with the other, further fired the feelings inside Billy. 'Aye, it'll do.'

Before this, he'd only had two kinds of women: one was the halfwit at the institute, but she was no more than someone to slake his need on and had sickened him most of the time; and the one he loved, Sarah, who'd no experience and he still wasn't sure of. This upper-crust woman was an eye-opener to him. There was no simply taking her, or having what he wanted; Theresa had needs and demanded that he satisfy them. She had him doing things he had never imagined – things he'd have thought repulsive, if anyone had told him of them, but which he found held intense pleasure and heightened his experience. This wasn't the coupling he'd known before. This was a ravaging of him, and he found himself wanting – no, needing – more. Aye, and he was glad he'd already had it twice in the last few hours, because otherwise he'd not have been able to last long enough to give a good show of himself.

But all that changed when he knew she was satisfied and he took his fill. His moment was upon him, when suddenly shock ripped away the feeling as Theresa pummelled him with her fists. 'No, no, you stupid bastard! Pull out – pull out!'

Her body writhed in an attempt to escape him, but he couldn't do as she asked as the strength of him ebbed into her.

Standing now, Theresa expressed greater fury with every garment that she fastened herself back into. 'You idiot, don't you know anything? How dare you come inside me! If you've made me pregnant, I'll have you imprisoned for rape, you . . . you imbecile!'

Grabbing her arm, Billy forced her to face him. She cowered against his raised hand. 'No whore calls me names, reet? You had what you asked for. You're a man-sucking bitch. You just try telling police as I forced you and I'll do for you. Aye, and for all your toffee-nosed family an' all!'

'No. No, I'm sorry. I'm sorry, don't hurt me. I won't, I promise, but please don't hurt me . . . Please!'

Billy threw her like she was nothing. She landed half on the sofa and half on the floor. Her screams filled the shed, bringing the walls crowding in on him. Everything had a red hue to it, like he was boiling inside. And this . . . this bitch had done that to him. Her flesh yielded to his vicious kick. His hand, without him knowing how, clenched the rough binding of a cricket bat. He raised it above his head.

A crack resounded around him, stopping his actions and bringing him back from the nightmare world that held him. Someone was nearby. That was a shot from a rifle, and a powerful one an' all.

Looking down on her crumpled, sobbing body, he sought to make his way out. As he stepped over her and grabbed his clothes, he told Theresa, 'You're done for. D'yer hear me? You're a dead woman. And so is the rest of your family, if owt comes from this. I'm telling yer, I'll do for the lot of yer.'

'Just go. Please, just go. I – I'll cover up. I'll get back to my horse and . . . tell everyone he threw me. Please, please, I beg of you. No one will ever know. Please believe me.'

Uncertainty clothed him as he clipped his belt into place and pulled on his coat. The hushed, fearful sobs of the posh bitch muffled any approaching sounds. 'Shut your rattle, woman. I need to hear if me coast is clear.'

She fell silent. He listened. Nothing.

Opening the door let in the cold air. Still and alert, Billy tried to decipher all of the sounds around him, but nothing indicated there was a soul about – not that Rita girl, or the shooter. Whoever that had been must have bagged his prey.

Running like he had a pack of wolves after him, he made it to the edge of the thicket. Not having taken note of his direction, he found himself on the lane leading to Breckton. He'd run there in minutes and pick up the ale that Sarah had asked for, then he'd not call into his mam's as he'd said he would. Sarah could phone her.

As Billy entered the smoke-filled room of the pub, the clanging of a bell warned that last orders were being taken as it prepared to close for the afternoon. He'd only just made it. He'd have a quick jug, and excuse his lateness to Sarah with the fact that others had wanted to congratulate him and buy him some drinks.

Rita was sat on one of the benches, her eyes looking at him over her glass. He had to find out if she'd stayed around the shed and seen anything.

'Been out for a walk then?' he asked her.

'What's it to you?'

'Did you stay to see the fireworks? You'd have enjoyed that.'

'No. And don't tell anyone I were in that field, please, mate. I'll get bleedin' sent back home. That place is out of bounds, but I were curious to see it. I left the moment I saw you and Theresa arrive.'

'You didn't follow us then?'

'Nah, why should I? Everyone to his own is my motto. I don't interfere in anyone's business.'

'Good, and you'd better keep it that way.'

Lacking the patience to talk to her any more, Billy moved away, satisfied she'd not seen anything. No one else spoke to him, but that suited him, as he'd nothing to say to anyone. He'd too much to think about, and needed to calm his turmoil.

Sarah mustn't suspect. No one must. He'd make up some story about taking a shortcut through the thicket and feeling fear overcome him; as his past flashed before his eyes, he'd ran and caught his shirt on some brambles, and hadn't wanted to go to his mam's in that state. Sarah would understand, even if it gave her memories of Billy murdering her sister. She'd forgiven him for that – knew his mind had been unbalanced by all he'd gone through. It was worth the risk anyroad, as he had no other story he could come up with for the state he was in.

*

'By, you look happy, Megan, lass! That's first smile I've seen on your face in days. Who were that on the telephone?'

'It was Sarah. Oh, Jack, she sounded that happy. I couldn't believe it. She were wondering if Billy were still here. He'd left her two hours since, on a mission to come here to tell us as they were all right and to pick up a couple of bottles of ale from the pub in Breckton for them to celebrate with. Any-road, he opened the door while she were on. He'd been held up at the pub.'

'See, I told you not to worry. What did she say?'

'It were more how she sounded, but she said they were very happy and everything was fine. I'm more than relieved, I can tell you.'

'I can understand that, Megan,' Issy chipped in. 'I were reet worried an' all. Billy seemed in a mood most of the day, yesterday.'

'It were natural, Ma. He ain't used to crowds and social occasions. Sarah knows how to handle him. Anyroad, we'll keep an eye on the situation.'

Something in Jack's glance towards Issy as he said this, and how Issy acknowledged her understanding with a knowing nod, made Megan realize that for all Jack's bravado, it seemed he was of the same mind as them after all. Well, it was comforting to know that at least he wouldn't think she and Issy were being silly, if they feared for Sarah.

'Reet, I'm going in search of a pot of tea. Does everyone wan—'

'Ma!'

'Issy, love! Oh God! Jack . . . Issy, what's wrong? Issy, oh, Issy. Come on, love.'

Issy's body had sunk back into the chair that she'd been in the process of lifting herself out of. Her eyes stared in fear.

Her mouth hung slack on one side. Her arm swung limply down towards the floor.

Megan's mouth dried with the horror of the knowledge that was hitting her. She'd seen this before. *Oh no. No, Issy . . . Dearest, dearest Issy . . . Please, God, don't let this mean she is having a stroke.*

17

Theresa

Facing the Consequences

'Oh, for goodness' sake, Theresa, what the hell is the matter with you? You've moped around for weeks. Are you missing your rough boy?'

'No. I can't wait for the bloody telegram to drop onto his mat, telling his wife he's copped it, to tell the truth.'

'I see. Well, unlucky you. Me, I'm getting on very well with Louise. In fact I am looking on her as marriageable.'

'No, Terence!'

'I think *yes*. The more I get to know her, the more I know she's everything I'm looking for. I'm going to get Mater to ask her to dinner and—'

'I won't let you. I need you – all of you. You won't marry, Terence, you won't!'

'Good God, are you serious? For heaven's sake, old thing, you can't mean that. Why?'

'I do. I – I'm pregnant; at least I have missed a monthly and I have other signs. Yesterday and today I was sick as soon as I lifted my head off the pillow.'

'What? No! Oh, come on now, don't cry. How did it happen? Don't say . . . You really did have him then? Bloody hell, Theresa.'

'I know. Oh, Terence, what are we going to do?'

'To tell the truth, darling, I don't know. We'll have to tell Mater . . . no, Pater. Yes, Pater will be best. This kind of news could send Mater over the edge. Pater will know what to do.'

'I can't let him know who it was.'

'No. No, of course not. Um, whom shall we say?'

'I was raped? Yes, and I don't know who by. That day when I fe – fell off my horse. We'll say that's when it happened. Say I didn't want to hurt Mater, didn't want to have her suffer, and thought, hoped and prayed it would come to nothing, but it has.'

'You've thought all of this through, haven't you? Wait a minute. Theresa, he didn't . . . Good God!'

She was in his arms. He could feel fear shaking her limbs as sobs racked her. *Oh my God, that brute hit her! He caused the massive bruise that covered her thigh.* Theresa's fear conveyed itself to him. The man had murdered before. Was he still capable of doing so? At this moment he could only thank the war that had taken that bastard away from them.

Stroking her hair away from her face brought to the fore the love Terence felt for her. 'My poor darling. Pater will sort it out, he will. We'll talk to him tonight.'

'So, you won't ask Louise over?'

'But why not? How can that have any bearing on all of this?'

'Because Pater may send me away, and I would want you to come with me.'

'No, Theresa, that's impossible. I can't. I'm only exempt from call-up because I'm a farm—'

'But you must – you must. I couldn't bear it; I couldn't go through it all without you. We could go to America. Pass ourselves off as man and wife.'

'For God's sake, Theresa, are you mad?'

Standing up out of his arms Theresa squared up to him. She looked formidable as she said, 'You won't let me down, Terence, you won't. If you do, I will tell everything. Everything!'

'Theresa, no! What are you saying? You're not yourself, old thing. Think about it. Theresa?'

Moving towards the door, she did not stop at his plea, but used what she thought might yet persuade him. 'I'm going to talk to Pater right now. I'll get Watson to drive me over to his office.'

'Oh no you're not! Theresa, for God's sake.' Angry as hell at her, Terence knew he had to calm down, to save this disaster from happening. 'Darling, my love, please don't. Don't leave me with this shocking news that you have given me. Come back into my arms. Let's talk it out some more. There will be a solution.'

He watched her hesitate, then turn back to him.

They were in his bedroom. He'd bathed and been about to dress for the evening when she'd barged in. It was early to be dressing, at only three p.m., but he'd had enough of the drudgery of the farm for one day. Besides, he'd bedded the ravishing Rita just before he'd come in and had felt unclean. Rita filled a need in him at the moment. Her raw sexuality satisfied him beyond anything he'd ever dreamed of having, but he feared her intentions. Her resistance to him pulling out of her when he ejaculated had nearly caused an accident and had unnerved him. He'd almost had to use brute force to disentangle himself.

The anger he'd experienced had frightened her. It had put it all on another level, as Rita had declared her love for him and had also said something rather strange – something about his sister not wanting him. That she knew who Theresa did want. That she'd seen stuff as would make his hair curl. It had all sounded very sinister. What did Rita know? God, life was complicated. And now this.

'So you won't leave me to deal with this on my own then, little brother?'

'Come here.' Sitting on his bed, he tapped the place next to him. 'You look all in, my darling.'

Theresa didn't do his bidding, but instead went round to the other side of the bed. Sitting then swinging her legs over, she lay down and indicated that he should do the same. Kicking off his slippers, he went gladly into her arms, laying his head on her breasts. 'Hmm – different, larger.'

'A symptom of my condition, and not comfortable at all. Listen to me, Terence, I feel frightened. Billy Armitage was raw and inexperienced in the needs of a woman, just desperate to satisfy his own, but I taught him things. It was good, but then he wouldn't, well ... He turned brutal. He ... he kicked me! Oh, Terence, he – he threatened to kill me, and you, and—'

'No! Oh God, Theresa!' As he held her close to him, feelings he'd never before had in his safe, cocooned world shook Terence's every limb. 'Do you think he meant it? Why did he say it? What angered him?'

As he heard how his sister's anger at Armitage had flared up in the first place, and why, and the way it had turned the brute's mood, his fear deepened. The man wasn't mentally stable, that much was certain. Armitage should have expected her anger, after not taking care to protect her. And after all that talk of him being well again, and of what had happened being put down to a temporary unhinging of his mind. Someone had missed something somewhere.

But what should I do? What can I do? How many others

143

would suffer at this man Armitage's hands? *His wife even?* The girl had seemed such a fragile thing, and very pretty, but what if she angered him? But then she must know how to handle him. Besides, her class of women was used to the odd clout – expected it, even. If he did anything about it, it would mean revealing what had happened between Billy and Theresa. He couldn't do that. It had to be kept a secret, otherwise . . . But then again, why should they keep it quiet? Surely the police would pick up Armitage and that would be the end of it? Yes, that was the solution. 'Theresa, we have to tell—'

'Tell what? Whom should we tell? No. No, no, no!'

'But it's the only way. Think about it. You tell Pater that it was Armitage. Stick to your story of not telling him about it sooner because you had hoped nothing would have come from it and you hadn't wanted to cause unnecessary upset to Mater, but now you find yourself pregnant and you have to. Pater will get the police onto it. They will pick up Armitage, the army will discharge him and he will rot in prison. It's our only chance. Think about it, darling. If he is not exposed and he survives the war, he will have this hanging over you forever.'

'No. You didn't see him. I have to keep it a secret. Please, Terence, I know what I am doing. What if they bail him? What if anyone saw me enticing him at his wedding? Look, I have thought about it – thought about nothing else – but every time I come up with possibilities of this or that happening and a disaster ensuing. The only safe option is to keep quiet, seek Pater's help in getting us away from here, have the baby, give it away, then return home and hope to God that Billy Armitage is killed in the war. If he isn't, we could go and live in York or London, and just visit here. That way he won't be able to get a hold over me again. *Please, Terence, please.*'

For a moment there wasn't an answer in him. It felt like his whole world had crashed around him. He'd had his own plans mapped out: marry Louise and persuade Pater to buy Tarrington House, which had recently come up for sale and had once belonged to Aunt Laura's husband's family. He wanted to settle down to family life. Into that equation, if everything on the sexual front didn't come up to scratch, he saw himself making visits to Rita, which he could carry on after she'd gone back to London – as she would after the war, if not sooner. Now all of that looked as if it would go by the board. Well, no. For once, he wouldn't allow Theresa to pull his strings. He doubted she would tell. And if she did, nothing had really happened between them – no thanks to him, of course, as he'd have had her many a time and would have thought nothing of it, but she'd always held back from the ultimate sin. Pity, that. They would have taken it to places he could only imagine – were bound to have done, with the illicit nature of it all and the feelings that lay between them. Even thinking about it, and despite him being as cross as hell with her, gave him a twinge.

Turning on his side and placing his leg over her only increased the feeling. She didn't move or object, but then Theresa liked to have this power over him. He moved closer and could feel her soft body against the hardness of him. Her arm tightened around him, drawing his head onto her delicious, rounded breasts. *Oh God, why were we born brother and sister?*

Lord Crompton's face had a frightening hue to it. Theresa cringed under his gaze. 'Pater, Pater, I – I'm sorry.'

'No, no, my darling girl, no. None of this is your fault. You have shown such courage. Oh, my dear, how did you keep this to yourself? And all to save your dear mother from further harm.'

The warmth and love of his arms soothed her. 'Oh, Pater, help me, help me.'

'I will, my dear, of course I will.' He steered her to a chair and, once she was seated, sat down himself. Terence had to remain standing, as Pater only had two chairs in his office: the high-backed one their father had sat Theresa in, and the hard wooden one he sat in to work at his desk on estate business and even household accounts, as Mater was no longer able to take responsibility for such things. This chair scraped along the polished wooden floor, grating on Theresa's frayed nerves as he pulled it up to sit next to her. With his hand holding hers, he asked, 'Are you sure?'

'I am, Pater, though I haven't seen a doctor.'

He looked away from her and glanced at Terence. 'How long have you known? Didn't you think to share this with me?'

'Only just this afternoon, Pater. I said immediately that we should come to you.'

'Good man. You did the right thing. So, my darling, you have been in a very lonely place. How did you bear it? And you have still more to face, but this time with our support. Terence and I will be here for you through all of this.'

Terence didn't hold her gaze. *Is he going to go back on our deal? After all I've let him do to me?* The thought of how far they'd gone disgusted and yet thrilled Theresa. It had been all she'd ever thought love-making between a man and a woman should be. And, best of all, it had bettered what had happened between herself and Armitage, giving her hope of blotting out what Armitage had done to her afterwards. She also hoped that having this intimate relationship with Terence would quiet the longings she'd experienced for what Armitage had awakened. Despite the side of her that was repulsed by the sin she and Terence had committed, she wanted it to happen again. And it could in the future, over and over, many, many times. Her eyes found Terence's and her heart fluttered. Oh, how much she loved him.

'Have you any ideas about what you want to happen, Theresa?' her father's voice cut into her thoughts. She saw Terence's body stiffen. The look he gave her held a desperate plea but, despite this, she was going to say what she wanted to happen and if Terence objected then she would carry out her threat and expose what had happened between them.

'I – I thought, if Terence and I went to America.'

'No, Theresa. I said—'

'Pater, Terence and I—'

'Have discussed this, Pater, and I haven't been able to come to a position where I can agree.' Theresa saw fear shadow her brother's eyes as he hastily blurted out, 'I – I'm not saying it is out of the question.' Anger shook his voice. 'But . . .'

'I can see the idea is disagreeable to you, Terence, as it is to me. No, Theresa, that just isn't going to happen. Even if Terence agreed and wanted to, I would block it. I cannot possibly have you both on the other side of the world while everything is so uncertain. Who knows what is going to happen? Let us have a quiet moment. I need to think. The only two certainties I have at present are that, above all, both you and your mother are to be protected, Theresa, my darling. That is why I am not asking you if you have any idea who did this, because knowing would mean that it has to come out in the open.'

'I don't, Pater. It is as I said: I was riding at a gentle pace near the woods when a man jumped out. He wore one of those woolly hats you see the miners wear under their helmets. It was pulled down to his eyes, and a scarf covered the bottom half of his face. He spooked my horse by screeching. It – it threw me, and then—'

'Don't, darling. Don't go over it again. I understand. The thought of you feeling so vulnerable, so afraid, causes me guilt. A father should be there at all times, and I wasn't.'

'You couldn't have been, Pater.' Terence had stepped forward and put his hand on Pater's shoulder.

On her twin's face Theresa now saw even more anger. He must be thinking her such a bitch, to have had what she craved, and then to make Father suffer like this because it had all gone wrong. But she didn't need him to remind her.

Anger of her own boiled up inside her. *How dare Terence? Wasn't it his games with me that brought me to this? He awakened me to the point where I've now committed incest, to gain what I craved.*

Terence cringed physically under her look, but carried on soothing their father. 'Neither of us could have been there. It is heartbreaking, after all that Theresa has been through. All we can do is try to put things as right as we can, so that she doesn't suffer too much more, and so that none of it will affect Mater.'

'Thank you, my son. Now, we must put our mind to a solution. Your mother will be looking for us all – you know how she hates us to be late for dinner. She thinks it rude to the servants.' After a moment he lifted his bowed head. 'First thing is to get medical treatment for you, dear. And that begs the question of whether you want to keep your child.'

'No, no, I don't. I can think of nothing more repulsive than having his . . . I – I mean, that man's child. But neither could I kill—'

'Oh, no, no! Nothing like that occurred to me. I wouldn't even suggest it. I couldn't do such a thing, nor could I put your life in such danger as taking that action would mean. No, I needed to ask, as it affects our decisions.'

'Please consider me going to America, Pater, please. It is the perfect solution.'

'Absolutely not! With Germany threatening to invade Belgium at any moment, and us agreeing on the coordination of British and French war production, there is already talk of trying to persuade the Americans to help us. If that happened, the war would cut us off from you. Not to mention the battles raging in the Atlantic and escalating in the air, happening at this very moment and making travel horrendously dangerous. The worry of the journey alone would kill your mother. I'm sorry, I know you are panicking and want to get as far away as possible, but please don't keep going over that idea.'

The lines in Pater's face deepened and Theresa knew she was lost. The dream of living with Terence as they would want to live – as she wanted to more than ever, now that they had cemented the feeling between them – died within her. But then . . . *Yes, that might be an idea.* 'What about Switzerland?'

'My dear, you are not thinking straight. You can only see the need to escape, but you have other needs. The baby, we have to consider the baby.'

The baby was the last thing she wanted to consider. If she had it now, she would throw it into the nearest ditch! An overwhelming feeling of hopelessness filled her. Her fate was in the hands of these two men. They loved her above everything, she knew that, but neither man – not even her beloved Terence – really had her wishes at heart. Terence was afraid, even more so now; and Pater worried more about the effect everything would have on Mater than on how it would affect her.

'I need to make enquiries, but I think Scotland may be an idea.'

'Yes! That would do us, wouldn't it, Terence?'

'I can't come with you, my dear, I can't. But I will come up to visit you every chance I get. How would that be?'

The urge to claw at him seized Theresa. And the word 'traitor' came to mind. He shrank from the implications of her look. But no; for everyone's sake, she'd accept this. His visits would have to be often, and he'd have to agree to drop Miss Louise Rothergill. She'd allow him to carry on his pleasure-seeking with the trollop Rita, but him marrying Louise was out of the question.

No, Terence could never marry. Neither could she. They could have their lovers, but would live out their lives together, under the pretext of being nothing more than spinster and bachelor twins. That would leave them free to live as they really wanted to. Of course all of this couldn't happen while Mater and Pater were alive, but until then they could carry on their secret visits to each other. These thoughts cheered her and had her agreeing. 'All right, Pater, but what do you have in mind?'

'I'm thinking to rent a place. Employ a full-time nurse for you, and other staff, of course, to see to your every need. Then arrange with one of the convents that deal with adoptions, to take the baby. You can go under the guise of being a widow.'

'That's not fair, Pater. I'll be all alone. I can't go through this without at least one of you. Terence, you will *have* to come with me.'

'No, I can't! Pater, please . . . ?'

'Theresa, darling, we can't change our minds on this. I will make sure that Terence visits you often. I know it's abhorrent,

150

but maybe those around you will come to think he is your young man, if neither of you let on that you are sister and brother.'

'What? Why on earth should we give that impression, Pater?'

'I know. I shouldn't have suggested it, but I'm thinking of your sister's future, and how we can get round everything without causing a scandal.'

'But I don't see how me pretending to be anything other than Theresa's brother can make a difference. They won't know her there. None of our acquaintances have anything remotely to do with Scotland.'

'Hear Pater out, Terence. I'm sure he isn't thinking that you should pass yourself off as my beau; just don't tell anyone you're my brother. Then if the time comes when we need to hoodwink anyone, you will be in place.'

'That's right. I'm trying to think ahead and plan for when the birth takes place. Until then it will be plain sailing, but once the baby arrives, we will have a big problem. We want everything to look normal.'

Warming to his idea, Pater began to embellish it.

'Once you have recovered from the birth, Theresa, you can leave the house with your baby. Terence will have been visiting on a regular basis, and we would hope that the staff and local people will have begun to make certain assumptions. On that score you won't have to pretend, as by the very fact of you being twins, you are highly affectionate towards one another, so you can let people surmise that you have found happiness with him. Maybe take them into your confidence, saying that your marriage was an arranged affair, but that you did have a true love. So when you leave, everything will seem as it should. You will just be someone who has fallen in love.

Terence will be seen to have accepted your child, and from that moment we can put in place plans for the baby, without anyone being the wiser. I could come with Terence to collect you, and I will take the baby to the convent and you will travel home with Terence.'

'Good gracious, Pater, how on earth did you come up with all of that?'

Terence had a blush to his cheeks. His stance looked uncomfortable, whilst Theresa rejoiced at the wonderful opportunity Pater had given them, without knowing what he had done.

'I don't know. It all just seemed to occur to me. The only problem is your mother. What reason will we give her for you leaving, and how will we keep her from visiting you – or, for that matter, explain you not visiting her?'

'We could say I am going to do war work. There must be something that is secret enough that I wouldn't have to tell her about it?'

'I'll look into that. Only last week Queen Elizabeth broadcast a message to the women of the Empire, calling them to join the war effort. You will say you are answering that call. Yes, and as long as it is something safe, Mother won't worry over you.'

'And I could visit now and again at first, whilst I am not showing. Then we can take it from there. After all, her health isn't good enough for her to travel, and you don't like to leave her, so I think she will be happy with the fact that Terence is visiting and bringing back news.'

The look Terence gave her at this cheered Theresa. There was no resistance in him now. His eyes held hers, and within them she read the promise and the hunger. A smile from deep within her, such as she hadn't experienced for a long time, found its way to her face.

'Oh, my darling daughter, I am so proud of you. And so happy to see your face light up like that. Thank God we have found a solution. I will get straight onto it. You will be leaving within weeks, so no more worrying. And try to forget the awful experience you went through. We can do nothing about it, only protect you from further hurt.'

'Thank you, Pater. I love you very much. You are the best in the world.'

As she stood, her father took her in his arms. Over his shoulder she connected with Terence. His look remained on her, holding what she wanted to see. Her world felt like it had been put back together. Billy Armitage had never happened, but Terence had – and he'd continue to happen, for now they had crossed the last divide.

18
Issy

A Blessed End

Issy watched Sarah lift the spoon towards her. Unable to talk and tell her about the pain in her hip, or to ask her to move her to ease it, she tried to concentrate and gain comfort from the glow Sarah had about her. Who'd have thought Billy could make their Sarah happy? But he had done, there was nothing so sure as that. It shone from her. And her having a young 'un inside her suited her. Not that it showed, but Sarah had told her that she'd missed her bleeding and was certain she was pregnant, and the news had obviously given her a deep happiness, though it must bring back to her the babby she'd lost. Issy knew that feeling, and she hoped that Sarah wasn't like her and Cissy, having difficulties in carrying babbies to full time. But then, for Sarah, losing her first might have been a result of the shock of what happened the night of the party, and not an underlying problem.

Issy felt troubled as she thought of the violence shown by Billy, and of what she knew him to be capable of. But he'd changed, hadn't he? What had happened wouldn't keep happening, would it? Naw, there was no way that Billy had hurt Sarah since. Sarah's happiness told of that.

Knowing Sarah was happy meant she could die with a peace in her. *How I wish that day would come* . . . This existing in a world that her loved ones couldn't penetrate was like visiting hell. Anyroad, with all the prayers she said and all her begging for forgiveness, she hoped it was just that – a visit.

In a way she was glad of this time. It'd given her a chance to look back at everything – to see where she'd not been at her best, and to ask Him above to turn a blind eye to them times. Like when that gypsy took her down. By, he'd woken in her feelings she'd carry to her grave, but it had been sinful of her to latch onto them like she had done. If she knew anything, though, she'd not meet him in heaven. If she made it there, that was. By, he was a bad 'un, and he'd got his just deserts at the end of a rope.

Mind, all in all, she couldn't have been a bad 'un herself, as she'd been hard pressed to think of a lot of stuff to beg forgiveness for.

Issy's past and that of those she loved came to her in waves of memories. She thought of how she had been adamant about moving away after her daughter Cissy married Jack. She'd always carried guilt over that, but had thought they would have a better chance without her living with them. In hindsight, maybe if she'd stayed she could've saved Cissy from dying in childbirth. And she knew she could have been a help to Megan during the time she'd suffered so much at her first husband's cruel hand. But there was no changing things; she'd done what she thought was best at the time.

Bridie – Bridget's mam and Megan's grandmother – came into her mind. By, that lass suffered at the hands of the gypsy an' all, even though he was her one true love. It just shows what others can do to a person. That poor lass. And she died so young, and yet old in herself, by what Bridget had told her.

The hope lay inside Issy that Bridie had had time to ask for the forgiveness of God. It was unbearable to think of anything else for her.

Eeh, that pain seems to be spreading up me insides. She'd have to try to indicate to Sarah that she wasn't comfortable. Sometimes, over the last few weeks since this had happened to her, Sarah had understood her needs.

'I've a letter from Billy, Granna. He's got his posting, but he's coming home for a twenty-four-hour leave before he goes. I'm that excited as he'll be home in two days' time.'

Oh, lass, I'm pleased for yer, but just look up at me. See me pain. Oh God!

'He doesn't say where he's going, but most likely France, and with what the news tells us, we must have troops heading for Belgium from there. We wouldn't let Hitler invade them without a fight, would we? Here, Granna, try to take . . . Eeh, what is it? Aren't you comfortable? I'll fetch Dad and ask him to lift you, eh?'

Thank God for that. This pain's making me sweat. Aye and making it hard to breathe an' all.

Megan came into the room with Jack. Together they lifted Issy. By, she'd love to take hold of them and give them a hug, but all her energy was drained. The room swam around her. Her heart drummed in her ears, taking these dear folk away from her. The swirl dragged her into its centre. Her pain had gone, and the tug on her heart blocked the sadness of leaving them, as the hole had opened up to a tunnel and, at the end of it, a beautiful light shone around some very dear faces: her ma, her Cissy, and little Bella, and Tom. *Eeh, Tom . . .*

'Oh God, Jack. Oh, Issy. Issy, love. Issy!'

'Ma, Ma? Eeh, she's left us, Megan, thou knows. She's gone.'

'No, Dad. Oh, no!'

'Come on, me lassies, we should be glad for her. Look at her. She's a lovely smile on her face. It ain't been easy for her these last weeks. I'd not have a dog live like Ma's had to. Not able to do owt for herself, and not able to talk.'

'She took it all in her stride. You could tell that, bless her heart, but yes, you're reet, Jack. She's at peace now, and it's only our selfishness as wants to hold onto her.'

Sarah reached out and took hold of her Aunt Megan's hand. Her dad's arms tightened around them both. A tear dropped off the end of his nose. It matched the silent ones falling in an avalanche from her own eyes, and she could see that unshed tears were stinging her Aunt Megan's.

There were no words to comfort, other than the ones her dad had said. Granna did look happy. But she was going to miss her. Her granna had been one of the constants in her life.

Megan's body began to shake.

'Megan, lass, you're laughing!'

'Aye, I am. I had it in me head to tell you of a joke me and Issy shared just a few days afore the stroke took her, and it's just come to me. Oh, Jack, it were funny. It were the last bit of real fun we shared together. It were me thinking of Fanny as brought it to me mind. I were thinking how this will hit her, and how sad she's been since the stroke happened to Issy, when you'd think as she'd be relieved not to have Issy on at her all the time.'

'Eeh, lass, I don't know how your mind works at times, but I reckon as Ma'd like us to share a joke with her as she leaves us. They say as the spirit stays in the body for a while, so she'll hear you, thou knows.'

Sarah couldn't quite make out how she felt about this turn

of events, but she supposed if it helped these two people she loved beyond any others, then she'd not object.

'It were the day as we were to fetch our gas masks from Breckton Town Hall. Issy said . . . Oh dear, it was so funny. Issy said she didn't feel up to going, so would I fetch hers? I said, "Well then, if you ain't going to come, what about Fanny's?" I'd asked her this as Issy had said she'd fetch Fanny's gas mask for her. Oh, I can't—'

'Go on, Aunt Megan, hearing you laughing and telling us about sommat funny Granna said is helping.'

'Well, Issy said, "Oh, you've no need to worry about our fannies; we can stuff them up with brown paper . . ." Oh, Jack, oh dear – it were so funny. I thought I would burst me sides.'

'What?'

Sarah saw that her dad looked mystified, but the joke hadn't missed her. She doubled over with her Aunt Megan and laughed so much that it verged on hysterics.

'Anyway, I said, "Oh, Issy, you are naughty." Then we heard someone coming, so I said, "Don't say anything, if it is Fanny. You know she can't take a joke." Then Issy said, "I won't. I'll just ask her to start saving all the brown paper bags as grocer delivers food in, and tell her as we women'll need it. We have to stop the gas getting into our bodies if that Hitler sends it!" Well, I thought I'd be sick with the expanding of me belly and not being able to draw me breath in.'

Without warning Aunt Megan's body crumpled. Sarah felt her dad's arm release her as he lurched forward to catch Megan, his voice full of concern. 'Aw, me little love, me little love, come on. Come and sit down. Sarah, get a glass of water, lass. It's all been too much.'

A few minutes later, with Aunt Megan recovered some,

Sarah knelt at her feet and held her hand. 'You were like a daughter to me granna. And she loved you so much, Aunt Megan, just like I do, as you're like a mam to me. I'm going to miss hearing you two having a laugh. You were always at it. You kept her going through the worst of times. She were always telling me as she didn't know what she'd have done when me mam died, if it weren't for you.'

Aunt Megan could only pat her hand.

'Well, we've had these few minutes with her, and I'm glad as we were able to laugh, though you'll have to explain the finer points of that one to me, Megan, love.'

'Oh, Dad, you daft ha'p'orth. Granna had pretended to take it as if Aunt Megan were asking what to do about . . . well, thou knows.' She nodded down below. 'You know what she were like.'

'Eeh, I see it now. By, she were a one.'

He laughed as he stood up off his haunches and went over to Granna. 'Eeh, you were a lass, Ma. A proper lass. You had us laughing when we shouldn't have. Well, I reckon as we've paid that back now. Brown paper! How you thought of them, I'll never know.' His hand stroked the still face, then he gently closed the half-open, unseeing eyes. 'Well, you'll carry on making us laugh, thou knows, cos we'll allus talk of you, and that will include the humour of you. It has to, as that's what you were all about, Ma – that and love, kindness and wisdom. You go to your rest, old girl, and I hope you meet up with your Tom once more. If there's any truth in all this as they feed us, you should do.' He bent then, and kissed her cheek.

Aunt Megan had risen. The colour had come back into her cheeks. She joined Jack. Together they straightened Granna's body and made her look comfortable on the gleaming white pillow that Granna loved.

It took all Sarah's willpower to join them. Somehow, touching Granna would give a truth to her having gone, and she didn't want to. But she knew she must. She had to let her go. She'd heard tell as them as had passed over needed that, so they could find true peace – the letting go by, and of, loved ones here on earth.

'D'yer want a mo alone with her, lass?'

'Aye, I'll stay a while. Are you fetching doctor?'

'I'll send one of the girls for him. We'll be back soon, but I know as your granna'd like a moment with you.'

When they had gone, Sarah got onto the bed and lay with her head on her granna's shoulder. 'Ta, Granna, for all as you've been to me. I'm glad as you lived to see me wed. Me and Billy will rub along all right together, thou knows. He were a different man once we sorted some things out that were between us. I know I have to tread carefully with him, and I'll miss your guidance on that. But he went through a lot, Granna, and I were there, so I understand him. Can I share a last secret with you, Granna? I can't share it with anyone else. But, thou knows, Billy ain't me true love. Oh, I love him, but more as a brother really. No, me true love is Richard, but I know as I can't have him.'

Megan walked away from the door, her heart clogged with sadness for the two women she'd left in the room – one whose life was over, and without whom she didn't know how she was to live; the other whose life was just starting, but wasn't really. Not in the way it should be.

She loved them both equally and had stood a moment outside the room to make sure Sarah was all right. What she'd heard had confirmed what she knew to be a truth. Hearing it had made her heart heavy – even more so than it was already.

Oh, Sarah, lass, I remember the pain of what you're going through. Please, God, don't let her go through what I did. But somehow, God, if you can do so without hurting Billy, can you think about bringing to her the same outcome as I had in the end? Can you make it so as she spends her life with the one she should be with?

Megan met Fanny along the landing, her face bright with a smile that said she must have missed bumping into Jack.

'I heard all the laughing, so thought I'd go and get you a tray. Eeh, it were a good sound. How is old Issy?'

Telling Fanny was painful. Saying it for the first time was always going to be hard, but this woman had found a special place for Issy in her heart.

'But . . . I heard you and Sarah squealing with laughter.'

'Aye, I know.' Could she share the joke with Fanny? Would it help or, like so often, would she be hurt? She decided to share it.

After a moment, Fanny laughed out loud. 'Eeh, if I'd have heard her! By, she were a one. A – A beautiful . . . Oh, dear.'

'That's right, Fanny, she were, and she only had a laugh about you, and with you, cos she loved you. She did, very much, thou knows.'

'I know. And I think as it were fitting to share that joke together, and with me. And it were good for Sarah, I'd like to bet. Little lass were that happy when she came in, and now that's been taken from her. Though when you think it were going to be taken anyway, as Billy's coming home is only for a short time, and then her worries will start.'

'Aye, that's the sad part of it all. All the young men going away and we don't know if we'll ever see them again.'

'Oh, I'm sorry, Megan. We tend to forget that, besides having wives, these lads have mothers an' all.'

161

'Aye. Have any of your family gone into the services, Fanny?'

Walking to the front room together, where she knew Jack would be, and talking about this and that with Fanny helped. Not least because, in doing so, she could be sure the joke hadn't made the woman feel as though they were taking the rise out of her. This was confirmed as Fanny was about to leave the room, when she turned and, with a tear in her eye, said, 'Eeh, thou knows, if I'd have heard Issy come out with that one, and she hadn't known I had, I'd have collected some brown paper and presented it to her. I bet her face would have been a picture! But, thou knows, she'd have had sommat to say. She allus did.'

Megan smiled. She'd registered the sob, and seen the hanky hastily taken from the pocket of Fanny's pinafore, but she let her go. They all needed private moments, and she felt this one was Fanny's.

19

Sarah

A Visit of Love

As she made her way home, Sarah's heart and mind were assailed with mixed emotions and thoughts. Her dad and Aunt Megan had wanted her to stay, but she had a lot to do to get ready for Billy coming home, and keeping busy seemed the best thing. There would only be today to make everything as right as she could for him – bake some pies, finish knitting those socks for him to take with him, along with the scarf she'd already completed – as tomorrow she'd have to go into work to see to the wages for the staff. No matter what, life had to go on. Folk needed their dues and there was a war to fight.

Taking the shortcut across the back field, she climbed the five-bar gate. Hesitating a while with her feet on the third bar and gazing over the surrounding countryside, she pulled her coat tighter round her body against the cold and allowed herself a moment to take in the beauty surrounding her. Everywhere looked lovely, clothed as it was in frosty white, and glistening in the low winter sun. Granna had loved sights like this and she could hear her saying, 'It don't seem as though there is a war on. Nothing's changed.' But it had. Most of the lads from around the area had gone to various training stations, and girls were working the land and doing the kind of factory jobs the men usually did. The sense of being safe had gone, as had Granna . . . Her granna was no longer with them. A sob clenched her throat. How was she to live life without her granna by her side?

The icy wind pinched her wet face and helped to calm her. She had to get on. Granna was at rest – she knew that from the serene look on her face when it had relaxed into death. It gave her hope that Granna had met up with her Tom again. Funny, she couldn't think of him as her granddad, as she'd never met him and had only ever heard of him in terms of him being Granna's Tom.

A thought came to her of how Granna had once told her of a lad called Denny. Granna had been engaged to him and then he'd been killed in a mining disaster. How did that feel? A shudder rippled through her that wasn't due to the cold. Would she know the same thing to happen? No! *Not Richard!*

With this fear came the realization that she'd rather it was Billy that was taken, and a shameful feeling that threatened to eat into the heart of her. But it didn't stop her begging God to keep Richard safe, and to make it possible for them to be together one day. It happened for Granna, didn't it? Not that it was the same, but she'd loved Denny, hadn't she? Then, after losing him, she'd found love again. Oh God, it was like she was willing Billy to die – and her carrying his babby an' all. Not that she hadn't wished all of this before, but Billy didn't seem to deserve her to wish it now.

Her thoughts went to the day after their wedding, when he'd come in from his walk. He'd said he'd got caught up in the pub, but there had been something different about him. She couldn't put her finger on what, but it showed in his love-making that night, and every night after. He'd done things to her – things she never knew men and women did together. Thinking of them, her cheeks flushed and a trickle of anticipation sparked deep inside her. There, that proved she did love him. But then why hadn't she missed him, like she should have? Because she hadn't. But then the thought occurred to her that her body had missed his making love to her. Shocked at this thought, she shook it from her. *Reet, come on, get yourself home, lass. The right one or not, Billy will be coming home.* They would be sharing just a few hours of married life together, and then he would be gone again. She'd to live with that, as it was to be her life's pattern for God knew how long.

For the rest of her walk home she concentrated on praying hard for Billy's safety and for everything to be all right between them while he was home.

As she lifted the latch to her door, the enormity of what had happened hit her again as she realized that her granna had never made it to her cottage since it had been done up for her and Billy. And now she never would.

Through eyes misted with tears, she set about carrying out her plans. Some two hours later, and with a cup of tea by her side and pencil and paper ready to make out a shopping list, she felt better and more positive about the future. She refused to allow her thoughts to mull over anything, now that she wasn't being active.

The rattle of the door knocker made her jump, and then the sound of Richard calling out almost froze her to the spot.

'Hello there.'

He'd opened the door and entered without waiting to be invited to do so, but where had he come from?

'How does it feel to be a little housewife then? Oh, sorry. Did I startle you?'

'Yes, you did. I – I wasn't expecting anyone. How did . . . ?

I mean, what are you doing here?' It was as if she'd conjured him up! The thumping of her heart against her ribs hurt. The sight of him hurt.

'I'm on my way from Glasgow to Biggin Hill. A bit of a detour, but I wanted to see you before it all starts. The fighting, I mean. I'm a fully qualified pilot now; I just need lots more practice and then I may see some action. So I couldn't go without seeing you. Is Billy . . . ?'

'No. No, he ain't here. He's due back in a couple of days. He's got a posting an' all, so—'

'Are you all right? You look dreadful. Has something happened?'

Richard's concern undid her. The tears she'd fought overwhelmed her as she told him of her granna's passing. Somehow, in the telling, she found herself in his arms. His lips kissed little caresses into her hair and onto her face, his voice soft and full of love.

'I'm so sorry, my poor darling, my love.'

Nothing in her wanted to stop this. It seemed right, as though it was where she was meant to be. Instead, she clung to him and drank in all that he was.

'Try to think of her at peace now, in a better place. If I know Issy, these last weeks have been hell for her. It was awful to think of her as Mother told me she was, but then I did hope to see her one more time before she passed away.'

'I know, you're right. It ain't as I would have her suffer any longer, but she were everything to me.'

'I'll always be here for you, my darling.'

'Oh, Richard!' She pulled out of his arms. 'We can't. I – I mean, it ain't right. I'm married. I couldn't have done anything else.'

'Why? Why did you marry him, when you knew how I felt

and knew how you felt for me? I don't understand, and maybe in a way it is why I am here. I need to understand, Sarah, please.'

What could she say? That she'd married Billy out of fear of what he might do if she didn't? Was that even true any more? Yes, she'd been afraid of him, and that fear had been compounded on their wedding night, but since that had been sorted . . .

'It's not too late. You can divorce him. We are meant to be together, Sarah. You must see that I love you beyond all there is. You fill my every waking hour. You are my motivation. I want to help save the world, to make it a safer place for you and any children we may have—'

'Stop it! Stop it, Richard. This is wrong. What about Lucinda? Besides, I can't leave. I – I'm pregnant!'

He slumped onto the nearest chair, then looked up at her. 'Sit down, my darling, sit a while with me.' He pulled another chair away from the table and took her hand the moment she sat down. 'Me and Lucinda – well, it's over. We're good friends, that's all. And it doesn't matter. Leave Billy, leave him now. I will take your baby as my own.'

'Please don't go on, Richard, there's not a way for us. We were for finding love too late.'

'You do love me then?'

His face held hope – a hope she had to dash. This was dangerous; she could only imagine what would happen if Billy found out. 'A – a little. I have a feeling for you, but it ain't like I have for Billy.' The lie stung her as much as it did him. 'Me and Billy have been together all our lives. We've been through a lot an' all. That stuff binds you. It holds you close against all the odds. I can't leave him.'

Richard had let her hand go. A tear dropped onto his

cheek. She watched it roll down and curl round his nose, joining the trickle of water there, its path engraving on her heart the love he felt for her. But she must reject him – for his own safety, and Aunt Megan's, as well as her own.

Wiping his face with the hanky he'd taken from his pocket, Richard stood and nodded his head. 'Well, I'm glad I came. I had to hear that from you. I have my mind made up now. Please forgive me. I won't bother you again. I can't get a train until tomorrow, so I'll go up to the house and see Megan and offer her some comfort in her loss. I'll stay at the inn in Breckton overnight, so you have no worries, if you planned on dining with them. Goodbye, Sarah.'

For a full five minutes she stood looking at the door after it closed behind him. Her body ached from the tip of her head to her toes with longing and loss, but she knew she'd done the right thing. Richard would find someone else. And, being the man he was, he'd make whoever it was happy. She needed to settle down and build on what she'd already achieved with Billy. But saying all this to herself didn't help. When at last she moved away, she dragged herself up the stairs and allowed her body to fall into the comfort of the soft mattress and let herself weep. For her granna, for her own lost love, for Billy and all that life had done to him, for her little Bella, and for her mam and all that had happened to her Aunt Megan, until the emptying of herself took her into a deep sleep.

20

Theresa

Undenied Feelings

Watching Rita spreading the straw on the stable floor, then straightening, rubbing her handkerchief over her forehead before pushing her hand into her blouse to wipe her breasts, gave Theresa feelings she did not want to have. Her mouth dried. Impatience with herself for harbouring such thoughts, which should be repulsive to her but weren't, made her snap out an order. 'You there, come over here and help me to mount my horse!'

An insolent lift to the girl's chin tempered the anger in Theresa. She didn't want to alienate her.

'Sorry, didn't mean to snap. It's my frustration with having to ride side-saddle. Not something I like doing.'

'That's all right, love. 'Ere, put your foot in that stirrup. That's it, now steady. There you go. I ain't seen you ride this way before, Miss . . . Oops, watch out!'

Theresa slipped back down to the ground and into Rita's arms. For a moment she held her breath. The girl was so near, so desirable. Making a play of having fallen, she made herself look flustered.

'You're all right, love. No harm done. I expect you're not used to it, and that riding skirt is a bit much. You should've put your pants on, like always. What's with this side-saddle lark anyway?'

'I . . . Oh, it's my father's idea. He thinks it isn't good for a woman to straddle a horse. Silly, I know, but I thought I would humour him. At least until I left sight of the house.'

Having to think of some feasible excuse while unfamiliar feelings assaulted her made Theresa want to turn away, but Rita's gaze held her transfixed. A smile played around the girl's ruby-red painted lips, further confusing her. Theresa blurted out the first thing that came to her.

'I – I've changed my mind. I think I'll go for a walk instead. Thank you for trying to help me.'

'Anytime, Miss. And if I can be of help in any other way, just ask.'

This last was said in a softer tone, giving innuendo to what she suggested. Theresa felt the heat of her body rise to her cheeks. Was the girl meaning what she thought she meant? Something in her wanted to try; she'd heard at school of two girls doing things together, and the idea appealed. 'I may need help in other ways. What kind of things can you do?' *Safe ground, just in case.*

'A lot of stuff. Some as has to be done in private . . . Then I'm handy with helping a lady with her clothes. All sorts, you might say.'

Deep in Rita's eyes Theresa read a message. It conveyed itself to her inner being, pulling at her nerve ends like a harpist plucking strings. 'Perhaps I'll leave my exercise till later and you could come with me. I have a number of items of clothing I need mending. We used to have a woman, but after she left, things just piled up. I'm leaving soon. Do you think you can do some of them in time? I'll pay you, of course. It would be a private arrangement, something you could do in your own time. What do you think?'

'Sounds just the ticket, Miss. I'd like to earn a bit on the side. Where're you going? Is it a long trip?'

'I – I'm going to take up some war work. I can't say where. Or what. Will you stable my horse for me and then follow me? I'll wait for you, and I'll make it right with my brother if he says anything about you leaving your work.'

Just watching Rita lead her horse away, and the way her body swaggered, set up a trickle of anticipation in Theresa. *Ha, what will my dear brother think of this new turn of events? Serve him right to have to share his prize filly and know he isn't the only one she desires.*

With Rita a couple of paces behind her now, and leading her to who-knew-what, everything inside Theresa came alight. This was going to be a new experience, and one she thought she would relish. The need to please, which she always felt with a man, didn't apply. They were women; they would please each other. The excitement of something different, of kissing and touching a woman, assailed her with delicious feelings that she wanted to savour.

They reached her room without coming across anyone. Not that it would matter, as she had a legitimate reason for taking Rita there. Once inside, Theresa took a bold stance. 'I haven't done anything like this before, have you?'

'Yeah, I've done it all, mate. It ain't nothin' to feel shy of. Just relax.'

Theresa propped herself higher on the pillows. Smoke from their cigarettes curled up into the air above them. Mixed feelings assailed her. The experience had been like nothing she'd ever imagined. Wonderful! Sort of shared, but in a different way, as they'd taken each other to pleasures that no man could ever understand. There had been no need for any pretence or worry over how long it took, as they each knew what was needed and, realizing it took time to achieve, coaxed and loved it to fruition. But despite all of that and the extreme enjoyment of it, there remained in her a slight repulsion at what she'd just partaken of. Not that she was going to let that put her off doing it again – she couldn't, as she knew she would need to, and with Rita. Especially with Rita. Yes, she and Terence would have to share the girl. Ha, that would add to the excitement. See who won Rita's affections the most times, though she supposed it would be Terence. What girl – including herself – could resist what he had to offer?

'That were a big sigh, love. Glad to have made you happy, cos you certainly made me pop me cork. We'll have to get together again, what d'yer think, eh?'

'I think we will, Rita. I wouldn't want to think that was the one and only time. Now, come along, get yourself dressed. One of the servants will be up soon to run my bath.'

'One of them? 'Ere, I thought as you had one all to yourself. Well, next time you tell 'em as you can manage, and we'll have a bath together, eh?'

The thought of this disgusted her. 'I don't think so. And I used to have a maid to myself . . . Well, at least my mother did, and I shared, but all of that has gone now. Everyone has to economize, even us. Now get going, you naughty thing. Go on – hurry.'

Rita laughed, but did as she'd been bid and got off the bed, showing all she had in an exaggerated, open-legged crawl as she did so.

'You're more than naughty. You're a sex tease. Stop that,

and get out of here. I'm getting scared now. Just look at the time!' Rolling off the bed, Theresa went over to the wardrobe, donned her silk dressing gown and gathered the items of clothing she'd put to one side for mending. 'Take these with you. They all need some attention. I'll ask whoever comes up to help me to make sure you have use of the sewing kit. I have no idea where it is kept. No one will object. They are all overworked as it is, so they will be grateful that one pressing job has been taken out of their hands. And by the way, if that other girl wants to do extra work, I'm sure my mother would be glad to hear about it.'

'I'll tell her. Here, can I take the rest of them fags? They're a sight better than me roll-ups. They taste like heaven. Just like you.'

Clothed now, Rita hovered over the dressing table, picking up jars and perfume decanters. With one perfume bottle she squeezed the bulb, letting the mist go behind her ears.

Fury beyond words took hold of Theresa. 'Don't you dare take liberties, girl! Leave my stuff alone, and please don't think for one moment that what happened between us elevates you above your status. Now, go at once, or I will ring the bell and have you removed.'

'Here, keep your knickers on, mate. I were only trying it. And I don't need no elevating, ta. With you out of the way, I'll have that brother of yours all to meself, so I can get what I want through him. War work – ha, I'll bet.'

'What do you mean? How dare you! Get out!' Her fury had no effect on the damn girl. Theresa watched, appalled, as Rita scooped all of the cigarettes out of the box on the dresser and shoved them into her pockets. Her laugh as she left the room annoyed Theresa beyond measure. *The little vixen! Does she know about me and Terence? Has Terence told her? And,*

God, what did she mean by her parting shot? But, no: Terence wouldn't say anything – he wouldn't dare – and Rita couldn't know about the baby. How could she? All the same, they'd have to take care, as she had a feeling little Miss Rita could be dangerous.

Throwing the frock she'd selected to wear onto the bed, along with the chosen accessories, didn't help to calm Theresa's nerves, nor did Molly's comments when she came through the door. 'My, what've you been up to? It looks like a cat fight has gone on in here.'

Molly had been with the family forever, so Theresa allowed her the liberty of straight talking, but reprimanded her for being late. 'I fell asleep and had a restless dream, that's all. If you had come when you were supposed to, you would have had time to tidy up.'

'Eeh, don't worry about that, Miss. I'll send young Annie up to see to it, and she can lay a fire in here an' all. It feels right chilly. I'll light the oil stove in your bathroom – that'll warm it up for yer whilst you have a soak.'

'Thank you, Molly. Forgive me. I woke up out of sorts with myself. I've been trying to make some decisions since the Queen's "call to arms", as it were. And it meant I didn't sleep well.'

'You ain't thinking of going off to do war work, are you, Miss?'

'Yes, I am. Father made enquiries for me. He thinks it is a superb idea and will do me – and hopefully the country – some good. But I haven't said anything yet, as we had to handle Mother with care. I go very soon. I need you to bring some trunks to my room and start to pack for me. I've engaged one of the Land Girls to do some mending for me, as you are short-staffed, so will you see that she has use of the sewing kit? Oh, and it is all right for you to tell the others now. Mother is resigned to it, and happy that I am not going to be in any danger.'

'Well! You've took the wind out of me – I never thought. But I'm proud of you, Miss. Just keep safe for us.'

Theresa was touched by this. She'd never been one for having much to do with the serving staff and hadn't thought any of them would say anything like that. 'Thank you, Molly, but there is no need to worry. I'm only going to be doing paperwork and such, but I can't tell you any more.'

Being able to tell everyone was a relief. They hadn't long until she left, but enough time to get used to the idea – not that she'd had much longer herself, as her father had sorted everything in days, instead of weeks. But her story of not wanting to upset her mother would account for why the staff hadn't been told sooner. None of them would guess her departure was a sudden thing, which was just as well. Their curiosity – not to mention the speculation they might indulge in, in particular if one of them happened to come to her room while she was bending over the lavatory pan – might have exposed the truth.

Ugh, the very thought of the sickness that had taken her of late, the minute she woke, disgusted her. *God, why do women have to pay such a high price for their indulgence, while men get off scot-free?* This thought made the enjoyment she had found with another woman even more appealing. Maybe she'd lean more towards that, after the baby business was over and done with. In any case, she'd make sure she had one more encounter with the delicious Rita before she left. Maddening as the girl was.

Best of all, and making this whole business bearable, was that her beloved Terence would visit her often. After all, Pater had practically given them permission! Ooh, she couldn't wait. *Perhaps he'll even visit me tonight?* Yes, she'd flirt with him over dinner. Discreetly, of course.

21

Sarah

Laughter Brings Healing

The phone ringing woke Sarah. Disorientated, she rolled off the bed and headed for the persistent shrill sound. Unhooking the receiver from the wall, she'd no time to announce her number before her dad's voice came to her.

'Eeh, lass, you had me and Megan worried out of our wits. We've rung twice already, and Richard were just about to set out to check on you, but I said I'd give it one more go. Are you all right, lass?'

'Aye, I am, Dad. I fell asleep. What time is it? I were meant to go to the shops.' The painful throbbing of her heart let her down. Hadn't she convinced herself she didn't need Richard? Then why this thudding at the mention of his name?

'We wanted to ask you to come up to the house to have dinner, lass. Megan forgot, with all that was happening. Anyroad, the undertakers have been now and taken Granna to the chapel of rest.'

This statement awoke in her the reason for the heavy feeling that something terrible had happened, which lay in the pit of her stomach. She allowed the short silence to continue, and could sense her dad trying to compose himself. A small cough and he went on, 'Me and Megan are going later, just to make sure as she's all right, but they have folk there all night, so she'll not be alone.'

'That's good, then. Look, I'm reet tired, Dad. And tearful an' all. I'll just get a bit of sommat here, and be on me own.'

'No, Megan won't hear of it, and neither will I. Get in your car and bring your nightclothes. You're stopping here, as is Richard. He wanted to book in at the pub! Felt he'd be in-truding, but that ain't how it is at all. It'll be good for us all to be together. Oh, and while I'm on, can you take him to the station on your way into work tomorrow? Lad were going to book a cab, but Megan says as you'll pass right by there. She said as you've no need to go in till later, and only just to do the wages – no need to put a whole day in. That'll be that then, and you can come home and finish owt you haven't done for Billy's arrival home the next day.'

There was nothing she could say. The last thing she wanted was to take Richard to the station – to see him off, to stand and wave as he disappeared – but what objection could she possibly come up with? It stood to reason, as Megan and her dad would have a lot to see to, so they'd not have time. 'All right, Dad, that's fine. I'll be there in the next half-hour. See you then.'

Part of her jumped into life at the thought of seeing Richard again, but the sensible part of her dreaded it. How would it be? To sit at the table opposite him and make small talk, and to know he was sleeping in the room across from hers?

Sarah was surprised at how relaxed they all were, and how cheerful. She hadn't expected that. But having enjoyed the first course of Fanny's delicious oxtail soup, as they tucked into the excellent steak pie the laughter over their memories of some of the things Granna had said and done lifted any morose feelings they'd had. It was exactly how her granna would want them to be.

'Eeh, I remember once, taking her to meet yer Aunt Hattie for the first time . . .' Aunt Megan wiped away a tear, put there by her laughter. 'We stood outside her "house of ill repute", as you might call it. It were a grand place. The sight of it stunned Issy. She stood a moment with her mouth open, with me embarrassed and afraid as to how she'd think of Hattie, then she turned to me and said: "Eeh, they say as we sit on a pot of gold, don't they, lass? Well, it looks like it's right, an' all." But then . . . Oh, dear, I can see her now, she winked and said, "Mind, I reckon as I've sat on mine too long now – it's all dried up and won't be worth nowt!"' The room erupted. Richard didn't show any sign of being embarrassed. But then they'd all been subject to Granna's coarse ways at times – Richard included – so it wasn't like he hadn't any idea what was coming.

It took a full five minutes for them to compose themselves, the last of which saw Richard looking at Sarah. She dabbed her eyes as though they needed more attention than they did, just to help her adjust, then went straight into a story of her own. 'Only a few days before her stroke, Granna had another go at Fanny. She . . .'

By the time Aunt Megan fetched their puddings they were all exhausted, and not a little deflated. Laughing about Granna had helped, but only for a short time, because soon the stories had them all longing for her to be amongst them again – not how she was at the end, but how she used to be.

'Well, Jack. How about you and I have a brandy and one of those nice cigars you bought in, for the last time we visited? Leave the ladies to do what they have to, eh?'

'Good idea, Richard. I'm not allowed to touch them when

you're not here. I have to make do with me roll-ups. Mind, I still enjoy a hand-rolled cigarette, even though I could afford sommat better. Let's be really bad lads and go into what I call the "posh parlour".'

'Hmm, are you sure?'

'Go on with you, the pair of you – taking the rise out of me. Aye, course you can, and me and Sarah might just let the pots grow mould overnight and sit here and enjoy a nice sherry, instead of seeing to them.'

'Eeh, you're pushing boat out with that, lass. And if Ma were here she'd join yer, only she'd have more than one.'

Sarah supposed they'd always make references to her granna, but she wondered if there'd ever come a time when it wouldn't hurt as much. Deep in thought, she hadn't noticed Richard move towards her. His hand touched the bare skin on her back where the cut of her frock draped, and it was as if someone had put a match to kindling. Her body jumped away, but her heart stayed with his touch.

'I'm sorry, I – I didn't mean to startle you. I just felt you needed comfort, and perhaps your old – young – step-uncle could be the one to do it.'

Aunt Megan saved the day. 'Well next time, little brother, see as you warm your hands. And while you're at it with your comforting, I reckon as we both could do with a hug.'

With this she came close, and Richard enclosed them both in a cuddle Sarah never wanted to come out of.

Her dad broke it up by saying, in a voice that betrayed how the gesture had moved him, 'Well, come on, then, lad. Eeh, it were a good omen as brought you to us tonight, when we most needed you. Let's away and have our brandy.'

Once the men had gone through, Sarah came down to

earth. Controlling the longings inside her, she turned to her Aunt Megan. 'Would you mind if I went up? I'm all in.'

'You will be, love. Early days of carrying are allus the worst, and it ain't that long since you were poorly.'

'I know. It's hard to think of that time. It scares me an' all. Me mam lost babbies, and so did Granna, and now me.'

'Don't worry, love, as that won't help owt. We'll take care of you. Just take it easy. You can stop work and rest all you can – we'll manage.'

'No, not yet. I'll cut me hours, but I'd never get through without being with you and Sally, and Phyllis and Daisy and the rest of them, not with Billy away and everything.' How those words came to her she didn't know, for though she felt relief at the realization that she could make a go of things with Billy, and wasn't filled with the dread she thought every day would hold, being married to him wasn't what she really wanted. Not what her heart wanted. But then the relieved smile on Aunt Megan's face was enough to make it all worth it.

'Come here, lass. You've a lot to face. We all have, but know as I'll do me best to be a mam and a granna to you, and to help you get through. I have a big place in me heart where you've sat since you were born. Every day I think how proud your mam'd be of you, and I love you like you were me own.'

Snuggled up in Aunt Megan's arms, Sarah told her, 'And I love you an' all. I love you as if you were me mam, and have done all me life. Thanks, Aunt Megan. Thanks for always being there for me.'

A feeling of being safe entered her. Nothing could happen to her while Aunt Megan's protection cocooned her. Granna had gone to her rest and deserved the peace she'd found after a long life, but Aunt Megan would be there for her for years and years to come. The thought gave Sarah the comfort she'd felt drained of, since that moment earlier when Granna had taken her last breath.

Crossing the landing to the bathroom the next morning, Richard stopped in his tracks and stood transfixed, as though lightning had struck him. Sarah walked towards him, the contours of her body caressed by the rippling of her silk dressing gown and her hair flowing freely around her shoulders, like he'd never seen it before. The shock of the encounter nearly undid him, as his whole instinct was to open his arms to her. Pain as his clenched fists dug his nails into the soft flesh of his palms didn't do anything to release the urge to do so. Taking a deep breath, he steadied himself.

'Good morning. Did you manage to get some sleep?' He knew she had, by how fresh and bright she looked, but could think of nothing else to say.

'Aye, I did. I were surprised to find as I had, as I wasn't expecting to. And you?'

'After a time of thinking things through, I did, thank . . . Oh, Sarah, I—'

'No, Richard. We've to find a way to live with this. We've to put it behind us, thou knows that. There isn't a way as we can avoid each other, but we can survive it. I'm to give my best to Billy, and you will find someone, I'm sure. We can't put ourselves through this every time we see each other. The strain's too much to bear.'

Looking at Sarah – so young, so beautiful, and yet with a fragility belying the strength she tried to portray – he felt shame at his actions. To keep declaring his love, and wanting her love shown to him, wasn't fair on her. She was trying to do the right thing, and so should he. 'I'm sorry. I promise I will try not to lay my feelings bare again. It won't be easy, and I may slip up from time to time, but know, Sarah, my love, that even though I behave in the future like you are no more to me than a step-niece, underneath my feelings for you will be as deep as ever and I'll be there for you. You only have to give me a sign and I'll be by your side.'

'I know, but that ain't how it should be. You should get on with your life, as I can't ever part from Billy. It wouldn't be right, and it would cause hurt to me Aunt Megan, and she's had enough of that in her life.'

Every fibre of him was alert to her, to the extent that he could taste her fear and knew that her staying – and even marrying Billy in the first place – was rooted in that fear, and this frustrated him beyond words. There wasn't any way he could remove it. He knew what Billy was capable of; God, he couldn't bear thinking of it, and it angered him that all those around her knew of it and yet had allowed their marriage to happen. It was like they had sacrificed Sarah for the sake of peace, and to keep Billy on an even keel. How could they have done it? Even his mother and father hadn't counselled against it.

'I'll see you at breakfast, Richard. And I'll be ready to take you into Leeds station whenever you need me to.'

With this she walked past him, vulnerable in her dignity, putting him to shame for his uncontrolled outpourings of forbidden love for her. She belonged to another, whatever the rights and wrongs of that, and was doing her best to fight the love he knew she held for him. He *must* do the same. But how?

22

Sarah & Richard

A Fateful Goodbye

'Sarah, you look lovely. That coat suits you so well. I haven't seen it before.'

Sarah smiled and did a twirl for Richard. It felt safe to do so, as he hadn't spoken in anything other than a friendly voice. 'Aunt Megan made it for me. I love it.' The rich brown coat, calf-length and of the finest wool, was complemented by astrakhan sleeves and collar in a chocolate colour, a couple of shades darker than the coat fabric. As Sarah came out of the twirl, she said, 'And look, I have a hat to match!'

As she put on the Russian-style hat, Richard drew in his breath. 'Hold on a mo. I'll be back.'

'Where are you going? We'll be late for the train.'

'Just don't move.'

A few minutes later he came back into the room carrying his Box Brownie camera. 'Stand over there by the window. I have to have a picture of you. That's perfect.'

Something in her niggled, telling her this wasn't right, but then what harm could it do?

'I'll treasure that. As soon as it is developed, I'll put it in my wallet and carry it everywhere'

'Richard, don't—'

'Oh, there you are. Me and Megan were looking for you.' Her dad interrupted her protest. 'We wanted to say our good-byes, lad.' His voice caught in his throat as he shook Richard's hand. 'Have a safe journey, and keep yourself safe.'

'Yes, above everything take care, little brother.'

Sarah smiled. She knew how much it meant to her Aunt Megan to be able to call Richard 'little brother', after not even knowing that he existed for most of his life.

'I will. Now stand by the window, you two. I want a pic-ture of you. I'm going to carry my family with me wherever I go. Old Luftwaffe won't get me, with all of you protecting me.'

The journey felt like their last, and Sarah knew that was how it must be. Talking didn't come easily: the weather, the time of his train, how long it would take Richard to get to Leicester-shire, the little time he'd have with his mother and father; and, finally, his fears. This last shocked her and rocked her foundations. Richard had always seemed so much older, wiser and more educated than her and Billy, so she'd thought of him for most of her life in the same way she'd thought of all the grown-ups around her: invincible, capable of coping with all that was asked of them, and beyond feeling fear of anything.

'What I feel,' Richard said, trying to qualify his statement of being afraid, 'isn't a cowardly fear. I'll do my duty, and in some ways I'm excited about the prospect. I love flying, and I'm good at it. It's this thing about being ready to die for your country. Everyone seems to put that on us as if it comes naturally to us and we're all longing to do so, but I'm not. Oh dear, that doesn't sound right, either. Of course I am, but—'

'I understand your meaning, Richard. Your fear is of the

unknown. If death comes, what will it be like, what will *you* be like, will you be brave or frightened? I know, cos I'd thought about joining up meself and I had them thoughts. Still have them, even though it's not possible to go into the forces, with me being married. But it's like there's an unknown future for us all. Will we be caught in a bombing raid? How will we cope if anything happens to . . . I mean, none of us knows what that's going to feel like. And the not knowing has unnerved us.'

'Yes, that's the word. That's how I feel: *unnerved*. Oh, we're here.'

His voice held disappointment and matched her own feelings, as for the first time in a long while she'd relaxed in his company and had enjoyed sharing his thoughts and outlook. And there'd been an absence of the tension that now clogged the atmosphere.

When they reached the station, that atmosphere changed. After a silence Richard asked, 'Sarah, I know I shouldn't ask this, but will you allow me to kiss you? I know – please don't be angry. I know I'm breaking my promise to you, but . . . what we've been talking of, the possibility of death and never seeing loved ones again, if I could have the memory of what kissing you feels like, I could face that. Because at the moment it happened, I would think of it and take it with me.'

'Richard! I thought better of you than to try blackmailing me in that way. The answer is no. No, and I'm more than angry with you for asking and trying to put me in a position as I feel guilt at refusing.'

'Well, I'm not going to apologize. I didn't mean it as blackmail. I was only asking the woman I love – and who, though denying it, loves me – for what any two people in love share every day. I just wanted it to happen the once, that's all.'

A giggle came to her at this. This was a side to Richard she'd never seen before, like he was a spoilt child. In some ways it brought him down to her level and made him seem more normal. 'Come on, I'll come up to the station with you and, if you're good, I'll give you a peck on your cheek and wave you off.'

'You're laughing at me.'

'Yes, I am. And you deserve it an' all. By, you've a side to you, Richard Chesterton. Cheek of you! You ask for what it would be sinful of me to give, then act like you had a right, and all in a way as a child would as couldn't have his own way.'

'Is that how I sounded?' He laughed with her now and the moment of tension lifted. It put them on a better footing – one she felt more comfortable with, and she thought he did too, by the look of the grin on his face. Eeh, she'd take a mental picture of that grin and keep it with her. That way she could bring it to her thoughts whenever she felt the need for him.

Smoke belched out from the engine standing at the platform. Remnant wisps of it floated around them and clung to the inside of the station roof, lingering and giving a nasty taste as it descended, before it dispersed.

Going onto the platform was something she knew she shouldn't have done, but she had felt compelled to. Around them was the bustle of people, some running after a departing train, others milling around holding hands with loved ones, not talking, just being together. Sarah felt all her emotions compounded: this was truly a goodbye. Not just for a while, but a severing of their feelings. It had to be.

Any conversation they might have had proved impossible against the chugging of a goods train passing through, and the arrival of another passenger train on the far platform, all against the backdrop of a disembodied voice explaining where the trains were destined for or had come from.

Richard leaned towards her. 'This is my train. I'll just put my bags on board, then come and say goodbye.'

Reality hit Sarah. *Goodbye* . . . God, she was going to be doing a lot of that – they all were.

'There, that's that. Well, I've come back for that peck you promised.'

The grin was back in place. His eyes sparkled with it. *It's going to be all right. I can do this . . .*

But then Richard's arms were around her, his face close to hers, and his voice, a whisper, brushed her cheek, and she was lost. Held so close to him, the rough material of his uniform chafed her face until his hand lifted it towards his. His eyes had darkened with the intensity of the feeling he held in them. 'Sarah . . . Sarah.'

Nothing prepared her for his kiss. Had she ever lived before this moment? Had what folk said about the earth moving all been true? Every sound faded. There was no longer any smell or smoke burning her throat. There was just—

'What the fuck d'yer think you're doing? Is this it then? When me back's turned, you two are at it? Fucking let go of her! Didn't I warn you once . . . You—'

The sudden intrusion stunned her. *Billy! Oh, dear God, no! How?*

Richard's body was yanked away from hers. Billy stood in a stance ready to strike out at him. As if in a frozen moment, Sarah could only observe; numerous emotions hit her, leaving her afraid, desperate and confused. Her mind couldn't explain where Billy had come from. *His leave begins tomorrow, doesn't it?*

A fist jerked past her and Richard stumbled backwards. Billy threw another punch, but this time it didn't find its mark, as another arm hooked around his. Standing back, Sarah saw two men in air-force uniforms holding Billy in a grip he couldn't escape from. 'Now then, army-lad, there's no hitting one of ours, so if you don't want to find out what a good pasting feels like, you should get on your way.'

They threw Billy's body forward. He landed on the floor face-down, his rucksack pinioning him there.

Richard's voice came to her. 'Sarah, I'm sorry. Forgive me. Write—'

'Come on, Flight Lieutenant, on the train with you. We've got you out of the trouble it looks like you had coming to you. So just count how lucky you've been, and get out of the way of things.'

With one last longing glance in her direction, Richard did as they bade. One of the men followed him onto the train, and she could see him sitting in the carriage with Richard. The other helped Billy up, saying, 'Now then, mate, I don't know what's gone on here, but if this is your young lady, then I can't say as I blame your reaction. But as it stands, the lieutenant is one of ours and we're going to defend him. How you take it forward with the girl here is up to you, but us men are fighting a war with the Germans, not with each other, and we can't excuse you hitting an officer.'

Billy stood up. He brushed his beret like he was wielding a whip, his eyes, deep and evil, staring into hers. 'I think as you've sommat to say for yourself, Sarah. Well, you'd better have, cos this lot ain't going to be explained easy.'

What could she say? What words would get her out of

this? She'd been caught in the arms of the man Billy hated most in the world, and she knew had always hated. She couldn't have committed a worse sin in his eyes. Shame washed over her.

'Well, say sommat, or is your tongue as covered in shit as the rest of yer?'

'Don't talk like that, Billy. Not in public. I accept I've to take your anger, and you saw what you saw, though it weren't all what it looked.' *At least it didn't start out to be, but it was soon everything I've ever dreamed of. But what price will I pay now?*

'Ha, not all that it looked? Well, first we'll get home, then you'll tell me how it were.'

His nails dug into her wrist. The pain this caused aroused anger in her. 'I'm coming, Billy, there's no need to hold me like that or to drag me. At least let us leave with some dignity left in us.'

'There's no fucking dignity coming your way.'

'Don't threaten me, Billy. I told you afore, if you even think of beating me I'll go to me dad.'

'Aye, and you just try setting him on me and see how far it gets you, cos it won't get you far – nor him neither – cos I ain't above knocking him off his pins if he tries to stop me disciplining me own wife.'

They were in the car park heading towards her car, when this gave her temper its final shove. Yanking her hand free, Sarah stood staring at him. 'Disciplining me? Have you gone mad? Or is it that you've always been so? That's it, ain't it, Billy? Me and you know how your mind still works, don't we? Well, I'm not standing for it. You just try it. And don't forget I'm carrying your child, thou knows.'

'Ha! Mine or his? Get in the car.'

'I'm not going anywhere with you, Billy. I'll get on the bus and get to work, where I'm supposed to be. Here, you take the car. I'm sorry for what you saw, but I'm telling yer, it weren't my doing. It were just one of them things when you're saying goodbye. I can understand how it made yer feel, and I know I'm to have the wrath of you, but what you have a mind to dish out to me at this moment, I'm not for taking. You go home. Think about it, then when I come in we can talk about it. I'll make it up to yer, I promise.'

'You can never make this up to me. You've no idea how to go on. I've had better in the bloody institution than what you give under duress. I'll take meself home, but I have a couple of places I can call on to get me pleasure, and you don't deserve any more of me, so don't expect it.'

Not knowing what he referred to, and thinking he was just trying to get revenge, Sarah walked away from him.

She hadn't gone far when dust and pebbles showered her as Billy drove within inches of her, at a pace she thought would burn the engine out. Leaping out of the way, she caught her heel. The ground rushed towards her. Not caring about her bloodied knees or her stinging hands, she held her stomach. *No, no! Don't let me babby be hurt . . .*

Arriving at the cottage, Billy had no inclination to go inside. Everything in him sagged with the weight of his Sarah not being faithful to him. And he'd never have known, if it hadn't been as that Rene had took ill.

The leave he'd been given had started from last night, but with Rene having a day off and her promising him they'd spend it together before he went home, he'd told Sarah it didn't start until tomorrow. Not that he wasn't eager to see Sarah, but Rene was something he couldn't pass up on. He'd clocked her on his first day, when he'd gone into the NAAFI. She lived near the camp in Aldershot and worked in the NAAFI, serving food and snacks to the soldiers. The swagger to her hips, and seeing her rounded bottom sway from side to side, dried many a man's mouth, but it'd been Billy as she'd set her sights on.

The pleasure of her was ten times what he'd had with Sarah, because what Rene gave she gave willingly and she was hungry for it. There was no coaxing, like he'd had to do with Sarah. Mind, he'd had an improvement with Sarah, specially when he'd tried the stuff that Lady Muck up at the big house had taught him.

Sarah had liked that, and he'd looked forward to picking up where they'd left off. Now she'd spoilt it all and he was going to make her pay, and when he had, he'd find a way of getting at Richard, the lieutenant air-force shit! By, he had something coming to him, did that rat. And he wouldn't care if it took him a lifetime to achieve it – he'd see Richard got his just deserts.

The thought cheered Billy. He'd always liked the feeling of the power he could wield over others who were weaker than him, though not if it was through the redness. Funny, he still called the hot, searing sensation that took him at times *the redness.* He'd given it that name when he was a youngster and had first experienced it, because that's what it was like: a red kind of mist that clouded his thinking. And in its pain it always held a message – something he had to do – like it was consuming him and his only release was to do as it bade. No one understood it, or they seemed not to. Not even the high nobs, the so-called psychiatrists.

It'd started to gather when he'd seen Sarah in Richard's arms. But the shock of Richard's air-force mates grabbing him had cleared it. He was glad of that, because he hated the feeling. He hated it that much that he could end his life, when the redness was on him.

23

Theresa

A New Chapter Begins

The two trunks that had littered the floor for the last few hours, while the maids had packed them, had gone and now, as Theresa stood looking around her room, a sadness etched itself in her. *All neatness and order restored, like I've never been here.*

Letting her eye travel towards her bed, she smiled. *Ahh, but I have.* Pleasure rebounded through her. What her bed hadn't seen, and what she hadn't experienced in it, wasn't worth talking about; and, though naked of her knick-knacks and pictures, the room – even in its impersonalized state – was still permeated by her personality.

The silk drapes, a delicate silver-grey painted with pink and purple rosebuds with long stems, were elegant and a beautiful complement to the Regency pink-and-grey striped wallpaper. The light-grey, thick-pile carpet blended the two together, giving an overall picture that mirrored her own natural elegance and beauty. A dramatic contrast came in the deep, rich-purple silk bedspread, and in the stripes of the upholstery of her chaise longue and chair, a reflection of the diverse needs within her.

Recognizing and indulging those needs had given Theresa an understanding of her former husband. Something in her had wanted to reconcile with him. What he offered allowed her to express all of her sexuality in whatever way she felt the need to do so. If it hadn't been for her newly formed plan for her future with Terence, and who the real father of her baby was, re-engaging with her marriage could have provided a safe haven for her child. After all, she had spent a night in her husband's house, and others would think that they had consummated the marriage even though they hadn't, and that that one time had been enough to make her pregnant. But things were as they were, and now she had to face a lonely existence in Scotland, between Terence's visits.

In some ways she was glad she'd decided to go today, instead of tomorrow. She'd rung an old friend who lived about halfway on her journey to Scotland and, without having to think about it, had jumped at the chance offered, not to just stop off for an hour, but to stay a night with her. She hated long goodbyes and knew that, with everything ready and nothing more to occupy their thoughts, that would be the order of the day. This way, she could make a quick exit and have the excuse of breaking up her journey. She was especially glad of these new plans where Terence was concerned. Last night had been wonderful with him and Rita, and a fitting goodbye in itself. It would be spoilt by another day of regrets.

As if her thoughts had conjured him up, Terence tapped on the door and entered. 'There you are, old thing. Your carriage awaits you. Come on, it won't be so bad. I think the house Pater acquired for you looks lovely in the pictures the agent brought round. I envy you. Dumfries and Galloway is a superb area, beautiful and dramatic. It will suit you very well. Besides, my love, you're not going to be far from Stranraer. I've checked trains and I can be with you in around six hours from leaving here, which is a lot quicker than being driven, as you have to be, to transport everything you need with you.'

He came further into the room and closed the door.

'Come here, my darling. I need to say a proper private goodbye, and to promise you that I will come as often as I can to see you.'

As she went into his arms she told him, 'You did that last night – the promise and the goodbye. And, my darling, I will keep the feelings you gave me within me, until I see you again. Oh, Terence, my love.'

They clung together as they came out of a kiss she thought she would die from, because of the pleasure it gave her. *How quickly the familiarity of his visits to me, with the full expression of our love, has made it all seem a normal thing for us to do. As do his kisses – the kisses of a lover: deep, demanding and yet giving.* No longer did she berate herself with the sin of it.

'My sweet girl, I love you. We are bound together always.'

'You mean that? You promise you won't pursue Louise whilst I'm gone?'

'You're a funny one. You don't mind me having fun with Rita, and yet you hate the thought of me going after Louise!'

'It's different. If you married, and I know the relationship you have nurtured with Louise is designed for that outcome, then everything between us – all our future plans – would end. I can't bear that.'

'I know, and it won't happen. But how are you going to manage without what Rita gives you?'

'I will. I'll think of your visits and will live for them. You know, I didn't expect you to understand, and that's why I didn't tell you before last night, but you catching me and Rita together and joining us . . . well, I wish we could do it again. I loved it, and so did you.'

'No! You're wrong, I didn't. Well, I did at that moment: the excitement of watching you, I have to admit, felt exquisite. But afterwards – well, it took me longer than you know to get over it, and what I had found out about you. I didn't sleep at all, and it still doesn't sit right with me. Besides, I think Rita is dangerous. She's dropped more than one hint about me rewarding her for her silence.'

'Oh God, and now we have given her proof of what she speculated about.'

He'd shocked her by saying that he'd not liked the side of her that needed the Ritas of this world, but Terence had to get used to it. She was what she was. But they'd been careless, both of them. They'd traded a half-hour of pleasure for the knowledge of what they were to each other, their forbidden selves. Something had to be done.

'Look, darling, don't worry. We'll deal with it. Just humour Rita, and let her think you're going to play ball. Say you will sort her out the next time you get your allowance – anything to keep her quiet, and to give me time to work out how we get out of this one. The bloody bitch! I could kill . . . Wait a minute. What about Armitage? When I went to his mother to have my last fittings done, she told me he is due home tomorrow. Gave me another reason to feel glad I am leaving today, actually. Anyway, how about you make sure your path crosses his? Offer him a good amount. I'll help out with it. Get him to sort Rita out.'

'Sort her out? What are you suggesting? God, Theresa, sometimes I feel I don't know you at all.'

'Oh, come off it, little brother. I'm no worse than you.

Don't tell me you haven't some scheme or other to rid us of her?'

'I may have, but it's not the same thing at all. You're proposing murder.'

'I am not! I just thought Armitage could threaten her, though he'd have to do more than that, as his departure would lift the threat. Get him to give her a pasting – just as a taste of what you are capable of arranging, if she steps out of line. I know that would deter her. After all, I have been on the end of Armitage's violence. He terrified me. I think if Rita had a similar experience, we would have no further trouble with her.'

'Well, yes, that might work. Anyway, you'll have to leave it with me to deal with. By the way, talking of his mother, we've just heard that Issy Grantham, Jack's mother-in-law, died yesterday. Good old age and everything. Anyway, let's get you in the car and on your way. You have a long journey ahead of you.'

'One more forbidden kiss first, my darling. I need us to part on the lingering feel of our love for one another, not the frustrations Rita has brought into our lives.'

Depression settled in Terence as he waved to Theresa until her car rounded the bend on the driveway and disappeared from his view. *How am I to exist without my Theresa by my side?* Unlike her, he hadn't ever had any concerns over what they did together, and would have done it years ago if she'd let him; but now that they had, he didn't know how he was going to live without her.

Thank God their erstwhile farm manager, Earnshaw, had returned. Oh, it wasn't good news for the man himself, of course. Collapsing while training and having to be medically discharged from the army had devastated him. Lucky in other ways, though, as it appeared that the medic on hand had been trained in the technique of re-inflating a collapsed lung and had saved Earnshaw's life, but the incident had been the end of his war ambitions. But what a stroke of luck for himself. Now he could take a more relaxed approach to running the estate.

Pater had reinstated Earnshaw financially, but had not given him his old position back, citing his health issues. *Of course the real reason was that Pater just didn't want me going to war, so I had to keep the farm manager's post.* All in all, everything has worked out very nicely, and he now had a lot more freedom to come and go as he pleased.

Thinking of this, Terence decided he would take a ride out this afternoon – go over to Fellam's to offer his condolences on the death of Fellam's mother-in-law and then, whilst there, he'd take a look around. Under the pretence of seeing how things were faring with the horses, he would check out the plans that were forming in his head. Plans that, if they went well, would solve all his problems.

When he'd discussed his intentions with Godfrey and Cecil, they'd called it 'spiffing' and said it was sure to work. They congratulated him on getting to know Fellam's place and finding the right spot for the fire to start. Both had hated the thought of the horses suffering, but knew there was no choice. Just destroying the buildings wouldn't be enough, as buildings could be replaced. It had to be all or nothing.

Yes, he felt better now and, with or without Theresa, life held promise. He just couldn't wait for the opportunity to present itself. He was certain he had the right person for the job.

With a smile now playing around his lips, Terence went

inside to change into his riding gear. His visit to Fellam's could have a twofold purpose: with luck, he might just bump into Louise. Despite what Theresa wanted or didn't want, he knew he'd have to marry. There was the question of an heir, for one thing, and to date Louise presented the best prospect in that quarter that he'd come across.

24

Hattie & Megan

A Feeling of Dread

Hattie sat her velvet hat on her head and pulled it down over her ears. Harry had his back to her, but his stance told of his worry. 'Harry, love, I told you: you can come with me, if you want. I'm not at doing owt behind your back. But it's sommat as I've got to do. Thou knows that.'

'Aye, I knows it, but it don't mean as I have to like it. I'm scared. What if meeting up with Arthur doesn't put you at rest, as to your feelings for him having long gone? Cos they haven't, have they, Hattie?'

'I can only be honest with you, love. You know how it ended. You know how me heart were broke. You knew when you took me on, it weren't all of me as you were getting, but you were willing to take what I could give.'

'Aye, I knew all of that, but it don't make the hurt less. We've been everything to each other. We've built a life together. You've been happy with me, ain't you, lass?'

'More than I ever dreamed were possible after what went on, and you allus said as that were enough for you. I – I have to know it is enough for me.'

'Oh, Hattie, love, I can't bear this.' Harry's body slumped. His hand gripped the chair next to him. His legs buckled.

'Harry, oh God. Harry, my love.'

Before she reached him, he'd sat himself on the chair. Sweat rolled from his forehead, a tinge of blue ringed his lips, and his eyes seemed to have sunk into their sockets. Shock held her rigid for a moment, then she moved towards him. After a moment of sitting on the chair with his head forward, Harry recovered a little. 'I'm all right. I just had one of me turns, that's all. I didn't mean to scare you.'

'Turns? What turns? Harry, my darling, you're not well. What's happening?'

'It's nowt. Just sommat as happens now and then. I feel a panic come on. Like when I were in the trenches with Arthur. And then it's like all me stuffing goes from me body. It passes. Happen it were talking about Arthur, and the fear of losing you. And yet I can understand how you feel. I loved him too, thou knows. I stood loyal to him through all he went through, and I felt just as cast aside by him as you did – though of course my love wasn't of the nature of yours. It was more admiration for the bravest man I'd ever come across, and born of Arthur's nature and how he was with us, who were below him in rank and served him. All of us would have done anything for him. But one thing I never prepared meself for was falling in love with the same woman as him, and facing losing her to him.'

'You ain't going to lose me, Harry. I just need to put me old feelings to bed. I never had a chance to do that. I don't want to feel me insides jump out when I catch a glance of him, or see his name.'

'But that's just it, Hattie. You sought him out. You bought that posh paper just on the off-chance there'd be news of him, and his doings, in the society pages.'

This shocked her. He'd known! He'd taken her on about

202

buying *The Times* on occasion, but she'd never guessed he'd known the reason why. Deflated now, she sat down next to him. 'I don't know what to say, love. I've betrayed you.'

'Naw, lass. It ain't as bad as that. I understood. But it just seemed like you were thinking of him as he were one of them film stars or sommat. It never felt real. I tolerated it, and I liked to take a sneaky look meself, if I knew he were featured. But now it is real. He's free of his wife and he's come looking for you – and you want to go to him.'

'He never did love me, Harry. Not how you've done. Not with all of himself. All the time we were together, he must have been longing for his wife, as the moment she'd have him he went back to her. Aye, and without the guts to say a proper goodbye, just that letter. That's all I got: a letter. And, thou knows, it's what kept me pain alive, cos if Arthur had faced me, I could have hit him or sommat, but I had no way to get back at him.'

'And now you have. But is that what you'll do?'

His handkerchief looked soaked with his constant wiping of his brow, and the weariness of him tugged at Hattie's heart. In an instant, she made up her mind. 'No, it ain't. In fact, I'll not even go to meet him. He can stew, just like we did when he left us.'

'Well, that ain't quite right. He did leave you the house and a good settlement on me. But are yer sure, me love? For all me upset, I want you to do as your heart says you must.'

'Eeh, Harry, hark at you. You've tried your best to stop me, and now I'm in agreement, you're trying to persuade me to go! There's no accounting for yer. Come here.' Putting her arms around his clammy body aroused her fear. These turns seemed more than panic attacks. 'Harry, I'll not go. And I'll not ever leave you, I promise you that.'

The gentle hold he'd had on her tightened, but he didn't stand. It was like he didn't trust his legs to hold him.

'Look, Harry, love. I'm going to call the doctor. It ain't right how you are, and I'm heartsore as me actions have caused it. I love you, my Harry. More than I've told yer. Aye, and maybe more than I've shown, but I do. You've been like a solid rock I could lean on, and that's what I've done. But you can lean on me now, love, and I'm allus going to be here for you, so as you can.'

'Eeh, me love, this is a grand day. And, aye, I reckon as it is time as I saw the doctor. I've had more than sweats, which I know many of them as survived the hell of the last war have. I've had pains an' all. In me chest and down me arm, and that ain't right, is it, Hattie?'

A sick worry landed in the pit of her stomach. No, it wasn't right. And she'd heard tell of them symptoms afore, and the outcome hadn't been good. *Oh, Harry, Harry, I can't bear to lose you* . . . This thought brought her up sharp. The truth of it zinged pain through her. Why had she been so blind, clinging onto something as flimsy as being a paid mistress to a man she thought had loved her, but who'd left her the moment he had the chance to? How could she have let Arthur's shadow taint the beauty of the love Harry had for her?

'Stay where you are, me love. I'll ring the doctor now.'

The phone had only tinkled an indication of being put back on its stand when it rang out. For a moment Hattie hesitated. But no, Arthur wouldn't ring. Her failing to turn up would tell him how she felt about meeting up with him. Unhooking the receiver, she placed it to her ear and leaned forward towards the mouthpiece. A voice, so familiar and yet with a different note to it said, 'Oh, Hattie, at last!'

'Megan? What is it, love? You sound like you've been

chasing me forever and not caught me. I've been here or at work. Is there sommat wrong?'

'Aye, there is. Oh, Hattie, there must have been a fault on the line between here and Leeds. I couldn't get through to you, though I tried all day. Operator were no help. She just kept saying as she couldn't connect me.'

'Well, you've got me now. What is it, love? Is Issy . . . Oh, no! It ain't Issy, is it? Oh, love.'

Listening to Megan telling her of Issy's passing, Hattie knew her face was dampening with the tears she'd tried not to shed this good while – ever since hearing of Arthur's wife's passing – and the thought came to her, *Well, that's two gone.* Not that she'd ever met Arthur's wife, but in a way she were part of her life. *Oh God, who is going to be the third one?* Because deaths always came in threes, and you couldn't count Sarah's little babby, as it wasn't even formed right. *Please, please, don't let it be my Harry . . .*

'Eeh, Hattie, love, it never rains but it don't bucket down, as Issy would have said if she could, bless her.'

'Aye, and she were right an' all.'

'How is Harry now? We came as soon as we could. Jack's just parking the car. Have they said owt yet?'

'Naw, they know it's his heart, but they haven't said how serious. Eeh, Meg, love, I'm to blame.'

'Don't be a daft ha'p'orth, love. How can you be to blame? It's just one of them things. I just wished as it hadn't happened to Harry, though.'

'It weren't, Megan, I know that. It were me carry-on over the years, harbouring feelings for Arthur. He knew; Harry knew and it made him insecure. He told me it were like a constant threat over his head, and he's never felt like he were the right one for me. Imagine the strain of that on him. Oh, Meg, what have I done?'

'You haven't done anything, Hattie, love. Only the best you could have. None of us can help what goes on inside us. It seems as though we're tuned into stuff we have no control over, but it's how we react to it that matters. You've never sought Arthur out, or left Harry short of your affections, so you've nowt to put on yourself. Come here, love.'

Hattie's body trembled in her arms and Megan felt heart-sore for her. She'd been there, and knew what it felt like to be with the wrong bloke. 'He'll be all right, love. Keep your chin up. Harry's going to need you to be strong. And we'll all help, thou knows.'

'You have enough on your plate, with Issy's passing and Billy coming home tomorrow, and then him going off to fight.'

'Aye, but it were strange, yer know. I saw his letter, so I know Billy were due back tomorrow, but when Jack rang the barracks to ask for him, so we could tell him about Issy, they said as he'd left on leave last night. But he ain't showed here . . . Oh God!'

'What is it, love? You looked feared to death.'

'It's Sarah and Richard. Sarah took Richard to the station. What if Billy arrives back and sees them?'

'Well, there's nowt for him to worry over, is there?'

'You saw how he behaved at his coming-home party. He hates Richard. He thinks . . . Oh, Hattie.'

'Look, Meg, there's another saying Issy had: don't meet trouble halfway, as it may not be travelling your road. It'd be a bit of a coincidence for him to arrive at the same time.'

'Not such a one at Breckton, Hattie. The station is only

small, and there's only trains in and out in the morning and evenings.'

'Reet, I can see your worry then. Look, I'm all right now. You go and give Sarah a ring. There's one of them public phones down the corridor. Have you got some coppers for it?'

Megan searched in her bag and found the two pennies she would need. 'Aye, I have. I'll not be long, I'll just make sure as Sarah's all right. If she is, she should be in work by now, or at least the girls will have seen or heard from her.'

When Sarah answered the phone, Megan felt some relief, but still wanted to have confirmation that nothing was amiss. 'Sarah, love, are you all right?'

'Aye, Aunt Megan, I'm fine. *You* sound het up, though. Is sommat wrong?'

'Everything, it seems.' She told what she knew of Harry's condition.

'Oh no. Poor Hattie, and Harry, of course. Eeh, Aunt Megan, when will it all end? Tell them how sorry I am and give them me love. I've tried to ring you a couple of times as I have some news an' all. Billy's home a day earlier than expected.'

'I know, and that's what I rang you for. You've seen him, then?'

'Aye, at the station.'

What Sarah didn't say spoke louder than what she did, and unease settled inside Megan. Something wasn't right, and yet Sarah sounded fine as she asked if Billy had been to see her and Jack.

'He may have, but we've been out all day.' She told her what they'd found out when they'd rung the barracks.

'Oh God, I – I never thought. How could I forget? Eeh, Aunt Megan, I never told Billy about Granna.'

'Don't worry. We'll call in.'

'No, don't do that! I – I mean, he may be resting. He's had a long journey.'

'All right. But, Sarah, is there something wrong?'

'No. No. Billy were a bit upset as I couldn't come straight home with him, that's all.'

The dread increased. 'Look, come over to ours if he's in one of his moods when you get back, love.'

Disloyalty nudged at Megan's unease. It were as if she was saying as her son could be a danger to Sarah, but then she couldn't help the feeling. She had enough experience to draw on to make it true to her. As she came out of the phone box, she met Jack.

'By, lass, you needn't have come to meet me, but it's nice as you did.'

His squeeze calmed her. 'I didn't, as it happened, love. I came this way to call Sarah.' She told him about her fears. The colour drained from him.

'And she said as Billy were all right, even though he'd seen her at the station with Richard? I mean . . . Eeh, Megan, thou knows as he can see what isn't there. He can put a picture where there ain't none.'

'I know, and I'm worried. Sarah were a bit vague about his reaction, as if she was holding something back.'

'Aye, well, I'll go over there later and it might be a good idea to have them over to dinner.'

She told him how Sarah had counselled against them going over, but agreed about dinner. She should feel angry at Jack's mistrust of her son, but she couldn't. *Why did Billy give a false date to the start of his leave? And what happened to change his mind about coming home earlier than he planned*? These questions increased her worry, because she knew that, like his dad before him, Billy always had a motive for what he did.

25

Megan

Memories Evoked

'Oh, Megan, Jack. It's good news. Well, sort of.' Hattie had brightened some when she met Megan and Jack in the hospital corridor, and this lifted Megan. 'The doctor's been to see me,' she told them, 'and he said as the murmur in Harry's heartbeat is serious, but with plenty of rest and taking life easy, there's no need for it to worsen or have a massive effect on his life.'

'Eeh, that's good, lass,' Jack said. 'Here, let me give you a squeeze. Some good news at last.'

Watching her beloved husband hug the woman she loved most in all the world, Megan smiled. The smile didn't reach deep down, though. There was too much sadness in her for that. Aye, and fear. All of Billy's life she'd defended him against the concerns of those she loved. He hadn't deserved it, as he'd hurt them all at some time or other. She'd never been able to make up to Issy or Jack for him murdering their beloved Bella. And she had a shame in her over Billy's treatment of Hattie and the girls. But none of it came near her worry for Sarah.

Their steps echoed off the whitewashed brick walls of the

hospital corridor, and the sound took her back years. 'Eeh, Hattie, what does this remind you of, eh?'

Hattie laughed her lovely, deep laugh. 'I know. By, that were a long time ago. We were just thirteen and being sent out into the world.' The pressure on her arm tightened. 'Megan, love, we've come a long way since then, but, thou knows, for one moment when you put the scene back in me head, I had the same feeling as I did knowing the Reverend Mother were at the end of that other corridor waiting for us.'

'Aye, I did an' all.'

'Uh-huh, I think I'll go ahead and get the car out the front. I know what you two are like when you start.'

Even though Megan joined Hattie in giggling at Jack's reaction to them walking down memory lane, none of it touched her – not *really* touched her, to the point of lightening the feeling inside her. *What's the matter with me? It is as if my own doom is on me!*

'Thou knows, Megan,' Hattie's voice brought her back and helped dispel some of the fear in her, 'the bit of me past as holds Arthur is hard for me to banish. He were, and is, a big part of me.'

'I know, love, but keep trying, cos you and Harry deserve uncluttered love, like the love as I found with Jack, though it pains me as Cissy had to die for it to happen.'

'She were a lovely lass, weren't she? And a happy one an' all, and I reckon as she's the happiest she's ever been now, what with her ma coming to her and knowing you and Jack are together and looking out for Sarah.'

'Have I, though? Looked out for Sarah, I mean? I shouldn't have let it happen, not her marrying Billy. I shouldn't.'

'Enough of that. You couldn't have stopped it. Lass loves him, and allus has done.'

'But she don't – I mean, she does, but not in the way me and Jack, or you and Arthur— Oh, I'm sorry, love, I shouldn't have said that.'

'Eeh, don't worry. I know what you mean, but what are you on about, saying as Sarah don't love Billy in that way? You don't mean . . . Richard! So it were no accident, him calling her "darling" that night?'

'No, but I didn't know – not for sure – until after. I swear, Hattie, I would have done sommat. I would.'

'By, Megan, it's like a wheel turning round, but it ain't one of fortune, but of constant heartache.'

'I know. Oh, Hattie, give me a hug. One of your hugs as puts everything right for me.'

Clinging to Hattie as if she would save her from whatever she had to face, Megan felt some comfort from the strong grasp of her arms around her. 'Thou knows, Hattie, I don't know if I've ever told yer or not, but I love you. You've been me world. You've allus been there for me. The very best of friends and a sister rolled into one. Ta, love. And I do love you.'

'Eeh, yer daft ha'p'orth. You've spilled me tears as I were locking up for later. But, ta, love. And I knew it anyroad. And I love you, Megan. By, where have all the years gone since we walked along that other corridor in the convent, aged just thirteen? Two little girls with dreams of our future. And to think as you achieved both of yours: you *did* find your mam, and you got your frock-design and making-up place. And yer know sommat: I've not done bad, either, considering. Cos though I didn't find me mam, you shared yours with me, and both Issy and your mam have been like a mam to me an' all.'

'If owt happens, Hattie, I – I mean—'

'Give over. What's got into you the day? Happen it'll be

losing Issy. Well, it's natural, after someone close dies, to feel as though you can't hang onto owt and it's all going to go away. But it ain't, love. I'm here for you, and so is Jack and your mam, and all of us. Come on. If it's a good cry as yer need, get Jack to drop you at mine. We can go over all our lives and have a good chinwag, if yer like. How would that be?'

'Ta, love, and you're right, but I'd better not. I'd best go home. Jack wants us to have Billy and Sarah over for dinner, so I've that to see to. Anyroad, Billy don't know as yet about Issy, so I need to tell him.'

Megan held Hattie's hand as though she'd never let it go as they continued along the corridor. A shudder, not caused by the wind coming in as the doors opened, ricocheted through Hattie's body, leaving a cold place near her heart. It were as if whatever dread Megan had in her had transferred itself to her. Once outside, she hugged Megan again. 'I'll come over and see you tomorrow, love, after I've visited Harry.'

The hug Megan gave her crushed her, but she'd have it no different. Megan needed a prop, she could tell that. She'd always be that to her, just like Megan had always been a prop for her.

They'd always been there for each other.

Crossing the pebbled yard towards his stables, and leaving Megan to go indoors to start preparations for dinner, Jack saw Dorothy coming out of the furthest stable. He called out to her, 'Everything all right?'

'I think so, Jack, but you might want to call the vet in. I've just checked up on Betsy Girl, and she's very restless. I've fetched her in earlier than usual. I'm not sure, but how she is, I think she could have her foal any time now.'

'Thanks, Dorothy. I'll ring him. Should I have me worries over her, d'yer think?'

'No, she's doing fine. Oh, by the way, your son-in-law came over looking for you both, but said he'd come back later, and that Mister Crompton was snooping around.'

'Snooping? Mister Terence? That's a funny word to use.'

'Well, it's how I would describe his actions. I don't know what his game was. I came across him around the back of the stable about an hour ago. He seemed to be checking the structure. Jumped out of his skin on seeing me, and made some petty excuse about when he was here last. He said he'd meant to mention to you about a damp patch. So he thought, as you were out, he'd take a look to see if it had worsened.'

'Don't worry over it. He's allus struck me as a funny one. I'll ring him later. Now, let's have a look at Betsy Girl and see how much you've learned about fillies' habits when they're about to drop their foal.'

She grinned at him. Lass had a lovely smile. He didn't know all the circumstances of her loss, but he felt for her. *Happen when this lot's over, she'll find someone to be happy with.* Dorothy was a good-looking lass. He'd always thought so, but when he'd seen her at Sarah and Billy's wedding with her glad-rags on, he'd thought her stunning. Some lucky bloke had a treat coming to him with her. And if it was a farmer, or someone who had stables, he'd get the bullseye, because she'd picked up all the tasks around here as if she was born to them.

Guilt entered him at his next thought, as it hadn't been the first time it had come to him. But in many ways he wished Megan were more like Dorothy. To have had her support around the stables, working alongside him as he'd built it all up, would have felt like someone had iced his cake. But then he knew it was a selfish thought, as Megan had always had her own dream, and realizing it had made her happy.

As he turned back towards the house, the 'posh one' – as they called Louise – shouted over to him, 'Mr Fellam, may I have a word?'

'Hello, Louise. What can I do for you, lass?'

'I wanted to ask if you would mind me going out to dinner tonight? Mr Crompton invited me to his home. I have sort of said yes.'

'Mind? Naw, lass, you can do as you like, once work's all done, you know that.'

'Yes, I know, but this seemed a bit different. It's not like going for a walk or whatever.'

'You go, and have a good time. Eeh, he'd right suit you, young Terence. He has his ways, a bit on the lazy side, though he did help me out when I were trying to get arable side going. But then he's top-drawer, so has no need to put his shoulder to the grindstone.'

'It's only dinner with his family, Jack, not a marriage proposal!'

Her giggle had him smiling. All these lassies brightened his day. He'd been lucky to get such a good bunch of Land Girls, and had had no trouble with any of them, though they had their moments when they turned the task of laying fresh straw in the stable into a free-for-all, throwing it at each other and wrestling in the bales, but they were only letting off steam.

'Well, you never know; and you could do worse,' he told her. 'He's well set up, thou knows. Anyroad, I'm to go and ring vet. Betsy Girl has reached her time, and Dorothy says as she's a bit agitated.'

'Oh? I'll go and see her. See if I can soothe her.'

Lass had a love of the horses – a deep love – and she could ride them as good as any jockey he'd seen an' all. Happen she'd keep Betsy Girl calm.

With talking to the girls and dealing with everyday things, some of Jack's worry left him, but it came right back with the look on Megan's face as he entered the kitchen.

It wasn't as if anything had happened, other than that Billy had refused to come over and didn't want them visiting. He'd said he were tired and just wanted the night with Sarah. But even that set a fear up in Jack. It might not have done, but when Megan worried, he did too, as she had a sort of sixth sense where that son of hers was concerned.

'I'll not be a mo, love. I can see as you're upset, but I have to make a phone call to the vet.'

When he put the phone back on its hook, he turned back to Megan. 'Now then, lass, what's happened, eh?'

'It's Billy. He hardly said owt when I told him about Issy. Well, not like you'd expect. He just said, "Oh, well, it ain't like you didn't think it were going to happen, and she'd had her time." And he sounded agitated, but then none of me news were of the kind to cheer him, I suppose, what with how things are for Hattie as well. He's funny over Hattie, for some reason.'

Trying to soothe her, and himself, Jack made light of this. 'Happen as lad is just tired. Sarah'll sort him out.' And though he didn't like to think of that side of things, where his own little daughter – as he still thought of Sarah – was concerned, he made a joke. 'Lad's been deprived, thou knows. All he wants is to cuddle up with his bride and get some release, make him feel like a husband again, rather than a fighting machine. He'll be right as owt tomorrow. Stop worrying and give me a quick cuddle. Only a quick one, mind, as I've stuff to see to.'

The tension in her body matched his, but holding each other helped. It was like they knew something was going to happen, but couldn't stop it. Nor could they express it. After all, nothing more had gone on than that Billy had seen Sarah waving Richard off – an everyday thing in family life, especially these days. They were just being silly and overprotective, and Jack supposed that's how they would always be.

26
Sarah & Sally

A Friendship Deepens

Sarah looked up as the door of her office opened. She'd been trying hard to concentrate on balancing the books, but nothing fitted with anything else, though she knew it was due to her own lack of concentration.

More than once she'd stared through the internal office window, to where the girls were working, and had watched them, heads down, guiding material through the sewing machines.

The knock on her office door was a welcome distraction and Sally entered. 'I've made you a pot of tea, love. You look all in.'

'I am, Sally. Me life just seems filled with complications.'

'D'yer want to talk of it? I'm a good listener. Comes of me early days when, if I opened me mouth, it were shut for me.'

Wanting to talk about anything except what had happened at the station, Sarah picked up on this from Sally. 'I don't know how you got through everything, love. Though it ain't as if you have really, is it? I mean, you don't want to give of yourself – like in having a boyfriend, or owt.'

'Is it that obvious? But then, you're right, so it must be. Problem is, when something happens like it did to me, it sort of shuts you down. I can love folk. I love Hattie like she were me mam. Mind, she has been really, cos I can't remember that much about me own mam, nor about me sister Janey. I suppose it hurts too much to do so.'

'Aye, I understand, as same thing happened to me: I lost me sister. Anyroad, I'm sorry. I shouldn't have took the subject up with you.'

'It's all right. Don't worry over it. I should speak of it more, but I've never had anyone as I could talk to. I can't talk to Hattie as it hurts her too much. She still feels full of guilt, no matter how I try to reason with her. Occasionally, something will trigger a conversation about what happened, but her remorse is such that I don't feel I can open up about my deeper feelings. I'm always trying to convince her that she had to do what she did. That I understand how she trusted the police when she convinced my poor mam to agree to use me as bait to expose the child sex-ring that Lord Byron was mixed up in. It wasn't her fault that the police held back from swooping in in time to save me from the rape.'

'I can't imagine what that felt like. If you ever want to talk about it, I'll listen. I – I don't know as I could take your pain away, but I do know it helps to unburden yourself.'

'Ta, Sarah. Maybe if I can do that you can convince Hattie that she weren't to blame – the police were. After all, once she realized the police were waiting for the whole gang to be assembled and that that had put me in grave danger, she risked her life to save me. I mean, I wouldn't be here now if it weren't for her actions.'

'It's funny, but we have a lot in common, don't we? I lost me mam and me sister and so did you, and both our sisters were murdered.'

'Can you remember yours?'

'No, not always. I try, and every time I see a Mongol child I like to think it is Bella. I remember more of the things we did, and how she was, than what she looked like. What about you?'

'Not really. I'm the same as you: it's more an impression of her, but the events – they're like an open sore in me.'

An urge came to Sarah to take hold of Sally's hand. When she did, it felt cold, as if it had never, ever been warm. Suddenly she wanted to hug this girl whom Hattie had adopted, and who seemed always to have been in Sarah's life, and yet, though a friend, she'd never really been close to. Sally moved at the same time and they came together. The hug held love. 'Oh, Sally.'

Tears spilled down Sarah's cheeks. She brushed them away whilst Sally clung to her as if she'd never let her go.

When they did release each other, they started to giggle. The giggle built into a belly laugh that doubled over their bodies. 'Eeh, Sally, we're a pair of dafties. But I feel as though we're special friends now, and I'm in need of one of them.'

'Me, too, lass, and apart from Hattie, and a bit as I feel for Harry, I've a feeling in me as I haven't experienced in a long time. Like I can love another. I know it's childish, but . . .'

Sarah curled her little finger around the one offered by Sally, and they shook on it, like two little girls in the playground, before bursting out laughing again.

For Sarah, the laughter held a release from the pain of her granna going, and from the fear of Billy, and the shame of what she'd done with Richard, but it didn't even begin to touch the part of her where she held Richard in her heart. Nothing could free her of that, and she didn't want it to.

'Thou knows, Sarah, there's sommat as I'd like to share with you. Well, two things. I said as I couldn't give meself to anyone, but I've not been able to get Megan's stepbrother Mark out of me head. Oh, I know as he's a couple of years or so younger than me, but—'

'Sally, you dark horse! Well, I've a mind as he feels the same. He never left your side at that dinner party. Oh, what a mess that turned out to be an' all. I'll tell you what, I'll find out what his address is. I know he's in the navy, but I don't know if he's at sea yet, and then you can write to him.'

'I don't know as I could.'

'Of course you could. Start writing as a friend – someone concerned for him – and I reckon as things'll soon develop from there. Anyroad, you said *two* things?'

'Aye, I know we had a laugh about it that evening, but I was serious about wanting to join up. I have a talent as no one knows of. Not even Hattie, and it could be of use. You see, I can speak French.'

'What? French? How?'

'When I was forced to live with me aunt, she put me to mending, and that's how I learned the skills I had when I came back to you all. You remember? I used to help your Aunt Megan when she first set up? Well, back at me aunt's house, I had work come in from this lady. She were French, and she took it on herself to teach me her language. I just seemed to have a talent for it. I were speaking it in no time. We had long conversations and never a word in English. I think it was because that was the only learning I had. I couldn't read or write and had no education, and so me brain just soaked up the only academic skill it was offered.'

'And you can still speak it? You remember enough of it?'

'Yes, I've allus gone over it in me mind, and at night I even talk to meself in it. Then, just recently, I got a book out of the library and started to learn to read and write it. It didn't seem a problem at all. I could understand and hold a conversation with no difficulty. So I thought, as we were hooking up with the French for this war, it might be as they could use me in the forces.'

'That's amazing, Sally, though I don't want you to go. I feel as though I've only just found you proper.'

'I know. I feel like that too, like I've never had a friend afore and now I have. I know we have been friendly and attended parties and been part of the same family, but not like this. But me urge to help is very strong. Only problem is getting Hattie to agree. On top of that, I feel as though Megan really needs me here.'

'Yes, she will miss you, especially as I'm . . . well, I'm pregnant again!'

'Again?'

'Aye, again. And it'd be nice to share that with someone an' all. Aunt Megan and Aunt Hattie know.'

At the end of her telling, Sally held Sarah's hand again. 'By, you've had it rough, lass. But everything's all right now, eh?'

Something held her back from telling Sally it wasn't. 'Aye, things are going along. It's not easy, with how everything is. Anyroad, I'd best pack up now, it's on half-past two. I've done the wages and stuff, and Billy's at home waiting for me. He came home a day early.'

'Well, then, what're you doing here in the first place? Get on home, lass: your man is waiting.'

It was easy to fake laughing with Sally. Everything seemed easy with her, and Sarah wished she'd found this way of them being friends a long time ago. But then it hadn't been possible to get under the solid wall Sally had built around herself.

It had cracked now, though, and she was glad of it. It was going to be good to have someone of her own age to talk to.

The bus trundled along, taking Sarah on her journey home. Though full of fear at what she'd face, her mind was more occupied with Richard and the kiss they'd shared. He'd be home in Market Harborough now. How she wished she was there with him, and he had his arms around her, keeping her safe. *Oh, Richard . . .*

27

Richard

Feeling his Shame

'Darling, you're home! And so is Mark. What a coincidence.'

'Well, not really, Mother. Training has finished for a lot of us, and we have a couple of days before we take up our postings, though of course I will still be training for a while longer yet. Where is Mark? Has he any idea when he will be going?'

'A hug would be nice, Richard. I've missed you, you know.'

'Sorry, Mother. Come here. Oh, it's good to be home. Is Father in?'

'Is everything all right with you, my dear? You seem very agitated.'

The need came to Richard to unburden himself. 'I'll tell all over a cup of tea. I've done something I am rather ashamed of. Not sorry for, but afraid of the consequences.'

After telling them, he hung his head in shame. He felt that emotion intensify, just by being surrounded by his family – all honourable, decent people who wouldn't dream of behaving as he had.

'Good God, Richard! Not a good thing at all. You may very well have put Sarah in a lot of danger. I'm surprised at your appalling behaviour.'

'I'm sorry, Father. I don't know what possessed me. Is Billy still dangerous? I mean, still capable of—'

'I think so. Never should have been released, in my opinion, but when I spoke to the fellows in charge of his case, they said there was no evidence to keep him in. They feel he is the army's responsibility now. But I didn't like what I saw at the dinner party: the look Billy had in his eyes, and his irrational thinking. Not only that, but he acted upon what he perceived. Though what you are telling us now, Richard, has simply confirmed what I thought. This is very bad form on your part. I've suspected how you felt for a long time, but why leave it this late? Damnation, man!'

'Edward!'

'I'm sorry, my dear. I'm just worried, and feel let down. I think we should contact Jack and warn him.'

Never had Richard seen his father so angry. His shame turned to humiliation. To have been bawled out like that, in front of everyone. But then, it didn't matter. Sarah mattered, and he'd put her life in danger. 'Oh God.'

The feel of his brother's arm around his shoulders comforted him. 'Come on, Richard, it may not be as bad as all that. Father, have you some of that whisky left? That nice syrupy one we had in our tea, before we went away? I think Richard could do with a drop. Poor chap was only following his heart, you know.'

'You don't follow your heart with a married woman. Yes, there's some whisky in the cabinet – and pour me a stiff one whilst you are at it.'

'I don't want anything, thanks, Mark. I'm tired out, but I must keep a clear head. Father, I'll ring Jack. It is only right that I do so; I need to salvage something from all of this. But may I say: this wasn't a flippant thing. You are right, Father, I do love Sarah. I should have spoken up. It just didn't seem right to do so.'

Feeling wretched enough about it all, Richard could have done without his mother chipping in. 'Poor Megan and Jack. They have enough on their plate. Oh, Edward, I'm frightened. I have this feeling.'

'Please, don't start that, Bridget, dear. You have feelings every day that something is going to happen to Megan. You're paranoid about her. She'll be fine. Well, not fine, of course, but it is Sarah I'm worried about. Billy will see this as her betrayal of him, and I honestly think she is in grave danger.'

'I want to go up and see them, Edward. I don't want to wait until the funeral. I should be with them. Issy meant so much to Megan and Sarah, and to me, and Jack adored her. I can't imagine what they are going through.'

'All right, my dear. Yes, I think we should, but it has come at a bad time. The boys . . .'

'We'll come. I – I mean, I will. I can get to Liverpool from there easier than from here, and I have six days left of my leave.'

Richard suspected Mark had an ulterior motive for wanting to go, but had no inclination to goad him about it. The contents of his stomach were threatening to evacuate, and his head swam. Possibilities stabbed him with the horror of what could happen. God, he wished he had more leave. Not for the first time he felt the restrictions on his life. *Bloody Hitler!* How easy everything had been before that fateful broadcast saying 'Britain is now at war.'

'What about you, Richard?'

'I can't come, Mark. I'm due at Biggin Hill the day after next.'

'And a bloody good thing, too. Having you there would only complicate things.'

'Father, don't you think I know that I have done wrong? Can't you see how this is crucifying me? We are talking of the woman I love being in danger through me expressing that love. God, I feel bad enough without your constant condemnation.'

Slamming the door released some of Richard's tension. Standing looking at the phone compounded the dread in his heart, but before he had time to ring Jack, the door opened and his father came through. 'Richard, I'm sorry. I . . . well, I am angry with you. It was a silly action on your part, but I have suspected your feelings for a long time, you know. So maybe I am as much at fault. I should have broached the subject and helped you to a solution. Love is a very powerful emotion, making you act out of character. Still, all we can do now is try and save the situation.'

The stiffness and anger had left his father's body. His arms were open. Like a child, Richard felt drawn to them. The hug held comfort and love, and the tears he hadn't wanted to shed spilled over.

'Come on, my boy. Make the call. Let's do what we can to rescue the situation.'

Although he groaned inwardly, he didn't say anything. His father stood by as he dialled the operator, his face showing concern of the kind that deepened Richard's own worry. *Where's the bloody operator? She never answers when you want her, but is always there when you're having a conversation. Poking her nose into everyone's business!*

The ringing continued: monotonous, persistent, demanding an answer. At last he got through, and after reeling off the number he wanted, there was a 'Will try to connect you.'

A painful pounding set up inside his chest as he waited. No one answered. Images of the phone in Megan and Jack's house came to him. He pictured the empty hall, and begged for the doors to open and for either Megan or Jack to cross over to the phone and answer him. It didn't happen.

'I'm sorry, caller, there is no answer from that number.'

He snapped with frustration. 'For God's sake, let it ring a little while. You haven't given them time to get to it. I'm sure someone will answer.'

They didn't, and his worry increased. Every possible scenario clogged his brain.

'Richard, you know this is very bad form regarding poor Lucinda, don't you?'

'Oh, Mother, please! Don't you think I know everything you and Father are saying is true? Do you really think I need all of this? I've behaved badly, but sometimes there is a moment in life when nothing else matters but what is before you. That moment happened at the station. I can't explain it. Besides, I have been truthful with Lucinda. We have an agreement. Neither of us is sure, and we are not holding each other to anything.'

'You will have to tell her how your feelings lie now.'

'Where they have always lain, you mean. I know I will.' He sank onto the bottom step of the stairs, his hands supporting his aching head. Desperation filled him. *What can I do? What should I do? Please, God, keep Sarah safe.*

28

Terence

A Plot Comes Together

Terence walked across the farmyard. Rita came into view, her cockney twang irritating him for a moment as she called out to him, 'Oi, yer not avoiding me, are yer? I've been looking for yer.'

'Far from it, Rita, dear. I have come in search of you. I want to have a talk with you.' Despite his resolve, the usual ache came to his groin as he looked at Rita. The little minx stood in a pose in the doorway of the barn, one hand stretched upwards holding the door jamb, the other on her hip, her body at an angle that showed off her best assets to the most seductive advantage.

'Right, mate. What can I do for you, eh?'

Her giggle, high and mocking, further disturbed him. 'I can't talk here. Besides, you're not going to like what I have to say.'

'Oh? That ain't got a good sound to it. Where shall we go then? We could go up to the loft. Me and Penny have been putting hay up there to give us somewhere to rest out of the way of them lot in the kitchen. Nosy blighters.'

'No, let's go into the stables. There's no one around at the moment.'

The stables were altogether a better place, Terence thought. Too many intimate moments had passed between them in the loft, and he hadn't been up there for a while. His recent visits to Rita had been to her bed, whenever he wanted her. She'd get rid of Penny for an hour.

A picture flashed through his mind of Rita with Theresa. He shuddered at the memory. Theresa had deceived him. Not that it had been going on for long with her and Rita; she'd sworn the last night was only the second time. And not that he'd stop her in the usual run of things – or mind, even – but lesbianism! God, he hadn't expected that of her. Clever, too, the scam she'd sorted out to cover taking Rita to her own bedroom for their frolics. He'd had no chance of doing that, and hadn't wanted to, either. Any lady, other than Theresa of course, that he ever took to his room would have to be of a much better class than this whore.

'Right, mate. What's on your mind, then?'

'First, your little tricks haven't passed Theresa and me by. We know your game – gathering and storing information – but it won't work.'

'Oh, right, and who's going to stop it working? I know what I know; and what I know, the society columns would pay a bleedin' fortune for. Even more so, now your sister is carrying a kid. So you can bleedin' stick that in your pipe and smoke it. Hey, let go! Don't even think . . . Argh!'

Rita was surprisingly difficult to hold, considering her small stature. Her strength shocked him, but he held onto her arm and twisted it up behind her back. He couldn't remember ever feeling as angry as he did at this moment. And never had he treated another human being – let alone a woman – as he was treating this bitch. Vitriol spat from him. 'You vile, filthy scum. You tell anyone what you know of me and my sister, and your remains will never be found.' *How can she know about Theresa's pregnancy?* 'Have you been snooping? Listening to conversations, eh? Well, a listener hears no good of herself, or of others.'

'Let go! 'Ere, who d'yer think you are? How d'yer think I bleedin' know? I saw the changes in her body, that's how. Her breasts were much bigger, and the nipples were huge and dark – not like normal, but like when a woman's got a baby inside her. Let go of me arm or I'll scream, and that'll fetch your dad down. I saw him go by a minute ago . . . Argh!'

'Shut up and listen to me. You've heard tell of the murderer back in our midst, haven't you? Well, I'm going to pay him a nice little sum to get rid of you.'

'Don't be bleedin' daft, mate. You're better off paying me for me silence than getting mixed up in a murder. You can trust me, honest. Besides, I know stuff about Billy and Theresa, and I know that you know, so if I tell him that you know he might do for me, but he'll come after you as well. He won't want to risk his wife finding out what he got up to. Wait a minute. It's his, ain't it? I'm telling you, mate, none of us want to get mixed up with him.'

Terence let her go. *Why the bloody hell didn't I think of that? Billy Armitage would think exactly as Rita has put it. There is nothing else for it: I'll have to go down the path of paying her off. But then, will the blackmail ever stop?* His mind went from one thing to another as plans formed. But as he looked at Rita on the floor at his feet, rubbing her arm, a sick feeling of self-disgust hit him – not only for the degrading and brutal way he'd treated the girl, but for the credence he'd given the plans in his head. *What kind of man am I? God, I don't know myself at times.* He turned away from her to hide the tears brimming behind his eyes. How low was he prepared to go? Incest, woman-beating, murder, and a willingness to destroy a man's life's work? 'Rita, I'm sorry. I – I don't know what came over me.'

'Bit late to have a conscience, mate. You've near pulled me arm from its socket. I can have you for that, yer know.'

'I – I just wanted to protect my sister.'

'Well, you've a fine way of showing it. I wouldn't like no brother of mine behaving how you have towards her. Now, how much are you offering? It has to be a good bit, mind.'

'How do I know that will be an end to it? What about when you want more money? Will you be back with your vicious threats then?'

'That's up to you. If you pay me enough, no.'

'What is enough?'

'Oh, I should say as them society gossipers would give me a thou—'

'A thousand! Are you mad? I don't have that kind of money – far from it.'

The fresh-smelling smoke from the cigarette she'd lit, once he'd helped her to her feet, curled towards him, mingling with the smoke she blew out from the deep drag she'd taken. As if switching a light on inside him, it fuelled an idea once more. With it came clarity about how he could put an end to this. He gave his mind to the details as he listened to her droning on. She clearly thought she had the upper hand.

'Well, you'll just have to go to Daddy, won't yer? Cos that's me price. I want to set meself up in a little business in the East End after this bleedin' war is done, and with a place to live as well. If you can't sort it by that time, then it's a poor doings – and not just for me, cos I could write a book about what goes on around here. "Confessions of a Land Girl".'

'Look, you'll get your money, but you have to do more

than promise your silence. I have a job I want you to do.'
Tapping his pockets, he located his own cigarettes. Taking his
time to light one, he watched Rita, noting her uncertainty.
Before he spoke, he blew his own satisfying drag of smoke
towards her. 'I need you to accidentally set a fire – or, rather,
make it look like an accident.'

'What? Are you off your head? What fire?'

As Terence told her his plan, all self-disgust left him. The
idea was perfect: get Rita to set the stables alight, then follow
her and make it look like he'd caught her in the act. With his
testimony she'd go to prison, and if she let on about him and
Theresa, her accusations would sound preposterous to everyone and would be looked upon as the ranting of someone
deranged. *Yes, it is perfect.*

'You need to do it tonight. There is nothing to it. It will
look like you have been foolish by discarding your cigarette
butt whilst visiting your friends – nothing more than that.'

'But what if it don't catch alight?'

'It will. You'll go to the barn and soak this handkerchief in
petrol.' She took the handkerchief he handed her. Put it in a bag,
so it doesn't touch your clothes: a brown paper one with handles
will do. There must be some of them in the kitchen. Ask the
housekeeper for one – just make any excuse as to why you want
it. The petrol will soak into the bag, so make sure you hold it
aloft and take care not to get it on you, or your hands. We don't
want anyone smelling it on you. Check and make sure, and if
you can smell anything, there's a tap at the end of the barn – use
water from that to clean it off. You will need to approach
Fellam's farm by going over the fields. You will come to the back
of the stables, and no one will see you until you emerge around
the front, by which time you will have left the bag in a discreet
place. When you depart from there, you light a cigarette. Throw

the lighted butt-end at the bag, and whoosh! When that happens, run. Get as far away as you can. No one will see the flames until the stable is well alight.'

'And what about Penny? How am I meant to go visiting without her? She follows me round like she were me bleedin' keeper.'

He hadn't thought of that; it was a complication. However, Rita hadn't refused to set the fire. And excitement settled in him. This could really happen. He'd have to solve the problem of Penny, though. He'd have to keep her occupied. Maybe flirt with her. Not a bad prospect, actually. Since her physical transformation, she'd tickled his fancy more than once. He liked the innocence of her. Yes, the more he thought about it, the more he liked the idea. 'Leave her to me. I'll find a distraction for her.'

'You ain't going to—?'

'That's my business. If you want your money, you just concentrate on what you've got to do.' He wouldn't have time to do anything with Penny as he had to get ready for Louise coming to dinner. But he could play with her for a bit; get her ready for another time – anything, as long as he kept her out of Rita's way. But right now he just wished Rita would stop putting up obstacles. He wanted this sorting, but she hadn't consented yet and still had the upper hand.

'I ain't saying as I'll do it, but if I do, what about me money?'

The thought came to him to say *You'll have no need of that where you're going*, but instead he took a lock of her hair in his hands and twirled it round his fingers. 'You'll get your money, sweetie, and a whole lot more besides.'

'I need to know when, and I ain't settling for anything less than a thousand.'

'Okay, but I can't fund it all at once. I can find a couple of hundred, then make a regular payment to you from my allowance each month. It'll add up to what you want, over time. I'll work out the details. I need to find a way that you can't touch it until you leave here, and yet stop you having it if the conditions of our agreement are not met. That way, I think I'll be assured of your silence.'

'You're quite the gangster, ain't yer, mate? Well, I like gangsters. I were mixed up with a mob of them in London. That's why I come up here. I needed to get away for a while, but some of them blokes couldn't half make a girl happy.'

'Ha, well, you've jumped out of the frying pan into the—' He couldn't finish the saying, because the irony of this hit him and laughter seized him, shaking his body and doubling him over. Through it, he heard her cackling laugh join with his.

The air had cleared. They were co-conspirators now, and he liked the feeling. He felt safer with that than with having Rita as an enemy. But that only went so far, because he'd think nothing of betraying her. Nothing at all.

29
Billy & Sarah

Vengeance is Mine

The sound of the door opening and Sarah calling out, 'I'm home, Billy,' as if nothing had happened, set his blood boiling. She needn't think as a couple of hours had made any difference, and if it had, it had only worsened how he felt as he thought everything over.

'And about time an' all. We've sommat to sort out, and it won't get sorted with you going off like you did . . . Don't walk away from me, Sarah.'

'Is there a point in me stopping here? You seem set on having a go at me, and in the mood you're in, it ain't a good idea to try to sort anything out.'

At this he moved and positioned himself between Sarah and the door. Her face showed fear, but she needed to feel scared, after what she'd done. 'I'd never have believed it of you. You, having an affair behind me back, and us not married five minutes.'

'I haven't, Billy, and I'll not have you thinking it. I were just saying goodbye to Richard, that's all. Look, I'm sorry – he kissed me before I realized what were happening. It happened and I can't change it, but I didn't kiss him back. I were just going to pull out of his arms when you came on us.

Let's just forget it. It weren't meant, not by either of us. It were just a goodbye kiss. Let's not fall out on your first night home.'

'Fall out? Fall out? I'll bloody kill you. You've been carrying on with him behind me back. I knew it. I bloody knew it.'

'I haven't, Billy. I haven't. He's been away all the time you have. He was on his way down to Biggin Hill and called in on us, that's all. And with me granna – I need to tell you about me granna.'

'You don't have to bother. I know.'

'Well then, you know that me dad and your mam had such a lot to see to. And that's how I came to be taking Richard to the station on me way to work. I couldn't refuse.'

'Couldn't refuse? Didn't want to, more like.'

She shrank back from him as he stepped forward, her plea desperate. 'Please, Billy, don't be angry.'

'Don't?' He was unable to stop himself repeating everything she said. His eyes burned in their sockets as the mist descended, putting a red cloud around Sarah and searing his brain. His mind wouldn't let him control it. Spittle wet his chin, but he couldn't draw it back into his mouth.

Terror was written all over Sarah's face and resounded in her scream. 'Billy, no . . . No, please, please.' She cowered beneath his raised fist. The blow caught her shoulder and sent her reeling.

He stood over her. The heat in his head blinded him, and flashes of his dad came into that heat: hitting his mam, making her bend to his will. Well, he'd no need to imagine any more. His own woman lay on the floor at his feet, and his blood surged through his veins with the same passion those thoughts had aroused in him. He had to live the scene he'd witnessed –

he had to. He knew his body would be more gratified than it had ever been before.

Sarah's pleas filtered through to him. *Yes! Plead, you bitch!* Her anguish intensified the feelings consuming him.

'No. No! Billy. Not now, Billy, no.'

No? No? She is just like me mam. He remembered she'd said no to his dad. Everything was as it should be; it was going to happen.

The searing heat in him urged him on. Sarah was no match for him as he grabbed her and pinned her arms above her head. She writhed beneath him, fighting him. *Yes, yes!*

Letting go of one of her arms, the punch he wielded squelched into her chest. Her body doubled over, moaning and gasping for breath. The punch had felt good, and it made her easier to handle. Tearing her blouse released her breasts.

The redness in his head increased. It told him things, giving him ideas and singeing his anger. *Has she shown them to Richard?* He thrust his head forward and bit into the tender flesh, tasting her blood and savouring the pleasure that her screams gave him.

Pain ripped the tender, agony-filled parts of his head as Sarah grabbed his hair and yanked his head back. The slap he gave her made her let go.

'Stop it, Billy! Stop it, *please*! Oh God, help me . . . Help me . . .'

'I'll stop when I bloody want to. Your body belongs to me. You're me wife. You've no reet to give other men pleasure of it.'

Flashes of his dad came to him again: the blows he'd rained down on his mam, and how he'd thrown her backwards over the edge of the table, forcing her legs open with his knees.

The same fear he'd felt then cracked Billy's chest now as he remembered sitting on the stairs, watching. He'd shifted his position and the stair had creaked. He'd thought his dad would hear and turn on him, but he hadn't. And the shivering, frightened little boy that he had been could do nothing but watch.

Sarah was like a rag doll as he pulled her to her feet and dragged her across the room. Her cries fuelled the burning desire to have everything as he remembered it, and it pumped feelings through him with a force he'd never experienced before.

Her body thudded onto the table. Her face took on a blue hue, but he couldn't stop. Not now. His mind registered her struggle and welcomed it. Holding her with one hand, he found the edge of her knickers with the other.

'Not like this. Please, Billy. *Please*, don't.'

Yes. Yes. Everything was right. She had her breath back and was pleading again. The feeling this gave him was fantastic, and the heat in his body filled his brain to bursting. An intense, searing pleasure surged through him. Obscenities gushed from him as his mind and body became one. This was what it was all about: he'd beaten his woman into submission, and now his reward took him to places he'd only imagined. He burst with joy as his release came, splintering his body and his soul.

Gasping for breath, he slumped down onto Sarah. The experience had fractured every part of him. 'Oh, Sarah!' He couldn't take his weight off her. He didn't want to. His love for her weakened him, shattered everything that was him. The redness left, and the pain – the agonizing and yet beautiful pain – faded.

Sarah's sobs penetrated his peace. Confusion clouded in on him as shame at what he'd done washed over him. Had his dad felt this? Yes, Billy knew he had. He'd heard him saying sorry, and saw him trying to soothe his mam. And his mam had said it was all right and told him to go and have a fag while she made him a sup of tea. So it was as it should be, for him to feel as he did; it was natural and a part of it. He'd do the same as his dad. He'd make things better. 'Sarah. Aw, lass, I'm sorry. I'm reet sorry. Come here, lass. Don't cry.' He took her gently in his arms. 'Aw, lass. Come on now, come on.'

Standing away from her, he adjusted his trousers, then lifted her as gently as he could. She didn't resist, and this compounded his worry for her. He'd get her to their bed, bathe her wounds and take care of her.

Laying her down, he climbed on the bed and lay next to her. 'I'm sorry, lass. Forgive me. Oh, Sarah.' His body, heavy with shame, found blessed relief as the soft bed took his weight. The redness had wrecked him, leaving his mind quivering. Tears prickled his eyes. He doubled over, trying to ward them off, but a flood of tears swamped him and he wanted to scream out, *Help me, help me*.

Billy's sobs reached Sarah's distressed mind, but she couldn't move. Nor could she speak. Pain and fear tightened her chest and burned her body with hurt. Things she'd heard and known of the past came back to her, as did the sickening memory of Billy's enjoyment of what he'd done. He'd relished brutalizing her, just as she'd heard his father had done to his mam – Megan, poor Aunt Megan. As the realization of this hit her, she knew with certainty that this would be the pattern of her life if she stayed with Billy. She couldn't let it be. She had to get help. Aunt Megan would help her, she would understand.

Through Billy's anguish one word came over and over

again: *sorry*. He was sorry. But then *sorry* wasn't enough for her, and never would be, though she knew she had to pretend as it was. If she didn't, he'd likely get angry again.

She put her hand out towards him, and he uncoiled his body. He turned to her, but his movement brought a whimper from her as it cut deeper into her pain.

'Oh God, I've hurt you bad, Sarah. I'm sorry, lass.'

Inside she stiffened, ready to ward him off, but she fought the urge to do so as his hand undid her ripped blouse. His gentleness surprised her.

'Oh, Sarah, lass.'

Her breasts seeped blood, and the skin that wasn't broken was pitted with red marks.

'I'll make you better, lass.'

Better? She would never be better from this. Her body would heal, but inside? In her mind? Would that ever heal? And there was something else she hardly dared to give thought to. *What about my babby? What if he's harmed my babby?*

'I'll see to yer, lass. I'll clean yer up. Wait there.'

Returning with a bowl and cloth, he set about bathing her. A soreness ached in places she hadn't known he'd inflicted harm on, but his voice, low and urgent, held a note she didn't dare defy. 'Me mam's not to hear of this, thou knows, Sarah. Nor your dad, or anyone, d'yer hear me? You've no marks on your face, so if you wear long sleeves and them trousers as I hate to see you in, that'll stop them knowing owt. Right, you're all cleaned up. Now get off the bed and get dressed. Just in case they come calling. I told them not to, but that ain't stopped me mam in the past.'

Sliding her feet off the bed sent pain searing through Sarah's ribs. 'I can't, Billy. Just let me rest. Ring them later and tell them as I'm sick. Tell them it's due to me pregnancy, so it don't worry them none. Aunt Megan knows as I take with the vomiting.' Now, as she came round a bit, some of her fear left her and anger trickled into her. 'I'll tell you sommat, though, Billy. If you've harmed our babby, I'll never forgive you, never.'

There was no retaliation from him. He sat on the edge of the bed next to her and tried to take her hand.

She pulled it away. 'Why, Billy? Why? It ain't normal to do what you did.'

'Oh, here you go again, with saying as I'm not normal. Well, I know I'm not and if you were inflicted with that as takes me, you'd not be either. But I'll tell you sommat for nowt: it has to have a trigger, and you and your ways were it.'

His standing up and bending over her intimidated her, but she stared back at him. Something came over her that made her not care any more. After a moment Billy turned his back on her and headed for the door.

'I'm going out. I have to get out of the sight of yer, as when I look at yer I see *him* with his arms round you, and I can't stand it, I can't.'

This last came out on a sob. Guilt trickled into her. She'd to take some of the blame on her own shoulders, she knew that, but then, no matter what she'd done, she hadn't deserved the punishment he'd meted out. Nothing deserved that.

The sound of the door closing behind him raised hope in her. If she could get off the bed, she could ring her dad and . . . But what if *he* went there? They'd tackle him, wouldn't they, and then? No, she couldn't risk it, as she'd an inkling of what Billy would do if Aunt Megan and her dad took him to task, and it didn't bear thinking about. But then what else could she do? Could she risk that? What if Billy hurt them? But what choice did she have?

I have to have their help. I have to . . .

30

Megan

The Ultimate Sacrifice

'Are you all right to get that, Megan? Or does you want me to come and answer it?'

'No, I'm fine. It might be Sally calling from work. I told her to ring if anything cropped up. With me taking leave unexpected, I've left things in the air a bit.'

Jack had come out of his office, which was a grand title for the little room where he kept all the books and stuff to do with his business. Not that he tackled such things, but sometimes he went in there as other men might go into a shed. His own little den, as it were. He needed one at the moment, she knew that. Somewhere he could cry a few private tears.

He stood watching her, no doubt curious as to who it was on the phone, even though he'd been reluctant to answer it himself.

'Sarah! Hello, love. Eeh, what's wrong? Sarah? What is it? Is it Billy?'

The front door opened. 'Oh, here's Billy now.'

A distraught Sarah begged Megan not to let Billy know it was her calling. Unsure how to cover up, or to let Jack know not to say it was Sarah, she turned her back on the front door and, with what she hoped wasn't too much hesitation, changed her voice and sent a grave look Jack's way. Her brain worked faster than she'd ever known it to as she said, 'No, like I were just saying, I didn't expect to see him today, but it's a lovely surprise to have him come over. It'll do Jack good an' all. He could do with some company to take his mind off things. How's Harry, love? Have you been back to the hospital?'

The agony of listening to Sarah's sobs whilst keeping up this pretence nearly undid Megan. But she knew she had to, and knew she'd to think of a way to get to Sarah an' all. Fears assaulted her, blocking her thoughts, but then an idea came to her and she voiced it as if speaking to Hattie. 'Aye, that'll be fine. No, it's no trouble. Yes, I know. But don't worry; knowing my menfolk, they'd rather have time without me. I'll set off now. I should be with you in an hour. No, we hadn't planned owt. Sarah and Billy didn't want to come to dinner, so we were going to have a light supper later.' Warming to her theme, she almost believed it herself. 'No, honest, love. None of us feel like eating much, anyroad. Just let me greet Billy. Poor lad gets home after six weeks away and his mam stands chatting to folk she could talk to anytime. See you in a while, eh?'

Jack looked at her, a question puzzling his face. Returning the receiver to its cradle, Megan ignored him and put her arms out to Billy. 'By, it's grand to see you, son, and you'll be a tonic for your Uncle Jack. He were a bit down just before you came.'

Billy's face held a tinge of red high on his cheekbones. His expression had its customary sour look, and he reluctantly allowed her to kiss his cheek. Without giving any of them time to react, Megan grabbed her coat from the stand next to her. 'Look, I have to dash.'

Crossing her fingers as she piled yet another lie onto the

others, she added, 'It appears Sally's stranded. She can't get that damn back door of the shop to lock. I'm the only one who seems able to do it! The others have all left, and Hattie can't go to help her as she's just leaving to visit Harry.' She'd reached the door when the thought came to her that she'd said to the imaginary Hattie that she would see her in a while. 'Once I've done that, Hattie asked if I'd come along to the hospital with Sally, and I said I would. You two have a good natter. Sarah won't be expecting you back that soon, will she, Billy?'

Billy grunted at this and shrugged his shoulders. His eyes bored into her. Megan's nerves clenched in fear. *Please, God, let me get to Sarah and help her before Billy decides to return home*. She was convinced he'd done something terrible to the poor lass.

Jack crossed over towards her, blocking Billy from her view. He spoke over his shoulder to Billy. 'Make yourself comfortable, son. I'll see as your mam's car's all right. There's a sharp frost in the air.' With his voice normal, but his face still questioning her, he opened the door for her. Once outside, he pulled the door closed behind them. 'What's going on, love? That weren't Hattie, were it?'

'No. Oh, Jack, it were Sarah.'

Jack's arms enclosed her. Megan clung onto him, drinking in his comfort and wanting to stay locked in his embrace and not have to face the awfulness of whatever Sarah was going through. Painful memories shuddered through her. 'I have to go to her, Jack. She were sobbing and begged me not to let Billy know she'd rung, but I know nothing more, as I had to talk over her and come up with what you heard. D'yer reckon as Billy knows it were her?'

'Naw, he couldn't. I had no idea and I even heard you say

'hello' to her. You had me right confused. Just get off, love, and do what you can. I'll keep Billy here till you phone. I feel like strangling him, but if it turns out it's just a tiff that's upset Sarah, she won't thank me and I'd end up making things worse.'

Megan agreed with this, though she'd an idea it wasn't a tiff. Not from what she'd heard. 'I'll contact you as soon as I can, love. Just so you know what's happening.'

Jack tightened his grip on her.

The trepidation that had been with Megan all day coiled deeper into her. 'Oh, Jack, I love you. Can you ever forgive me?'

'What for, lass? Thou's done nowt.'

'I have. I should've done more to prevent them marrying. I – I suspected Sarah was doing it out of fear, and now I know for certain she were. And I put that fear in her path, as I were the one as fought for Billy's release.'

'You did what any mam would do. Now I'll clear your windscreen and crank your engine for you. You have to hurry to Sarah, me little lass. You have to see as she is all right.'

'I love you, Jack Fellam.'

Once the engine jumped into life, spewing fumes from its exhaust and curling white billows of smoke into the frosty air, Jack took hold of her again. Megan clung to him, but as she did so, she saw the curtain move and knew Billy was watching them. Her blood ran cold through her veins.

'Well, lad, that were unexpected. One minute me and your mam are all settled for a quiet night, and the next she's gone out and you're here. I must say as I'm reet surprised to see you. Your mam said as you weren't up to coming round. Any-road, it's a good surprise. Come on through. Like always, there'll be a kettle on the boil. We'll have a pot of tea; it's near on freezing out there.'

Billy followed Jack into the kitchen with an uneasy mind. Something wasn't right. Jack had been mystified when the caller had turned out to be that Hattie. And he had a good idea why. He'd heard more than his mam had thought. Why would she say to Hattie, 'Is it Billy?'

Anger flared in him. Sarah – the bloody bitch! She'd telephoned his mam when he'd told her not to tell them. But he was stuck now. He'd need all the cunning he had used in that institution. *By, I had them fooled on many occasions.*

'I can't stay, Uncle Jack. I were tired, but I thought better of not coming to see you both. I wanted to say as I'm sorry about Issy. I know as it must have hit you and Mam hard.'

'Aye, it has. Ta, lad, that's reet kind of you. But take a minute to rest up. We've had a new foal delivered in the last hour and I've to go out to the stables. I thought you might come and take a look with me?'

'I would, but I promised Sarah I wouldn't be long. She wanted to come, but she's all in. Babby seems to be knocking her about. She couldn't stop being sick earlier, so I don't want to leave her for long. I just couldn't not come over to give you me condolences.'

'Well, what're you up to tomorrow, then? I'm up for a bit of shooting, if you are. There's not much around, but we might get lucky. Or we could just do some target practice – you used to like that when you were a lad.'

'Aye, I'm good at it an' all. You'd not stand a chance at beating me. I passed that part of me training easy.' A thought came to him that made the sweat stand out on him. It gave him the solution he needed. He'd seen his Uncle Jack's guns hanging on the wall of the storeroom, next to various types of saddles and stirrups and that kind of stuff, and above them on a shelf were boxes of ammunition.

Excitement tingled through him and shook his body. Yes, it was the only way out; he couldn't live, knowing that the minute his back was turned she'd be off with that Richard.

'Are you all right, son? Is everything reet with Sarah and you?'

For a moment he couldn't answer. A voice in his head screamed at a pitch that had him cringing against it. It tore painfully across his forehead. He wanted to rip it out of him, but he had to fight to keep calm. If he didn't, he'd not be able to carry out what the voice demanded. And he had to do that. It was the only way to rid himself of it.

Breathing in deeply, he managed to reply, 'No, I have one of me headaches. You know how bad they get. I'll have to get home and lie down for a bit.'

'Why not go into the posh parlour? There's that comfy sofa you could lie on, and I could ring Sarah and tell her.'

'No, I have to go.' It was taking him over. The intensity of it was like one of them explosions they had mocked up during training. Over and over he could hear, *Kill them . . . kill them both*. And he answered the thought, as understanding came to him. *Yes. Yes, that's it!* And he knew that by doing as the voice said he would find peace, his final peace. It was them – Sarah and his mam. They had done all of this to him, and he had to do them in. He had to.

'Billy. Billy, lad . . . Come on, now.'

With these concerned words, the heat cleared. A strange peace descended, giving Billy the knowledge of what he had to do. He needed to get out of here, find a gun and get on his way. To do that, he'd to sort out his Uncle Jack, and there was only one way. His eyes rested on the bronze statue of a woman and child standing on a shelf under an oval mirror – a fancy thing, too fancy for the likes of his mam. But then she considered herself something. Well, in this instance she'd provided him with his means of escape.

He had to look like he was playing along, then he could catch his Uncle Jack unawares. 'Thou knows, I think as I will have that pot of tea.'

'That's good, lad. Eeh, them pains have plagued you all your life. Thank goodness they've gone for now. How they let you through the medical, with your condition, beggars belief. Anyroad, let's go into the kitchen then.'

As Jack turned to lead the way, it took only a moment for Billy to curl his fingers around his chosen weapon. The resulting thud had a sickening note to it, and it didn't sit right with him to see this man he loved, beyond any, buckle and fall. But he'd to focus. He had a job to do.

The gun in his hand had a magnificent feel – clean-cut lines, two barrels, long and sleek, a lovingly carved stock and a chamber holding the bullets. Two, that's all he'd need, but he had more in his pocket and had taken only seconds to load it. He held it in readiness across his chest, his finger resting on the trigger. His pace quickened when he knew he was out of sight. His head burned again, giving him the message that he was right to do what he intended. They must die.

His ma had had it coming for a long time. He hated her. She hadn't protected him from his dad's brutal ways. She'd driven his dad to hate Jack, and driven himself to kill his dad to protect Jack. But he understood his dad now, because Sarah was doing the same thing: messing around. And with that arsehole – the man he despised more than any other, and had always done. He hated Richard's fucking guts. One day he'd do for him as well. Aye, one day. The thought warmed him; it'd give him something to live for after Sarah had gone.

The cottage came into view. Mam's car stood outside. Billy quickened his pace. The beads of sweat ran down his forehead and dripped off his brow, and some found their way into his open mouth and salted his tongue. The blinding pain was etched into him. His mind recalled the first time that pain had come to him, the exquisite sensation of it weeping from him once the thick branch smashed into that fat sod Bella's head. Her ugly, flat face swam before his eyes, then his dad's image came to him, and he heard the satisfying crunch as he squelched his dad's head to a pulp. The memory took some of the pain from the heat and increased the sense of facing his most magnificent moment; and with that came a clear knowledge of how he'd kill his mam and Sarah.

Taking his finger from the trigger, he let his hand glide along the polished stock of the gun until he held the cold steel of the double barrel. Gripping it with both hands, he sliced the air as if it were a sword. Adrenaline pumped around him. He'd never been so honed, felt so in tune with himself. His body had reached the higher level of his mind. Every sinew of him knew what part it had to play.

Entering the cottage yard brought the red mist back into him, almost as though it was a sponge soaking up his conscious thoughts, blocking his ability to think straight. He hadn't wanted this – not to be cut off by the red fog from the act of killing them.

His heart pounded in time with every step he took. Nothing about him wanted to hesitate, to think again. The redness commanded him, telling him that peace would come with his actions. As before, it would sear the feeling – the pleasure – onto his very soul. He'd remember it forever.

He moved with stealth. He could hear them; could hear Sarah's sobbing voice. 'I know, Aunt Megan, I know, but I feel me guilt. I love Richard beyond words, but I promised meself to Billy. I couldn't let him down. Oh, I've made such a mess of things and—'

The scream rose from deep in the pit of his bowel, surging the redness to the forefront of his brain and catapulting him into the room. Their shock gave their ugly gapes the likeness of the devil incarnate. His mam cowered beneath him – her terror-filled eyes reflected the blood-red that was swimming around his brain. Then he heard the squelching crunch as the butt of the gun smashed into her face.

Now the heat enclosed him. It comforted him, gave him more strength, congratulated him and urged him on. His mam's face had gone, and now her head split open and gushed blood all over him as his second blow finished her off. Spittle filled his mouth, thrill zinging through his veins. Never had he felt more alive. He turned towards Sarah. No sound came from her. She had slumped forward, her breasts squashed into rounded mounds meeting in a deep crevice. He would torture her, make her suffer like she'd made him suffer.

Sliding his hand along the barrel, he grabbed the stock. Sticky blood coated his fingers before they curled around the trigger. Pointing the gun at Sarah's head didn't get any re-action from her. Still she did not utter a sound, or close her gaping mouth. Had he ever thought her beautiful? He stuck the barrel into her mouth. 'You bitch! You've betrayed me.'

Her eyes widened, the look in them changing from one of horror to sheer terror. He remembered the gutting knife in his belt. He'd taken it from the shelf at the last minute. He whipped it from its sheath. The skin of her breast indented as he pressed the tip into it. A laugh gurgled up from his belly.

This was the best time of his life – better than killing the bitch at his feet; better than smashing his dad; better than when he'd killed Bella.

Yes, that's who Sarah reminded him of at this moment. He'd tell her: 'You look as ugly as that fat sod of a sister you had. Remember her?' His own laugh interrupted him again. He let it release, then looked back at her. He wanted to taunt her some more, but his laughter wouldn't stop. It hurt as it rebounded back at him. He cringed against it, hearing it echo around the room. He wanted to control it, but he couldn't. A weakness took him. He wanted to hit out at the image of his own face as it stared back at him from the mirror on the wall, hideous and twisted in mirth. But before he could, a great force pushed him and his body smashed into the wall. The laughter stopped, and he was crying.

Through his tears he saw the twisted and agonized face of his Uncle Jack and heard his thick holler, 'No! No!'

The sight of this man – the only good thing in his life – crumbling to the ground and crawling like an injured animal towards his mam tortured Billy's very soul and wrenched from him the realization that his beloved Uncle Jack hated him. *No, I can't take that. Don't, don't hate me – not you, not you!* Billy's hand reached out. He needed something to hold onto. The feel of polished wood sent a message through him. Now the cold steel of the barrel showed him clearly what he must do.

Through an excruciating haze of pain, Jack saw the glint of the barrel. He felt no fear; all emotion had frozen inside him. A crack resounded around the room and bounced off the walls. Sarah's scream reverberated with it and then died, turning into a helpless wail. Blood splattered Jack's face and ran along the floor towards him. Billy's hideous eyes stared at him. No face – just staring, glassy eyes.

He heard his own wailing join Sarah's and felt his body slump, leaving him with nothing inside him. His arm reached out and held the still-warm body of his Megan, and then his mind closed down. A deep black fog swirled inside his head and took him into nothingness.

31

Rita

The Flames of Hell

Rita looked towards where the rifle shot had come from. It was a normal sound for around these parts and one that wouldn't usually bother her, but it frayed her nerves more than they already were.

The bag she'd just placed in the undergrowth, next to where a supporting wooden beam stood out from the rough stones of the building, looked huge and highly visible. Hesitating, she wondered if she should squash it down, but that might mean the petrol seeped through onto her foot. Shaking with fear and indecision, she stood still, listening. The gunshot didn't seem to have disturbed anyone else.

Though it was only just on five o'clock, darkness had crept up and the air held a bitter sting in its coldness. The girls' voices came to her, giggling like children. They must be outside, but she had no idea why. Or were they in the stable itself? Blimey, if they were, she'd have to get them out of there before she left them.

Trying to summon some courage, she moved away from the wall and strode out around the barn. Now the girls' location became clear. The floodlit yard showed the stable door ajar, and she heard their squeals of delight and an annoyed snort from one of the horses.

Heading towards the entrance of the stable, she glanced up at the house. A light shone from the top of the door and from one of the rooms to the right of it, but there was no car in the drive. She supposed one of them must be out. She wished they both bleedin' were. She didn't want any folk around when she did the deed. Not that she could help the girls being here, but she just hoped none of them came out with heroics to try and save the animals. She couldn't have anyone being hurt on her conscience; it was bad enough to think of the poor bleedin' horses. But then what was a bit of animal flesh, compared to her ticket to a better life?

'Ahh, he's lovely. Look at him. I can't believe he can stand, and him only a few hours old.' This was from the young one, Iris.

'Oh, they are not like our babies. He will be half as big as his mother in a few weeks.' The replying voice was that of Louise, the posh one.

Jealousy still lay in Rita over Louise. She had everything – looks and money – and now she was going to take bleedin' Terence if she'd read the signs right. It was Louise who spotted her looking in the door.

'Rita! Gracious, they haven't brought you over in the car, have they?'

'Fat chance of that. Me, in the toff's bleedin' car? I don't think that's going to happen. No, I walked over. Got a bit fed up. I've never been in such a boring place in all me life as that Hensal Grange. What you up to? You were all gawking and cooing over something. I could have crept up on yer and murdered the lot of yer.'

'We've had a foal born last night. Come and look. He's beautiful.'

'Nah, I ain't interested in bleedin' animals. Besides, I'm freezing. Any chance of a cup of Rosie Lee?'

'Yes, love. Come on – come up to our flat. It's lovely and warm up there.' Mildred came over to her and linked arms with her. 'We'll make you more than a *cap*, as you call it. We'll make you a pot full.' They all laughed at this.

She'd found that Mildred and Iris were the friendliest of these girls, but all of them seemed a cut above her and Penny. Although they were all from down south, she and Penny were the only ones from the East End.

'I won't come up,' Louise said. 'Terence said the car would be here for me between four-thirty and five. That's why I thought it had brought you, Rita.'

The twinge of hurt she felt at Louise assuming she would be brought over here by the family chauffeur was nothing to what hit her when, in answer to her question as to the reason the car was coming, Louise replied, 'I'm invited to dinner with him and his family at Hensal Grange.'

Seething with jealousy, she couldn't keep the sarcasm from her voice. 'Oh, well, I hope you has a nice time, I'm sure.'

'I'm sorry – have I offended you in any way, Rita? I didn't mean to.'

Offended her! She could have scratched the girl's eyes out, and Terence bleedin' Crompton's, the bastard! As it were, she felt like saying: *Yes, you have actually, as your so-called fancy man is having the bleedin' time of his life with me, whenever he fancies. And at this moment he's probably having a go at Penny!*

The thought of that fuelled Rita's temper even more. Terence had come across the yard just as she was leaving. He'd saved the day, as it happened, as she had Penny in tow and didn't know how to get rid of her. He'd said he wanted to talk to Penny, explaining that he'd not had a chance to get to know her, and had steered her into the barn.

As she'd left them, all she could think of was the bed up in the loft. It had taken all her effort not to have a go at him. She'd wanted to, just like she did now with Louise, but the thought of the threats Terence had made stopped her. If she was to get out of this with what she wanted, she'd have to carry out his instructions to the letter – and spoiling his chance with this posh bitch didn't come into that. He'd been a different bloke when he'd come on rough to her, holding her in an armlock and warning of the consequences, and she believed he'd meant it.

Putting a cheeky smile on her face, Rita told Louise, 'Nah, I'm not offended. It's me way. Take no notice of me.'

Dorothy made and poured the tea. As she took it from her, Rita wished that she dared take three heaped spoons of sugar to steady her nerves, but the stuff was getting hard to come by and there was talk of rationing, so she just took one and stirred it well.

Sitting having a laugh with them all eased some of her dread until Dorothy said, 'Has anyone heard Jack come back yet?'

Mildred and Iris shook their heads. 'I heard a car just now, but I reckon as that was Louise leaving. Why?'

'It just seemed funny how they all left, that's all. That son of Mrs Fellam's arrived, then she took off like she was in a hurry; not ten minutes later the son left, then not long after that Jack tore across the yard and jumped the fence by the barn over there. He was running like something possessed across the fields – or, I should say, staggering in a hurried fashion towards Sarah's cottage.'

Iris, her eyes wide, said, 'I don't like that Billy. He seems surly.'

'Nah, and he ain't one to like, neither. He's a murderer.'

'What?'

Three voices said this in shocked unison. Rita was stunned to realize they didn't know. How could they have missed all the tales about him? But then this farm was four or so miles from the village, so they might not hear the gossip. 'He's killed two, as I heard, and I can see as none of you know about it. Well, it happened a long time ago.'

By the time she'd told them all she knew, Iris was quivering, Mildred sat with her mouth open, and Dorothy looked as though Rita had told her a bomb would drop any minute. Dorothy found her voice first: 'Oh God! It doesn't seem possible. I mean, Jack's let him marry his daughter!'

'I know. And I have it at first hand as Billy's still dangerous. I've seen him rape someone.'

'Rape!'

'Yes, Mildred. I keep me bleedin' nose into everything as goes on and I snoop around – and that's not all I've seen. It's bleedin' fantastic what these country folk get up to, I'll tell yer. London ain't got nuffing on them up here, and that's with all the gangsters and the barrow boys, and everything you can think of to compare it with.'

A whimper took their attention. Iris, white-faced and trembling, sat huddled in her chair, tears running down her face.

'Aw, come 'ere, love. You're safe. He ain't no random killer. He has to have something against yer. Don't be worrying.'

The tone of Dorothy's voice as she said, 'I'm worried – I'm scared out of my wits' sent a chill through Rita's bones, and her voice shook as she asked, 'Why's that, Dorothy?'

'Well, why should all three – Mrs Fellam, her son and Jack – go towards the cottage one after the other, not together, and all looking agitated?'

'That's not all. Oh my God!'

'What is it, Mildred?'

Mildred's face had paled. 'I – I came out of the stables for a few minutes to have a fag. Just as I got to the door, I saw that son of Mrs Fellam's coming out of the storeroom. He – he had a gun!'

''Ere, come on. Don't be daft. He was probably going shooting.'

'No, Rita. Something is wrong.'

'Look, if there is, there's nuffing you lot can do now, is there?'

'If you want to go to the cottage, I'll come with you, Dot.'

This from Mildred set Rita feeling agitated. They'd expect her to go with them, but she couldn't. Her frantic brain sought a good reason why not, and suddenly one occurred. 'Well, I think you're daft and will look stupid if you turn up and they're all sitting enjoying a cup of tea. What're you going to say then, eh? Besides, what about Iris, 'ere? She's scared out of her wits. You can't leave her alone.'

'Will you stay with her? We'll be back as soon as we can. It takes about twenty minutes to reach the cottage and get back.'

'Well, I think you're out of your minds. It'll only look as though you're poking your noses into family business and—'

'I don't care. I just feel something is wrong. I don't know what, but I'm going over to that cottage, and that's that.'

'All right, keep your hair on. I'll stay, but I can't stay for long. I have to be back to bed the cows down.'

'You won't leave me, Rita, if they're not back, will you? Promise me you won't leave me?'

'Nah, if they're not back, I'll take you with me. How's that? Then it will serve them right when they have to fetch yer.'

She'd hardly said this when the door closed behind Mildred and Dorothy. *Bloody hell, what do I do now?*

Terence sat in his car, his limbs stiff with cold. His fingers, though encased in gloves, were aching and tingling. His breath curled like smoke, causing patches of mist on the iced windows. *Where is that bitch? God, I'll kill her if she flunks this.*

And what would it look like if he didn't have the fire as his reason for not being home when Louise arrived? His parents would be furious.

He'd spent half an hour with the virgin, Penny, doing what he called 'priming' her, giving her a few kisses, compliments and endearments, all said and done with gentleness and easily pretended. He'd found her innocence – and, yes, her vulnerability – more than appealing. It wasn't long before he was no longer putting on an act, as Penny had begun to have a deep effect on him. It had been her shy and confused reaction that had prompted him to take things easy with her, for fear of spoiling something quite unique, and which, he knew, would be better for the waiting. Getting out of the house afterwards had been a simple matter: a message left for the parents to say he had remembered that he was due at a late-afternoon parish council meeting, but he'd be back in plenty of time to greet Louise. Not being there was out of the question – a faux pas of the worst order. And now it would happen. He'd seen the family car pick Louise up, but there was nothing he could do about it. The moment had him sweating with fear that their driver would have to wait and might get out and wander around, but Louise had come out of one of the stables the moment the car glided to a halt.

Now he sat here like a bloody idiot. Where the hell was Rita?

One thing had pleased him: he'd passed Mrs Fellam going out in her car, and then just as he got here, he'd seen Fellam crossing the field towards their daughter's cottage. All a bit strange, he thought, as they'd left the door to the house open. Then, just now, two of the Land Girls had left and gone that way, too. Still, he couldn't worry about whatever had taken them all away; at least none of them would be around to do anything about the fire or, worse, would be hurt in any way by it. Though there was one other girl who must still be here. Oh God, the fact that someone might get hurt hadn't really occurred to him before. But no, he couldn't start imagining something like that. He'd get help here before anyone tried any heroics. That's if there even was a bloody fire! *Come on, Rita, for Christ's sake.*

Sitting back and trying to relax his taut sinews, Terence thought about how, for the first time since he'd been a member of the parish council, it had been of use to him. His father had put him forward for the job once he could no longer continue in the role himself. Not that the role meant anything – not to him, it didn't. He rarely attended their bloody meetings. Oh, he'd put his face around the door, but always with a ready excuse. After looking at the agenda, he'd give his views on each item and then leave.

Pater might or might not know there was no meeting, but that was of no real consequence. He would understand why Terence had used this as an excuse when he presented them with the made-up reason he'd had to leave – one he could not share, for fear of upsetting Mater. He would say he'd come to the farm because he had suspicions over something Rita had said to him. Which brought him to the last part of his plan: that, as he drove up to Fellam's farm, he could see the flames, and all his fears came true.

He'd tell them that when he got nearer, he saw Rita standing watching the flames take hold, then turn and run away. He'd then say he stopped and ran towards the fire, but it was already too fierce for him to tackle. And, this was the best bit: with Fellam out of the way, he could say he went to the house to raise the alarm, but no one answered; and, in his panic, he didn't think of using their phone, even though the door was open. So rather than waste any more time, he drove home as quickly as he could to phone for help. He smiled to himself at this, because he knew that however quickly he got help to the scene, it wouldn't save the stable – not with it being seventy per cent wood, and dry at that. So his mission would be accomplished. And more than that, Rita would be out of his hair.

As to Rita's alleged motive, that had been a bit more difficult to come up with. He'd come to the conclusion that he would have to shame himself a little. He would say he'd had an attraction for her when she'd first arrived, and he'd been silly enough to show it and confide in her his dearest wish to have his own stud farm and tell her the reason why he couldn't have it. Then, he would make out, the girl had become obsessed with him and had tried many tricks to compromise him. Even to the point of making herself useful to his sister, having seen how close Theresa and he were.

He'd say Rita would hang around him, making any excuse to talk to him, and – out of politeness and because he had given her the wrong impression, and because of his desire not to hurt or embarrass her – he'd made time for her, while being careful to keep to propriety. He'd go on to say that he had begun to sense her sexual frustration, and she'd got to the point where she would say things like 'I'll do anything for you, guv – anything. You only have to ask, yer know.' He'd say that at first he thought she was offering him sexual favours, which had prompted him to distance himself from her and to be very cold and businesslike in his dealings with her. But it hadn't worked, and Rita had started to intimate that she could help him in his quest to achieve his dream.

He'd tell them that although he'd had fears, he couldn't discuss them with anyone – he would have looked foolish, and there was nothing he could back it up with, other than his own concerns and intuition.

The final nail in her coffin would be relaying his suspicions about what Rita intended and how he had been alarmed when, after telling him she was going to visit the girls over at Fellam's, he'd found that the drum of petrol kept for the tractors had been interfered with. The cap had been left off, and there were small stains of petrol on the floor leading out of the shed. This part of his story would have the ring of truth, as he'd asked Earnshaw if he knew anything about what he'd discovered. Of course he did, as Terence had made sure he was around to see Rita coming out of the shed.

He would need Penny on his side. She knew too much about his relationship with Rita, and that mustn't come out. But he felt confident that he could get her to keep quiet. If she didn't play ball, he'd say she was a liar; that Rita ruled Penny and made her tell lies about him. He would be believed. After all, he was the son of a lord. Rita and Penny were just East End scum.

He also needed to account for his own presence at

Fellam's, so he'd worked out to say that, whilst getting ready for dinner and mulling over the incident of the tampered petrol, he'd had a horror-struck moment when Rita's real intentions had dawned on him – she'd said she would help in his quest to achieve his dream! Could that mean she intended to destroy the main obstacle standing in his way? Hence he'd made his excuses and dashed over to Fellam's. It was fantastic, and the story was flawless – except that he'd been here ten minutes already and the bloody deed hadn't yet been done. Christ! How was he going to explain the time-lapse?

Taking his glove off and running his finger around his collar, Terence flinched at the cold touch of it, as his agitation mounted. *Such a perfect plan, with every bloody 'i' dotted and every 't' crossed, and that . . . that—*

His thoughts were suspended as the barn door opened and Rita appeared. Hardly breathing, he watched her make her way around the back of the stables. He waited a moment. When she didn't reappear, he got out of the car and hurried after her.

It was done! The flames licked at the wooden prop, caught the grass and took hold quicker than he could have imagined. Elation gripped him, but so did fear about his position. Running like he'd never run before, he made it back to his car in seconds. He cranked the engine, which, still being warm, fired up on the first turn of the starting handle. *Thank God!*

Sweating in a lower-class way that appalled him, he reversed out into the space behind the barn, his wheels spinning on the pebbled surface. *Please, God, don't let me get stuck now.*

32

Louise & Terence,
Dorothy & Iris

A Searing End to an Era

'M'Lord, there is a Land Girl from Fellam's at the door, with some distressing news that requires your urgent attention.'

Lady Crompton jumped in, before Lord Crompton could answer. 'Really? Oh, dear, where is Terence? Where *is* he?'

Louise stood up and went over to Lady Crompton's chair. Sitting on the stool next to it, she said, 'I am sure he is all right, Lady Crompton.' Then, turning to Lord Crompton, she asked, 'Would you like me to see who it is, and what is wrong?' Her heart pounded with worry. What could have happened? They were all safe when she'd left.

'Thank you, dear, but I think we should have the girl sent in. Please see to it, Frobisher.'

'Yes, m'Lord.'

Comforting his wife, Lord Crompton sat on the arm of her chair and put his arm around her. 'Daphne, my love, please don't upset yourself too much. Let's hear what has gone on first, shall we? It can't possibly have anything to do with Terence. He is at a meeting. It's very bad form of him, and not like him at all not to be home when he has a guest. But that doesn't mean you should jump to conclusions, dear.'

A tap on the door stopped the speculation, because when it opened, Frobisher announced Mildred. One look told of her anguish. Louise ran to her. 'My dear, what is it?'

'Mrs Fellam . . . Jack . . . Sarah . . . Oh God!'

'What? Has something happened to them?'

Mildred's body swayed. 'Oh, Louise. Megan, sh – she's dead!'

'Oh my God!'

This, from Lord Crompton, increased the goosebumps on Louise's skin. She opened her mouth, but nothing came out. Mildred, having released the shocking news, revealed everything she'd seen. 'He's dead, too, that son of hers; and Sarah's in a bad way. She's obviously been beaten and she's in shock, curled up like an animal in a corner of the room. And Jack, poor Jack. He – he's just rocking back and forth, and a terrible noise is coming from him. His m – mouth is frothing, and his eyes . . . Oh, Louise.'

Lord Crompton was by her side, and together they caught Mildred. Neither could speak as they helped her to a chair, but before they could gather themselves to say or do anything, the door crashed open and stopped them.

Terence, looking just as distraught as the rest of them, stood framed in the open doorway. 'Pater. Oh, Pater, there's . . .' His head swivelled and he gaped at Mildred.

'We know. Dear God, how did it happen?'

'How can *you* know? Where did *she* come from? She couldn't have got here before—'

'What are you talking about, Terence? Look, we've no

time. I have to telephone the police and an ambulance. Where have you been? You're never here when we need you!'

Terence looked from Louise to his father's retreating back, then back to Louise. His face held utter bewilderment. She sought to enlighten him. 'There's been . . . Look, something appalling has happened.'

'I know, but how could this young woman have got here before me? I—'

'I was at the cottage, sir. I saw them – the bodies . . . the blood . . . Oh—'

Louise only just managed to get out of the way of the vomit that exploded from Mildred's mouth. A moan behind her had her turning and, seeing the state of Lady Crompton, she shouted at Terence, 'See to your mother, Terence. She has had a massive shock.'

'But . . . ?'

'Frobisher, we need water for Lady Crompton and for my friend Mildred. And please bring someone to clear up this mess.'

Behind her, Louise heard Terence speaking. 'Mater, dear, it will be all right. Come on, my dear.' As she turned to look at him, his face had a bewildered expression. 'What was the girl on about? The – the cottage? I came to tell of a fire.'

'What? Oh dear, everything is so confusing. I'll tell you what I know, but a fire?'

'Yes. Dear God, where is Pater? We need to get everyone fighting it . . . The horses. That bloody Rita, she—'

'Look, Terence—'

'Whatever it is will have to wait, Louise. I have to phone the fire brigade. I have to get help.'

When Terence returned, followed by his father, who now looked as though someone had punched him in the stomach,

Louise told him what Mildred had said. At the end of her telling, she thought Terence would faint. His face had the pallor of death. His mouth hung open and he dropped his head into his hands.

'What is your news about a fire? Where? And what girl? Terence, please, I have to know.'

After hearing him out, Louise felt sick. Had the world gone mad? Two deaths and a fire – and God knew how many horses. *And the new foal . . . It is all unbearable, unbelievable.*

Dorothy held onto Jack's body. Her own body trembled, and her eyes held the unspeakable horror of the room, even when she closed them against it. She'd tried to get near Sarah, but Sarah had kicked out and screamed 'No!' in an awful, howling wail, whilst shrinking away from her. But although this meant Dorothy hadn't been able to comfort her physically, she hadn't given up trying to coax Sarah out of the blank stare fixed on her face. Using gentle words of reassurance, which she didn't feel, brought about no change in Sarah.

Inside, Dorothy begged and begged for someone to come. *Anyone, but please, please come.* Make the horror go away, or remove her from it.

'Jack. Come on, Jack, let's get downstairs, eh? Will you help me with Sarah? We need to get her out of here. Please, Jack.' His head felt heavy on her shoulder as he cringed against what she'd asked of him. Oh, why had Mildred run? Why hadn't she used the phone here? But then, Dorothy couldn't blame her. If it hadn't been for the pull of Jack on her heart, she'd have run, too – run as far away as she could.

These thoughts showed her what needed doing, and made her realize she was behaving just as stupidly. It must be the shock. The practical side of her had closed down, as she'd responded only to the emotions surging through her, making her want to comfort and make things right for the man she loved. Yes, she could admit it now. Feelings that had lain dead inside her, since her husband had died in the accident, had been rekindled the moment she'd first laid eyes on Jack. Working with him on a daily basis had deepened the strength of the emotions he had awoken in her. Finding him like this, sitting in a hell she thought none of them would ever recover from, and with his life in devastation all around him, it had only occurred to her to console and reassure Jack. But now she knew she must do something to get help, and not just rely on Mildred doing so.

Easing Jack's body away from her, she rested him against the wall. There was no protest in his hollow moans. Straightening her stiff limbs to get the life back into them took her a moment, and then she stood up. Without looking over to where the two bloodied, staring-eyed corpses lay, she made her way out of the room and down the stairs.

The operator took an age to answer. When she finally heard 'What number do you require?' all she could do was gasp, 'Help me, help me!'

'What's wrong, lass? Tell me as clear as you can. Is it police you want? Where are you? Give me the number you are calling from.'

She read out the number written in the centre of the dial on the phone. When she stated the address, she was relieved to hear the girl say, 'Oh, right, love. Well, there is help on the way. I've dealt with calls about the trouble at that cottage already. Lord Crompton made them, and about the fire, so don't worry – someone'll be with you soon. So what's happened then? Only his Lordship didn't give me details or owt.'

'I – I'm sorry. I—'

Dorothy replaced the receiver, unable to engage in conversation about what was happening. All that mattered was that help was on the way. But then a question came to her. Fire? What fire? Suddenly she registered that the windows were lit with an unnatural light for this time of the evening. Looking out, she saw the glow of a huge fire coming from the direction of the stud farm, and it was too much for her to take in. Slumping against the wall, she slid to the floor. *Oh God, no . . . No!*

For a moment her mind couldn't sort out all the horror around her, and in its confusion it told her stories of invasion, of bombs, of troops of German soldiers torching buildings. But then another thought hit her: *Iris and Rita . . . the horses. Please let them be safe!*

Iris woke and looked around her. Her head hurt. Had Rita hit her with something? No, she wouldn't. Why would she? But what had caused the blow to her head when she'd turned to go across to the kitchen area? And where were the others?

Fear clutched at her. Her head began to clear and to give her a picture of events: Louise leaving; Dorothy worrying about the family and thinking something was wrong; Rita being agitated at Dorothy and Mildred leaving. Then, when they were alone, Rita being cross with her for being afraid to stay alone on the farm. Rising to make a pot of tea, then feeling a massive blow on her head.

When she stood on shaky legs and tried to move, her foot hit something on the floor. *A brass candlestick.* It must have been Rita! Rita had hit her, but why?

Unshed tears of panic made her eye sockets feel as though they'd filled with sand. Only one candle remained alight. It flickered, its wick having reached a pool of melted wax. The thought of it going out spurred Iris into action. She must find another candle. She couldn't bear the darkness; she'd not survive that. But then it wasn't dark . . . why? Everything in the room glowed. Not with a still glow, but a dancing yellow glow.

When she got to the window, what she saw halted her thoughts and gave release to the scream she'd knotted inside her since waking. Flames licked the black sky. The sound of crackling and spitting penetrated her mind and mingled with the terrified neighing of the horses. Her thoughts filled with the beautiful beasts, their huge liquid eyes and the pleasure they gave her when they nudged her body whilst she fed and groomed them. *No! No, they can't die!*

Smoke swirled around Iris, catching and burning her throat, smarting her eyes and making it difficult for her to see. But she didn't care. Nor did she heed the searing heat as she neared the stable. Only the desperate, terrified screams of the horses pierced her thoughts.

Once nearer the building, she saw that one half of it wasn't yet alight. There was a door at the far end, and if she could get to it, she could release the horses from the bays in which they were trapped.

Close to the door, another sound confused her. A pounding sound. The doors rocked on their hinges to its rhythm. As she lifted the latch, sudden clarity came to her, but it came too late. A huge, powerful, petrified horse stampeded towards her. Her body hit the ground. A tremendous weight crushed her. Pain stung every part of her until a zinging noise enclosed her and the light around her became blackness – a blackness that sucked at everything she was, before swallowing her into its raging, swirling centre.

33

Hattie

A Final Goodbye

Hattie stood by the open grave, a lone figure, too encased in grief to cry and too drained to think. Megan's coffin lay on top of Issy's. 'She'll be a comfort to you, Megan, lass.' The words croaked from her parched throat.

Is this what happens when your heart is splintered? At this moment it felt as if hers was damaged beyond repair, and it wouldn't be possible to feel anything ever again. But then, she did feel something: she felt hate – a hate so vivid it consumed her, and it was directed at Billy.

Why had they been afflicted with him? How could someone so blackened by evil have come from Megan's pure self? From a young age he'd vandalized the lives of Issy, Jack and Megan, and now he'd done the same to hers. He'd deprived her of so much that she held close to her heart. He'd torn her apart.

Oh, Megan. Megan . . .

Her body folded. Strong arms grasped her. They'd all stood back, allowing her a moment, but now Richard was by her side. 'Hattie, come away now. You're frozen.' He held her close to him.

A wet droplet hit her cheek. It had fallen from his eyes, and felt like one of those wax seals must feel to the paper they stamped. Because the tear stamped her with a seal of sadness that she thought she would never let go of.

As Richard turned her away, she saw Edward holding Bridget: two figures stilled by grief. And beyond them, a crowd of about one hundred stood with their heads bowed, all of them from Breckton. Miners, their wives and the Irish community were paying their respects to two of their own: two women who had made their mark through love and character. And there, too, were the business folk of Breckton, as well as the remaining four Land Girls.

Anger seared Hattie as she looked at these girls. Anger at the one called Rita, who'd caused so much devastation. How glad she was that Rita was now locked up. *I hope she never gets out while I'm alive!* And anger mixed with pity at the terrible injuries caused to the poor lass who had tried to save the horses. She was in a bad way, and not expected to live.

Neither Jack nor Sarah were there. Both remained in hospital – Jack all but shut down, and Sarah a trembling bundle of fear who could barely function. And no Harry. Poor Harry seemed weaker by the minute. Oh God, where had her world gone?

As Richard guided her away, Hattie looked back. The wind swayed the naked boughs of the tree under which the grave lay. She felt the same back-and-forth movement going on inside her, churning her up and taking her in one direction and then the other. But her heart jolted her as she turned and saw a figure dressed all in black, standing on the edge of everything. Arthur! He'd come to support her. She'd have to go to him – she needed to.

'Richard, there's someone I need to talk to. Will you tell

everyone as them at Hensal Grange have put on a wake, and as everyone's welcome?'

'Yes, but are you sure you will be all right?'

'I will, ta, love. I have an old friend as has come to be with me. I'll come up to the Grange in a little while. You go and look after your mam and dad. Poor Bridget. She's taken this hard.'

'She has. Her happiness seemed complete on finding her daughter, Megan. It was strange for me at the time to have this older half-sister suddenly, but Megan brought me so much love and seemed to bring sunshine into all of our lives.'

'Oh, Richard, we'll get through this, lad. We'll get through.'

'But what about Sarah? Hattie, it was all my fault.'

'No, lad. No one knew more than Megan what you were both going through. You just be there for Sarah, lad. It's going to take her a long time, thou knows. But if she has you – the man she loves – watching out for her, that's going to help.'

'You knew?'

'Megan told me.'

'Megan knew?'

'Aye, and she weren't without feeling guilty, bless her. She thought she should have stopped the wedding. But no one could change Sarah's mind. Poor lass.'

'I think it was because of her fear. She knew if she crossed Billy, this would happen. She went through with the marriage to prevent it, then I—'

'Richard, you must stop this. You've got to, lad. Guilt can consume you, and you've no time for that, neither can you give time to it. You have to be strong. I can't do this on me own. I need you to help me to prop up Sarah and Jack, and there's no one better.'

'Thank you, Hattie. I'll try. I promise you, I'll try. I'll just go to Mother and Father now. I'll see you up at the Grange.'

Hattie watched him go. For all her words, she knew Richard did carry some of the blame on his shoulders, and he deserved to. He'd taken what was forbidden. But then hadn't they all? No. She'd not think of him as deserving guilt, for Sarah had kissed him back. Her ramblings had told Hattie that much. And two people who loved each other, snatching an illicit kiss, didn't deserve what it had brought down on them two. No one did.

'Hattie, I don't know what to say.'

'There's nowt anyone can say, Arthur. Me world has been shredded. I've nothing left.'

'You have me, my love. I'm back. I'm here for you.'

'Oh, Arthur. It's not reet that you can get through all of this pain and give me a warm spot of hope. It's not reet for me to feel that.'

'I know, but I'm glad you do. You have a lot to deal with. Don't shut me out. I don't expect anything other than to be your friend, for the time being.'

'And that's what I need most in all the world, as two of me best ones lie back there in that grave, and my Harry is fading fast. If you can replace them in just a small way, then I'd welcome you back into me life on that basis. Don't expect more from me, though.'

'My love for you is not a selfish love. I know that now. It can manifest in many ways and can adjust to what you most need, my dear.'

'At this moment, I – I want help. Help me, Arthur, help me; please take away my pain.'

She was in his arms. He held her close. As wrong as it was,

it felt so right that he should come back to her when she most needed him. And, despite everything, Hattie hoped with everything that was in her that Arthur would never leave her again.

34

Theresa

Another Curtain Falls

'Terence, I know what it is I want to do.'

'About what, darling? Move up a little. I know you need a lot of room, but you needn't take up all of the bed.'

Shifting her bulk as best she could, Theresa moved over. *Not long now. Four weeks at the most and I will be rid of this curse in my womb – rid of the longing, and love, I have for it.* Banishing these thoughts that hurt so much, Theresa answered Terence, 'About my life after. And this is going to shock you. I am going to join up.'

'Good gracious!'

'I know, but I have this overwhelming urge to help since that awful Dunkirk business. If we are going to win this foul thing, we should all do our bit.'

'Don't look at me. I am "doing my bit", thank you very much. Supporting Jack Fellam with the running of his farm, as well as Hensal Grange estate, is war work.'

'Oh, I know. Anyway, how are Fellam and his daughter? God, what a bloody awful thing. Even though it rid us – and the world, come to that – of that evil bastard Billy Armitage, and of the threat Rita had become, it must have been hell to go through.'

'Fellam gets through each day, and that's about it. His daughter seems as though she doesn't exist. She's empty, vacant. Oh, I don't know, it is hard to describe. That chap in the RAF, some relation or other – or at least he was a relation to Fellam's wife – seems to have a thing for her. He's stationed at Biggin Hill, one of Churchill's lot that we all owe so much to. He comes up whenever he has a minute off. Or it seems that way, according to what Louise—'

'Louise, Louise, bloody Louise!'

'Look, be reasonable, darling. You know I have to see her. God, she is the only one keeping things going on Fellam's farm. Well, with the sterling help of Dorothy, that is. You remember – the older one, widowed or some such. Anyway, besides coping almost on their own, Louise helps me with Fellam's three remaining horses, which I am caring for at our stables. That other poor girl who was injured so badly has finally gone home from hospital.'

'Oh? She recovered then?'

'Well, she'll be disfigured for life, and her mind is affected. The evidence she was able to give helped to convict that evil Rita, and it was accepted that what she could remember was consistent with her injuries. The doctor who was giving evidence said that the girl had received a single blow to the head, apart from possibly banging it when the horse charged her. She'll never walk again, poor thing. So no, I wouldn't say she has recovered.'

'And you have no conscience about any of it? God, Terence, you take the biscuit!'

'Why should I have?'

'Oh, come off it. Don't tell me you didn't plant the idea in Rita's mind. I know we wanted rid of her, but we said we would use Armitage. What changed your mind?'

'I didn't. I told you, I threatened Rita with setting Armitage on her. That's when she said she'd put things right for me, and would never cause me harm. Anyway, that bitch has got all she deserves, and I hope she rots in prison. What if anyone had believed her story? My God, it doesn't bear thinking about!'

'Well, they didn't. They believed yours, so you are nice and safe. Bet you miss her, though. Between visits to me, that is?'

'No, well, actually, I have been meaning to tell you . . . Penny—'

'Bloody hell, Terence, you bastard! Do tell.'

Listening to his conquest of 'the virgin' stirred feelings inside Theresa. She snuggled closer to her twin.

With her so near her time, and finding love-making uncomfortable, they'd reverted to their old ways of giving pleasure to each other. Terence knew her needs. And her love for him knew no bounds.

As Terence lay back and drew deeply on his cigarette, stroking the hair of a contented Theresa who was now resting her head on his chest, he thought about Penny. She'd turned out to be something! 'Giving' was the word he'd use, and grateful – a loving combination. Something he hadn't experienced before and found he enjoyed. Yes, Penny was more than a substitute for the artful Rita.

These musings left him suddenly, as his mind registered what Theresa had said. His curiosity piqued, he asked, 'So, which force are you going to join?'

Theresa lifted her head and looked at him. 'You needn't sound so amused. Anyway, pass me your ciggie; I need some smoke in my lungs.'

He watched the tip of the cigarette light up as she drew on it, and waited as she exhaled the smoke.

'The army.'

'For goodness' sake, Theresa, stop being silly. Join some volunteer group or something if you must, not the army!' The agitated puff that he took of his cigarette filled his lungs and calmed him. He felt immediate regret at his sharpness with her. 'Sorry, old thing, didn't mean to snap. Come here, snuggle up to me.'

'No, I'm all sweaty. I'm going to take a bath. And you may as well get used to the idea, as my mind is made up. There is no point in you even trying to change it. The minute I recover from dropping this beast inside me, I'm signing on the dotted line.'

'But you can't. I won't let you. Theresa, this is a silly notion. You going out to save the world – you're not equipped. You'll get yourself killed. No, I won't allow it and neither will Pater, and it would be the end of Mater!'

Her look held disdain. 'The least said about anything I do affecting Mater, the better. I'm angry. Boiling angry at the way our lives are dictated by how everything will impact on Mater. That maxim has ruled us for far too long, Terence. We have to stand up against it. I'm going to.'

Terence had no argument against this and, by the look on Theresa's face, she would brook none. *I'll leave the question alone for now. There's plenty of time. Theresa will forget this silly notion.* Feeling sure of this as he listened to the bath water running, he stubbed out his cigarette and lay back to relax. He felt at one with himself. His future looked bright. He'd ridded them both of the evil Rita – though there had been a few hairy moments during the trial, especially when the defence council had tied him in knots.

Sweat broke out over him at the thought of the moment when he thought the truth would come out. But then Penny – poor smitten Penny – had saved the day. She'd told the court that Rita was lying about her relationship with him. That she'd never seen Terence Crompton act in any way other than politely and respectfully towards them both. That she knew Rita fantasized over her relationship with their boss going further, but she never witnessed anything that made her think anything had happened between them.

Smiling, Terence thought of Rita's horror and defeated look as she listened to this. *Ha, I owe a lot to you, Penny, and I'm going to see that you get your dues. In fact, I'll take great pleasure in giving you what you most desire.*

Laughing now, Terence swung his legs off the bed. Going to the bathroom, he looked at his beautiful sister. Her naked body half-immersed in the water was wet and shiny, and her hair hung in dripping strands, as if she'd dunked her head. Her face looked angelic. An overwhelming love for her swept over him. Kneeling beside the bath, he traced the mound of her stomach. The child within moved, as if to acknowledge him.

Terence's heart lurched. The love he felt wasn't solely for Theresa. Taking his hand away, he stood up. *What is the matter with me? I must suppress this feeling I have for this unborn child. I have to . . .*

35

Harry & Hattie

Harry Gives his All for Love

Hattie stood by Harry's bed. The hospital ward was hushed around her, the silence broken only by the soft tread of the nuns and Harry's laboured breathing.

Dear Harry, how strong he'd been for her through these last painful months.

Every day Hattie had thought her spirit would be crushed under the burden of it all. How had it come to this? But she couldn't dwell on it, couldn't think of the horror of what had happened and her devastation – the loss of her life as she'd known it. Everything, everything as she knew it, had gone.

A further thread had snapped when Sally joined up. Not that she'd have it any different, as the lass wanted to do her bit, and Hattie was proud of her for it. But it beggared belief – Sally knowing all that French stuff and studying books, so she could actually use it to help in the war effort. A translator, her Sally! Still, she was safe in what she was doing, which wouldn't have been the case if she'd been to France and knew of the life they lived and the country's geography. Then they'd have had her over there, doing God-knows-what, most likely in constant danger. Sally was upset that she hadn't been accepted for such work, but she enjoyed the job they'd given her. Eeh, she'd always known as Sally was a clever lass; it had shown in how quickly she'd caught up with her learning, once she'd come back to Hattie. From that time, Hattie had thought Sally was really meant to work with her head, not her hands, even though she did a good job with both.

Aye, and I've to do the same, if I'm to keep everything going. Megan's factory, as well as me and Harry's emporium. But all of it is draining so much from me. Oh, dear Lord, I miss Megan so much. I miss life as it was.

Maybe that was confusing her, where Arthur were concerned, but all Hattie knew on that score was that she needed him – really needed him – and the thought shamed her.

Harry stirred. His agitation showed in the way he picked at the sheet with his long, thin, yellowing fingers. His voice, weak and shaky, was difficult to understand. 'Ha – Hattie?'

'I'm here, my love. Don't try to talk. I know everything as you want to say.'

'I – I must. Hattie, be happy. Ar – Arthur . . . It's all right—'

'What? Harry, what're yer saying?'

'I – I know. And I . . . want you happy. G – go to him.'

'Harry! Oh, Harry. I'm sorry.'

'N – no, it's all right. I want . . . P – please, go to Arthur. He loves you.'

'Please don't say this, Harry. I can't bear to see the hurt in you. I never meant—'

'You gave me happiness, my d – darling. I will die at – at peace . . . if I know you are happy. Please, Hattie.'

'Don't leave me, Harry. I love you. Please stay, please . . . Harry.'

'I – I love y—'

'Harry! Harry, listen to me. I love you like I've never loved another being.' Despite everything, she knew what she said was the truth and came from her heart. Her love for Arthur wasn't anything like what she had for Harry. She could depend on Harry; he'd never let her down. Arthur held her soul, but he could destroy it as if it was nothing.

'I – I know, my love. But . . . go to Arthur. Th – things change. I – I want you happy.'

With the last vestige of her world collapsing, Hattie felt she had no choice but to utter the words she never thought in a million years to say to her Harry. But she had to give him peace. 'All right, my love, I will go to Arthur. Now don't fret. Save your energy, get well, and make it as I don't ever have to leave you. I can't bear to be without you. No. No, Harry, don't go . . .'

Harry's grip on hers slackened.

Hattie's heart thudded painfully, causing her throat to constrict with each intense beat. 'Oh, Harry, no, no, no—'

An arm took hold of her, trying to drag her away. She fought against it and escaped, flinging herself onto the bed, where she snuggled into the still body and kissed the unresponsive waxy features. The hand grabbed her arm again. 'Come along, dear. He is at peace now.'

But she didn't want him at peace; she wanted Harry here with her. She wanted him to hold her, to . . . 'Oh, Harry, my love.'

A voice that she could not see the owner of spoke from behind the curtain, championing her cause. 'Sister, leave them a moment. They'll be all right.'

'It isn't right, it's—'

'Who are we to say what is right?'

'Yes, Doctor, but Matron wouldn't—'

'Matron won't know. Now come away.'

The hush of earlier descended again, this time with nothing to disturb it. Into that hush came all of Hattie's life: the wasted, rotten part after leaving the convent; the vile happenings, and her time as mistress to Arthur – Lord Arthur Greystone, as she now knew him to be, although back then she had thought him to be Captain Faraday. That deception still hurt. He'd found her on her patch, when she worked the streets. She could remember so vividly how he came up to her, limping and with a scarf covering most of his face. She'd seen a tear trickle from the stretched socket of his left eye and had been mesmerized by his sweet, gentle voice as he had said, 'I – I will understand if you can't, but I need—' She'd understood: the so-called 'Great War' had left so many young men badly injured. Her heart had gone out to this one. 'Of course, love. Where shall we go?' she'd asked him. He'd summoned his cab, driven by Harry. Harry had smiled at her as he'd helped Hattie into the cab. Everything had seemed as though she was entering a different life, and she was. As time went on, she and Arthur fell in love, and she had thought of him as her lifetime companion; but he had gone back to his wife, the moment she could bear to look on his much-improved facial appearance following the skin grafts he had been through.

Now Arthur was back, but did she want him? At this moment it seemed that the only really good thing had been meeting Harry, through her association with Arthur. And now Harry – faithful batman to Arthur, and loyal and wonderful husband to her – was gone. Oh God!

Twice in the last year Hattie had felt alone, and when Harry had collapsed again a few days ago, she had known that the final nail was being driven into the coffin of her devastation. Now, as she left the hospital, the feeling of being abandoned by all those she loved engulfed her.

Arthur had waited in his car, as he'd promised, and as she looked at him, all doubts left her. No matter how wrong it seemed – no matter how it would look – she knew she'd go to him and become his mistress again. And she knew she'd do it with Harry's blessing an' all.

Arthur stepped out of his car and put his arms out to her. Hattie went into them. As she did so, a draught caught her legs. A nun's habit had caused it, and the loud 'tut-tut' she heard came from the wearer. Anger made her turn on the Sister. 'Aye, you can look with disdain on us who are sinners in your eyes, but by God, you should look inside yourselves, for a lot of life's misery is caused by the likes of your lot. I should know, being a product of one of your convents and dragged up by them like you.'

The nun put her head down and walked on. Hattie felt a moment of guilt as she remembered the love given to her and Megan by Sister Bernadette when they were young. Sister Bernadette had been different, hadn't she? But no, in the end her lies and deceit had been the start of it all. Of Megan not being with her mother, Bridget, all those years; and how she herself had been sent to work in a place where it was known the master was partial to taking the virginity of young maids. Sister Bernadette hadn't challenged the Reverend Mother's decision to place her there. She probably thought that pray- ing would be enough to keep her safe, but it hadn't been. Memory shuddered through Hattie. No, she'd not think on Sister Bernadette as being any different from the rest of them, because in the end her true colours had come to light.

Arthur didn't tell her off for her outburst, or try to calm her. He just asked gently, 'Hattie, dear, has Harry gone?'

'Aye, he's gone. Your way's clear.'

'Hattie!'

'Eeh, I'm sorry. Aye, me Harry has gone, and he gave his blessing to us. But if you hurt me again, Arthur, he'll haunt you, and you'll have no peace as long as you live.'

'I won't, Hattie. I told you. My pain at our parting equalled yours. I endured deep agony every day at not being with you and knowing you were with Harry. I would have been back sooner if it hadn't meant hurting him. Please believe me, dear – there was nothing I could do.'

'I will try, Arthur, but it didn't seem to stop you when you were freed up. You came back into me life quick enough then.'

'I only meant just to see you, and not for you to see me. I – I couldn't help myself.'

'Oh, well, no matter. Like I say, Harry went happy, knowing you would be back with me. But tell me: it is what you want, isn't it? I am more than a mistress to you this time?'

'You are much more. Much, much more, my darling. I have never stopped loving you. I admit I had a moment of joy when I met up with my wife again and she wanted me back and still loved me. It clouded my judgement. The thought of being accepted back into the only circles I had ever known, and of being myself again, all added to the illusion, which made me think it was what I wanted. Then one day, a few months after I had left you, I woke up in the night with a terrible sense of loss. My heart felt like it would break, but it was too late. You had Harry, and everything in your own and dear Megan's life seemed so settled. You all looked so happy. Harry was ecstatically so.'

'How did you know all that?'

'I had people watching you all and reporting back to me. They were business advisors and friends.'

'The business advisors! I wondered why they approached us. We were just four people setting up a small business – folk who wouldn't normally attract the attention of advisors.'

'I asked them to approach you, but of course Lord Crompton saw them off. I didn't know at the time that you had such an influential banker behind you. I relaxed as regards your ventures, once I did know, and by then I had all the information I needed about you all and how well your lives were turning out.'

'My God, Arthur, if only—'

'No, don't say it. I wouldn't have wanted you to leave dear Harry. You were his world.'

'Aye, and he were mine for a long time. Oh, right enough, you were never far from me mind, but he and I found happiness together, and I need to grieve his loss. I'm not ready, not altogether ready. Oh, Arthur, take me pain away.'

'Hattie, my dear.'

The world turned into a shimmery haze as she looked through the tears that had filled her eyes. Her legs gave way. Arthur supported her weight.

'Come on, my dear.'

How she got into the car she did not know, but once there she knew where she wanted to go.

As they turned into the churchyard, the sun dappled its way through the boughs of the tree laden with leaves, throwing a pattern onto Megan and Issy's grave.

Hattie thought of what Megan had told her about the first time she'd lain with Jack. How the trees above them had thrown a shadow that looked like a lace canopy, as the sun had filtered down just as it was doing now. 'So your lace canopy is still there for you, love. I'm glad. I hope it's protecting you, like you said it always did. I – I've come to tell you . . .' She could get no further. She sank down. The soft grass, cut and nurtured so lovingly by Jack, accepted her. Her fingers dug into it. 'Oh, Megan, help me.' With these words, the very heart of her – the place she'd kept so tightly bound, so that it couldn't escape to destroy her – broke free.

Sarah's voice came through her despair. 'Aunt Hattie? Oh, Aunt Hattie.' She felt Sarah's body as she lowered herself to kneel beside her. 'Don't, Aunt Hattie, please don't. If you break, what is there left?'

Sobs that weren't her own – deep and wretched – penetrated Hattie's misery. The sound gave her a small amount of strength. She took Sarah's frail, thin body into her arms and they clung together. Sarah's belly dug into her own soft middle and she felt the life within it move – a new life. Out with the old, and in with the new: that's what people said, wasn't it? Well, they were all being given a fresh start, with what Sarah carried, and the little mite wouldn't have any of its grannies there for it. Well, she could do that for Megan and Cissy. She could help Sarah through this and be a granny to her child. The thought gave purpose to her life.

'Eeh, Sarah, lass.' Pulling herself up, Hattie helped Sarah to rise. Arthur stepped forward with a big white hanky, but didn't speak. Wiping Sarah's face first and then her own, Hattie said, 'By, lass, I could do with a cuppa. I've sad news to tell, but I feel better for the comfort of you and Megan and Issy.'

'Harry?'

'Yes. Dear Harry. This two hours since.'

'I'm sorry. Oh, Aunt Hattie, it feels as though everyone will be taken from us.'

'I know, but it won't happen. We have to be strong, lass.

You have to find yourself again and live on for your child, and for Megan and Issy. We both do. How does Granny Hattie sound, eh? Cos that's what I'd like to be. It would honour me if you'd let me stand in for Megan and Cissy.'

'It sounds grand. Like I've been given something back. A granny for me babby! Come on, Granny Hattie, I'll make a start by taking care of you when you most need it.'

They walked together towards the churchyard gates, arms linked, just as Hattie used to with Megan, and it felt good. 'We can do this, lass, me and thee. We can get through, and by doing so we'll help your dad, I know that. It won't be easy, but if we pull together and don't shut ourselves down, or shut each other out, it can happen.'

Holding her breath, Hattie waited for Sarah's reply. She prayed it would be a positive one, for she'd seen a difference in Sarah in these last few minutes. Like she had a purpose again. Please, God, let it be so.

'You're right, Aunt Hattie. I already feel like something has changed. As if something has opened up inside of me . . . Ouch!'

'What?'

'Babby kicked me! Eeh, it were a good 'un an' all, like it were saying, "About bloody time."'

'Ha, Sarah Armitage, you swore! By, Issy'd have the soap out if she heard you!'

They giggled. It was a nervous sound at first, but then it became a deep belly laugh that doubled them over. Hattie thought, *Harry, lad, your passing has brought about a miracle, cos I never thought to hear Sarah laugh again, but her having a purpose in looking after me has done the trick. We're going to be all right, me and Sarah, and as such we can be a strength to Jack.*

36

Richard & Mark

'Blood, Toil, Tears and Sweat'*

Richard sat back on his haunches, as did all the fellow pilots of his squadron as they waited for the signal to scramble.

Last night in the pub the talk had been of a big push by the Germans to knock out British defences in the air and at sea. Intelligence suggested it would begin any day now, and rumour had it that it would be worse than any of the missions they had flown so far, including the cover and back-up they'd given at Dunkirk.

Now and again he caught a glance thrown by one of the others, and each time he read fear – a fear that matched his own. He hadn't thought it possible to feel such gut-wrenching terror; or at least he hadn't at first, but each mission he flew, each time the count of those not returning went up, that terror increased. When would it be his turn? The next mission, or the one after that? What would it feel like: the flames licking at the cockpit, singeing his hair; the tumbling and somersaulting of his aeroplane; the ground, and certain death, coming ever closer? Or would he take a direct hit – a gunshot to his head or chest? What would that feel like? He imagined a

---

* Winston Churchill, 13 May 1940.

292

burning explosion, and then nothing – a preferable way of dying, if he had to die at all.

A noise, urgent and piercing, had him on his feet, disintegrating the fragments of concern and sending adrenaline through him. He was ready – ready with a fearless urge not to let the side down, and to defend his country against the tyrant who would destroy it.

Already in his flying gear, he grabbed his helmet and goggles and pelted across the tarmac. *This is it! God protect us.*

Barnie and Archie sprinted past him. They were really good men: funny, loyal and dependable. Barnie had been a solicitor, in the other life they used to lead – the normal life – and Archie an accountant, with a wife and child. God, what happened to that 'normal' life? Where had it gone?

No time to think: chocks away, engine whirring, groundsman waving him forward; and now, like a flock of birds, they soared into the sky, eyes piercing the wisps of clouds for any sign of approaching Luftwaffe.

Christ! Coming towards him was a moving sea of planes. 'Ready, gunner?' he asked himself. Giving himself roles, naming those roles and talking to each person made him feel less alone. 'Ready! One at three o'clock. Dive!' His Spitfire responded immediately. He shoved the joystick forward, swooping down like an eagle going for its prey. The Messerschmitt appeared alongside him, the pilot's face visible – young, stocky, with a determination woven into it as he disappeared. 'Christ, if he gets behind me, I'll cop it.' Hearing his own voice urged Richard into action and, surging upwards, he avoided the barrage of gunfire. Now the plane was ahead of him. 'God forgive me!'

The Messerschmitt couldn't manoeuvre like his Spitfire

had, and it took the burst of gunfire that he unloaded into it. The plane exploded into a ball of flames – whining to a screaming pitch as it plunged to the earth. Then it was gone. *A job I had to do.* Richard tried to convince himself of this. He had to, in order to carry on, but knew he would pray for the soul of the pilot and his family for the rest of his life.

Turning his plane back towards the others, he saw a Spitfire take a hit. 'Oh God, Archie. Bail out, Archie! For Christ's sake, bail out.'

It didn't happen.

Tears blurred Richard's vision, turning the blazing inferno of Archie's falling plane into a kaleidoscope of colour. He blinked them away and refocused on the chaos around him. Planes dived and turned, spun and rolled. Others exploded, and some dropped from the sky – a dead pilot at the controls. It was a nightmare, a searing hell, and all to the sound of droning engines and the rat-a-tat of gunfire.

Doing all that was asked of him, Richard protected himself and his fellow pilots as they did him. Adrenaline carried him forward as he talked his way through. 'One at nine o'clock! One tailing Barnie. One behind me . . . Dive!'

At last the Luftwaffe turned what few planes they had left and flew in a southerly direction, beating a retreat. Richard released his breath and, with it, the tension that had held him. 'We made it, gunner,' he told his imaginary other self.

Without warning, a rogue Messerschmitt came from nowhere, looming ahead, then dropping low. Richard put his Spitfire into a climb, arched over and tucked in behind the other plane. He muttered his sorrow to God, then opened fire. The tail of the Messerschmitt caught a direct hit and, like a huge firework, trailed flames as the plane dived once more. This was one pilot who was not giving up. Richard turned, rising higher as he went. 'Where the hell is he? Christ, he's behind me!'

Too late. A searing heat engulfed him.

In the mid-Atlantic fear beat in Mark's heart as he scanned the horizon. Intelligence had informed them that there were U-boats in the area, but where were they? The palms of his hands sweated. His instincts told him danger was close. Yet all around him seemed as it should, as the gunboat that he served on escorted the fleet of ships carrying freight across the Atlantic.

Mark's hand went to his breast pocket. Patting it gave him the comfort of the familiar sound of the crinkle of paper. Just knowing Sally's letter was there calmed him. He knew its contents word-for-word:

Dearest Mark,

Ta ever so much for writing. And, aye, I feel the same as you do. It's a feeling I never thought to experience.

I don't know how much you know about me, and what happened to me when I was only a child, but I'm thinking you are the only person in the world I can open up to. Me saying that might not seem much to you, but when we talk, you will understand that it is.

Just knowing I can tell you of it makes me know how deep my love for you is.

Keep safe, my darling. Fight through it all, for me.

With all my love,

Sally xxx

Sally loved him!

Although the letter was months old now, that declaration

never ceased to amaze him. What she spoke of, concerning her childhood, he had no idea, but it didn't matter. He could deal with whatever it was. Nothing mattered any more, not like it used to. Not the so-called difference in their standing, or their age, for Sally was three or so years his senior. Nothing mattered. War was a great leveller.

For a brief moment his mind went to his brother, and Mark wondered how he was faring. It was rotten luck for Richard to have fallen for someone who already loved another, and having to endure her marrying someone else. Sarah would have been perfect for Richard – much better than Lucinda. Not that there was anything wrong with Lucinda, except that she could be overbearing, and he imagined marriage to her would be on her terms only. Thank God that Richard had dealt with the problem, though there was still a worry that the relationship between them was on hold, rather than over. As if they were both hedging their bets.

'There, sir, at twelve o'clock!' The panic-stricken voice cut into his thoughts and caused his heart to plunge. Following the direction given to him, Mark turned his eyeglass on the sea. Zooming towards them: a white torpedo.

37

Richard & Sarah

The Toll of War

'You're all right. A few bruises and some bad burns, but nothing that will take you to your maker. Must have been your lucky day, sir. Right, let's get these dressings changed.'

'H – how many did we lose?'

'No official figure, sir, but we took a hammering.'

'Archie Greaves?'

'Don't know any names, sir. Sorry, been too busy with the wounded.'

The medic worked with efficiency, bathing and re-dressing Richard's wounds, chatting away in a light tone as if this was any other day. As he wiped away the tears trickling uncontrollably down Richard's cheeks, the medic said, 'Don't take on, sir. They died heroes. The second wave hasn't so many coming at them, as you lot crippled them.'

'Is it still going on?'

'Yes, sir. Your lot chased them back, but they returned. That Hitler seems determined to knock us hard so he can step onto our soil, but that'll never happen. Never! Now get some rest. They'll need you in some role or other before long.'

Need me? Oh God, when will it end?

As the medic walked away from his bed, whatever drug

he'd given Richard began to take effect. His pain eased and the room spun around him, throwing images at him as it went: a ball of fire; smoke, choking smoke; the rushing of air; his cheeks billowing back towards his ears; finding the cord to his parachute; tugging it . . . then nothing. As these pictures faded, Sarah's face came to him as clearly as if she stood in front of him. Big eyes, sad, empty – tugging at his heart. Would those eyes ever twinkle with laughter again?

'Oh no, dear God! How is Bridget taking it all?'

Sarah froze. Richard! No – please not Richard! 'Dad, what is it? What's happened?'

'Hold on a moment, love. Sorry, Edward, Sarah's here. She just came into the hall. I need to tell her. Oh, all right, I'll ring back. Aye, we're reet. Well, as reet as we can be, that is.'

The ding of the receiver as it was put back on its hook sounded like a death knell to Sarah. Her mouth dried and her body shook. She wanted to scream, *Don't tell me*, but no words would come from her.

'Come and sit down, lass.'

As she followed her dad through to the sitting room, it seemed he'd grown back to the man he'd been before . . . Her mind wouldn't give her the 'before'. She'd never been able to think of it or acknowledge it, and she never would. If she did, she would go mad.

Once they were in the room, her dad slumped into the chair. 'It's Richard and Mark.'

'No!'

'They're injured. Mark more than Richard. Mark's in danger of losing his sight. And he . . . he lost an arm.'

The tears that dropped from her dad's eyes and ran down

his cheeks struck a terrible fear into her. She willed him to tell her of Richard.

'Richard's burned. His arms and thighs. And he's bruised, very badly bruised.'

'Oh, dear God!' Her utterance was one of relief. They were both alive. Broken, but alive. 'When did it happen?'

'Two or three days ago – I'm not certain, I didn't take it all in. But both on the same day. It beggars belief. Look, lass, we might have a lot more to face. None to top what has happened to us already, but we've to be strong. I know I haven't been, not up till now, but I am now. Megan and Ma would want that of me.'

'It's all right, Dad. I know. But yer know, despite it all, the worst that could happen to me hasn't done. And even though what went on near broke me, it didn't come near what I would feel if I lost Richard. And that helps me to understand how much more than me you're going through.'

'Eeh, lass.'

She was in Jack's arms, feeling his tears drop into her hair. She knew his words had been bravado and wondered how he'd found the strength to say them. For such a good man to have loved and lost two women: her mam, Cissy, and now Megan. And to have known such tragedy in his life, even as a young man, losing his brother and father to war and his mam to a broken heart. It didn't seem right.

A shrill ringing intruded on them. For a moment she couldn't think what it was, then she realized it could be Sally ringing. Sally often rang on a Saturday afternoon, to check up on how she was doing and tell her how much she liked her work, and to talk of Mark's love for her. How would she tell Sally what had happened?

Picking up the receiver and hearing who it was released

some of her tension as Richard's beloved voice came to her. 'Sarah?'

'Oh, Richard, my love. Are you all right?'

'Yes, I am. I wanted to ring you to reassure you. A bit bandaged, and my limbs are painful, but lucky really.'

The catch in his voice caught at her heart. 'But you're alive, my darling. And you will heal, thank God. But poor Mark. Oh, Richard . . .'

'I – I know. It – it's still touch and go with him.'

'Where is he? Can we go and see him?'

'No, he's still on the hospital ship. Look, I'm getting out of this hospital in the next few days. They need the beds, and I can recuperate at home.'

'Eeh, that's good news, love. Will you come up and see us?'

'I need to be with Mother and Father. It has rocked their world, both of us having been injured at the same time. They lived with the possibility of something happening, of course, but now it is a reality, and Mother in particular has taken it very hard.'

'I'll come down. I have to see you.'

'I want you to so badly, but it isn't safe. You are so near to having the baby, and the shock of this and the journey will be too much.'

'I'm fine. I have three weeks to go yet and I have petrol, so I can drive down. They'd class this as an essential journey, wouldn't they? It's not like I'm travelling for nowt. Me man has been injured fighting in the Battle of Britain, and I need to be with him.'

'Oh, Sarah, you called me yours?'

'Aye, I did, and if you'll have me, that's what I am – and have always been – Richard.'

'Have you? Sarah, I love you with everything that is in me.

300

But I can't bear anything to happen to you. You must take care and, well . . . not just you. You have to take care of your baby, as he or she, whatever it turns out to be, is precious to me as well. I – I hope you don't mind me saying that?'

'Mind? Eeh, Richard, it's the next best thing to you saying you love me. None of what happened is me babby's fault, and he or she deserves all the love we can give.'

'And that's what will happen. We'll take care of, and love, the baby together. I'll always be there for you both, my darling.'

Sarah felt as though her heart would burst, such was the happiness seeping into her. But then Sally came into her mind. 'Oh, Richard, thank you. You have put me back together again, but, though I don't want to spoil this moment, my heart bleeds for Sally.'

'I know, darling. Do you think Mark knows how she feels about him?'

'Yes, she has written to him.'

'I'm so glad, as he will have that to hold onto. You know, when something bad happens, you need something. I thought constantly of you, my darling.'

Sarah swallowed hard, as tears threatened.

'And this will be good news for my parents, too. They'll be so happy to hear about Sally and Mark. We'd all guessed how Mark felt, but weren't sure about Sally. I didn't say anything to them, when you confided in me how Sally had told you of her feelings. I don't know why. Perhaps because they hadn't really connected then, but now that Sally has written and Mark knows, I'll share it with Mum and Dad. It will give them hope that Mark has a lot to fight for, and I know they will do what they can for Sally.'

'That's good. I'll contact her. Maybe she will get leave, on compassionate grounds. We'll all take care of her. Richard, I have to see you. I'll set out tomorrow. Will you be home then?'

'Yes, darling, but please take care.'

As Richard rang off, telling her over and over again how much he loved her, Sarah thought of what he'd also said many times during their conversation. *Take care.* Yes, she would take care. *I'll take care of the love I've been given, and of all those who need me. It's taking care of folk that's made me strong again.*

In some ways Sarah thought it was wrong to feel this happy, when all around her there was suffering, but she couldn't help it. And she never wanted to stop feeling this way.

38

Richard & Sarah

Bound by a Tiny Life

Richard winced as he tried to swing his haversack onto his back. Failing to overcome the soreness of the action, he opted to carry it by its straps.

'Letter for you, Flight Lieutenant.'

'Oh? Thank you.' Richard recognized the handwriting – Lucinda! He'd no time to read it. He was cutting it fine as it was to make the train.

Aching in places he didn't know he could ache, he made it to the station with a few minutes to spare. Around him was the hustle and bustle that the country had become familiar with: men and women in various uniforms – the able-bodied amongst them going about their business with a purpose that gave a false joviality to them. But despite their valiant attempts, he could almost smell their fear. Then there were the walking wounded: bandaged, hobbling on crutches or, in the case of one poor chap, carried on a stretcher. Several youngsters, looking no older than sixteen or so, made an attempt to salute him. An older man came up to him and offered his thanks. 'Churchill has said we owe you, mate, and I reckon as we do. You take your time getting better.' His wife wiped away a tear as she smiled at him, adding, 'He did his bit in the last lot, so he knows what you're going through. Come on, Alf, the lad looks tired. Don't try to get him talking.' With that, they were gone.

The 'last lot' – in the so-called Great War. How much worse that one had been, even though it hadn't been fought at home.

In some ways he was lucky. At least he put his feet on English soil every evening. And he could see Sarah whenever he had enough of a break to make the journey. That poor couple had probably spent years apart, as was the fate of so many today.

These thoughts ground his own pain deeper, as emotions of every kind assaulted him. Fear for Mark vied with happiness at the prospect of being with Sarah again – and with that thought came the sense of something having changed in her. He'd detected it in her voice, or had it just been concern for him that had taken her out of herself for a while? Whatever it was, Sarah had told him she loved him and that made his heart sing.

His life should be complete, and would be, if he could rid himself of the guilt that was his constant companion. Guilt that had never left him for the way his selfish taking of a kiss had led to such devastation in Sarah and Jack's lives. He wore that guilt every day, itching away at him like a hair shirt. Added to that, he felt more guilt over the young men whose lives he'd taken. Oh, he knew he'd had no choice; and he would kill again and again, if asked. But that didn't assuage the feeling that he was wrong to have caused so much pain to their loved ones. Nor did it sit right with his chosen profession of doctor. He wanted to save lives, not take them. Mark, too, was on his conscience. Lovely, funny, kind-hearted and sometimes irritating, Mark didn't deserve what had happened.

Why had these terrible injuries been inflicted on his brother, while he'd escaped with bruises and burns? But, he knew, this was guilt by association, and he and all young men who survived battles would experience this, as brothers and friends fell.

Finding a seat on the train hadn't been easy, but then a young man of about seventeen stood up, wearing an oversized army uniform and looking fresh-faced and ready to die for his country. His smile was full of confidence. 'Have my seat. You look all in. Caught one, did yer, sir?'

'Thank you. Yes, I did. It brought my aircraft down, but I managed to bail out. Didn't know much about it after that, though they told me I landed in a tree and had to be rescued from quite a high point. Have you just enlisted?'

'Aye, I weren't old enough at first.'

'Well, good luck. And thanks again for the seat.'

'You're welcome.'

Settling back, Richard closed his eyes and hoped, without appearing rude, that this would indicate he didn't want to engage in conversation. The hard bench seat didn't aid restfulness, and Lucinda's letter demanded to be read. He hoped with all his heart that she had finally accepted there was no future for them, as her letters often held hints that she was still available for him; and, to his embarrassment, at times she had added, 'Even just for the fun we had last time.' Richard's face reddened as he remembered, too, how Lucinda had referred to the feelings he had for Sarah, which he had confided to her. 'It may be that you just feel sorry for the girl,' she'd written. 'And that feeling is like a red rag to a bull, where you're concerned, as you tend to think everything is your fault and that you have to put it right, or be there for everyone. Just be careful, darling, and give yourself time to assess your true feelings.'

Richard smiled as he remembered these lines. Well, I don't need time. I know my own mind and so does Sarah. I think we always have.

A small dread sat in him as he unfolded the letter and received the usual whiff of perfume. She always wore the same one, and the smell permeated everything she touched. 'Dear Richard,' she began – hmm, that was a change from 'my darling' or 'my sweetheart', her usual form of address to him:

At last I know what you have been trying to tell me! I know because it has happened to me, too.

My dear friend (as that is what I hope you are, and will always be), I now know I am not in love with you. I have fallen in love for real. Yes, truly! The darling man is Winston Fellowes. I know: who'd have thought? He has been out of the country, working for some bank or other, but the war has meant he had to return. Oh, Richard . . .

By the time he'd read all she had written, Richard felt like laughing out loud. The relief was enormous. He just hoped poor Winston felt the same for Lucinda as she felt for him, otherwise he was in for the long haul of trying to disentangle himself.

At last! With a peace he hadn't known for a long time, he relaxed back into his seat and watched the houses give way to rolling green fields bordered by darker green hedges. Here and there gold-coloured horses, the sun glowing off their backs, grazed on the lush grass. The scene gave truth to the saying that Kent was 'the garden of England'. And yet this beauty, this tranquillity, was really a carpet of death and destruction, accepting bodies falling from the sky as the battles raged above it.

A niggling backache plagued Sarah as she drove, sometimes peaking to a point where it caught her breath and she had to stop.

But at least these stops served the purpose of cooling the car's engine a little, and on one of them she'd remembered to top up the petrol from one of the cans. Her dad had put two in the car, each only half-full, so they wouldn't be too heavy for her. This was just one of the things he'd fussed over, but then she couldn't blame him.

As she got out of the car the damp air clawed at her, but she stamped her feet and wrapped her arms around herself. She just had to ease this cramp in her side.

The exhaust fumes hung around and nauseated her. Sarah thought of her dad, and how he'd worried so much about her making this journey. Dorothy had helped to settle him. She had a way with her, where Dad was concerned. She liked Dorothy – well, all of the girls, really. What Dad would have done without them, Sarah couldn't give her mind to, as she'd been no help to him herself. Her world had closed down, and nothing inside her had existed until that day with Hattie at the graveside, when something had happened to make her want to pick up her life again.

How Daisy and Phyllis had coped at the factory whilst she'd been in this trance-like state, she'd never know. Thank God for Aunt Hattie. They were always saying it, just as Aunt Megan had: Hattie was a lifesaver, a solid rock in everyone's life.

Sarah supposed that seeing others' need of her had been the trigger, especially catching Hattie looking like a broken woman the day Harry died, when Sarah had come across her in the churchyard. Well, whatever it was that had made the difference in her, she was glad it had happened. Yes, she'd had to let in the pain of everything, as she allowed herself to feel again, but even that had helped her to recover.

I'd better get back on the road . . . Oh God! The pain shot around to the front of her stomach and cramped Sarah's whole body. *My babby. My babby's coming!*

Once the spasm passed, Sarah made it back to the driving seat. She knew she wasn't far away from Market Harborough, but could she make it the rest of the way? From memory, she felt certain the last village she'd passed through had been Kibworth Harcourt. Funny names they had around here for their villages! She remembered her dad and Aunt Megan giggling over them each time they visited Granny Bridget's. Happy times, memories to savour. *But best I don't dwell on them for now. It will undo all I've achieved, if I do.*

At this moment she was glad that the games they'd played with her on the journey, making up funny stories about the places they'd travelled through, had served to plant the route in her mind. With that knowledge, she at least had some idea of where she was, despite all the road signs having been taken down or, as she'd discovered, turned around in some instances, in a ploy intended to confuse in the event that the country was invaded.

As the pain eased, Sarah knew she couldn't just sit there. She either had to turn around and go back and get help, and maybe find someone who could call Richard, or carry on and hope she made it. Her decision to carry on coincided with another pain creasing her. Sweat ran from her forehead and trickled down her body as she wound her window down and screamed, 'HELP ME!'

'Are you all right, me duck? Can I be of help to you?'

Squinting through the pain brought into focus the kindly face of a man – a working man with a cloth cap on, holding his bicycle with one hand and her window with the other. Somehow she managed to say, 'I – I'm in lab . . . labour. Help me, help me, please.'

'Right, you stay there.'

It occurred to her to scream that she had no choice, but he'd pedalled away, leaving her clinging onto the steering wheel as another blast of pain waved in an intense circle around her middle, gripping her stomach as if it would crush it.

'There you are. A lovely little girl, and your man is downstairs, ducky. Ooh, look, she has red hair. You haven't, and neither has your man – poor thing, him all bruised and burned. Anyway, it must be a throwback. You get them—'

'All right, Brenda, give the girl a chance.'

'Sorry, Nurse, but it ain't every day a baby is born in me house, not nowadays anyway. There were plenty when I were younger, as you well know.'

'Yes, you had your share, but all grown now and doing well. So, come on, shift yourself and put the kettle on. This young lady could do with a nice cuppa, after what she's been through – you should know that. And tell that young man he can come up.'

The nurse smiled and winked as she turned to Sarah. 'Don't mind Brenda, me duck. She's the salt of the earth.'

'I'll never be able to thank her. Eeh, to take me in like that and let me give birth on her own bed. And look at the mess I've made! I'll make it up to her, I will.'

'She'll not expect anything. You've given her a bit of

excitement. She'll live off this tale for a long time, bless her. Oh, here's your man.'

Richard stood in the doorway. Her heart came into her throat at the sight of him. Pale and drawn, he looked half the man she'd said goodbye to when he left for Biggin Hill just a few weeks ago. 'Eeh, Richard.'

'Don't cry, love. Everything is all right. You – we have a lovely little girl.'

'Aye, she's bonny. Just look at her. She has Aunt Megan's hair, all red and curly. Oh, Richard, I'm sorry, I—'

'Don't, darling. It does no good to dwell on it all. You've made such progress.'

'I know. But I think it's that progress that's letting me cry – feel even, if you can understand that? Come and see babby. You'll see the likeness.'

'She's beautiful. And yes, she does look like my lovely sister. I'll always take care of her, of both of you. I feel a surge of love for her.'

'Oh, I'm glad, Richard. And you calling her ours an' all, that warmed me heart. Thou knows, I think your mam will see your grandma Bridie in her, as well as Megan. As from what I can remember, they say as your granna had red hair and blue eyes. Just look, our babby's eyes are the bluest blue.'

'They are. Ha! I'm sure she winked at me.'

'Eeh, Richard, you daft ha'p'orth.'

A silence fell between them, as all that had happened seemed to create a gulf, then Richard stepped forward and took her hand. 'I was going to ask you in a more romantic setting than this, but, Sarah – my love, my life – would you marry me?'

Her heart felt as though it would burst. With tears soaking her cheeks, she nodded her head.

39

Theresa

Another Girl

The violence of the pain tensed Theresa's whole body and her scream echoed in her own ears. Terence stood looking down at her, his face a mask of shock and horror. 'What shall I do, old thing?'

It came to her to tell him to *bugger off*, but his concern for her stopped her. This was something she had to do on her own. She'd prepared herself mentally, knowing she had to be strong. Her rejection of the child had taken her a whole nine months to perfect, and this was the most telling time for her. Soon her baby would be here: a living, breathing being coming from her. Her baby. *No! I mustn't think of it as my baby. I must find the hate and the repulsion, or I will be lost. I must think of it as nothing but a bastard, begotten of a bastard of the first order! Hate is the only emotion that will get me through this.*

'Just mop my brow and be here for me, Terence. I – I . . . Oh God, aargh!'

'Actually, I think you should leave now, sir. Go for a walk or something. It will all be over in no time.' The doctor moved forward, his tray of instruments gleaming in the sunlight filtering through the window as he placed it down on the table next to the bed. 'Nurse, is everything ready?'

As the doctor and nurse busied themselves, Terence left the room. Theresa saw him glance back at her, his look one of deep love. *Once this bloody war is done, and the part I intend playing is done, we'll find a way to be together. Nothing can stop that.*

'How is she?'

Terence thought his father had shrunk in stature. This had been a lot for him to handle, and keeping such a massive secret from their mother hadn't sat well with him. 'Oh, you know Theresa. She's making sure we all know what she's going through, but she will come out with flying colours. Is everything ready, Pater?'

'Yes. I have everything in place.'

'Your plan is excellent. I have read up on these things, and it is not uncommon for a mother to reject her baby, so the staff here – though they might be shocked – will know it is something that happens. And coupled with the story of Theresa's supposed husband's death, just before she came here, they will find it plausible. Yes, I think we are home and dry. Naturally we would want to take her home to convalesce and to take care of her baby. Yes, I think everything will go smoothly without anyone being the wiser.'

'There is just one thing I would like to change: I thought to get the baby cared for near to us. I thought then we could keep an eye on its welfare?'

'No, Pater.'

'I know. That was silly of me, and I realize it now, but thought I'd test the idea out on you, since I haven't actually made any changes. It feels wrong, but I suppose it will be best to cut all ties. I can't bear, though, to think of the child not having the best we can provide.'

'You've made provisions for its future, haven't you?'

'Yes, and in the end I decided to approach a convent in Glasgow.'

'So near? What if someone sees you and realizes?'

'That's very unlikely. I didn't know what else to do. I was worried about taking the child on a journey on my own, and couldn't involve anyone else. The nuns understood my distress and the need for haste in the safe disposal of the child, once I told them what had happened to my daughter – the rape and everything – and how ill her mother is. In any case, if someone from here realizes, what can they do about it? As it turns out, what the nuns will arrange is ideal. It appears they have ties with an Irish convent that links up with women all over the world who cannot have babies. They tell me there will be no problem in making sure the child goes to a good home. I have made provisions for a regular donation to both convents.'

'That was a big sigh, Pater. This isn't easy for you, I know, but—' A scream reverberated off the walls around Terence and stopped him in his tracks. 'Oh, dear, I never realized it was—'

'Come on, old thing. Women can cope with it. They just have to let us know, that's all. Let's go for a walk. Get ourselves out of earshot and out of the way.'

Though his father said this in a jovial way, Terence knew it was far from what he was feeling. His eyes showed his anguish.

'Pater, it isn't going to be easy parting with one of our own.'

'I know, my son. But then what choice do we have? It would kill your mother, and besides, we can't have Theresa's chances of finding happiness blighted any more than they already are. Speaking of which, I have news on the divorce papers. They are all ready for her to sign, at last. And from what the solicitor told me, it seems the settlement is going to be a very generous one. My poor darling Theresa. She has been through so much.'

Before them stretched endless countryside, dramatic in its backdrop of hills and mountains. The cap of snow on each hill glistened in the hot sun, giving it a touch of magic and yet realism too, as it told of how cold it must be at that altitude.

Terence found he couldn't speak. The beauty surrounding him compounded his protective feelings towards this soon-to-be child of Theresa's, almost as if he was the father and his child was to be wrenched from him.

'Well, my boy, the war keeps trundling on. Many a good man lost . . .'

This from his father, after a period of silence, surprised Terence. He'd wanted to keep his thoughts on Theresa, not talk of the war. 'Pater, I – I'm sorry, I know you would rather I was one of them.'

'No, no, my boy. I wouldn't have you joining them. Of course I could have come up to scratch and dealt with the daily fear we would have felt for you, but your mother couldn't. And you are doing a very good job helping to feed the nation. It has to be done.'

'Pater – well, there is something you should know. Theresa has plans. I – I haven't been able to dissuade her . . .'

Shock at what he revealed had his father searching for and finding somewhere to sit. Perched now on a tree stump, he looked up, aghast. 'Theresa?'

'Yes, she has been on about it for weeks now. I thought it

would pass, but no. She's even written to Derwent. You remember him? He's an older brother of Royston Smith who was in my set. Derwent Smith took a shine to Theresa when we attended a party at their home. Theresa went out with him a few times.'

'Of course, I know the family well. But why did Theresa contact him?'

'He's working at the War Office. It appears he has just the job for her.'

'What? Good God! And you didn't think to inform me of this before?'

'I told you, Pater, I thought I could spare you this. I've tried to change her mind, but Derwent has only fired her up even more.'

'How? What has he told her?'

'It seems there is a need for people with the knowledge Theresa has – her language skills and her familiarity with Europe, especially France.'

'No! No, she can't – not after the lengths we are going to, to cover all of this up and protect her and your mother. She cannot, and I will not allow it.'

'I don't think we can stop her, Pater. The work is vital to the war. Theresa wants to do her bit and—'

'I will bloody stop her. I'll keep her a prisoner, if I have to.'

'Pater!'

'Oh God, Terence, why didn't you tell me?'

'Pater, there is nothing to be served by blaming me. I did what I could. I honestly thought I could dissuade her, but, well—'

'Well what? What possible excuse can you come up with this time?'

His father's look withered Terence. His words cut deeply

into him and showed him the truth. Whatever his father said to reassure him that he'd done the right thing to get out of going to war, Terence suspected that, inside, his father was ashamed of him. Guilty about him even, when it came to dealing with his friends, men whose sons were serving and losing their lives. But he couldn't be something he was not, and he had put everything into his work since the war had become a reality. 'It isn't an excuse, Pater, just an observation. I think the thought of parting with her child is cutting Theresa to shreds and, as such, has led to her searching for something to give an edge to her life, to assuage what she envisages the pain will be. Putting herself in danger and being responsible for the safety of others will serve to give her no time to think of anything else.'

'And having come to this conclusion, you saw fit not to discuss it with me?'

'Will you always be ready to think the worst of me?' Terence's anger surprised him as it boiled up against this adored man, whom he'd never been able to fully please. 'I cannot be something you want me to be, Pater. I am what I am. I am no different from millions of others. If the circumstances had been that I was forced to go to war, I would have gone and conducted myself just as they are: afraid, but doing what was required of me. I had a way out and I took it, but that way out suited you as much as it suited me. Theresa is looking for her way out, and if this is it, then you have to allow it. We will find a way of protecting Mater, but maybe your constant stressing of the need to protect her isn't what she needs, either. Maybe Theresa and I are the people we are because of it. Maybe Mater could have weathered the storm by now, but your constant ministrations to her have kept her shielded and unable to cope!'

If he'd thought his father was shocked before, it was nothing to his reaction now. His face paled to the colour of the snow-tipped mountains. His eyes rounded to reveal the whites bordering the irises. 'Terence, I – I don't know what to say—'

'No, neither do I.' He turned away, and the world around him blurred. Terence blinked, allowing the tears to flow and his heart to cry, for he was losing a lot today. His whole life. Because today he'd lost something of his father, and today marked Theresa's freedom to go her own way; but it also marked his loss of the child he'd watched grow in her womb, whom he had stroked and patted, talked to and joked about. A child who had become real to him – and, yes, had become his.

A cry of the kind that could only be made by a baby filtered down the stairs when they returned to the house. Terence felt joy surge through him. His father had hardly spoken to him in the last hour or so – the only effort had been an attempt at an apology, something about being under a lot of strain. But Terence hadn't felt inclined to let him off the hook, and so the uncomfortable feeling between them had prevailed.

'Well, Pater, the next generation has made its entrance.'

'Don't talk of the child like that. We must never acknowledge it. We can't.'

'I know, but you must acknowledge Theresa's heartbreak concerning it. She will never admit to it and will behave as if she can't bear the child near her, but I know that deep down she feels differently. If you realize that, then you will be able to understand her motives for the other business she is planning, and deal with it in a way that limits the damage to Mater.'

The nurse swept into the room, stopping all further attempts to get through to his father. 'There you both are! You are a grandfather, sir. It's a bonny wee lass. Will you come up to see them?'

'Yes, thank you, Nurse.' As they went up the stairs, Terence held his breath. Please let Theresa be playing her part of being repulsed by the baby. They couldn't deal with any more complications at this stage.

As planned, she had refused to hold the child.

'Don't worry about it, sir. Och, many women take like that at first. It wears off the moment the child is put to their breast.'

'That thing is not coming anywhere near me, so you can forget that stupid notion, Doctor. I told the nurse to fetch milk from a wet nurse the moment the baby was born. I hope she is carrying out my wishes?'

'Aye, it's done – don't carry on, now. Haven't I told you not to be upsetting yourself, lassie?'

The doctor looked alarmed. Terence went to speak, but his father stepped in. 'It has all been too much for her. You know she was widowed? Well, this is the last straw, I expect.'

'Pater, take me home. Please take me home.'

'There, you see. Everything runs its course. I had to bring her up here, as she couldn't bear to be at home, with so many memories surrounding her. Now she is begging me to take her back there. Yes, my darling daughter, don't upset yourself. Mother will be waiting for you. She will take care of you both. The nursery is ready, and nanny is in place.'

God, how could his father lie so convincingly? Terence watched as Theresa put out her arms to their father, tears streaming down her face. Only he knew they were for real – not because she didn't want her child, but because she did.

Walking over to the crib, he peeped inside. A tiny body wriggled, and a hand peeped out from under the swaddling that held her tight. He put out his finger, and her finger curled around his. His heart constricted. The tiny bundle needed them – her family – but there was nothing he could do. Her head moved to one side, looking away from him. It shocked him to see that she had red hair, tightly curled to her head. When she looked back at him, her eyes looked the palest blue, almost like a blind person's.

Megan, Jack's late wife and mother of Billy, came to mind. The child was the image of her. Terence didn't want a constant reminder of Megan, or what happened to her, in his life. Nor did he want her son's bastard growing up with them. But even as he thought this, he knew he'd give anything to have it made possible that she could.

40

Theresa & Terence

Their Paths Chosen

Three months had passed. Some of the time the pain of loss had visited Theresa, but throwing herself wholeheartedly into her new venture, her army life, had helped.

'You have come through your basic training with the highest praise, Theresa. That is good. Very well done. Now, I am in a position to suggest you as a recruit, but what I am going to tell you is highly confidential. You will tell no one, not even your family. Is that understood?'

'Yes, Derwent. You know you don't have to ask that!'

'There is a new organization called the Special Operations Executive, known as SOE. I have spoken to the senior recruitment staff there and they are very interested in you. I could have done so earlier, but, well, to be honest, Theresa, I wanted to be sure of your commitment and ability. I know that sounds disloyal of me, as we have been friends for a long time.'

'I understand. I haven't exactly shown any inclination to do anything other than be a society girl. Things change, though, and I have changed. I have had to weather a few storms that I can never tell anyone of, and they have given me a stronger core. I know now that I am up to this special work, whatever it is.'

'Yes, I believe you are. I had to let you go into the army and see how you fared, to check that out, but the reports I have received are of someone with spirit, courage and tenacity. Put those together with your knowledge of the language and the country of France, and Hugh Dalton, the political head of SOE, agrees with me that you could prove invaluable to us.'

'Thank you.'

'No, don't thank me. The work is highly dangerous. You will work behind enemy lines with the Resistance. You will be a key figure in communications and in the disruption of the Germans' operations. You could be killed at any time or . . . Look, I'm going to lay this on the line: capture is a real possibility, as are torture and execution. I believe our lot issue a pill.'

'Derwent, I understand. I am ready.'

'Oh, Theresa . . .'

'No, Derwent. You know we have been to that place, and you know I don't have feelings for you in that way. You married Felicity and, as I understand it, you are happy. Don't spoil that for some imagined excitement with me. I can assure you, I have nothing to give.'

'Well, talk about putting a man down.'

'I know no other way. I have to be straight with you.'

'Yes, of course. I shouldn't have spoken. Sorry. Look, are you all right? There seems something different about you. You've changed.'

'War changes everyone.'

As she walked along the corridor some ten minutes later, Theresa's boots squeaked on the polished linoleum. Her future was almost set but for the interview with the senior staff of SOE in some flat or other in Baker Street. Her heart clanged with the emotions Derwent's words had evoked. *Changed! My God, if he only knew how much.*

Her very soul had changed. It had been ripped from her in the form of something beautiful, tiny and so loved, and then torn to shreds by the parting, before being put back together and strengthened by her surviving it all. But for what? To protect her mother? Well, there was to be no more of that. Mother would have to stand up with courage, as all of them had to. Their country and their whole way of life were threatened, and she, for one – unlike her coward of a brother – was going to do something about it. *Oh, Terence!* How she longed to have him with her, and yet how repulsed she was by what had passed between them.

Never again. Whatever she had to face in the future, she would face with more than sheer guts. She would face it as her act of contrition. She just had to get through Terence's wedding to Louise. If she could face the possibility of capture and torture in her new role in SOE, then she had no doubt that she could face the wedding.

She had never thought he would go ahead with it. Always Terence spoke of being there for her, but as she had said to Derwent, *war changes everyone*, and it had changed them.

Terence was different, too, since the birth of her child. He'd been affected just as badly by the parting, which was strange, because he had no reason to love the baby. And yet it had all been as difficult for him as it had been for her, and in being so had created a schism in their relationship. It was one that had to come, she knew that now, but knowing that didn't make it easier to bear. A part of her had died – a part that would never spark into life again. Her life was given to the cause of her country now, and if that meant laying down her life, she was ready to do so.

Terence hated himself for what he'd been and how he'd treated people. And now that he was faced with Penny trying to change his mind, his guilt was compounded.

'Penny, you have to understand. There can be no more.'

'But you said you loved me. I gave myself to you.'

'And I do. You are very lovable, but only as a friend. I have asked Louise to be my wife. She is the woman I love. As you know, our wedding is next week. It's impossible to carry on as we have been doing.'

'Why? You will have to come over here from Tarrington House. You will still manage the farm and we'll be working together, so why can't we carry on as we are now? No one has ever caught us.'

'Because I was single then. Now I will be married. I'll have a family soon and, well, because everything is different now.'

'But when did it change? You always talked as though everything could carry on the same. Me and you, making love whenever we could.'

He couldn't tell her what had changed him. The feeling had been so profound, after the child had gone from them, as to give him a sense of honour and, more than that, guilt. Guilt was an emotion he'd thought would never bother him, but now it did. It lay in him as if he had a brick to carry around in his chest – guilt over the child, guilt over Rita, guilt over Penny and guilt over Louise, but none of it came near to the guilt he felt over Theresa.

Theresa felt it too, he knew that, and he knew their ultimate parting was imminent. If she survived whatever it was she was going to do – and all she'd tell him was that it was highly dangerous and would be carried out in occupied France – they'd never be together again.

They'd talked. It had been a strained affair. They'd apologized to each other and tried to kindle their love in a different direction, but it hadn't worked. They both knew the love they had for each other was as deep as it could be, but they both knew, too, that it was wrong. Theresa had always known that, and so the guilt was really his. He'd been so arrogant. He'd pursued the love as if it were legitimate, but it wasn't. It was vile, what he'd done to her. Vile what he'd done to himself, too. And so the only way was to separate.

London, she'd said. After the war. That's where she would settle, and she wanted to see him as little as possible – family dos, that sort of thing, but only when it was compulsory. He'd agreed, knowing she was right.

Now he had to put the rest of his life in order. He had to stop this affair with Penny, as beautiful as it was. He had to do something about Rita, although he did not know what.

With his impending marital status, his father was at last going to make over the business to him and a substantial amount of capital, so perhaps he could fund something for Rita when she came out of prison. But that was in the future – for now he had to devote himself to Louise.

He loved Louise. He hoped she would be everything he needed, and that she would fill the voids that Theresa and Penny would leave in him. He had no way of knowing if she would, as they had conducted their courtship with the utmost propriety, as was befitting of a girl of her standing and his own.

'Well?' Penny brought him out of his thoughts. 'You haven't got an answer, have you? And I don't think you mean it, either. Come up to the loft with me. Let me show you how I feel about you.'

'No! Look, I'm sorry. I can't. Something has happened, and it is something I can never discuss with anyone, but you are right when you say I have changed. Can you allow that in me? Can you look on what we had between us as a lovely interlude in both our lives? Something we won't ever forget, but something we won't hurt the other with, either?'

Penny was silent for a long moment. He could see the battle going on inside her, see the pain she was feeling, but he had faith in her goodness and that didn't let him down.

'You *do* mean it!' Her lip quivered. 'Well, I like Louise, so for her, I will do it. I'll carry on as if nothing has happened, but I'll miss you, Terence. I've never met anyone like you before. You've made me have feelings I never thought to know of.'

'I feel the same, Penny. But thank you for understanding. And I'll not blame you if you ask for a transfer to another placement.'

'That's what I was thinking of doing. I could make some excuse. Yes, I think it would be best all round. I should have known. I shouldn't have been so silly. You didn't hide the type you were – look how you had that Rita, and she used to say you had your sis—'

'Shut up! That's preposterous. You know what Rita was like – she said, and did, everything she could to get what she wanted. You should know that, from her ultimate act.'

Again Penny was quiet, but this time in a defiant way. Her look said that she knew, or believed, something different. He had to be careful. He had to keep Penny on his side.

'I'm sorry. I shouldn't have snapped at you. It is all such a sensitive area. I know the lies Rita spread, and the vile accusations she made, but you are above that; and Rita is where she should be.'

This seemed to do the trick.

'Will you help me get another placement? I'll need a good reason.'

'Leave it to me, Penny. I'll be sorry to see you go, but maybe it is for the best. Anyway, you need to get on with the rest of your life. Going away from here might be just the thing for you, and I wish you luck. And, well, thank you. I'll never forget what we had or what you did for me at the trial. I have an envelope here for you. I hope it helps you to find a good future for yourself.'

Walking away from her, Terence could still feel her hurt. But his guilt concerning her eased a little. The two hundred pounds he'd given her would see Penny right. It wasn't a good thing to do, as it cheapened her, but it was the only thing he could think of. In some ways, his old life had been much easier. Being a bad lot took no toll on your emotions. Trying to be one of the good guys did nothing but tear at you in every direction. Well, it was over now. He had to put all of it behind him and, as he'd told Penny to do, he must get on with the rest of his life.

41

Jack & Sarah

New Beginnings

Jack called out to the horse to stop. The magnificent shire obeyed, but snorted and shook his mane in protest.

Pressing his hands into the small of his back, Jack straightened up to soothe the ache there. He could ease the pains in his limbs from the physical work on the farm, but he never thought to do the same with those that fragmented his soul.

Looking across to the house, he saw an image that would stay with him forever: his Megan sitting on the bench with his ma-in-law. Megan waved. Jack lifted his hand, but let it drop down by his side again as the image faded. She wasn't there.

Leaning heavily on the plough, he dropped his head forward. Every day since he'd begun to focus on life again he'd faced a daily battle against the deep-seated horror and devastation that had paralysed him for months. Every hour and every minute he had to try and dispel the scenes playing over and over in his mind. As if they were being shown through a projector, they flickered in jerky movements in his head, putting all the players in place, vividly coloured against a background of red – red everywhere, spurting like fireworks, dripping like a tap that needed a new washer, a flowing river of blood.

'Jack?'

Dorothy's voice penetrated the self-destruction that had threatened to engulf him. He turned to see her running towards him, urgency in her pace.

'Are you all right, Jack? I thought . . .'

'I'll never be all right again, lass.'

'You will. I promise you. It'll take time, but I'm . . . we're here for you, Jack, all of us. And there is a future. Your Sarah has cemented that by bringing new life into the world, and by her marrying Richard in a few days' time.'

Jack looked into Dorothy's eyes and saw in their deep violet colour something he couldn't cope with. And yet part of him was gladdened by it. Though he didn't want the kind of love he knew she felt for him, he needed it. That kind of love said it forgave everything and would stand by you, no matter what, so he'd take some strength from it, even though he couldn't give anything back. 'I know, and you girls are like me saviour. I know you've been hit hard by what happened, and especially what happened to young Iris. You came as a four, and now you are three. And the horses an' all – you all loved them horses as much as I did. But when I hear the three of you giggling over sommat, it's like there is hope – resilience – and I can take some of that from you.'

'You can, Jack. I – we – have oceans of it to give you.'

'Ta, Dorothy.'

'Here, I've brought a billycan with some hot, sweet tea in it, and some butties. Mildred made them. She likes looking after us in that way. She's a real mother-hen type.'

'Ha, you hadn't better let her hear you say that. She thinks of herself as a bit of a liberator of women. She were talking to me for ages about political stuff and how the war will show women's worth, and it reminded me of my Megan – well, Megan thought like that an' all. She said as women had a role to play in all walks of life, and she proved it too, with running her own business. Her and Hattie, they are – were, I mean – well, Hattie still is – women ahead of their time.'

'There, you see. That's good, Jack, you talking about Megan. You should, you know, like you do of Issy, because Megan deserves that. Oh, I know it is painful to do so, but the more you do, the easier it will be. And it will bring her to you. Don't try to shut her out.'

'Eeh, lass, I forget you've been through it. We're akin in that.'

In remembering this, Jack felt a deeper sense of comfort from being with her. Her words weren't empty condolences said with the best intentions, but were meant, felt and experienced. Aye, he had a mate in Dorothy – a kind of soulmate, in a way, as she'd travelled the same road he was travelling, though for him this was the second time this kind of agony had visited him, and he wondered at the cruelty of life.

The day Sarah had dreamed of was upon her. She smiled up at her Aunt Hattie's reflection in the mirror as she stood behind her.

'Oh, Sarah, lass, you look grand as owt. Like a fairy princess. Eeh, if only—'

'No, don't say it. There is no *if only* today, Aunt Hattie. Today we must think of them as all being here. We must make it a day to remember. Just one in a sea of hell that we all survived.'

'Eeh, lass, it gladdens me to hear you say that. And you're right. They are all here – here in everything we are and have.

329

That frock, it's cut from the same batch as the one your Aunt Megan made a frock from for your mam, years ago. Megan kept everything, and she put labels on it all. It gives me a headache now, with storage and everything. But that one had written on its label "was used to make a frock for Cissy, 1918, for a social at the Miners' Club to celebrate the end of the war". By, it's pretty, and with it being silk and having such a soft, silvery sheen, it's perfect for today.'

'Aye, Phyllis has done a grand job of it, and the shawl Daisy has made is lovely. It's nice to think that material has a link to Megan, too. Daisy told me the label on the cloth was "used for my bridesmaid's dress when I stood for Cissy and Jack on their wedding day. Given to me by Madame Marie." That was who Megan worked for when you left the convent, wasn't it?'

'Aye, Megan loved her placement, and it was where she met your mam. Cissy were a grand lass.'

'I remember her. Which is lovely, as I can picture her in me head and talk to her. I do that with Megan now. By, Megan must have looked lovely in this gold.'

'She did. And, thou knows, that were the first time as your dad really noticed her. Oh, I'm not saying as he fancied her, or owt like that. He loved your mam to the exclusion of all others. But up until then, he'll admit it himself, he never saw anything in your Aunt Megan. It were sudden, like. He turned to greet your mam and caught a glimpse of Megan all dressed up, and it shocked him at how changed she were. He'd only ever seen her as Cissy's mate from work.'

'Well, that's a nice story, and he should never be ashamed of how things turned out. These memories are the ones we must hold onto today. Eeh, I'm so happy. And to think, like Aunt Megan, I'm finally getting the real love of me life.'

'Aye, and dressed in silver and gold, which is how I think of your mam and Megan, as Cissy had hair so light it were like silver, and Megan had golden hair. But both had hearts of gold, and both glowed like silver and always will.'

'Eeh, Aunt Hattie.'

'Aye, lass. We've a lot to be thankful for. Our lives were crossed by such good 'uns as Megan and Cissy, and Issy and my Harry, and many more. God rest their souls.'

'You've never told me much about Arthur, thou knows. I know as it ain't my business, but . . . well, it is all a mystery to me. And why isn't he coming today?'

'Well, it's a long tale, but Arthur was my first and – now this is going to sound reet bad – but me only real true love, in the sense of how Richard is to you. And yet I loved Harry, I did, and it wrenched me heart to lose him. Am I making any sense?'

'Aye, you are. And now Arthur is back in your life.'

'He is, but it isn't proper as we should be together. Harry's not gone yet. He still has a big place in me. But, thou knows, we have his blessing. Look, it's all too much of a long story to tell right now, but one day I will. Just to say that once a year has passed and I'm feeling in a more comfortable place with everything, then me and Arthur will be together. He has asked me to be his wife. I don't know if you know, but he is a lord. Well, anyroad, he's giving up all that peerage stuff and we're going to live just outside of Leeds. He'll support me in me businesses and carry on advising on Megan's, though. Oh, well, that's all for another day.'

'I know what you are thinking, Aunt Hattie, and I am in agreement, as I know Dad will be. Any time you are ready to make us an offer for Megan's business, the whole lot is yours and we'll be glad to be rid of it. We know it couldn't go to anyone better.'

'Ta, lass. I didn't know how to approach you, but now I can make plans. Phyllis and Daisy are going to be full partners in that side of the business, so that would have pleased Megan an' all.'

'Aye, and me. I'm so glad they've come down to Market Harborough for today. It's good that as many of us as can be are together. It comforts me.'

'I know, lass.' The door opening interrupted them, and Sally walked in. Aunt Hattie made light of the situation by making a joke. 'By, look at this, another princess! We have the full set now. Sally, love, you look a picture.'

'Always the bridesmaid.'

'Naw, love. Eeh, come here. You will have your day, I know you will. Mark will come round. He's a strong lad. He'll wake up, and the first thing he'll do is ask you to marry him, you'll see.' Standing up and taking Sally in her arms, Sarah held her close. 'Eeh, Sally, ta, love. I'd have understood if you'd have said as you couldn't stand for me, thou knows.'

'I'm sorry, I didn't mean—'

'Eeh, don't be. I know what you mean. But you have to have faith, love. Aunt Hattie's right. Mark will make it – he will.'

As if on cue, Granny Bridget came through the door. 'Sally, Sally, lass.' *It is funny how, when she's excited or sad, Granny Bridget reverts to her Yorkshire accent.* 'There's a phone call . . . it – it's Mark!'

Sally hurried down the stairs, her head refusing to let her thumping heart believe that the miracle had happened. Mark able to talk to her on the phone! She never thought the day would come. Grabbing the receiver from Edward, all she could say was, 'Oh, Mark.'

But Mark stopped her from saying anything further, as in a faltering voice he said, 'Sally, I – I'm not . . . the man I was.'

'You are, my darling. Inside, you are. Nothing can be at changing that. I love you, Mark. You're me world.'

'Oh, Sal, I – I love you.'

She didn't comment on the sob, but felt it mingle into her own tears. 'Mark, something wonderful is happening today. Richard and Sarah are getting married! They couldn't wait, not with how things are, and we none of us knew if—'

'It's all right, it – it's wonderful n – news. Mother told me. And it – it means you were there when I phoned. I didn't kn – know how I was going to – to contact you. Sally, I . . . I can't see.'

Again the sob. Her heart felt as though it would break. 'I'm sorry, my darling. I wish I could change that, but somehow we'll get through it. I'll be there for you. I'll be your eyes.'

'W – will you, Sal? You won't—'

'Don't even say it, Mark, let alone think it. I will be with you forever. I love you. In fact, I know it ain't the conventional way, as *you're* s'posed to ask me and be on bended knee an' all, but, Mark, will you marry me?'

The sob became a full-blown crying from depths she never thought to hear from him. Fear gripped her. Someone took the phone from him and said to her, 'I'm sorry, but he is too overcome, and this is dangerous for him. I'll have to end the call.'

'No,' Mark screamed from the background. 'I – they're happy tears. Please.'

'Well, calm down and I will, but if this sets you back,' the voice droned on. A caring voice, that of a man who wanted the best for Mark. She could hear that in his tone.

'It – it won't. My girl h – has just asked m – me to m – marry her!'

'Oh, right, love.' The male voice again. It became louder

and said, 'The answer is yes,' then faded again. 'There, I've told her for you. Anything else?'

The sound of Mark laughing lifted Sally and filled her with joy.

'Oh, and I'm going to be the bridesmaid!' This was the male voice again, said in an effeminate voice, and had her laughing out loud. By, whoever it was with Mark, he was a tonic.

'G – give me the phone.'

'Only if you promise no more crying, right?'

'Oh, Sally, sorry, l – love. The answer is yes! Th – thank you, thank you.'

'Reet, we'll fix it up. I'll be down to see you as soon as I can. Tomorrow. I have a few days' leave. I'll get the first train. I'll stop off to buy you a ring, seeing as I did the asking. You can get mine when you are well enough.'

'I will, my darling, I will. G – give—'

'Don't speak any more, sweetheart. I can hear you are exhausted. I know what you want to say: congratulations and love to Richard and Sarah, love to your mam and dad and everyone. Tell them you're looking forward to seeing – being with – them soon, and that you love me beyond anything! There, will that do?'

'Yes. Yes.'

The sob came again, but then she'd to expect that. No one could go through what Mark had been through without it nearly crushing them. She was to be his strength. He loved her. He was going to marry her, and that was all that mattered. Her world was complete. He managed another 'Goodbye, and I love you.' The last was all she needed.

The day had been perfect, made even more so by the phone call from Mark, and Sally announcing that she and Mark were to be wed. By, that had made Bridget and Edward happy, and her and Richard an' all. Not that Sarah had ever doubted that Sally would stand by Mark. But now Mark knew that too, and this would give him hope for his future.

Richard pulled the car up outside the small cottage that was to be their home, just a mile from his parents' house in the pretty Northamptonshire countryside. Part of Sarah was sorry that this had to be so, but Richard would need to continue with his studies when he returned from the war and it seemed the best arrangement. Before that happened, she would stay as normal with her dad, but would come down here to Market Harborough if her petrol allowance would let her to be with Richard when he could get away.

A murmur from the crib on the back seat reminded her that they were now a family. 'Uh-uh, Harriet is awake, and hungry no doubt. Richard, thank you for agreeing to her coming with us, on what is meant to be our honeymoon.'

'I wouldn't have it any different. She is "us" now. We can't possibly go anywhere without our little Harriet. When I am away, I shall think of you both together at all times.'

Sarah had heard the saying *one's heart swelled with joy*, and now she knew what it felt like.

'Come on, let's get in and get Harriet settled. I'll cook for us while you feed her.'

It was as if they'd been doing this all of their lives.

That feeling stayed with Sarah as they got into bed later on. No nerves entered her, just complete and utter love and desire. Up until now, they'd kissed and had come near to going further, but they'd waited. Sarah had needed that, after what Billy put her through. She'd wanted to know the respect and gentleness of real love, but in its rightful place within their marriage, so that there was no guilt attached to it – no illicit taking and giving. She wanted purity.

Richard's arms enclosed her the moment she slipped between the sheets. His kisses, tender and searching, landed in her hair, over her face and snuggled into her neck before he found her lips. They were *giving* kisses, not *taking* ones. They tingled a love through her and the feeling of being everything to her man.

His hands explored her and hers explored him, in the way they'd allowed themselves to before, but this was different. With the exploration of her naked body and the feel of his body pressing against hers, it was worlds different.

Her throat constricted until she could hardly swallow, and her breath panted, labouring with the sexual tension that had taken control of her. Now his fingers found the very heart of her, caressing her until she thought she would die with the ecstasy that took her into another world, a world she'd never entered before. And all to Richard's whispered words of love, telling her she was beautiful, and was his, and would always be so.

When at last he entered her, Sarah's very being let go. Flood after flood of feelings were released. Tears flowed down her cheeks at the utter fragmentation of the *her* she'd been, before this moment.

That person splintered into a thousand grains, as love and passion washed over her. And then, as the spasms of completeness passed, her body and soul reunited. Richard had made her whole again.

EPILOGUE
Eighteen Years Later
1958

42

Rita

Returning to the Scene of the Crime

Rita stood by the tree and looked towards Hensal Grange. Memories flooded back to her. Hatred and anger coiled in her stomach until the tightness of it hurt. *If it's the last thing I do, I'll get my own back.*

Fifteen years she'd served. Fifteen years of hell. And for what? For that bastard, that bleedin' bastard, Terence Crompton! Well, he was going to pay. Somehow she was going to make him pay.

Some of her anger was directed towards the huge banner-type sign over the gate, announcing 'Hensal Grange Stud Farm'. *So the bleedin' bastard got what he always wanted, then?* But at what cost to her, to Jack Fellam and that lovely girl, Iris?

Getting back into her car, she drove towards Fellam's farm. Her nerves frayed at the thought of the reception she might get, but Jack was a link – a source of the information she needed. If she played her cards right and went under the guise of being sorry, she just might succeed in getting all she desired. The downfall of the high and mighty.

She'd made good, since her release. Three years of freedom had seen her turn her life from nothing to having a good income from her market stalls. Her uncle had always done the markets and she'd helped him as a kid, learning the ropes, the best stuff to sell and where to sell it. She'd started off with antique jewellery. With the money she'd come out of jail with, and some that she'd got from working the streets of London for a few months after her release, she'd bought some good pieces to get her going. Now she had four stalls and a fair few regular customers. Some bought off her, some sold to her, and others borrowed money on the strength of the value of their stuff, then forfeited it if they didn't pay up. All in all, it was a good little number.

Recently she'd added another string to her bow – she'd set up a modelling agency. It was a game that covered a lot of different avenues: models for catalogues, models for calendars and playboy-type magazines; and besides these, she had others who came under the umbrella of 'escorts' who were willing to go the extra mile for a client, and who could please the opposite sex as well as their own. All of it raked in the money, as if the streets were paved with gold, and she'd only to take a shovel to get her share.

Turning her Triumph TR3, her bright-red pride and joy, into the lane that led to Fellam's, Rita saw that the sign no longer said 'Fellam's Stud Farm'. A pang of guilt gripped her. That Terence bleedin' Crompton had a lot to answer for. Well, when the day came that she did to him what he'd had her do to Jack, she'd have no guilt about it. She'd rejoice.

Pulling the car up a little way from the farm, she could see activity going on in the yard. *Good God! Is that Dorothy?* Yes, she was sure it was. And who was the young lady with her? Pretty thing, slender figure, a mound of red hair glistening like flames in the sunlight – similar to what Megan had, only a

richer colour. Probably about eighteen years old. She couldn't
be Dorothy's daughter, surely?

Feeling scared and more nervous than she'd ever felt
before, Rita coaxed her car along, getting nearer and nearer.
Dorothy looked up, shielded her eyes and waited. Stopping
just the other side of the gate, Rita got out.

'Dorothy, it's me – Rita.'

'Rita! What on earth?'

'Look, I know I shouldn't have come, but, well, I wanted
to say I'm sorry to Mr Fellam.'

'You have no right to—'

'I've done me time, Dorothy. I did fifteen bleedin' years,
and I swear to God the fire weren't all my doing. It were—'

'Fifteen years can never pay for what you did. You took
away Jack's livelihood, and you robbed that young girl of her
life.'

'But . . .'

'What's going on?'

'It's that girl – woman. The one who set the fire and—'

'Christ! What're you doing here, lass? Don't you think you
brought enough suffering on us?'

'I came to say as I were sorry, Jack. And I wanted to tell
you why it happened and who was really behind it.'

The moment froze. No one moved or spoke. Jack stood
looking at Rita with an incredulous expression that gave way
to many emotions. Dorothy held his arm, in the same way a
wife would. Was she his wife now? Rita supposed it was possible. She'd heard what had happened to Megan, and for it to
have done so the very night she'd caused so much devastation
only increased her guilt. And the girl – the beautiful nameless
girl – stood where she'd been the whole time, by the sheds,
watching with fascination on her face.

Rita could see that the barn had been rebuilt, but not as a stable. She supposed it was a cowshed, as she'd seen cattle in Jack's fields when she'd driven along the lanes. Regret punched her as she looked at it. *Why did I do it?*

'Look, you'd better come in.'

'No, Jack, we don't want the likes of her here. She—'

'Dorothy, love, we should hear what she has to say. I know as she has done us a great wrong, but everyone deserves a chance at making amends. No one can do more than that, can they? And fifteen years is a long punishment.'

'But it doesn't come anywhere near what Iris's term is. That girl will suffer till her death, as will her family. The injury you inflicted on her head means that she cannot cope without help.'

'I never meant for that to happen. I was made to do what I did by that Terence Crompton. He wanted me to destroy your stud farm, Jack, so as he could start his own. He said he'd see me right, said he loved me, but once he'd had me and I'd done as he'd wanted, he betrayed me.'

'Hark at you. Can you hear what you're saying, Rita? And all as if it should excuse you. Well, we heard it all at the trial, and we don't want to hear your lies again. Because even if you are telling the truth, it beggars belief that you think it a justification for your vile actions.'

'I don't, but all I'm saying is that bleedin' bloke up at Hensal Grange was behind it, and it looks as though he got what he wanted, don't it? *Hensal Grange Stud Farm.* His dad wouldn't fund him, not while you were in the same business, he wouldn't. The final straw were when his dad said he would see you through the war and make sure you had the funds to come out the other side. That made His High-and-Mightiness flip. He came up with the plan to make it so as you lost everything and it would cost too much to help you start again.'

'Dorothy, I reckon as we should welcome Rita in. She's nowt to gain by coming here. She's come because she wants forgiveness. I, for one, would like to give it her. There's been enough upset. We can't keep living with bitterness.'

'Well, if you say so, Jack. Come on in then, Rita, but don't expect much change from me. I've had a hard job picking up the pieces of what went on that night, and though it wasn't all down to you, what you did put the tin hat on it.'

Nothing about the farm that Rita could see had changed much. She'd never been inside the house before, but it was as she imagined it would be. Jack motioned to her to sit at the wooden table in the centre of the huge kitchen. He and Dorothy sat opposite her, and the girl stood behind Jack.

'Who's this then? She has the look of Megan. Well, sort of.'

'This is Harriet, me granddaughter.' Jack looked full of pride as he said this. 'She's Sarah's lass by her first marriage. Sarah's married to Richard now, Megan's half-brother – but no relation to Sarah, of course. They have two boys in their early teens.'

'Pleased to meet you, Harriet, I'm sure.' The girl smiled. She was a stunner. 'If you don't think me nosy asking, Jack, how is Sarah?' With Jack telling her that Sarah was well and happy, Rita felt she could ask about the others. 'And everyone else around at that time – did everyone survive the war?'

'Pretty much. A few tragedies, even amongst those who did come home, but I don't think as anyone you knew copped it. P'raps you'd do better to get on with why you're here, Rita. Making conversation isn't comfortable. It took me a lot to get over what you did. My insurance company refused to pay out, as arson wasn't covered. You hit me with a blow I couldn't take, on top of what else'd happened that night.'

'I know. And that made it an even worse atrocity, if that were possible. But I have no other motive than to see if you can forgive me. It's a lot to live with. And, like I say, I did me time. I wanted you to know that, though it don't excuse me none, I did tell the truth at the trial. I were daft to believe that sod Crompton, but I were young and looking to better meself. Having escaped the filthy, overcrowded hole that were me home in the East End of London, I weren't about to go back there. I never thought as I'd be capable of doing what I did, though. And, to tell the truth, I never really thought it through – what could happen, and how it would affect you. I didn't, Jack, and I'm sorry.'

'Well, lass, what you did were bad, but it came nowhere near what had gone just afore it, though in itself it caused me more heartache than I could take. But I appreciate you doing this. It can't have been easy for you and, as far as I'm concerned, I forgive you.'

'Ta, mate. That means a lot to me. I know you can't forgive me, Dorothy, and I understand. You thought a lot of Iris, and it were terrible what happened to her as a consequence of me actions. I take it you and Jack are married?'

'Yes, I stayed on after the war. We worked together for ten years before Jack came to love me, but to my shame I'd loved him from the moment I set eyes on him.'

'Oh, I knew how you felt – we all did, and you couldn't help them feelings. The thing is, you didn't act on them. We knew you wouldn't, not with him having a wife and being so happy, but you didn't hide how it were for you, where Jack were concerned.'

Dorothy blushed, and a look passed between her and Jack

that told of their love. Rita thought she'd never stop being sorry about what happened to Megan, but it was good to see the happiness that Dorothy and Jack had found together.

Although Rita knew everything she needed to know about Terence Crompton, she had to sound as though she didn't. 'I suppose High-'n'-Mighty Terence Crompton got married, did he?'

'Yes, he married Louise and they're very happy. They have three children: a boy and twin girls. It's best you forget it all now, Rita. You look like you've made a life for yourself. You have the trappings of money. So let things lie, eh?'

'I don't have much choice, Dorothy, but I'd like you and Jack to believe me story. What happened to Theresa Crompton then?'

'More than you can imagine! None of us knows the full story, as a lot of what she did was hush-hush and will remain so for a long time, but she worked behind enemy lines in the war. She's changed. Looks like a dropout when she comes to visit, which is on very rare occasions. Her looks have gone, her hair is like wire and she smokes constantly. I reckon as she's been through stuff we can't imagine. They captured her, you know. And it's said as she'd have been shot, or suffered a worse kind of death, but our lot and the Americans got there just in time to save her and all the prisoners from the prisoner-of-war camp she was being held in.'

'Theresa, a war hero! Blimey, how did all that come about? The pair of them twins were as lazy as anyone could get, and were into all sorts as would make your hair curl. Bugger me!'

'Aye, well, that's as maybe, but she's paid her dues for whatever it is you refer to. He hasn't, not by a long shot, if what you say is reet. Terence Crompton came out on top, as his type allus do. His dad passed on sudden, and he's come into the estate, besides having the best stud farm in the whole of the county and a good wife and happy home. He has a life to envy. It don't seem right.'

'You're right, Jack, it don't. What about his mam? She were a fragile thing when I worked there.'

'Funny that. She were, weren't she? And had been since her sister died . . .' Jack's pause spoke volumes. She'd never got to the bottom of it all, but she'd heard there had been a scandal surrounding Jack and Lady Crompton's sister back in the early thirties. Rita watched as he shifted uncomfortably, before he continued, 'Well, after Theresa went to war, Lady Crompton threw herself into charity war work and grew in strength. Everyone said it was Theresa's efforts making her feel guilty, and it brought her out of herself. She's still very active in the community and lives over in Tarrington House now.'

'That's good to hear. You say Theresa visits, so where does she live then?'

'Somewhere in London, we think. By, lass, you've a lot of interest in them all.'

'Nah, not really – just making conversation.' She hoped they believed her. Jack sounded suspicious, and the last thing she wanted was them thinking she was up to something. 'I am interested to know how Mildred and Penny went on, though. Have you kept in touch?'

'Yes, they're fine. They both went back home. Both are married and have families and seem happy enough. Look, Rita, I'll be honest with you. I'm not wanting to keep in touch with you. Like Jack has, I will forgive you, but that doesn't mean we welcome you as a friend. Here, I've made you some tea and there's some cake, but I would appreciate you leaving when you've had them.'

'I get your gist, Dorothy. I couldn't fail to, with how blunt you put it, and I can't say as I blame you. It's enough for me that you're willing to forgive me. I live and work in London and am doing all right for meself, so I have no need to come up 'ere again. I have what I come for, except . . . Well, I wondered if you'd give something to Iris's family for me?' Rummaging in her bag, she found the envelope. 'It's a bit to help with her care, or just to make things easier for them. And tell them I'm sorry. I can't make amends, I know that, but this might help them.'

'I doubt they will take it, but I'll try. If they don't, I'll give it to charity. Is there anything in particular you'd like it to go to?'

'Horses. Anything to do with horses. I pay a regular amount to a charity as looks after clapped-out racehorses, and mares as have dropped that many foals they're knackered. It's in Sussex, but I bet as there is something around here as does the same thing.'

'I'll see to it for you. And, well, I know I've been short with you, but I do appreciate you coming. I'll see you out.'

'Right-o, Dorothy. Ta-ra then, Jack. I'm glad to see as you're all right now, and nice to have met you too, Harriet. Remember me to your mam – only tell her about me being sorry first, and I hope she understands.'

Once on the open road again, Rita relaxed. *You did well there, girl, coming over all contrite. They bleedin' well fell for it.* Her smile widened. She'd found out quite a lot, most of it useful. She regretted not actually seeing Terence bleedin' Crompton, but that would come.

When she took her revenge, he had to know it was her, but in such a way as he couldn't do anything to her, because him knowing would make her revenge all the sweeter. Now, to find Theresa. Her living in London would make it a bit difficult, as anyone could lose themselves there, but she had folk as could find out most things. She didn't doubt one of them would come up with an answer for her – they had to, because she'd never got over Theresa, and she hoped as Theresa felt the same. *Besides, Theresa may hate her brother as much as I do, and might make a useful ally.*

43

Terence & Louise

The Past Intrudes on the Present

Terence patted the rump of the magnificent stallion. The animal had sired two sure winners to date, and had just covered a mare that had previously produced a Derby winner. The resulting offspring could make him a lot of money. He already had owners from as far afield as the Middle East interested in bidding for the horse.

A voice he loved interrupted his thoughts. 'Darling, I have a letter from Theresa. She wants to come and see us. She has things to discuss – sounds ominous, don't you think?'

Terence turned and saw Louise walking in his direction, waving a letter. She still had the same graceful beauty that had attracted him to her all those years ago. He hadn't thought it possible then to love someone as deeply as he did her, and that love had sustained him through the years of longing to be with the one person he was born to be with – the person he'd been conceived at the same time as, had shared a womb with, and with whom he should have been able to share his life forever, if only it wasn't forbidden.

Waving in a gesture that said *Give me a moment*, he turned from these shameful thoughts. He needed to compose himself. His head trainer stood next to him, holding the mare, and Terence handed him the reins of the stallion. 'See to them, Gary. They've done a good day's work. Keep them apart, though, as we don't want Field of Joy getting agitated or worked up at the nearness of his mare. We may have him cover one of the others later, when he's rested. Perhaps Fancy Lady, as she's in her oestrous cycle as well.'

Trying to talk of run-of-the-mill things didn't help, as Gary was part of the past. Granted, he wasn't a main part, but one that served as a reminder: he had worked for Terence's Aunt Laura when she had a stud farm, and then with Fellam, but there was no stud farm for Gary to return to after the war. He was a good and a nice man, and Terence had felt obliged to take him on. But at moments like this, when he found himself vulnerable to being attacked by his conscience, anything that brought Fellam to mind wasn't good. *When will I be able to live with it all? Thank God Fellam doesn't know the truth.*

As it was, Fellam had been glad of the money Terence had paid him, for the goodwill of the business and the three horses that survived. *Christ, it's all years ago now! Nigh on twenty. It is history – the history of another person, not me. Well, at least not the me I have become.*

Making a huge effort, he turned back to Louise. 'Now, darling, you have all my attention.' Dealing with the practicalities of the horses had given him a moment's respite, though not much else. At least he felt able to deal with Louise's sudden appearance and her comments having caused him to visit the darker side of his mind, where his guilty secrets concerning his sister lay hidden.

'You seem distracted, darling. I should have waited until you came up for your lunch. Sorry. I just thought it strange, as Theresa only ever visits when she really has to. She doesn't invite herself, and what can she have to "discuss"?'

Sweat broke out all over his body, and fear lurched in his heart. *Does she want to bring up what happened in the past? Dear God, I hope not.* Their separation – an open sore in Terence – left him yearning to be with her, but at the same time he was relieved that he didn't have to bear Theresa's constant presence, as he knew he would give in to the dangerous urges that engulfed him.

'Terence?'

'Oh, I'm sorry, darling. I've a lot on at the moment – the stables, and everything. You know these summer months are our busiest, with all the mares coming into season at different times. It's difficult to switch my mind between that and the domestic stuff. Anyway, Theresa, you say? Writing to ask us if she can visit – never thought I would see the day. Well, as long as it is convenient for you, my dear, then it will suit me. I'll leave it to you to reply. Perhaps she's found herself a man at last, eh?'

'Oh, I hope so. She must be lonely. Do you remember how it was when she came back from the war? It was as if she'd suffered a bereavement.'

'Yes, but then maybe she had. A lot of people had wartime relationships, and I suspect most had to break up when reality hit them, once the war came to an end and they had to go back to their spouses. Anyway, no good speculating; just let her know she can come, and we'll soon find out what this is all about.'

'What if we have a dinner party whilst she's here? Invite a few likely males?'

'Good God, no! You haven't forgotten what Theresa's turned into, have you?' It broke his heart to admit it. 'It's as though she has a mental illness. She does the strangest things, and the way she dresses . . . Oh dear, it's all very upsetting.'

'I know, dear. Maybe we should get her to see someone. A psychiatrist?'

'She wouldn't agree. But you are right, she does need to. Sometimes it is as if she isn't with it. God knows what the poor darling went through in that concentration camp . . . Oh, don't let's talk about it.'

Louise's arm came round him. 'Look, darling, how about an early lunch? It's a lovely day. I can get Millie to set it up in the garden for us. What do you think? You look all in.'

A sudden urge came to Terence to block out all the bad things his memory held – his exploits with the Land Girls, his betrayal of Rita, the destruction and theft of Fellam's business and, most of all, his incest with and his worries concerning his beloved sister. Louise could help him do that. He could lose himself in all she had to give. He hugged her to him, trying to cement this thought to block out all the others. 'I have a better idea, darling.' He kissed the top of her hair. 'And I'll take the afternoon off, if you're free?'

'Oh? Well, in that case, I'll have Millie pack a picnic up for us and we'll ride over to the family field. We haven't been there for ages. Something in me wants to do that, darling.'

The thought of a peaceful afternoon in the haven that had always been kept as a special place for family only – a field about a mile from the house, fully enclosed with high hedges and its own summerhouse, and out of bounds to anyone other than those instructed to take food or whatever the family wanted there – really appealed. 'Me, too. Excellent. I'll instruct Gary to saddle our mounts whilst we change. Though I think we'd better do that separately or we'll never make it over to the summerhouse!'

She giggled at this: a pretty sound, and one that clutched at him and made him wish no one had gone before her. She was the only pure thing in his life – well, her and his wonderful son, soon to go to university, and his adorable twin daughters, away at school but due home for the holidays any day now. He couldn't wait. *Please, God, don't let anything happen to destroy it all.*

'Darling, why don't we have a party to celebrate Simon finishing school with such brilliant results and securing a place at Oxford? I don't mean at home – too much organizing, with the limited staff we have – but at that hotel just outside Leeds. We could coincide it with Theresa's visit.'

Terence had been almost asleep as he sat in his deckchair, relaxing. He looked down at Louise lying on the grass at his feet. 'A good idea. Yes, I like it. I'm very proud of our son. What about a shooting party the next day, for him and his friends? Give us a chance to look over some prospects for the girls?'

'Terence! Don't be so old-fashioned. If you think for one moment the girls will allow you to pick them a husband, then you have another think coming.'

He laughed at this. Louise giggled. A moment in the life of doting parents, he thought. Still, he'd like to have been an old-fashioned parent – one of those who ruled the household and had the last say on who could ask for the hand of his lovely daughters. He sighed. 'Another glass of wine, dear?'

'Mmm? No, thanks. You are funny sometimes, Terence. And you know something? I do love you. You know that, don't you?'

'You often say it like that, and it always worries me.'

'Worries you? How? Why?' Louise eased herself onto her elbow and squinted against the sun as she looked at him.

Terence was sorry now he'd said anything, as he didn't

353

know how to explain. 'Well, it sounds as though you didn't expect to.'

'Actually, I didn't. I mean, I did love you from the start, but your actions – well, I had an idea of what you were up to and with whom. I went crying home to my mother once. She sent me back, telling me I was being stupid, and the more *wild oats* you sowed before you settled down, the better it would fare for me. She said the time for me to put my foot down was when you made a formal proposal. But I never had any need to do that, as she was right. You seemed to have got it all out of your system, and I never suspected anything else from the moment you asked me to marry you.'

'Good God! You've never told me all of this before.'

'You've never questioned me before about how I express my feelings.'

'No. I've always been afraid to.'

'You've not really doubted me, have you, Terence, darling?' Louise sat up properly now, and frowned at him.

'A bit. Well, I don't know. I never felt I deserved love. Not anybody's. My father—'

'I know. But he did love you. He just didn't understand you. You were so different from him in every way.'

'Yes, I'm sure he loved me, but he never made me *feel* that I ever matched up to what he expected. You know, if I hadn't had Theresa's love . . . I mean, Mother didn't seem to feel anything for anybody. I sometimes think Theresa filled a gap in me – an emotional gap. Though all that has reversed now. Mater is so different and is a joy to be around. I wish Theresa could experience that; it would be so good to be a family again.'

'You were very close to Theresa, weren't you?'

This seemed to be getting onto dangerous ground. The

afternoon had been lovely. They'd picnicked, then made love, and now the feeling of relaxation and the aftermath of pleasure were being eroded. He sipped his wine, hoping to avoid giving an answer. He hadn't expected his innocent question about the depth of Louise's love to lead any further.

'Terence?'

'Oh, well, yes, we were. Twins, you know. Look at our two. Jacqueline and Josephine hate to be without each other, and they always seem to have a secret going on between them. In fact they are worse than we were. Both being girls, they can share everything.'

'But it didn't stop you. You and Theresa sometimes behaved more like lovers than—'

'For heaven's sake, Louise! What are you saying?'

'I – I didn't mean you were.'

Her shocked expression gave him the feeling that something was dawning on her. He'd protested too strongly. He laughed, but the laugh came out sounding nervous and false.

'I know. It's a sensitive subject. That awful Rita accused us of that at the trial, and it hurt. It hurt very much, and I think it contributed to Theresa never wanting to come back home. There's always those who will take the "no smoke without fire" attitude. She couldn't face it all.' *How silkily the lies slide off my tongue.*

'Oh, I'm sorry – I'd forgotten. Mine was just a silly observation: a way of describing the rapport you had between you, nothing more.' Louise rose and came and sat on his knee. 'I'll share your glass with you.' As she took it and sipped from it, the sun reflected off the base, sending a rainbow of colours over her soft skin.

He leaned forward and kissed the nape of her neck, murmuring, 'Should one kiss a rainbow?'

'What rainbow? Oh, never mind – if it is where you are kissing, yes. Yes, please.'

Suddenly they clung together as if to ward off something evil. Terence could feel Louise's anxiety in her clasp. It matched his own. He suspected she couldn't put a name to what worried her, just as he couldn't. It simply seemed there was something in the near future that could hurt them. It was a silly notion, but it lurked like a child's fear of the dark.

44

Rita & Theresa

A Bittersweet Reunion

The curtain quivered in Theresa's hand as she eased it back, just enough to see the street. *Yes, I'm certain it is her! What does she want? When did she get out of prison? Why does she keep coming and sitting outside?* It was like some kind of slow torture.

The interruption to her normal routine was too much to take. She needed Terence. Oh God, she hoped they'd received her letter and would ring. She should have rung them, but fear had stopped her – fear that if Terence answered she'd not be able to cope, and nor would he. This way he'd get Louise to ring her.

Theresa looked over towards her desk. Her book lay open. Her pen, dropped in anguish when she heard the car pull up outside, balanced on the edge of the unfinished page, taunting her with the words she hadn't yet written – words that tumbled her memories out of her, opening up raw, painful wounds and making her eyes bulge with the swell of tears.

At times she wasn't sure whether writing it all down was helping, but at other times she felt a compulsion to do so. *Oh, Pierre, what happened to you? And where is our son?*

A sob caught in her throat.

She had to stop this. Nothing could be gained by it. Pierre's family had taken their child, born secretly two weeks before their capture – where to, she did not know, and she had found it impossible to find out. So many displaced persons. So many documents destroyed, particularly those of anyone with a connection to the Jews. Pierre was of Jewish descent. His sole reason for fighting in the Resistance was to avenge his people.

Oh God, Rita's getting out of the car! The sound of the knocker sent a tremble through her. *Go away!*

It rattled again. The letter box lifted, allowing Rita's voice to penetrate inside the house. 'I know you're in there, love. Open the bleedin' door, won't yer?'

Unable to move, Theresa's blood felt icicled by the fear that held her. She waited, praying Rita would go away.

'I've come because I still love you, Theresa. I want us to get together again. You want that, don't you?'

Do I? Something inside warmed her at Rita's words. A tiny spot deep down where all had dried in a cold finality, never to be touched, never to be thought of again, flickered a sensation through her.

'You know you loved me, girl. Me and you were good together. We can be again. No one need know. I want you, Theresa. I want you in me arms, where you should be.'

Without her bidding it to, Theresa's body moved. The trembling in her limbs weakened her. She wanted to be sick, but something compelled her forward.

In one movement the door opened and she was in the warm, loving arms of Rita. Her frail bones pushed back against the banister that curved into the hall, her face and lips receiving kisses. It felt good. So good.

'Come on, love. Let's go up to your room. We can talk after. I've gotta have you. Oh, Theresa, me lovely.'

Shivering with fear and anticipation, Theresa allowed the stronger woman to guide her. Oh, how the tide had changed. How was it that she had once determined what happened to her, and who she let intrude on her inner self? Now hands undressed her, lips kissed and nibbled her, and she could do nothing against the feelings that were awoken, which snapped the fragile, twig-like core of her. Nor did she want to stop the crescendo of sensations that brought her world crashing around her, screaming from her as if a thousand symbols had clanged together. In shattering all that into a million pieces, Rita's loving of her put her together again.

'Oh, Rita, my love, my world . . . Help me.'

With this last plea came the tears – floods and floods of tears that swamped Theresa's face, her breasts, her whole self. An enormous release, which she thought would drain her of life itself.

'It's all right, love. I know some of what you've been through. We'll rebuild you. We will. Everything's going to be all right. Here, let me hold you a while. I need to do that. I've missed you, love. I've not been without this one and that one taking bits of me, and me taking bits of them – some of it good, some of it not worth the effort – but I've never forgot what we had together, and to me it were the best ever, and were meant to be.'

'Oh, Rita. I – I don't know what to say.'

'Don't say anything, love. There's nothing to say. We know what we have, and that's all that matters. I'm not going to lose you again.'

Lying on her bed, with her head in Rita's lap and Rita stroking her hair, Theresa knew something profound had happened. It was as if a missing part of a jigsaw had been found and clicked into place. It hadn't completed the whole puzzle, or even shown the finished picture, but it was a link to the rest, a beginning of the journey back to sanity.

'Come on. I'll run you a nice bath and you can soak, whilst I put the kettle on and make us a cup of Rosie Lee, then we can talk, eh? I've a lot to tell you, and I know you have a lot you need to talk of.'

Theresa allowed Rita to wrap her housecoat around her and to help her to the bedside chair. Exhausted, she leaned back in it. First thing tomorrow, she'd write to Terence and tell him she wasn't coming. Her suspicions had been correct: the woman watching her had been Rita; but far from wanting Terence to help her get away, and to warn him this woman was back in their lives, she knew she wanted Rita to stay; knew she wanted – needed – Rita, and knew, too, that she didn't want to share her with Terence ever again.

Right, mate, another mission accomplished, and not an unpleasant one, either. Theresa is back in the fold. Now to put my whole plan together and see if two and two really can make five!

Rita got into her car and waved to the puppy-like Theresa, blowing her a kiss and mouthing, 'See you soon.'

Looking at her watch, she judged she would have time to get a hot bath before she had to be in the office of her modelling agency. Not that she did many evening shifts. Too knackered, these days. It was enough to check over her club, sit in her private booth and see that clients were being taken care of. But she had a girl coming in for an interview and she always liked to look over new blood herself.

As Rita drove, she thought about the state she'd found Theresa in. If she hadn't been warned by them at Fellam's farm, she would have been shocked. There was still a glimmer of the beauty Theresa had once been, but it was almost lost in the too-thin body, the wiry hair; and the once-lovely eyes were now void of any happiness and held only pain.

Some of that had lifted as Rita had gently loved her, enjoying the feeling of rekindling everything Theresa had lit in her all those years ago. She'd never forgotten Theresa, and had used the images and thoughts of being with her again to help her get through the fifteen years of hell.

The sign above her agency office in Soho came into view: a small flag-like sign swinging in the wind, with a big red arrow attached to it leading down an alleyway between some buildings.

Rita parked and looked up at her home – a flat above the shop. Not what she had aimed for, but it would do for now and was a million miles away from the cell she'd shared with three others in Holloway. Her body trembled at the memory. Her determination to wreak revenge strengthened. *If it's the last thing I do, I'll make bleedin' Terence Crompton pay.*

45

Rita & Patsy

A Mirror Image

Refreshed after her bath and feeling as if all her dreams were coming together, Rita sat back in her chair in her bright office. It was painted yellow, with the walls adorned with photos of the so-called models she had on her books, and she thought the picture it presented was just right for her clients, who were mostly businessmen of an older age.

What she lacked was girls of quality. Some of the business gents were after a girl who was presentable enough to take out for an evening before going back to their hotel. She hoped the girl she was expecting would turn out to be just that.

Glancing at the clock, she realized she had time to repaint her nails before the girl arrived – and some thinking time, as it happened. She needed that. Her soak in the bath had eased the frustration at having received nothing back from Theresa, in a sexual way. The woman had taken all and not tried to give anything in return, but then Rita hadn't gone there expecting anything, so it was all a bonus. It was just that feelings had reawakened in her – stuff she'd felt for Theresa and Terence. She couldn't deny it. They'd both touched something in her all those years ago, and that something had leapt up and demanded attention the moment she was in Theresa's presence.

Anyway, enough of that. It was time to try and put some plans together.

First, how to destroy that bastard Crompton? Her favoured method was by fire, for hadn't he destroyed her by that means? Right. Fire it was. Now, the house or the stables? *Oh, fuck it! I'll do the bleedin' lot. But I have to pick me time.* No one must get hurt, not even Terence bleedin' Crompton. No, that wasn't in the plan. Not physically hurt, anyway.

Waving her hand of painted nails, Rita gave some thought to how she could achieve her plan. One thing she needed was information about the family's comings and goings. And she needed to make sure that Terence Crompton wouldn't be in a position to report her. Blackmail! For that, Theresa would play her role.

Evidence – that's what I need. Evidence of her own and Theresa's lesbian relationship. She would threaten to make it public, and prove she had been telling the truth about that at the trial. And just maybe she could get Theresa so dependent on her that she could get her to sign a confession, admitting incest with her brother. That's it! *I'll have Terence bleedin' Crompton by the balls at last!*

'I'm sorry if I'm early, only the train times didn't fit with the interview time. I can sit down and wait, though.'

The voice made Rita jump. She hadn't even heard the door opening. She'd had her back to it and had gone into a world of her own.

When she swivelled round, the sight that met her eyes more than shocked her. Her mouth gaped open. 'Harriet! What're you doing here? Wait a mo, it didn't say I was expecting a Harriet in the diary. Oh, using another name, are we? Well, I don't blame you, love, I can't see that Dorothy letting you apply to work in the likes of this place!'

'Me name ain't Harriet. It's Patsy. Who's this Harriet and Dorothy you're going on about?'

Rita couldn't speak. It was as if a ghost had walked in on her and taken all that she had out of her.

'You all right? Sorry if I'm not the right girl, but I do have an appointment. I saw your advert and thought I'd be just what you're looking for. I can talk to anyone, so I would make a good companion. I've had a good education – a better one than most of me standing – and I'm not shy. Besides that, I can put on a very posh voice when called upon to do so.'

Her giggle as she mimicked the top-drawer lot with this last sentence relaxed Rita. She found she could speak again. 'It's bloody uncanny, but I've met your double, girl. She lives up north and could be your twin. How old are you? Were you born in 1940? Let me see . . .' Doing a quick calculation from the time when Theresa had that Billy Armstrong, Harriet's father, she asked, 'August 1940?'

'I was, but . . . Hey, what is this? You're scaring me.'

Rita ignored this, her excitement growing as she pursued the idea further. 'Do you know who your parents are?'

'As it happens, I don't, but what's that to you? I don't think I want to work here; you're giving me the creeps.'

'Well, I think I know who they are.'

'What? You know me mam and dad? How? Who are you? How can you know that? You don't know me. All right, I look like this Harriet, whoever she is, but that don't give you the right to say you know who me mam and dad were.'

A sob on the last words pulled Rita out of the incredulous daze she'd been in. 'Sit down, Patsy, there's nothing to be scared of. Just give me a moment to think.' Rita smiled kindly at the girl. *I need to be careful, keep her on my side, as she could be useful, very useful. Because, as sure as day follows night, this girl is the daughter of Theresa and Billy Armitage – she has to be!*

Everything fitted. Besides the girl strongly resembling that Harriet, whom Jack Fellam had told her was the daughter of Sarah and Billy Armitage, the timing was right. *Theresa was definitely pregnant when she went away that time. I saw the evidence with my own eyes when we were naked together, and I witnessed her and Billy in that summerhouse.* At this thought, Rita felt a pang of guilt at making off when Billy cut up rough with Theresa. *Right, I'm to handle this with care.*

'Look, I'm sorry if I scared you. It's just me – I have premonitions about things sometimes. They come of a sudden and leave me with a headache. Just forget it.'

'No, I won't. I've been looking for me mam and dad since as long as I can remember. One of the Sisters at the convent told me I come from rich stock, and that was the reason that I had to have a tutor and extra lessons, even after the others had done their schooling. It were paid for and checked up on, and it had to last until someone adopted me. She said as I were taken a couple of times by folk who could give me the standing I should have had, but they brought me back because I have a temper and disrupted their lives too much.'

'That'll be your red hair and a trait you got from your dad. He were a rough one. You're better off not knowing anything about him.'

'But I do want to know. You have to tell me. And if it's his fault I were put in the convent, I'll hunt him down and make him pay for the years of loneliness I went through.'

This one statement made up Rita's mind. The passion put

into it told her all she needed to know. Here, walking in off the street, was the answer to her prayers: someone who had just as much of a reason to seek revenge as she had, even if she didn't know it yet. 'Right, Patsy, me and you need to have a good talk. Sit down. I'll get you a nice cup of Rosie Lee.'

'Ta. I could do with one. At this moment I could commit murder, I'm that angry.'

Better by the minute . . .

After Rita had told Patsy as much as she wanted Patsy to know, Patsy's reaction shocked her.

'So, me mam's still alive, but you know she won't have anything to do with me, and me dad were a murderer?'

Rita watched the tear trickle down Patsy's face and felt a moment's apprehension. Had she read this girl wrong? One moment she seemed like a hard nut who could take anything on her shoulders, and the next she had crumbled into a vulnerable wreck.

'Look, love, I've told you what I know, right?'

'No, you haven't. You haven't told me who they are or where they live, only about them.'

No, and I'm not giving you that information. That's something you have to work for, girl.

'I want you to take me to me mam. Tell me her name, and where she lives.'

'All in good time. There's other stuff – a lot of it that I haven't told you about. It involves me. And, like you, I have a reason to hate your mother and her brother, especially her brother. I need to get me revenge on them. Me need is like a scab that I can't leave alone. It itches constantly and I have to rid meself of it.'

'You scare me, but I know how you feel. I'd like to get me own back on them, too. They deserted me for no other reason than I'd be an embarrassment to them. If me mam had turned out to be poor and couldn't have coped with me, or ill in her mind because of what happened to her, then I might have some forgiveness in me. But to give me away as if I were nothing to her, just because of her standing in society, that sticks in me throat. I hate her and everyone to do with her. But what about me dad's family? What were they like and where are they? Wouldn't they take me back and welcome me as one of them?'

'You have a great-granny, your granny's mam. And a couple of half-uncles, and, well, I'm not sure about this, but maybe a half-sister, and that's it. But look, love. They know nothing about you. Don't even know you exist. They've been through life's grinder, them lot, especially your dad's widow. She's now married to one of your half-uncles, and her dad were married to your granny, so he's your step-granddad.'

'What? They're all related!'

'By marriage, yes. Oh, it all goes on up north, I can tell yer. But like I said, they've been through a lot, so it don't seem fair to put more on them.'

'Put more on them! I'm not a thing. I'm a human being, and nothing as they've been through has been my fault. Me being born wasn't my fault, and yet I've been made to feel like a sinner, a lesser person than others, all me life. Don't you think as I've been through enough? And how come the family is so complicated?'

As it happened, Rita did think the girl had been through enough, but she wasn't about to say so. She needed to make Patsy feel anger against all of those who should be taking care of her, so a few lies were called for. 'There's a lot of that goes on in the country. Makes your hair curl, but I know one thing: they'd hate you, because of who your dad was. And that's why I'm reluctant to put you through it. What your dad did made them all bitter and twisted. Even the girl I told you of – your half-sister, as is the image of you – has it rough. She's pushed from one to the other. Her mam rejected her. She's sometimes up north with your step-granddad – her granddad – and sometimes with a friend of the family, but she's always in the way, according to my sources, like she's a reminder to them of your dad and what he did. So I can't see them wanting another reminder of him.'

'But what about her? Me sister? We could look out for each other. At least we'd have someone of our own, and we could make our lives together.'

God, this is getting worse. It is as if everything I come up with digs me a deeper hole. Isn't there a saying that lies build a tangled web, or something like that? The girl is all questions. She's beginning to irritate me.

'Look, with all this emotional stuff, you ain't much bleedin' use to me. I want revenge on your mother's lot, and I thought as you'd be a useful tool to have by me side. But I've told you enough of me intentions to incriminate me, so I'm not happy about it all. I reckon as you need to tell me if you're with me or not; and if you are, then we can sort all the rest out after we've done what has to be done. No one need know you're involved. They need never realize you even know me. But you have to act out your part, right? No messing it up just because you want a bleedin' family. If you can give me a promise on that, then I'll tell you everything.'

The girl was quiet for a moment, a sullen silence that gave nothing away. When she spoke, it told of her calculating nature, and Rita liked that.

'So if I agree to go along with you, I get to know who all my family are and where they are, and get to have me revenge on me mam's lot, right? Well, I don't care about them, they're not worthy of me bothering about them, but I'm not getting involved in anything that's dangerous to them. All I want is for them to feel the same pain I'm feeling, and for them to know it's me, and I know who they are and what they did to me.'

'That's the deal. But if you don't agree to help me, then you can sling your hook and good luck to you finding them; I reckon it's impossible, seeing as you don't know their names, and most of what happened was at the beginning of the war. So where are you going to start looking, eh? You might say "up north", but up north is a big area, and I haven't told you where, so you'll not be much further forward than you are now.'

'I'll do it. But you have to keep your part.'

'You agreeing to help will make me keep my part, won't it? Because if you're involved, you will need to know more about them. Right, here's all you have to do. Contact your uncle, your mam's brother. I have his telephone number – I got it from the exchange. You tell him that you want to meet him, as you have information for him about the past. Now he's going to be as confused as hell and may come the high-'n'-mighty. If he does, say it's to do with Rita and the trial, and his and his sister's involvement with one another.'

'What involvement? Can't I tell him who I am?'

'The least you know about that, the better. And no, you can't tell him who you are. Not on the telephone. Out in the sticks, the bleedin' operators listen in to everyone's business, and what we have is for his ears only. What I told you will be enough to get a meeting with him. It's then as you can tell him more.'

'So when we meet, what do I tell him?'

369

'You tell him that you've met me, and what you know of yourself being his niece. You tell him that I have other knowledge that will bring his life, as he knows it, to an end. I don't care what it all sounds like: what I know is the bleedin' truth, and I want him to admit to it. I want to blackmail him a bit, so when I carry out the ultimate act, he knows who is responsible, but can't do anything about it.'

'The ultimate act?'

'Don't worry yourself about that. It won't involve you. Now, what do you think?'

'I don't think I have much choice. Me need to know where I come from, and any family I have, is too strong to turn this down. As long as you promise I won't be hurting anyone, just making them face up to the truth about their past, and you also promise to tell me who me dad's family are and where they live.'

'I'll say one thing for you, girl: you're a mixture of the natures in your background. Both your dad's mam and your mam's parents, though classes apart, were a nice lot. I don't know where your dad came from, though I did hear as his dad were a rough one. Your dad were more than rough: he were a psycho. But I can't see them traits in you. In fact I can't see much of him at all, except you saying you have a temper.'

'I don't know if I can trust you, Rita. You skirt around everything. I'll not do anything unless you promise me you'll tell me what I need to know. Don't forget, I'll know how to contact me uncle after this, so if you welsh on your part of the deal, I'll let him know you're planning more, and where he can find you.'

Blimey, this girl's got more of her dad in her than I thought. A tremble went through Rita. She had to tread very carefully with this one. The only hold she had on Patsy was knowing who her family were, but once she met Terence Crompton, she'd be able to find out the rest. *Christ, what if she tells him more? I've been a bloody fool to let her suspect what I have in mind.* 'You say *I* have to promise, what about you, eh? Well, I'm telling yer now, I've done fifteen bloody years for something that wasn't all my fault, and your bleedin' uncle got away with. If you turn on me, then yer'll know of it. There's nowhere you can go that I won't find you. I have men in my employ that would kill you on my say so, and that's what will happen. You're in this now, and you play everything the way I've told yer to, or you'll take the consequences.'

For a moment the girl looked terrified, but then she rallied. 'All I want is your assurance that you don't intend to physically hurt anyone. If you keep your half of the bargain, then I'll keep mine, and you'll have no need to worry.'

Patsy had spirit and cunning, aye, and courage too, Rita could see that. Damn and blast the girl; she had the upper hand. The ultimate plan would have to be abandoned. But none of that seemed important now. *If I go through with this, I'll have Terence and Theresa Crompton in me clutches again and I can do what I like with them – play them like puppets on a string. Destroy their peace of mind – that will be enough. It will have to be.*

46

Sarah

Going Home

Sarah gathered up the medical records and stacked them neatly back into the box. Another surgery done. She walked through to the treatment rooms to tidy up anything the doctors had left about and to sterilize the equipment they had used. She loved working with Richard and the other doctors as their receptionist and assistant. She'd even helped a couple of times when they'd needed her to calm some of the youngsters, and more than once she had considered training to be a nurse.

Richard had argued at first, saying it wasn't right for her to work. But now that the boys were away at school, and with Harriet having gained her A-levels and waiting to hear whether she would get a place at medical school and spending a lot of time up north with her granddad and Dorothy, there was little else for Sarah to do. When Mrs Pickles, the previous receptionist for umpteen years, retired, she'd begged Richard and his partners to allow her to stand in. Now she hoped they would keep her on.

Apart from anything else, the job at last provided Sarah with a way to get to know the real community of Market Harborough and the surrounding area and feel part of it. Until now, she'd only really met folk way above her standing,

Richard's peers. She'd coped well, even trying to moderate her northern accent, but she'd never felt comfortable or accepted. At times she could almost see the noses twitching with disdain as they looked down on her. Richard couldn't see it, and it had been the only thing with a bit of an edge between them. He thought she was being silly, and told her his friends adored her. Adored to make fun of her, more like. Still, as Granna Issy would have said, *You have to get on with it, lass.*

It'd helped when Bridget had confided in Sarah that at times she'd had exactly the same feelings. 'And, lass,' she'd said, using her northern inflection, something she'd done more and more since Edward passed away a few years ago, 'I've been on the outside inside for a lot longer than thou has.'

They'd laughed together at this. Sarah sometimes wondered if it was her influence that had brought out the Yorkshire lass in Bridget, but doing so seemed to be a great relief to Bridget, as if her *other self* – the posh lady – had all been an act. Sarah couldn't remember when she'd stopped calling her 'Granny Bridget', the polite title she'd given her as a child, but not doing so made Bridget feel more like a friend to her and gave her the proper status of her mam-in-law.

As Sarah went to go through the last door leading to Richard's consulting room, the telephone rang, sending her doubling back to her own desk.

'Sarah?'

'Aunt Hattie!'

'Hello, love, is everyone all right down there? It seems ages since we spoke.'

'Aye, we're fine. Ticking along, you know.'

'Oh, just ticking, eh?'

'Well . . .'

'I'm only taking you on. I've good news. I've had a call from Sally. She and Mark and the young 'uns are coming home in two weeks. She wondered if we could all get together?'

'Oh yes, we heard, too, from Mark. It seems he sold those songs he'd written. It's funny really, he always said as rock 'n' roll were an abomination of music, but now he's writing songs for them as sing it!'

'I know, but it's grand. He sounds alive for the first time. I mean, *really* alive. He were getting nowhere with that classical stuff he likes, and there was no money in it. Sally's always had to take in sewing work to help them make ends meet, and I think that made Mark feel less of a man than he already did, bless him.'

'I know what you mean. He copes well and doesn't dwell on it all, and he has a good go at whatever task he takes on. I s'pose he had to take his knock-backs, though. It's like that for all of them as try to make it in the music industry, or any of the arts really. Anyroad, they seemed to like America. Lucky them, I'd love to travel to foreign parts like they do.'

'Aye, well, Sally says as now Thomas and Marion are getting towards their teenage years they want to live back here. They want to make sure the young 'uns get a settled period in school and hope they'll go on in their education. I tell you what, though, love: I'm glad Mark's open to all the new stuff, as it means we can put some of me seventy-eights on the record player when we get together. I've just bought a new Bill Haley record. He's put all his old singles onto an EP. It's grand!'

'Oh, Aunt Hattie, you're a one. I thought you'd be playing Vera Lynn and Frank Sinatra?'

'Naw, that's for squares. My grandchildren think I'm hop, or hip, or sommat like that.'

Sarah laughed out loud. Hattie was a tonic. 'Talking of your grandchildren, has my Harriet been to see you?'

'Aye, she were here yesterday. Her and Arthur lose me, with their intellectual conversations. She tells us she's becoming a doctor.'

'I know, Richard's that proud, as I am. Imagine, eh, one of us becoming a doctor.'

'Talking of doctors. I have another reason for ringing. Well, you know how you're all on about how much you'd like to come and live back here? Even Bridget has said it since Edward passed on, bless him.'

'Yes. But, well, you know we can't. Eeh, don't get me started. Me heart longs to be back. I've never settled, you know. Not really. Even though there's a lot of bad memories up there, there's a lot of good 'uns an' all.'

'Aye, and memories are memories – good or bad – lass, and they're yours. They're where your heart is. Look, tell Richard there's a vacancy. A practice for sale, and I've had Arthur put a few words out in the right places.'

'What? But I thought Dr Cragshaw's son—'

'Aye, he did take over from his dad right enough, but he's getting on a bit himself and is talking of semi-retirement. Arthur was at one of them Round Table dos and got into a conversation with him. What d'yer reckon – would Richard be interested?'

'Oh, I think so. He's not comfortable working here. He just seemed to fall into it. His father influenced him. But he says there's not a day goes by that he doesn't have to ask one of his old school friends to take off their clothes!'

They both laughed at this.

'And yer know, even though it's been nigh on ten years since he bought into the practice, it never gets easier for him.'

'Eeh, he can strip this lot to his heart's content! None of them will know of him as owt different to being "the doctor". And, thou knows, we could do with another kindly soul.'

After controlling her laughter at the thought of Richard stripping folk to his heart's content, Sarah said, 'I don't think he'd like to be called that!'

'You know what I mean. Northerners need a special kind of handling. And your Richard has that gift. He won't look down on them, and he'll help the poor, I'm sure on that, cos National Health Service or not, they still get a raw deal at times, like as if they are second-class citizens and can wait if they need treatment. Anyroad, love, have a word and tell him to ring Arthur and he'll give him all the details. In the meantime, I'll keep me fingers crossed.'

'So will I, Aunt Hattie, so will I.'

'Oh, Richard, darling, I can't believe it! And Hartington House is up for sale an' all?'

Three weeks had passed since Sarah's conversation with Hattie. Richard had jumped at the idea of moving back up to the north and had arranged a meeting as soon as he could with Dr Cragshaw Junior.

'Yes, and I think we might get it.'

'Eeh, Hartington House is lovely. Me Granna Issy worked there as a young girl. She used to tell me tales of her days working as a cook for the family that lived there. It's a bit out of Breckton – about ten miles, I think – and about five or so from me dad, but it'll be perfect. Near enough to everyone we love, and just far enough away from your patients not to have them knocking on the door all the time. But can we afford to buy it?'

'With what I get for this house, you will.'

'Bridget – you'll come with us, then?' Looking from Richard to his mother, Sarah gave an exasperated sigh. 'You two have been at planning things behind me back.'

'Eeh, lass, we didn't mean . . . I – we – only wanted to—'

'Ha, I know. You didn't want to get me hopes up till you had a plan. I'm only at pulling your leg, Bridget, love. Come here.' Hugging Bridget brought a tear to Sarah's eye, as it did to Bridget's. They clung together longer than fitted the occasion and she realized they hadn't done this before.

'Me heart's back up in the north, Sarah, as are all the family, when you go. Mark and Sally are going to convert the outbuilding that's attached to Hattie and Arthur's house into a home for them. Eeh, it'll be grand.'

'Mother, you don't sound like you.' Richard laughed as he said this. 'It sounds so strange to hear you talk like that.'

'Sorry, love – the lass in me has outed. I suppressed her for a long time, for the love of your father and not to let the side down for him, but it's lovely having me own self back inside me.'

'Don't apologize. The more northern lassies surrounding me, the better, as far as I'm concerned.'

'I don't know how to take that, Richard. By, I'll have to be watching out for you.'

They all laughed at this. It was like a seal on the rest of their lives, as if they knew they were going home and all the bad that could happen had already happened and they were safe.

'So, how will it all work then?'

'I spoke to Mother on the telephone from Hattie's while I was up there negotiating the buying of the practice. I asked her not to say anything, as I wanted to tell you everything today when I got back. But, well, Hartington House is huge and there is plenty of room to make part of the downstairs into a flat for Mother. She will sell this house and, from the proceeds, help Mark out with his project and give us a good amount that we can use as a deposit, then—'

'A flat? Why would you want a flat? We've lived together all of these years.'

'Oh, I was on with thinking you wanted to move, and that move might mean moving from me as well.'

'Moving from you? No, eeh, Bridget, you're me family. Well, a big part of it. Leaving you behind was the only thing spoiling the thought of going back. I only kept quiet because I didn't want to make you feel that you had to come with us.'

They were in each other's arms again. 'Thank you, Sarah, I love you like you were me own daughter, as I do Sally. I must tell her that, next time I see her. I'm one for letting me actions speak, rather than words, but they don't always convey what I mean to.'

'In your case they do, Bridget. I've always felt your love. And I love you an' all, like as if you were me own mam, and like I loved Megan. I've been lucky in the women that stepped in for me own mam, thou knows. Silly that it's taken all these years for us to tell each other how we feel.'

'Well, when you two have finished – as touching as it all is – what does a man have to do to get something to eat? It's a long journey from up north, thou knows.'

This mimicking of them by Richard had them in fits of laughter again, as they went together towards the kitchen.

'Eeh, Richard, I'm that excited. When will it all happen, do you think?'

They were getting ready for bed after enjoying a quiet drink together once Bridget had retired for the night. Their conversation had been all about the part Richard would play in the practice in Breckton. It seemed that Dr Cragshaw Junior, as he was known, had secured the contract for looking after the pit workers, a partly privately paid service that would be very lucrative, and he wanted Richard to take complete charge of that. Richard was really pleased about this, as it would give him a chance to enter a field of medicine that he was interested in – lung diseases and their causes – and to have a direct bearing on the prevention of them. Besides, as he'd said, it would ease him in with the rest of the folk an' all. Any doctor looking after their menfolk was good enough for the rest of the community, so he'd have fewer problems settling in.

'It has to happen fairly quickly. At least, me going there does. Cragshaw can't cope and isn't keeping to the schedule in the contract. I've been avoiding this, but it may mean I go at the end of the month, which is the shortest time I can wrap things up here. But whether we will have the house by then, I don't know. It may mean you won't be able to come with me at first.'

'I ain't stopping here without you. Course I can come. We can stop at me dad's, as he's plenty of room, or with Aunt Hattie.'

'But what about Mother? I don't like leaving her.'

'She can come an' all. She'll love it. She's stayed at me dad's many a time when Megan was alive.'

'Yes, but maybe Hattie's would be best. Sally and Mark will be there too, and she's never stayed at your father's since he's been married to Dorothy.'

'That's settled then. Eeh, Richard, it's like all me dreams are coming true.'

'Have you been that unhappy here, darling?'

'I could never be unhappy where you are, me love, but I've been like a wheel missing a couple of spokes. I still ran all right, but I rattled a bit as I did so. I didn't run quite as I should.'

'Mmm, I think I know what you mean. Come here. I'll put those couple of spokes back in place for you.'

Snuggling into his arms, Sarah felt at peace. It was as if her world, which Richard had long ago put back together, had been made complete. Nothing could spoil her happiness. All the badness had gone, and she could think of nothing and no one that could harm them ever again. She wouldn't even put her mind to it. Instead, she gave herself to the exquisite pleasuring of Richard, filling her body with his as he brought her to sheer fulfilled joy.

47

Terence, Patsy & Rita

The Sins of the Past Return

Terence picked up the phone, expecting to hear Simon giving him the final arrangements for when he would be home. It seemed an age coming this time, as at the end of term Simon had asked if they would mind if he joined a group of boys on a trip to France. It would have seemed churlish not to let him. At seventeen and having done a wonderful job in his exams, achieving marks that would gain him entry to Oxford, the boy deserved to let his hair down. A niggling worry accompanied the decision, though, as some of Simon's friends looked more than weird with their shoulder-length hair and long sideburns. Not to mention their taste in music and dress! All those velvet collars and tight trousers – 'drainpipes', he thought they were called. And then the long jackets, and a shoelace for a tie! Good God, what was the world coming to?

The girl's voice coming down the line took him aback. 'Hello. You don't know me, but I want to meet up with you.'

The London accent made him quiver. 'What? Who is this?'

'Me name's Patsy, but like I said, Mister, you don't know me.'

'Then why should I agree to meet you?' The feeling deepened, as if someone had brushed the hairs on the back of his neck with a feather.

'Because I have some information you should know. It was given to me by Rita.'

With the mention of that name, shock surged through Terence's body. Good God! The hairs that had stood up on his arms now felt as though they were being pulled out, one by one. He had to think quickly. Louise was coming towards him. 'Where and when?'

'As soon as possible, and I don't care where.'

'All right.' He felt annoyed now. Angry even. Who the bloody hell was this girl, and what was that fucking Rita up to? 'Look, I go into Leeds on a Thursday on business matters. That's the day after tomorrow. Can you meet me there? There's a cafe-type place opposite the station.' Not the type of place he or any of his acquaintances used. 'I'll be there at around eleven. Now are you going to tell me who the devil I'm talking to?'

The phone went dead.

'Who was that, dear? Was it Simon?'

'No, though I wish he would ring. Damn!'

'What is it? You seem very upset.'

'The only thing I am upset about is that damn fly that keeps landing on me, and you and your infernal questions.'

'Darling . . . ?'

'Oh, leave me alone.'

Grabbing his hat and scarf from the stand near the door, Terence rammed the deerstalker on his head, wrapped his scarf around his neck and stormed out, answering Louise's hurt voice with a curt, 'I just want to be alone. I don't need you fussing over me.'

The house and its confines suffocated him. Louise suffocated him. He had to get out. He'd collect his gun and a couple of boxes of ammunition. He could always think straight when out shooting, and God knows there was plenty to shoot at. Rabbits abounded, eating what was left of the crops and generally making themselves a nuisance, attracting poachers, who'd then bag a brace or two of game birds. What the gamekeeper actually did, he'd really like to know!

It wasn't until he'd almost reached the thicket that Terence stopped and it hit him how terribly rude and unkind he'd been to Louise. He let his body sink down onto the ground. Damn and blast that bloody Rita. What did she want? A bloody pound of flesh, if he knew her! Well, he wasn't for giving it to her. She could do nothing; she had nothing on him. Yes, the years might have aroused her bitterness over it all, but there was nothing she or anyone else could do to him, was there? Wait a minute: that business with Theresa wanting to come to see him . . . She'd called it off, saying the problem was solved, but she wouldn't give any further information. Had she seen Rita? She wouldn't, would she? Theresa wouldn't betray him, surely? But then, God only knew what she'd do these days. She acted more strangely every time he encountered her.

He lay back. Tears trickled from the corners of his eyes and ran in cold slow motion down into his ears. He did nothing to stop them or wipe them away. Suddenly his safe world felt as though it might crumble. His past sins, which he'd tried to atone for but couldn't wipe out, piled up on the grass next to him. He couldn't face it all. He couldn't . . .

With a finality that took all feeling from him, he got up and walked into the thicket. Standing looking up into the tree that he'd always considered his favourite, his memory showed him a little boy, climbing its branches, Theresa scrambling behind him, higher and higher. Happy times, without a care.

Sitting under the tree, where its roots looked like gnarled feet, he unclipped his pen from his lapel. Taking his diary from his inside pocket, he wrote on the page for 3rd September 1958:

I'm sorry. I want Jack Fellam to know that I regret everything I did, and I hope he can forgive me. I want Theresa to know that I loved her more than I should have done, but have no regrets, except that the law prevented us being together as we were meant to be. I want my children to know I love them dearly and what I am doing is for them, to save them from the sins I committed and that are rearing their ugly head again. And my darling, darling Louise. I want you to know that you are, and have been since the day we married, my life, my love and my world. You are the purity to my evil, the angel to my devil. I love you beyond words, but staying with you would only bring sorrow down upon you. Forgive my outburst, and think of my last words as 'I love you to eternity.'

Dropping the pen and the diary onto the floor, Terence stood. The loading and cocking of his gun sent the birds fleeing their afternoon rest. No fear entered him. The inside of him was a void. A warm, floaty void. The metal taste of the barrel tingled his tongue. It was over . . . over . . .

'Hello.'

'Caller, please insert your money and press button A.'

Patsy did as the voice told her, inserting two pennies. 'Rita, he ain't come.'

'What? Bleedin' hell, what's he playing at? All right, get the next train back. I'll sort it.'

'I – I've just been reading the local paper. Th – there's a

report of a man from a place called Breckton. He committed suicide. He – he was a landowner.'

'What? No! What were his name?'

'T – Terence Crompton.'

'Christ!'

Patsy slammed the phone down. Something had told her it was her uncle. Oh God, she'd been a part of killing her own uncle. Tears streamed down her face. She leaned against the glass of the telephone box. What had she done? Loneliness and pain shrouded her. Her body folded.

A banging on the glass pane sent reality shuddering through her. A voice penetrated the place she'd let herself go to. 'Come on, love, I need to use the phone.'

'Sorry.'

'Eeh, are you alreet, lass?'

'I – I had some bad news. Can you tell me how to get to Breckton?'

'You'll need to catch a train. Breckton's quite a way from here. Take you a good three-quarters of an hour. By, there's nowt there, lass. Only a mine. Have you family there?'

'Yes. At least, I – I think I have.'

'Well, take yourself over the road to the station and some-one'll put you reet. Sorry I can't help any more. I've to ring the doctor for me little Aggie. She's got a temperature.'

Patsy nodded and left the woman to make her call. Cross-ing the road, she felt as if her legs wouldn't carry her far. She was no better than her dad, whoever he was. He'd been a killer, Rita had said; and now she'd caused a man's death. Oh, she hadn't known what effect calling him would have, but still, she'd been willing to cause him hurt; and she hadn't even known him, or the full reason Rita wanted to hurt him. Whatever it was, she realized it must have been bad. Something he couldn't face. But what? What would make a man kill himself?

'The next train ain't until around five-ish – ten past, to be precise. It takes the workers back to the villages and outlying areas and calls at Breckton. If I were you, love, I'd go and have a look around the shops for an hour or two.'

As she walked out of the station, Patsy looked at Leeds for the first time. Nothing about it had registered with her before. Just the cafe, that was all. The cafe where she was meant to meet her uncle. The tears threatened once more, but no, she'd to pull herself together. She couldn't go crying all over the place.

Leeds looked like it was a busy city; not like London as she was used to, but bustling all the same. The buildings looked similar: important, big, but a bit more tarnished. She supposed that was due to the factories and the mills. She'd seen a lot of them as the train had got nearer. All had tall chimneys belching out smoke. Buses pulled in and out of a lay-by across the road. On one of them she read 'City Centre'. Without thinking, she ran across and jumped on it.

Rita paced up and down. What to do? She couldn't stay here, that was for sure. Patsy had slammed the phone down in anger. Suppose as she took herself off to Breckton and found them lot? She'd only have to ask around a bit and she'd soon know stuff. Everyone in Breckton knew about the murders, and who'd committed them. Billy was notorious. Everything would lead Patsy to the Fellams and to her half-sister; she might even meet Harriet, if she was still staying with Jack and Dorothy. Knowing that bleedin' lot, with their family ties, they'd take her in and she'd tell them who had led her there and why. *If she tells Jack Fellam that I had plans to get even with the Cromptons, Jack's sure to ring the police. He'll not take any chances.* If they did that, Rita knew she'd be banged up again. She couldn't face that.

Running away was the only option, but what about Theresa? Would Theresa come with her? Leaving her behind would hurt. Rita longed to continue to rekindle what they'd had.

Theresa had welcomed her when she'd visited last night. They'd made love and talked of them being together forever. Rita couldn't think of giving that up. Perhaps she could persuade Theresa to move in with her somewhere near the sea ... Brighton, yes, the very place. It was cosmopolitan enough to accept their lifestyle. She'd heard that a lot of arty types lived there, and they were always open to anything. Dallied in it all, in fact.

With this thought, Rita dialled Theresa's number. A quivering, shock-filled voice answered. 'Rita ... He – he's dead!'

Thinking on her feet, Rita just stopped herself from saying that she knew and asked instead, 'Who?'

Theresa couldn't voice her words.

'Look, love, I'll come round.'

The phone went dead.

Theresa's whole body trembled. Rita couldn't get any sense out of her. Still playing the innocent, she shouted at Theresa, 'Look, tell me what happened. How did Terence die?'

'He – he shot himself ... Oh, Rita, why? Why?'

'Bleedin' hell!' Rita's shock was genuine; she hadn't expected that. She thought he would have taken pills or something, but to shoot himself ... That took guts, and that was something as she'd never associated with Terence Crompton.

There was a sadness in her, too. She hadn't wanted him dead. She'd thought there might just come a day when they could have picked up where they'd left off, because of all the blokes she'd been with, he was the best, just as his sister had bettered all the women she'd had. Despite these feelings she had to ask, 'Does anyone know why?'

'I – I think Louise said something about a phone call. I couldn't understand all she said, for she is distraught. She said something about a note.'

Christ! 'He left a note?'

'Ye – yes. Something about his sins coming back to haunt him. Oh, Rita, he means *me*. Me! Me! I killed him . . . I killed my darling, my own brother, my love, my lover . . .'

Her screams rose until they shattered the air around them and filled every particle of space in the room. They pierced Rita's ears and struck terror in her, because with the screams, froth appeared around Theresa's mouth, and her eyes glared as if made of glass, bulging from their sockets. The veins on her temple protruded, like blue, ugly, ever-growing worms.

Without thinking, Rita slapped the distorted face as hard as she could. The screaming stopped. Theresa gasped – deep, rasping intakes of breath. Her eyes stared, her mouth leaked foaming spittle. Then her body began to tremble uncontrollably. Horror curled Rita's insides.

This wasn't shock shaking Theresa's bones. If Rita knew anything, a fit had taken her. She'd seen this in the prison, as one of the inmates was prone to fitting.

Panic gripped Rita as Theresa's tongue swelled and protruded from her mouth, and her torso jumped as if someone had put a thousand volts of electricity through it. Nothing had prepared her for this. She had to get help. Reaching for the phone, she dialled 999, then left.

*

Tears blurred her vision. *Bloody hell, Rita, girl, it ain't like you to cry.* Brushing her eyes in a determined effort, she put her foot down on the accelerator. The car responded. She'd to get some things from her flat and get out of here. There was nothing left for her. She'd phone Bugsy. She'd always called Vince Yarman – one of the heavies she employed – Bugsy, because as tough as he was, he was afraid of any creepy crawly, often screaming like a girl at the sight of a bug. But he was the only person she could trust. The daft blighter loved her.

She'd get him to sell everything she owned while she lay low. Then, when she had all of her assets in cash, she'd take herself abroad. Australia. Yes, that'd be the best. She'd heard as you could get into that country, if you had money. They needed folk down there. She'd cruise over. Take Bugsy with her. They'd make out all right together. There must be a market for her line of work down there. It would all turn out all right.

Though she'd never forget Theresa. But what had changed her so much? But then, she knew what. It'd be down to what the bastard Gestapo had put her through. Theresa hadn't said anything, but last night, when she'd fallen asleep, Rita had gone downstairs for a drink and Theresa's diary had been open. What Rita had read had made the insides of her curl in horror. *Poor Theresa. Poor bleedin' blighter.*

48

Patsy & Hattie

Hope of Acceptance

The sign caught Patsy's eye: 'Hattie's Emporium'. It looked like a huge Woolworths. She still had over an hour before she had to get back to the station, and she couldn't think of a better way to spend it than looking around this shop. She wondered if they gave a free cuppa if you bought something, like they did in Woolies.

When she opened the door of the store, the noise of a loud bell clanging made her jump. Who it was meant to alert she didn't know, as all the counters – and there were lots of them – were built in a circular shape and had serving girls in the centre of them. Smells of all kinds tinged her nostrils: spices, perfumes and flowers. It was like she imagined Aladdin's cave to look.

Elvis singing 'Love Me Tender' blared out. The record had been out for well over a year and she'd seen the film, but with Elvis now in the army, everyone had to make do with his old stuff for a time. The music drew her to a counter with the colourful posters of current rock stars hanging from it. It was laden with boxes and boxes of records. She hadn't bought a record for ages. It'd be fun to have a look through.

'Any you want me to play, I will, love. I've a sales copy of each, so customers can listen before they buy.'

'Thanks. Have you anything by Cliff Richard?'

'I've got his latest, "Move It", and I reckon as it's his best an' all. You a fan of him and The Shadows, then?'

'Yes, love him.'

'Yer not from round here, are yer?'

'No, I'm from London.'

'What brings you up here then?'

A woman's voice interrupted them. 'Harriet, love, you didn't tell me you were coming in. I'd have come over and picked you up.'

Patsy turned round. A middle-aged woman with dark hair peppered with grey stood smiling at her. Small, but with a nice figure – a bit like the film stars with a big bust and a tiny waist – the woman wore a lovely blue costume. Patsy's heart thumped. Was she related to her? 'I – I'm not Harriet. Who are you?'

'Oh! I – I'm sorry. I—'

'Look, Missus, I know I look like this Harriet, and I've been told as I'm her half-sister. Are you related to her then?'

The woman's mouth dropped open. After a moment she seemed to pull herself together. 'No . . . well, yes, in a round-about way. She's me adopted granddaughter. Look, love, would you come to me office to talk this through? I can't think how you could be related to Harriet, but it's right as you're her double, so there's sommat to look into here. Come on, love, I don't bite, and I have a kettle and tea leaves in me room. You look like you could do with a drop of tea.'

'Ta, a Rosie Lee would be very welcome.'

'Ha, I remember the Land Girls during the war calling it

that. I guess you're from London then. They came from down south, only two didn't go back, they married locally.'

When they reached the office at the back of the store – an area partitioned off, but with windows giving a view of the whole shop – Patsy thought it likely she'd been spotted from there.

'You knew some Land Girls? Did you know Rita?'

'Well, I can't say as I knew them, not that well. They worked on me friend's farm – Harriet's grandparents' farm. But I do remember Rita. She worked on the local gentry's farm. She did a very bad thing. Do you know her?'

Without warning the tears welled up and swamped her.

'Eeh, lass, what is it? Patsy, come on, you can tell me. I'm known for sorting things, even when they don't look like they can be sorted. By, it's uncanny how you look like our Harriet. What's your story, lass?'

'I've done something terrible, and it were that Rita as made me do it, only I didn't know as it were terrible. I didn't know as it'd cause me uncle to kill himself.' At this, her sobbing took her over.

'Eeh, I can't make sense of anything you're saying. Look, I'll light me gas ring and get the kettle on. You calm yourself whilst I do so, and then you can start at the beginning. How's that, eh? By the way, I haven't told you me name yet. I'm Hattie.'

All Patsy could do was nod. Taking the hanky from Hattie's hand, she wiped her face. The whistling of the kettle seemed to fill the space around them. It was a comforting sound, one that said everything was all right. And somehow she knew this Hattie would see to that. She would put everything right.

'Now take a sip and, as soon as you feel ready, you tell your tale, lass.'

The hot liquid scalded her mouth, but soothed as it hit her stomach. It, and Hattie's presence, calmed her. Starting from the moment she had walked into Rita's office, Patsy told Hattie everything. The tears flowed as she explained how she thought she'd made her uncle kill himself.

'Eeh, lass. Whatever Terence Crompton's reason for taking his own life, it were nowt to do with you. It were more down to that Rita. She's a wicked person. Mind, I've heard tell that she recently visited Jack, the bloke who was the victim of all the wicked things that happened at the time. Look, I can see as it's my turn to start from the beginning. Rita . . .'

Horror gripped her as Hattie told of what had happened all those years ago. And to think she'd trusted that Rita!

'Now, if it's right as Crompton was your uncle, then that means the only person as could have been your mam was his sister, Theresa Crompton.'

'Where is she? Do you know, Hattie?'

'I only know she lives down in London somewhere. It was strange, but after living a frivolous kind of life, she suddenly left the area.'

'Rita said that – and she reckons as that's when I were born.'

'Yes, it's possible, but then later she went off to war and it's said as she were a heroine – even suffered capture by the Germans. But what's puzzling me is . . . Good God! Your dad must be—'

'Yes, the same dad as Harriet has. Rita told me that she witnessed him raping Theresa.'

'Well! You've took me stuffing out of me. So you are Harriet's half-sister. Eeh, you'll set something in motion with this, and here we were thinking as our lives had settled down.'

'I – I'm sorry. Only I have no one to turn to. I don't want to cause an upset.'

'Naw, lass. This isn't going to be easy, but no one will reject you.'

'Have I just got the one sister?'

'Aye. There are two lads, but they ain't related to you, only to Harriet through them all having the same mam. But you have a great-gran – your dad's gran, Bridget, is still alive. Eeh, lass, your dad has a lot to answer for, more than you know, but it ain't none of it your fault. Tell me, lass, where were you brought up? What kind of a life have you had?'

'I had various homes, from up in Glasgow to down in London, but it weren't too bad. The nuns in the convent were kindly, but it's just this feeling as no one wants you.'

'I know, lass. I were the same, and I never did find me family. At least you've got a bit of a chance now. There's no need for you to end up like I did. Look, the best thing I can do is take you home with me. I'll not let you go back to that Rita. Have you a home or sommat as you have to pack up?'

'No, I live in a hostel-type place. I just have me clothes.'

'Patsy, I can't say as how all of this will turn out, but I can say as I'm your friend from now on, lass. There's folk as will be hurt by you turning up, as it will dig up stuff they're trying to forget and will pile betrayal of another kind on top of what they have already dealt with, but—'

'They'll hate me, won't they?'

'Naw, these folk don't know how to hate. It'll just be strange, that's all.'

'I don't know how to act with family. I ain't never had any.'

'Aye, I know. I'll tell you me story one of these days. It ain't a lot different from your own. Look, let's get you home with me. Me man'll know what to do. We'll probably go and see this Rita, and find out where your mam lives and get your stuff from your place. At the moment I imagine your mam and the rest of your family are trying to cope with the death of Terence Crompton – your uncle – so we'd best leave it for a while.'

'The rest of me family? I thought you said I had none, except Harriet and me great-granny.'

'Well, that is about it, by my reckoning, as with them Cromptons not wanting you when you were born, it's unlikely they will want you now. Anyroad, on the side of your family, other than your mam, there's Lady Crompton – your grandmother. Then there's a boy and twin girls as are your cousins, that I know of. There could be other family as I know nothing of; bound to be. They're top-drawer folk and I don't mix in their circles. Me man Arthur were top-drawer, but he gave it all up for the love of me, but he'll know more about them. By, lass, I don't know how all of this is going to pan out. But come on; let's make a start on it by getting you back to my house, eh?'

On the way home Hattie felt as though she'd batted or answered a million questions. All of it beggared belief, and she felt out of control of her situation for the first time in a long while. Her heart went out to the girl, and just meeting Patsy brought back painful memories to her. How was she going to tell Sarah? And what about Harriet? God, Harriet had her life sorted – university, then medical school. How would all of this affect her?

'Were me dad a monster, Hattie?'

She had avoided umpteen different ways of asking such questions, but this one was too direct to dodge. 'I'd say he were, in a way. But only because his mind were that twisted, it made him so – he weren't human, not in the way we are. He seemed incapable of having feelings for anyone, unless it was hate, or unless it were for Sarah – Harriet's mam. His mind was like it were two halves, and the evil half won. I'm sorry, lass, but I can only tell you the truth. Harriet doesn't know it all – she's been told as he suffered mental illness, which of course is true. And that at times he went out of himself, which again is true. We've spared her, and will spare you, the worst of what went on. You have no need to know. Neither you nor Harriet are like him. He was different in all sorts of ways that you're not. You appear to me to be a nice young lady, who is understandably bitter about stuff. I were, and so were Megan – she were Billy's mam . . .'

And so they talked on and on, until Hattie was glad when they finally pulled into the drive of her house. 'Now, lass. Me daughter . . . well, me adopted daughter – see, we're a mixed-up bunch, so you'll fit in well.' Patsy smiled at this and it brought relief to Hattie. She'd thought the girl was without humour and would be very difficult to win round. 'Anyroad, her and her husband are staying with us, so I think it best I go in and tell them about you, then come out and fetch you in. Is that all right by you? Otherwise it's going to be such a shock and they'll all ask questions at once, and you won't know if you're on your head or your tail!' Another smile. 'Oh, there's sommat else: me husband, Arthur, and Sally's husband, Mark . . . well, they both suffered injuries. Arthur got his in the First World War, and Mark were blown up in the last lot. So they're both scarred and not pleasant to look on, till you get used to them; and besides that, Mark is blind.'

'Oh, poor things. But don't worry, it won't bother me. I'm sorry it happened to them, though. But I won't say anything. I'll just act normal.'

'You're a nice lass, Patsy. Now don't worry; everything will turn out. Like I say, I'm your friend now, and I never let me friends down, so I'll be by your side whatever you decide to do, or whoever you take on and confront.'

'Thanks, Hattie.'

'No, tears, now. I'll not be five minutes.'

49

Sarah

From Beyond the Grave

Sarah looked out of the window. There were things she would miss about Market Harborough. The lovely view from this window, for one. And she was aware how difficult leaving was really going to be for Bridget. She had spent most of her very happy marriage to Edward here. They'd brought their two boys into the world and raised them here. And though she said she hankered for the north, she was a young lass in her teens when she left there.

The phone ringing interrupted her thoughts. What was it about telephones? Somehow you always knew when it was going to be bad news, and this feeling came over her as she crossed from the front room to the hall.

Even Hattie's voice, as she said hello, set alarm bells ringing.

'What's wrong, Hattie? Is everyone all right?'

'Aye, they are, but I have news, and you're not going to like it, love, but . . .'

Sarah stared at the phone. Pictures came into her head of her wedding day, and of Billy talking to Miss Theresa. But surely not – not then, no, but . . . Oh God, the next day, when he was missing for ages.

'Sarah, are you all right? Look, love, you don't have to meet her. None of us wants you hurt. Not even Patsy, who's never met you. She understands, now we've told her everything that happened, but she wants to meet Harriet. What do you think?'

'I'll tell her. It – it'll be up to her. I can't keep from her that she has a sister. But if she wants to meet this Patsy, then I will too. And, well . . . I – I don't know. It shouldn't be affecting me, but it is. It's like the last slap in the face, like Billy's reaching me from the grave. I can hear him laughing. Oh God!'

'Oh, Sarah, lass. I'm sorry.'

'It's not your fault, Aunt Hattie. I'd not expect any less of you. No one knows more than you how the girl feels. And none of it's her fault, either. It's just that I feel like Billy's won. With one last thing he saved to hit me with, and I can't do anything about it.'

'Try not to think of it like that, Sarah. Billy couldn't have known about Patsy. Rita told her it were rape, so Theresa didn't have any choice in it.'

'I don't believe that. I – I saw something between them at me own wedding. I didn't register it then, but it's very clear now. There were always rumours about Theresa; things you'd not think on as true. But why, when Patsy came back to confront him, did it tip Terence Crompton over to suicide? I would never think of him as a man who would take his own life. He had everything: wealth, power, a lovely family. He must have thought Patsy's appearance would mean his past would come and smack him in the face and ruin what he'd got. Especially as it was Rita who'd set it all up. It all makes you think Crompton were behind the fire.'

'Aye, it seems likely. But like you said, though it hurts and is a lot for you to take on, none of it is Patsy's fault. It seems Rita used her. Oh, Patsy admits she wanted some revenge for her family having given her away, but I can understand that. Me own thoughts have gone down that line many a time towards me own, who did it to me, and it's the reason I never sought them out. Rejection hurts. The only thing I hang onto is how Bridget said as me mam wanted me. Patsy ain't even got that, but once she realized the extent of everything and what happened as a result, she's been almost inconsolable.'

'But what if Harriet rejects her? What then?'

'I don't know. I'll have to find a way round everything, as I can't just say, "Well, that's it, lass, sling your hook." I'm going to have to keep Patsy in me life and take care of her. After all, she's Megan's granddaughter, and that makes her bound to me as if she were me own. I'm sorry, lass. I hope you understand that.'

'Of course I do. And I wouldn't have it any different. It's what makes you the person you are: someone who is loyal and loving and . . . Eeh, Aunt Hattie.'

'I know, lass. And I'm sorry, I wouldn't have had owt disturb the happiness and peace of mind you've found. Talk it over with Bridget – see how she feels. Patsy is her great-granddaughter, thou knows.'

'Oh God, of course. It just gets worse.'

'It needn't. Give yourself a little time. I know you, Sarah. I know as you'll come to terms with it all. Richard'll help you. Patsy's willing to give you time. She understands.'

Understands? How could anyone understand? Sarah couldn't even understand her own feelings. Billy was nothing to her now; nothing but a vile memory and a source of pain whenever she thought of him. But this – it was like being asked to accept something from him back into her life. She'd never thought of Harriet as a part of Billy. Richard had helped with that – he'd been Harriet's father right from her being in her womb, and he'd sealed that the moment she was born. But this made her face that relationship for what it really was, and she'd never done that before. It made her think differently about who Harriet was, and she didn't want that. Oh God, she didn't want that!

'What is it, lass? I don't want to intrude, but I can see that phone call has upset you.'

'Oh, Bridget, it has. It was Hattie. And I don't know what all she has told me will do to you – and more so, to me little Harriet. And her just starting out on her new life an' all.'

'Me and Harriet? What's happened? What can affect us?'

'Eeh, Bridget.'

Bridget was quiet for what seemed like an age, after Sarah told her all that Hattie had revealed. Emotions of all kinds washed over Sarah while she waited: hate, pity and love. Love for this woman who'd been through so much as a young girl, and for all them years when Bridget couldn't find her child; then having to face the brutal murder of that child by her own grandson; and the loss of her soulmate, with Edward dying; and now this. For this Patsy didn't represent to them what she did to Hattie. It was easy for Hattie to see the girl from the perspective of her not being wanted by her family and having been brought up by nuns; but to them it was as if Patsy was bringing all the evil back into their lives.

'I don't know how we're going to do it, Sarah, but somehow we've to be bigger than this. We've to beat the evil by not letting it win. If I reject my great-granddaughter, I'll be no better than him as gave her life. Hattie's right. None of this is Patsy's fault; and, like Harriet, she came from me daughter. Me lovely Megan was her grandmother. So she'll have her goodness in her. Oh, I know Billy's strongly in the equation, but well . . .'

'I know. We have to remember that Billy was mentally unstable. Others can look at what he did and analyse it and come up with reasons. Maybe that's what we have to do. If we're ever to get any real and lasting peace, we have to think of Billy's evil self as being something he couldn't control, and that was the side of him that did all the terrible things.'

'He was possessed. But Harriet isn't, and from what you tell me Hattie has said about Patsy, she isn't, either. Her understanding and feeling no bitterness towards us shows that. Her willingness to give us time shows it. And her shock and horror at what her phone call to Terence Crompton caused shows it.'

'Are you wanting to have her in your life, Bridget? Are you saying we should let her be in Harriet's?'

'Aye, I am. Of course Harriet has to make her own mind up, but at the end of the day I've been given a gift. A great-granddaughter – and if she's anything like me first, who they say she looks like, then she'll enrich my life.'

'Then I can do it an' all. Given a little time, I can.'

'When will you tell Harriet?'

'I don't know. I think I'll leave it until after her holiday. She's so looking forward to it. Me dad's told her such a lot about Switzerland and the beauty of the journey there, since Harriet told him that her friend's family had invited her. And I think relating what he saw when he went there with Megan, to forgive that Laura Harvey, has helped him to quiet some of the guilt he held over all that happened.'

'Aye, Jack seems a lot better these days. I was talking to him for ages on the phone the other day. And though it hurt when he married Dorothy, I realize she has done wonders for him.'

'You didn't say owt about it hurting you, and you certainly didn't show it. It hurt me a bit an' all. It were like he'd shoved me mam even further back when he took a third wife, but I came to understand. He's one of them men as can't be on his own. He'll always need a woman by him. Someone of his own, who he can lean on and have love him. Like you – and us all – he's been through a lot.'

'I know. And I now know the loneliness you can feel, even with everyone around you, after you lose that special someone – the one you can share anything and everything with.'

'I can only imagine. Look, I'll make us a pot of tea and then we'll chat some more. Try to come to terms with a few things, because we'll need to, before we share it with the others.'

'I'd like to go up and meet the girl while Harriet is away.'

'Oh? Well, if you must. I think I'll wait till I see if Harriet is of a mind to, before I do. I don't want to make me mind up about her, one way or the other, until then.'

'I'll ring Hattie and see if I can come and stay. It'll get me from under your feet while you get everything ready for the move. There's only three weeks to go now. I've packed everything I'm not using, and I will take what I can to Hattie's with me.'

As Sarah went through to the kitchen, she marvelled at how Bridget had taken it all and at her eagerness to embrace this new blot on their lives. Because that's what Patsy was: a blot. Something she'd hoped wouldn't happen to them again. Something that had thrown a shadow over their happiness. At this moment she couldn't see a time when she'd accept the lass. A bastard of Billy's? No, that was the last thing she needed in her life.

50

Harriet

Joining the Threads

Harriet stared, her eyes wide with shock. 'A – a sister! How do you know she's telling the truth? She could be anybody. I – I mean—'

'Like I say, Aunt Hattie said Patsy is your double. She thought it was you, and even after the girl put her right, she couldn't believe her eyes. And besides that, your dad were seen with the woman who gave birth to Patsy. He were caught in the act.'

'I can't take it in. Do you think that was the reason my dad killed himself?'

Sarah couldn't answer. They'd told Harriet that Billy had taken his own life, and suspected she'd guessed there was more. With each passing year she'd asked more questions. Questions like 'So, me granny died of shock on the same day?' and 'They couldn't be buried together because taking your own life means you're a sinner and can't be buried in consecrated ground?' And on and on. Perhaps now was the time to tell her the truth.

Looking over at Richard, Sarah saw him nod. He understood and agreed. When he spoke, he gave her a lead. 'Harriet, darling, we haven't told you the whole story. We wanted to protect you. Now you are grown-up, it is right that we should tell you exactly what happened.'

'You mean there's more? I have a sister I didn't know existed, and now there's more to learn?'

'Yes, dear, there is.'

Sarah took a deep breath. She had to do this without bitterness and hate, but with compassion – compassion for her beloved daughter and in memory of Megan, because Megan deserved no less of her. She'd loved her son despite everything, and to taint his memory would be to taint hers.

'Your dad were two people. One were like you and his mam and Granny Bridget. Loving and kind, and everything you'd want and need in a dad. But he had an illness that split his personality . . .'

'Schizophrenia. You will learn about it in your studies.'

Richard brought some normality to what they had to reveal by taking Harriet through what the medical profession knew of the illness. It wasn't his field, but because of what Billy did to his mother, Richard's beloved half-sister Megan, Richard had studied the condition in depth to help to give him some understanding. He'd tried to talk about it to Sarah over the years, but she'd preferred just to close her mind. Now she was forced to listen.

'. . . and so, given this, Billy – your father – had no control over what this other half of him did. It took him over. And what we haven't told you, dear, is that this other half: it – it murdered your granny.'

'What?'

Sarah registered the shock and pain in Harriet as if it were a knife sticking into her own gut. Rushing towards her child, she held her, stroking her and sobbing her own tears alongside Harriet's. 'I'm sorry, me little lass, I'm sorry.'

'It – it's not your fault, Mam. It must have been awful for you. Well, for all of you. I just feel strange, like I've suddenly become someone else.'

'No, you haven't. Harriet, you are my child.' Richard had stepped forward and taken Harriet and now held her to him. 'You're not Billy's, and never have been. I was with you from the very beginning. I talked to you whilst you were in your mother's womb, and I loved you right from then. You are not changed by any of this.'

'I am more you, aren't I, Dad? That's right, isn't it?'

'It is, my darling.'

Sarah watched. She couldn't speak. Harriet and Richard. Harriet and her father – for that's what Richard was: her father.

'You are me. Just as much as, if not more than, the boys are, because we have something even stronger than blood ties. We have a love that stretches all of your eighteen years and the bit before you made your appearance. That doesn't change, does it? And look how the boys are not remotely interested in medicine, and yet you have a passion for it. That comes from me, and from my father.'

They clung together to the exclusion of all else – even her, Sarah thought as she stood still, not interfering. But then at this moment she'd have it no different; they needed to cement their bond once more, to overcome what could have created a schism in their love for one another.

After a moment Richard asked, 'Harriet, do you think you can look on Patsy in the same way? Not as an intrusion into your world, but as an addition to it? I think if you can, and she's as nice as your Aunt Hattie says, then knowing her and having her as your own will enrich your life.'

'I hadn't thought of it like that, Dad. I hadn't thought of

how she'll add to my life, but she will, won't she? A sister. Aye, as Mam would say, that'd be grand as owt.'

Their laughter penetrated the shield that Sarah had thrown up around herself from the moment she'd heard of Patsy's existence. It shook her pain and splintered it into tiny fragments that she found she could deal with. Her own laughter started as a smile, then spread through her body, and suddenly she could think on this Patsy not as a threat, but as someone they should welcome as Harriet's sister, Bridget's great-granddaughter, Megan's granddaughter and Richard's great-niece. And, as such, the lass must be a nice person. She couldn't fail to be, with all that goodness flowing through her veins. And, she had to admit, after listening to Richard's explanation of Billy's illness, for the first time in a long while a little understanding of Billy entered her. It broke down the ball of hate that had clogged a part of her mind and heart, freeing her of the shackles of the past.

When she went over to them both, it was as if they read all of this in her, as Richard said, 'You'll be all right now, Sarah. Everything will be all right.' And Harriet squeezed her and said, 'I understand now, Mam. I understand.'

51

Sarah

Building a Family Unit

'Eeh, look at them, Sarah! Who'd have thought?'

Sarah glanced through the window to where Bridget was pointing. A nice feeling entered her. It had been a long time coming. Oh, she'd pretended, played her part and kept everyone around her happy, thinking she was all right with everything, but deep down she hadn't been. Deep down the betrayal had sat in her, gnawing at her. But as she watched Harriet and Patsy sitting on the bench at the bottom end of the lawn, both laughing over a shared joke, something happened to nudge that knot of pain away.

They were beautiful. The sun danced on their rich red hair, and their faces glowed with goodness and love. They were soulmates in the way sisters can be, and all despite the evil that had spawned them. In some small part of her, she'd held that evil against the girl who'd come to them out of the blue and sparked such a change in their lives.

The change was not life-altering for them, but it had been dramatic and devastating for those over at Hensal Grange. You could say that all those involved in the tragic events triggered by lust, jealousy and hate over the years had been

409

touched by the appearance of this girl and by the one phone call she had made.

Now the Cromptons had left the area, without even knowing of Patsy's existence. Not that she and Richard had instigated that. Everything to do with Patsy's mother and her mother's family was the girl's own decision.

Louise Crompton had fled to her mother's after her husband's death. Theresa still lived in London; she'd suffered a nervous breakdown, and now lived the life of a near-recluse, according to a doctor friend of Richard who knew her well. And Lady Crompton had moved back to York, where she had brought her family from when she'd inherited Hensal Grange from her sister, Laura Crompton. The house had been sold, and the new owners had come full circle. They had once owned Hensal Grange Mine and had bought it from the Cromptons, but had now sold it on to the National Coal Board. They were millionaires and used Hensal Grange more as a 'country pile', as those who worked up at the Grange referred to it. 'Live in London, they do. Travel the world half the time. Eeh, they don't know as they're born,' they'd say.

Well, she was glad of that. That place, and the folk who had owned it and lived there over the years, had had a big hand in the events that had affected all of those she loved. From her Granna Issy, to Aunt Megan, to her dad – all had suffered through the actions of the Harveys and the Cromptons. Now they had one of them in their midst. For at the end of the day, Patsy was one of them.

Sarah watched Dorothy walk over to the girls. Funny thing, war. On the one hand it could devastate, and on the other it could bring people into your life to enrich it. Dorothy was one of the latter. What she'd done for Sarah's dad had been nothing short of a miracle. Aye, and she'd helped where Patsy was concerned as well. She'd accepted the girl from the off and had helped her to settle. In the first few weeks after Patsy came into their lives, Dorothy had taken her in at the farm, and that had been the arrangement for a while, just to give the girls time to get to know each other and to come to accept each other. Dorothy was what you'd term 'a quiet influence'. Different to Hattie. Hattie was up front, moved heaven and earth for you if you needed it, and made changes for the better in everyone's lives, whilst Dorothy worked at a slower pace and in a manner so that you didn't realize she was doing anything.

Hattie, Arthur and her dad walked over to the little group, and the six of them looked comfortable together, talking and laughing like they'd known one another all of their lives. Jack put his arm around Dorothy. He was a wonderful man, her dad. Capable of giving complete love, and of being loved. But something in him was afraid, Sarah knew that. That love had been snatched away from him so many times, by death and through the violent acts of war and murder. She tried to picture what it would be like if none of it had happened.

She turned her head. She hadn't noticed that Bridget had left her. On the dresser, amongst all the family photos, was a brown, faded one of her mam. *Eeh, Mam, you were beautiful, and you too, Aunt Megan.* Reaching out, she moved the photos of them, taken when they were young girls, and stood them side-by-side. *And now another generation of young women have found each other. My Harriet, yours and Megan's grandchild, Mam – and Patsy, Megan's granddaughter. How the world turns around, eh?*

It seemed to her that her mam's smile widened, and into the air around her came a tinkling laugh. It was joined by a

411

cackle, and then a giggle. *Eeh, Mam, you're with Megan and Granna Issy, and all three of you are here with us, I can tell that.*

A tear dropped onto her cheek, and through the haze of those that would follow, Sarah saw Bridget walk across the lawn. The others turned to greet her, but Patsy went towards her and hugged her. What must it feel like to grow up without anyone in the world belonging to you, and then to find you had someone like Bridget as your great-grandmother? Lass must feel as though she'd come to heaven.

Mark held Sally's arm as they joined the group. What a brave soul he was. And how Sally cocooned him in love and tender care. It warmed your heart to see them.

Music penetrated her thoughts: thumping drums and electric guitars. The teenagers – her own, and Mark and Sally's, who all thought they were the next rock 'n' roll sensation – were practising with their instruments in the garage. 'We're going to give you a concert later on,' Ian, her eldest son, had said earlier. Eeh, she wasn't looking forward to that!

A hand appeared on her shoulder. A loving hand with a gentle touch. A touch made for healing. Not just healing of the ailments of those in his surgery, but healing of her. Aye, and the loving of her. She turned and looked up into Richard's concerned face. 'Well, love, we have to let them go, don't we?'

'We do, darling. But it isn't an end – it is a beginning. Our girls,' he always referred to Harriet and Patsy as 'our girls', and had done from the moment Harriet had accepted Patsy as her sister, 'they're off into the big wide world of university. You know, I still can't believe they want to both take up medicine. Isn't that strange? Neither came from that background.'

'Well, Harriet was influenced by you, and I expect Patsy by a need to stay close to Harriet. How they both got into the same college, though, is nothing short of a miracle.'

'And a little nepotism. After all, both Father and I went there.'

'Aye, I suppose so.'

'So, no more tears. Let's go and join in the fun. This is a party. We're launching our girls into their new lives. They are taking the next step. Do you think you can do that too, darling?'

He knew; he knew some part of her had held back. Sometimes it was as if Richard was on the inside of her. There was nothing he didn't know about her or what went on in her head.

'Aye, I can. And not just in me head – forcing meself, so as to please others – but in me heart. I think at last I can open up me heart, to let Patsy into it and take her on as you have done. I'm sorry as it took me a while.'

'No, don't be. She understood. We talked about it, you know. She has a capacity to give a great deal of understanding to things. It's my guess she'll go into psychiatry.'

'Eeh, Richard, you and your medical world, it comes into everything. But I hope you're right. It will give her some answers.'

'And what about you? Have you found your answers?'

'I think so, love. I think so.'

His arms tightened around her and drew her to him. Encased in his love, she didn't need answers; she had all she needed to help her go forward. It was time she helped Patsy to have that, too.

Richard steered her outside. The girls were busy passing around sandwiches and seeing to drinks. Patsy brought a tray over to them. 'Champagne, but no caviar, I'm afraid, just cucumber sandwiches. Ha, if they could see me now!' Her face glowed. 'Help yourself, Richard, and what about you, Sa—'

'Mam. Call me "Mam". Because that's what I'd like to be, lass. You're a sister to me daughter, and I'd like you to be a daughter to me an' all.'

Richard took the tray from Patsy before she dropped it, as her jaw had dropped. A silence had fallen around them. Then Sarah's arms were filled with a bundle of joy. A nice feeling. She wasn't holding a product of evil; she was holding a lovely young woman. A daughter.

The clapping started somewhere in the distance, or so it seemed, but built into a loud cheer. Richard, his eyes glistening, put down the tray and came and held them both. 'And I'm "Dad" from now on, right?'

'Yes, oh yes – me own mam and dad. Me world's complete.'

'Eeh, Sarah, lass. That were a lovely thing as you did. It's grand to have Patsy as one of us, and now she really is.'

'I know, Aunt Hattie. I'm sorry I just wasn't able to give all of meself at first.'

Dorothy answered before Hattie had a chance to. 'No, you mustn't be sorry. Everyone understood.'

'You knew then, Dorothy?'

'I did – we all did. We talked about it, but decided you just needed time, and we were right.'

'You too, Bridget?'

'Aye, I knew an' all, Sarah, lass.'

Sally moved to Sarah's side and took hold of her hand and squeezed it. She understood more than most, as they'd talked through how difficult it was to accept and forgive those who'd sinned against you. It was good to have Sally living so close.

They understood each other, knew what the other was feeling, without being told.

Looking around at these four women, three of whom had been with her for almost as long as she could remember, and one brought to her by the war, Sarah realized how lucky she was. Some that she'd loved to her very core – her mam, her Aunt Megan and her Granna Issy – had been taken from her, but she was still surrounded by strong women, and strong love.

'Eeh, Sarah, that were enough to set me off. I couldn't talk for a mo. I'm glad as you're all right, love.'

'I am, Sally. I've never been more all right in me whole life. How could I not be, with having you all to protect me and bring me through?'

Aunt Hattie's arm came around her. 'Aye, we've always been about strength and standing together. We had to be. And it weren't just because we came from poor backgrounds; it were because we are women. It were how we got through, but, thou knows, times are changing. Look at lassies over there. Who'd have thought as them, coming from us who were at times considered the lowest of the low, could even think of going to university, let alone getting places there? Oh, I know as our fortunes have changed. We've made them do so, but still, it wouldn't have been heard of in my day.'

'You're right, Aunt Hattie.'

Bridget shook her head. 'Aye, you are, but I doubt as women's struggles are over. There's still a long way to go. Lassies are still having their babies taken off them if they fall pregnant out of wedlock, and men still say there's no such thing as rape. A clout round the ear to keep the missus in check is acceptable, and women can't do anything without their husband's permission.'

They were all quiet as they took this in. Sally spoke first. 'Well, let's hope things change soon. It will only take some strong young women to get together, like that Mrs Pankhurst and her suffragettes did. Maybe one of ours even?'

They all looked over to Harriet and Patsy. And Sarah thought: *Aye, they are the women of the future.* And without giving her mind to the horror that had gone before, she hoped with all her heart that things would change for women. Let them lassies know a different world. And she knew they were already putting a foot on the ladder towards that.

But then again, Patsy still had stuff to deal with. *And in my experience, and that of these around me, no one could just put sommat like that away from them. After all, even though I've given meself as a mam to the girl, Patsy has a real mam out there somewhere. A woman as is a mystery to us all, but she exists. Will it become a burning desire in Patsy to find her one day?*

'I know what you're thinking, lass. And if Patsy wants to seek out Theresa in the future, she must do so. We can only hope she doesn't get hurt. But it's true what they say: we can't predict the future; we can only learn from the past, and I think we've all done that.'

'We have, Aunt Hattie, we have. But, thou knows, there's always another day and there's always hope. Tomorrow doesn't have to bring sorrow.'

Author's Note

Tomorrow Brings Sorrow, though a stand-alone book, is the third in the Breckton series, which consists of: *To Catch a Dream*, *An Unbreakable Bond*, *Tomorrow Brings Sorrow* and *Time Passes Time*.

The use of the term 'Mongol'

In order to retain the authenticity of the dialect from the era in which the characters in the book lived, I used the term 'Mongol' to describe a Down's syndrome child. This term is now considered inappropriate, and of course I agree that it no longer is. However, the cause of a child being born with Down's syndrome wasn't then known and the medical profession termed such children as being Mongoloid, as they were thought to resemble Mongolians. Lay people picked up on the term and shortened it to Mongol. It was rarely used then as a derogatory address.

Then, as today, the loving nature of Down's syndrome children assured that they were accepted and loved. But, as today, there were the bigoted, ignorant and discriminatory people who did call names and make anyone who was in the minority feel less of a person.

By showing how things were in the days of this story and in the interests of authenticity, I have no intention of offending, and only wish to accurately reflect how my characters would have spoken.

Research

The research for this epic story of two sets of families – the rich and powerful Harvey and Crompton families, and the working-class Armitage and Fellam families – has centred around the coal-mining industry, workhouse life, the deep recession of the 1920s, stud farming and land management, the running of a country mansion, the ins and outs of being apprentice seamstresses and the running of a dressmaking business, culminating in this novel in how lives changed during the Second World War, with young people becoming Land Girls, special agents, pilots and naval officers.

Though mainly set in and around Leeds and York, and in the fictional town of Breckton (which, in my imagination, nestles somewhere between these two cities), the story also takes the reader to London, Ireland, Scotland, France and Poland – all of which I visited in search of atmosphere and the facts I needed. Switzerland also features, and I would love to have visited there too, but in the end I relied on my imagination, fed by the many beautiful pictures I had seen and my favourite childhood story, which I read and saw on television: *Heidi* by Johanna Spyri.

My research also took me to Caphouse Colliery near Wakefield, an experience that was both enlightening and terri-fying, as the rickety cage that I boarded descended into the bowels of the earth. It not only helped me to write about the conditions endured by the workforce – from young boys of twelve to men in their sixties – but also gave me the rare find of a real-life, late-nineteenth- and early-twentieth-century woman of power, Emma Lister Kaye, owner of the colliery, on whom I was able to base my rich and powerful character, Laura Harvey.

It was Eden Camp, near Old Malton, Yorkshire, that saturated me with different aspects of wartime life. It is a wonderful project, set in what was a camp for prisoners-of-war. Each hut walks you through a different experience of life during the Second World War, from the home front to the front line – you see, hear and feel the war.

I have scoured Leeds and York, and the surrounding countryside, to find the right mansions, old croft houses, mental institution and workhouse buildings that would fit my needs and become the background for the powerful story I wanted to tell.

Despite all this, I still had gaps in my information and needed help to trawl for little-known facts. These gaps were plugged by my own family, whose various careers and interests were a source of great knowledge, giving even greater depth to my work. They all have a special mention in the Acknowledgements.

I hope you have enjoyed the book and go on to read (or may already have done so) the rest in the series. Thank you.

You can find out more about me, and my books, at: www.panmacmillan.com/authors/mary-wood. And you can interact with me on Facebook: www.facebook.com/Historical Novels; follow me on Twitter @Authormary; or visit my website www.authormarywood.com, where you will find all my work and will be able to read the first chapters, and much more.

I look forward to hearing from you all, and to welcoming you as my friends.

Acknowledgements

I have been lucky enough to work with many wonderful, talented and skilful people during my self-publishing days, and now as a published author with Pan Macmillan.

In the course of the epic work of the Breckton series I have been advised and assisted by freelance editors Rebecca Keys, Julie Hitchin and Stanley Livingston, all of whom brought their own magic and expertise to my early editions; along with the talented cover artist Patrick Fox, who produced ebook covers for me back then. Thank you. My work brought you to me, but you have enriched my life with your friendship and encouragement. You truly helped me to climb the steps to my dream.

From those self-published beginnings, I have now seen all these works achieve traditional publication status, and for that I thank all at Pan Macmillan: the directors, editors, publicists, salespeople and cover artists, and all the teams that work with you. You are all amazing, but a special mention goes to my previous editor, Louise Buckley, for the help and support you gave me to make the transition to the traditional publishing world, and for what you brought to my books. I miss you and wish you happiness and success in your new career.

Special thanks to my new and present editor, Victoria Hughes-Williams, and your team. You have embraced me and taken me smoothly through the change of editorial team, and I love working with you. You have given me the support to help me settle and, most of all, the benefit of your exceptional qualities and expertise; to utter a modern phrase, you 'get me' and my books and what I am all about – a wonderful feeling, and I know we will continue to work well together. An author is made whole by her editor.

To Laura Carr and her team, thanks for sweeping my manuscripts clean and seeking out any detail that isn't correct. Without you, my books would be peppered with commas, and my poor characters would endure five-year pregnancies. Your eye for detail is amazing.

Thanks also to Kate Green, my publicist, who works tirelessly to promote me and my books and makes my book-tours go so smoothly that they are a joy.

I owe so much to you all, and thank you from the bottom of my heart. It has been an amazing journey, made all the more so by having you by my side.

And thank you too to a very special person, who listens to me when I'm down and then lifts me up to tackle another day; who fights my corner and encourages me. My agent, Judith Murdoch. Onwards and upwards, Judith!

No acknowledgements would be complete without mentioning my family. Here, I need to thank each one of you for the help and input you have given to the Breckton series.

My daughter, Christine Martin, researched timeline events, giving me the ability to keep the happenings of the world correctly placed. These facts are rarely centre-stage in a novel, but the mentioning of a well-known event or person can ground the period and is therefore essential, and needs to be accurate.

My daughters, Julie Bowling and Rachel Gradwell, along with Christine and my son, James Wood, read so many versions and advised me from a reader's point of view, without ever complaining that rereads were getting tiresome, while bringing me fresh ideas and giving me praise and encouragement.

My sons-in-law, Nick Martin and Rick Gradwell, were a source of knowledge on the Second World War for *Tomorrow Brings Sorrow* and *Time Passes Time*, providing little-known and hard-to-find facts that really helped me.

My daughter Julie's partner, Eddie Yates, provided me with valuable information about farming, which gave depth to the roles that the Land Girls would take.

My son's partner, the talented Scott Knowles, gave me the background of his beautiful voice, as I worked away in one bedroom and he practised in another.

And last but not least, thanks to my darling husband, Roy, who has taken over looking after me and our house to free up my time for writing. Without him, I couldn't achieve what I do – he is my rock.

I say the words 'Thank you' to you all, but they seem inadequate and cannot cover all that you give me. Your help – along with your love and support, and your belief in me – helps me to climb my mountain.

extracts reading groups
competitions books new
discounts extracts
competitions
books new
events books
extracts
new reading groups
interviews
events extracts
discounts
new books events
events new

www.panmacmillan.com

extracts events reading groups
competitions books extracts new